The

Mangler

of Malibu

Canyon

Also by Jennifer Colt

The Butcher of Beverly Hills

Jennifer Colt

Broadway Books
New York

The Mangler of Malibu Canyon

a novel

BROADWAY

PUBLISHED BY BROADWAY BOOKS

Copyright © 2006 by TESSERA PRODUCTIONS, INC.

All rights reserved.

Published in the United States by Broadway Books, an imprint of The Doubleday Broadway Publishing Group, a division of Random House, Inc., New York.
www.broadwaybooks.com

BROADWAY BOOKS and its logo, a letter B bisected on the diagonal, are trademarks of Random House, Inc.

This book contains an excerpt from the forthcoming hardcover edition of *The Vampire of Venice Beach* by Jennifer Colt. This excerpt has been set for this edition and may not reflect the final content of the forthcoming edition.

Book design by Caroline Cunningham

Library of Congress Cataloging-in-Publication Data
Colt, Jennifer.
  The mangler of Malibu Canyon : a novel / Jennifer Colt.—1st ed.
    p. cm.
1. Women private investigators—California—Los Angeles—Fiction.
2. Murder—Investigation—California—Malibu—Fiction. 3. Sisters—Fiction.
4. Twins—Fiction. 5. Malibu (Calif.)—Fiction. I. Title.

  PS3603.0467M36 2006
  813'.6—dc22   2005058158

ISBN-13: 978-0-7679-2012-4
ISBN-10: 0-7679-2012-0

PRINTED IN THE UNITED STATES OF AMERICA

10 9 8 7 6 5 4 3 2 1

FIRST EDITION

For Jenny Bent, agent extraordinaire

Acknowledgments

I'd like to thank my wonderful editor, Ann Campbell, of Broadway Books, for her contributions to this series. She has always exhibited patience, diplomacy, and sensitivity while dealing with me, which can't have been easy. She's also wickedly good with a pencil, demonstrating a high degree of intelligence and a great sense of humor.

As usual, I owe a great debt of gratitude to the friends and family members who have read and critiqued my manuscripts. I could not do this work without them.

The
Mangler
of Malibu
Canyon

I'm Kerry McAfee. My sister Terry and I are private investigators and identical twins. We may look exactly alike—long, reddish hair, green eyes, stick figures, freckled noses—but when it comes to personality, we're polar opposites. (One of us may even be bipolar, but that's another story.)

I'm talking about Terry, of course, a.k.a. Terry the Terror, Terry the Terrible, Terry the Pterodactyl from Hell.

I've always been the pleaser, the good girl. Polite and self-contained.

I was class president. She was class hellraiser. I like boys. She likes girls. I won't cross the street without a crosswalk; she won't cross the street unless there's something in it for her. I avoid confrontation; she'd rather be in your face than anywhere else on earth.

We live in Los Angeles, the land of the *New Age*. The kind

of place where you're likely to hear that *we* determine who we'll be when we come to earth. That before we incarnate, we choose our bodies, our life paths, our families . . .

NOT.

I did not choose the Devil as a sister. If it were up to me, I would have chosen someone like Jan Brady. Middle-of-the-road, average girl. No trouble, decent grades, inclined to marry the boy next door. Then I could be bad once in a while, instead of feeling like Siegfried or Roy, armed with a chair and a whip and a ton of hair spray, trying to keep my wildcat sibling in line.

She's my sister, of course, and I love her. But sometimes I wonder . . . If I weren't around, would she have turned out the same way? Did she develop into the person she is so the world wouldn't be saddled with two identical bores? And if she hadn't come along, might I have turned out a little more adventurous, a little more devil-may-care?

I guess I'll never know.

The detective thing just sort of happened. I had to work off Terry's legal fees after she got busted for cocaine possession (she hit a rough patch following the untimely deaths of our parents). Her lawyer, Eli Weintraub, Esq., became my mentor and surrogate daddy, the one who sent me down this path to perdition. I did legwork for him on matrimonial cases and the like, and after three years I qualified for a PI license. When Terry got out of prison, I hired her.

Who else would? She's dyslexic, completely resistant to authority, and has a criminal mind that approaches the genius level. Blessed with the gift of gab (some would say the gift of pathological lying), she can talk the fur off a lemur. She's also completely fearless, which causes me both envy and, well, fear.

We're not conjoined twins. Theoretically, we could go our separate ways. But if we did, who would look out for Terry?

Who would make sure she didn't self-destruct? And truthfully, the thought of trying to manage the future on my own makes my brain hurt. Our primary goal right now is making enough money to hang on to our little house on Beverly Glen, take care of our doggies, Muffy and Paquito, and have a little change left over for a great pair of shoes every now and then. The house, originally owned by our grandfather Pops, was willed to us through our mom and looks like something out of a fairy tale— a tiny wooden cabin beamed in from the Black Forest and plopped down right in the middle of Tinseltown.

Private investigation is the only thing we know, so that's what keeps the leaky roof over our heads and the martinis coming at the end of a long day. We may not be the most experienced Sherlocks on the block, but give us time, okay?

After all, we only hung up our shingle a year ago.

one

"*W*ell, that was fun," I said, taking a sip of dry Champagne.

"Huh," Terry grunted, not touching hers.

My attempts at cheering her up were falling flat. Here we were, flying first class to Los Angeles in a 767, drinking bubbly and nibbling lobster—the dregs of our extravagant Hawaiian vacation—and the brat was already sulking big-time.

She was wearing purple reflector shades that matched the floral print on her shirt, cut-off jeans that flared out at the knees, and neon pink flip-flops with white plastic flowers. Her toenails were painted mermaid green.

Terry'd gone native, and not only in terms of her dress. She'd left her heart on Kauai with a Polynesian hula dancer named Lailannii. The shades were to cover her puffy eyes; she'd cried like a baby all the way to the airport.

"We'll go back again, soon. I promise," I assured her.

"I am going back," Terry said, gazing down at the Pacific. "As soon as we get to LA, we'll get the money out from under the floorboards, I'll take my half, then I'm gone."

The money she was referring to—close to ten thousand dollars—was all we had left from our prior case. We'd retrieved it for a client who had subsequently shuffled off to the Great Buffalo in the sky. Since the client had no heirs, and since we were in possession of the money at the time of the client's death, Terry was convinced that it was legally ours. She'd argued that the IRS had their hands full sucking untold billions from the pockets of our fellow citizens, so there was no reason to bother them with our paltry sum. Before we left for Hawaii, we'd wrapped the cash in plastic bags and planted them beneath our little cabin for safekeeping. We then took the generous reward we'd received from an insurance company for returning a stolen painting by Francis Bacon, and blew the whole amount on three weeks of sunning and funning on the island of Kauai.

It seemed like a good idea at the time.

"I . . . I can't live without her," Terry said in a faint whisper.

I rolled my eyes behind closed lids. With her flair for the dramatic, Terry had already turned a vacation dalliance into a tale of soap-operatic passion worthy of Sweeps week.

"Why don't you take it for what it was, Terry? A *fling*."

"Don't tell me what my feelings are, Kerry! I think I'm in a better position to know what they are than you are!"

Due to the physics of the situation, she couldn't kick me, so she kicked the bag containing the memorial coconuts at her feet. She and Lailannii had found them during a walk on the beach and had carved their names into the hulls. To Terry they symbolized undying love. To me they symbolized a pair of big hairy nuts.

"Sorry," I said, grabbing a *People* magazine from the seat pocket in front of me and flipping it open. "Far be it from me to suggest that you shouldn't upend your whole life because of a few starry nights with a Polynesian hula dancer—"

"I don't need your condescending, racist attitude!"

"O-*kay*."

"I know what's real and what's not!"

"Lips zipped. Key thrown away. Forget I said anything."

Her hand flew into my line of vision and I flinched, thinking it was a fist coming at my skull. "Oh my God, is that Tatiana?" Terry said.

"What?"

She jabbed her finger into the second page of a photo spread in the magazine and sure enough, there she was. Tatiana Pavlov, the notorious beauty from our last case.

"It *is* Tatiana," I said in astonishment, flipping back to the opening of the article. The last time we saw Tatiana, she'd been ducking process servers and lawyers and a citywide dragnet designed to catch her mobster ex-husband, Sergei. And here she was being touted as the next big thing. The new one-name pop cultural phenomenon:

TATIANA!

Terry grabbed the magazine out of my hands. I grabbed it back. We wrestled with it for a moment, then it ripped in two. We each devoured our half of the article, then switched.

Tatiana had apparently been busy in the last few months. We knew she'd been dating a major Hollywood player and had managed to evade the police for weeks, only to resurface and be completely exonerated in a wide-ranging conspiracy involving a mainlining plastic surgeon, a silver-haired Beverly Hills attorney, and several well-heeled and very dead elderly widows.

But our girl had apparently become a media darling while we were lolling around on the island of Kauai. She'd landed a contract with Estée Lauder and bagged the role of the Bond girl in the next 007 movie. I wondered how much Tatiana's extraordinary looks had to do with her getting away scot-free in L'Affaire Butcher of Beverly Hills. She'd been guilty of fraud at a minimum, I knew, but the DA hadn't seen fit to bring charges. And the publicity had evidently brought Tatiana to the attention of the country's tastemakers.

"What a crock!" Terry said, laughing at the article.

It painted a picture of a tragic Russian folk heroine. Tatiana, we were informed in breathless prose, was a musical prodigy as a child—a pianist. But her fingers were dislocated by a cruel shopkeeper at the age of eight, when she was caught stealing a loaf of bread for her starving family of six brothers and sisters. Somehow she'd made it through a harsh life on the streets of Russia to immigrate to the United States, and had sworn on the tomb of Lenin she would make it big in the land of opportunity and bring her orphaned siblings along with her.

Whereas we knew her to be the worst sort of opportunistic, predatory man-eater, leaving a trail of carcasses in her wake as she went for the gold. The entire family back in the old country was probably the invention of some high-powered PR agent.

"Ha!" Terry guffawed. "You'd think she was the Mother Teresa of Moscow."

"Obviously, she got herself a publicist and a crack lawyer and a killer agent," I said, shaking my head in wonder. "Only in America."

"America will die like dogs!" a man shouted from the area in front of the cockpit.

Terry and I dropped the magazine.

A woman screamed and a baby squalled.

"Do not move!" We craned our necks around the seats in front of us to see a swarthy man tightening his grip around the neck of a wide-eyed flight attendant. He had a toothbrush pointed at her head, the handle filed to a lethal point, piercing her temple.

"Move and the airline whore gets an Oral-B in the brain!"

The man wore a cheap suit with a loud, patterned tie. He had crazed yellow eyes and a sweat-filmed face sprouting a five o'clock shadow at three A.M. Hawaii time.

There was a flash of movement behind me. A passenger from the main cabin rushed forward into first class, a sandy-haired guy in a Hawaiian shirt with a face like boiled lobster. Suddenly, another man jerked up in his seat and smashed the would-be hero in the face with a shaving kit. There were two of them.

Joe Tourist went down in the aisle.

"Do not move or you will die like the red-faced American pig!" the man with the toothbrush screamed. Holy shit! Were we being hijacked? Were these two clowns going to force their way into the cockpit with a toothbrush and fly us into the space needle at LAX?

The pilot's shaky voice came over the speaker:

"Ladies and gentlemen, please remain calm. We have contacted the authorities on the ground and are currently taking evasive measures . . ."

This isn't happening. This isn't happening, I chanted uselessly in my mind. My mouth was dry and my mind was blank, and all I could hear was the ocean of blood roaring in my ears.

As the flight attendant struggled in his grip, the man with the toothbrush addressed the horror-stricken passengers. "American infidels!" he shouted. "Do exactly as we say! We are in control of the plane!" He jabbed the toothbrush into the flight attendant's temple. She cried out and blood trickled down her ashen face. He turned to her and growled, "Now, you will talk to the pilot and you will tell him to—"

Suddenly, Terry made her move. She jumped to her feet with a coconut in her left hand, wound back, and then, with all the power that had made her a legend on the girls' softball circuit, she fired one of the coconuts at Swarthy Man, smashing him square on the side of the head.

He went down on the cockpit threshold, never knowing what hit him.

A well-known TV actor who was ten years past his prime and seated a few rows in front of us threw himself on top of him. Two more first-class passengers piled on like linebackers.

Meanwhile, an enraged Joe Tourist scrambled to his feet and took a flying leap at the shaving-kit-wielding man, knocking him ass over teakettle onto the laptop of a shrieking executive before decking him with a right hook.

The flight attendant stumbled toward the cockpit, only to find another hijacker rising from seats at the head of first class to stop her. He grabbed her around the neck with both hands, choking the life out of her.

I quickly reached for the other engraved coconut and clambered out into the aisle. I swung the coconut up two-handed and fired it toward the third man's head, where it hit with a sickening cracking sound. Blood dripped down the side of his face as he swayed on his feet. Then his eyes rolled back in his skull and he collapsed onto the lap of a plump blonde with orchids in her hair.

The flight attendant reeled away from her attacker, gasping for breath. The blonde pushed the fallen hijacker's sticky, limp form into the aisle with a disgusted *"Ugh!"*

We looked around. It was all over. There was a momentary silence as the passengers of Flight 222 took a collective breath. Even the screaming baby was quiet.

Then the pilot's voice came over the intercom again, sounding relieved and triumphant at once.

"This is your pilot speaking. The hijackers have been subdued. I repeat: The hijackers have been subdued, and we have alerted the authorities in Los Angeles. Go back to your seats and thank whatever God you believe in that a tragedy has been averted."

The crowd erupted in cheers. A few people began to cry. Off-key choruses of "America the Beautiful" were belted out as the crew moved quickly to bind the hands and feet of the three men and pull them, unconscious, to the rear of the plane.

After the commotion had died down, Terry and I took our seats again.

I looked out the window and saw the brilliant blue ocean undulating beneath us, the pure azure sky giving way to a hazy brown blob that beckoned us back home to Smogland.

"Well, that was fun," Terry said, her mood considerably brighter, as she picked up the pieces of the *People* magazine and settled back to read the latest showbiz gossip, while sipping the dry Champagne.

two

"*We* already told everything to the guys from the FAA, the airport police, and the LAPD. . . . Can't you get their notes?"

Terry was good and cranky after hours of debriefing up here in the airport security office at LAX. An army of stained Styrofoam cups was arrayed on the table in front of us, and I was so wired on bad coffee I thought my head was going to spin off the top of my neck and whiz through the air like a beanie cap propeller.

"I'm sure you can appreciate that in these matters, the FBI has to be in the loop," the cute guy in the dark suit said.

Or something to that effect.

I wasn't really listening. I was pondering the absence of a gold band on the left hand of Special Agent Dwight Franzen. He had blond hair in a buzz cut with a little cowlick over his forehead, and a squarish face with a broken nose that hinted at a violence beneath his friendly manner. The flawless skin made him appear younger than the mid-thirties I pegged him at, and I noticed he wasn't drinking the coffee.

Probably Mormon. Lotta those guys in the FBI are Mormon. Six kids and a nice frumpy little wife, dutifully homeschooling them. Or maybe six frumpy wives dutifully homeschooling eighteen kids. Duh, there's no wedding band. He'd have to have them piled up to his second knuckle.

"Pardon me?" Special Agent Franzen said in my direction.

"Huh?" Surprised out of my reverie, I looked over at Terry, who stared at me, frowning.

"Tired, huh?" Agent Franzen smiled, showing dazzling white teeth that overlapped a millimeter in the front.

I nodded. "Extremely."

He jotted something on his pad. "Now, which hijacker was wearing a wedding band?"

I said that out loud?

"I ask, because that's not something you usually see on Yemeni terrorists."

Terry got it now. She smiled wickedly and nodded at me. "Oh, she probably hallucinated it, Agent Franzen. You know how some girls just seem to have marriage on the brain . . ."

I rolled my eyes heavenward. *Why me?* I put my elbows on the table and buried my face in my hands, peeking out between my fingers as the heat rose in my cheeks.

Agent Franzen laughed good-naturedly and looked at the ring finger on his left hand. "I'm not married," he said, "if that's what you were wondering."

He chose to ignore my humiliation and continued with his questions, and Terry and I spent the better part of an hour reliving our citizens' arrest at 30,000 feet.

"Poor guys," Terry said when the interview was wrapping

up. "They signed on for seventy-two virgins, but they'll be taking it up the wazoo from a hundred feds instead."

"Yeah, my heart really bleeds for them," Franzen said, closing his notebook. "You know, this is gonna be big news. You girls are gonna be hounded by every reporter on the West Coast for a few days. Next time I see you, it'll probably be on the cover of *Newsweek*. Or maybe *Time* magazine's 'Twins of the Year.'"

I felt an onrush of panic. "We can't! They can't . . . they wouldn't!" I sputtered.

"What's the big deal?" Terry said. "Don't want your fifteen minutes?"

I sighed, shaking my head. "Tell me something, Terry. How are we going to do our job with our faces splashed all over the media? How are we gonna get things done if everyone sees us coming, if everyone knows who we are?"

She shrugged. "I'm gonna be in Kauai anyway. Maybe we should sell our story to Hollywood and hang up the gumshoes."

"Oh yeah, like anybody would believe it," I said. "Milk-bomb-throwing redheads. Sorry, but they're not making *Lucy* episodes anymore."

"We could be blondes . . . or brunettes," she said, really getting into the fantasy. "I always wanted to be a sexy brunette."

"With our luck, they'd cast the Olsen twins as us."

She made a face. "Right. No sale."

"You've got a point," Franzen said, laughing. "You might have a problem being anonymous PIs, but you could probably choose your duty at the Bureau after this."

"No, thanks," Terry said quickly, her felon status no doubt springing to mind. Probably they frowned on hiring people at America's foremost law-enforcement agency who had done time in the hoosegow.

"It's a nice thought, Agent Franzen," I told him, "but we'd better stick to the private sector."

"Call me Dwight," he said, giving me a look that almost melted the gum on my shoes.

"Dwight," I repeated dreamily, wondering for the first time where that name came from. Sounded like Tweety Bird confirming a cat sighting: *Dat's dwight, I taw a puddy tat.*

"Hold on a second." Franzen got up and ducked out the door behind us. "Uh, it's what I thought," he said when he came back in. "Security's still got the airport locked down, and there's a mob of reporters outside. They're shouting questions about the redheaded twins at any airport official who walks by."

I slumped in my seat. "Oh no."

"Don't worry," he said, picking up a hand radio. "I'll get you past them."

We punched eyeholes in the WH Smith bags that Agent Franzen obtained for us, then pulled them down over our heads. Shuffling our feet awkwardly, we were escorted by Franzen and three rifle-toting national guardsmen down in the elevator, across the airport lobby, and out the front doors.

The guardsmen shoved their way through the throng of reporters on the sidewalk, forcing them to give us a berth. I heard my own rapid breathing inside the bag and felt panic's clammy hands on my spine as the newspeople surged toward us, shouting:

"Are those the twins?"

"Give us a statement, ladies!"

"Your public wants to know more about you!"

Our public?

A boxy sedan screeched up to the curb, another dark-suited

man at the wheel. Franzen threw open the back door and shoved us into the back seat, our legs getting jumbled and our elbows jabbing each other as we clambered into the car. The door slammed behind us and the reporters began thumping on the window, raising a ruckus again.

"How'd you do it?"

"Give us your names!"

"What's your background?"

Our FBI driver yelled, "Ready?"

We nodded our shopping bags and he peeled away from the curb, burning rubber to the end of the terminal.

Ten minutes later, Terry and I removed the bags. I looked up and saw the driver's small brown eyes laughing at us in the rearview mirror. His meaty neck dripped over the edge of a white oxford collar, a pinkish scalp shining through the thinning bristles of his buzz cut.

"These bags, they're state-of-the-art FBI disguises?" Terry said to him. "That must really throw 'em for a loop when you infiltrate the mob."

The driver chuckled.

"I'm starting to get ideas about Tony," she said in a dead-on New Jersey accent. "He used to wear a Lucchesi's Meat Market bag over his head, now it's WH Smith. That don't strike you as fishy?"

He grinned. "Hey, sometimes you gotta improvise. Like you, with the terrorists. That was some fine footwork, ladies."

"Thanks," Terry said. "It was pure instinct."

"Wish we had more like you. So—" He waved to the windshield. "Where are we headed? I am at your command."

I looked around and saw that we were stuck in a mass of

motor vehicles manned by frustrated drivers creeping north on the 405 in a haze of hydrocarbons. Home, sweet home. "East on Santa Monica Boulevard, please."

"Hey," Terry asked the driver, "is somebody getting our luggage?"

"It should already be at your house."

She smiled at me and whispered, "Skycap service from the FBI. Is that great or what?"

I wished I could share Terry's childlike enthusiasm for the adventure that had been thrust upon us. But I wasn't so sure I was ready for this. The world had become strange enough in the last few years, and now we'd just fled our hometown airport under siege, like Michael Jackson after a baby-dropping junket. I didn't want my life further altered—I just wanted to go back to the way things were. And, truth be told, I was also a little bothered that the cute FBI guy hadn't driven us home himself.

"Hey," Terry said, pointing to my handbag. "Look."

There was a business card tucked into the outside pocket. I pulled it out and looked at it, my heart speeding up. Special Agent Franzen had slipped his card into my bag when I wasn't looking. I felt a thrill, like a second-grader who's just received a valentine card from the cutest boy in class. Or what I imagined that might feel like, since it had never happened to me.

I smiled in spite of myself. "Sweet," I said.

"Kerry's got a boyfriend," Terry sang mockingly.

I jabbed her in the ribs with my elbow. "Shut up!"

"*Ow!*" Terry yelled. "That hurt!"

"Hey!" the driver called, frowning at us in the rearview mirror. "Am I gonna have to come back there to separate you two?"

"She started it," I said, making a face at Terry. But I felt a surge of giddiness as I slipped Dwight Franzen's card into my wallet for safekeeping.

$\mathcal{T}$*erry jumped out* of the sedan before it had pulled to a complete stop. She ran up the walk to our house, yelling, "Puppies! Puppies . . . !"

Our FBI chauffeur turned in his seat and raised his eyebrows at me.

"Haven't seen our dogs in a few weeks," I explained. "Thanks for the ride."

"My pleasure." He gave me a two-fingered salute. "You girls are a couple of model Americans."

"Uh, yeah . . . thanks."

I slammed the door and ran up the walk. As promised, our bags were sitting on the porch. I hauled them inside, where Terry had already greedily snatched up both dogs, one in each hand. "Mommy's home!" she said, nuzzling them.

"Yeah, but don't get used to it," I told them, "'cause she's throwing you over for a chick in a grass skirt." I grabbed Paquito, a Pomeranian, out of her grip. "I'm the one who really loves you," I whispered into his oversized ear, petting the lustrous brown and white fur that had just regrown after a stint of the "puppy uglies," wherein Pomeranians lose their coats at six months.

Muffy, a pug, was slobbering all over Terry's face, the corners of her wall-to-wall smile reaching all the way to her silky ears. "Don't you listen to her," Terry said. "You guys are going to love it in Hawaii."

"Don't even joke about it!" I said. "You take these dogs, I'll track you to the ends of the earth. There won't even be enough DNA left to identify you when I'm done with you!"

She stuck her tongue out at me. "Where's Uncky Lance?" she said, baby-talking to Muffy.

Lance Manley was an actor/bodyguard we'd met on our last case. He had dubious qualifications for both professions, but seemed to have done all right by us as a dog-sitter. Lance was as loyal as a golden retriever and almost as intelligent; a great guy, but there was a *Back in Five Minutes* sign permanently attached to his forehead.

Just then he came hulking in the back door, blocking all light with his six-foot-six frame and massive shoulders. Drill a couple of screws into his neck and he could be a stunt double for you-know-who.

"Hey, girls, welcome home! I was out on the deck bagging some rays."

He gave us a hug, mashing us against the retaining wall of his chest and smelling pleasantly of suntan lotion. His blond brush cut was newly streaked with highlights from the sun (or Sun-In).

"Just in time," he said. "I got a slew of auditions in the next couple of weeks. Things are really heating up with my career. My agent says I'm just about to happen."

"Great." I peeled myself out of his grip. "So were the dogs good while we were away?"

"You bet," he said, giving Paquito a pat on the head.

Terry pulled some twenties out of her pocket. "Thanks a lot, Lance. Here's a hundred. And we have more inside the house—"

Lance reeled back as though he'd been hit in the chest with a two-by-four. "Money? You want me to take *money*?"

Terry looked over at me. "Uh, yeah. We said we'd pay you, remember?"

Huge hands cut the air like flying mattresses. "Whoa, whoa, whoa. Lance Manley would not even be standing here today if it wasn't for you girls."

He had a point—we *were* kind of responsible for Lance's being alive. But I didn't want him feeling obligated for the rest of his life because of it. And it could be argued that his own bumbling attempt at rescuing our family was the reason that *all* of us were standing here, even if he did kind of flub it.

I decided to give him the credit anyway. "Lance, you were the one who saved *us*, remember?"

His iceberg-blue eyes went off into the distance while he turned the memory over in his reptilian brain. "Yeah," he said in a raspy Eastwood voice. "I guess I kinda did." Then his eyes snapped back to me. "Hey, did you hear about the stuff going down at the airport? They broke into *General Hospital* with the news. Some guys tried to hijack a plane from Hawaii, and apparently some redheaded tw—"

His jaw unhinged itself and dropped four inches.

"Omigod! It was *you*?"

Terry and I shrugged modestly.

"Did you put bags over your heads? No offense, but that looked really goofy. They're calling you the Smith twins, 'cause the bags said WH Smith."

"*What?*"

"Come look!"

He ran to the TV and clicked it on. Sure enough, there we were, stumbling through the media mob in our state-of-the-art disguises. Really goofy didn't cover it. *Complete losers* was more apt.

Terry rolled her eyes. "We should have let them take our picture. Now this is going to turn into a *thing* . . ."

Right on cue, an excited CNN announcer wondered, "Who are they? *What* are they? How did they subdue a plane full of terrorists? The answer—unknown. Their identities—a mystery."

Cut to a female reporter holding a microphone in the face of Joe Tourist, who was running a hand through his lank, sandy hair. "I don't know who they were. Some kind of kung fu babes or something. They went flying through the air just like the people in those martial arts movies. . . ."

"What did they look like? Can you give us a description?"

"Oh, pretty cute, I guess. In their twenties. Not much meat on 'em, though. Kinda flat-chested."

"What?" I shouted at the screen. "What's that got to do with anything?"

The reporter yanked the microphone away from him. "We'll have more on the mystery of the twin avengers when we return."

"Twin avengers?" I moaned, collapsing on the couch. "Oh my God, our lives are *over*."

Lance's small eyes were popping out of his head. "Wow! I didn't know you two had black belts!"

"We beaned the terrorists with some coconuts," Terry said, laughing. "We didn't fly through the air."

"But this makes a much sexier lead-in," I said, wondering how long it would take for the story to fizzle. Surely if they had no one to interview, nobody willing to go on the air and blab endlessly about the incident, the furor would die down. The newshounds would move on to fresh meat.

"I wouldn't worry about it," Terry said. "The public has the long-term memory of a gnat. Quick—what was the name of the girl who sued Clinton for sexual harassment?"

"Paula Jones," Lance and I answered.

"Yeah, well. It's time we went to the bank anyway. Kerry, go get the flashlight."

"Right," I said, glad to have something to take my mind off the news broadcast.

I retrieved the Mag flashlight from the kitchen while Terry pried up the floorboards in front of the stone fireplace with a Swiss Army knife. She had scraped the sealer out from between the boards back when we were kids, and since then the crawl space had been home to secret caches of everything from treasure maps and comic books, to beer in later years.

"What's down there?" Lance said. "I mean, besides spiders and stuff."

"My aloha money," Terry said, wedging herself down into the dark hole.

"Take more than money to get me down there," he said with a shiver.

"It's close to ten thousand dollars."

"Oh." He leaned over the opening, suddenly cured of arachnophobia. "Need any help?"

Terry took the flashlight and ducked out of sight. We heard her scuffing along in the crawl space for a few seconds, then a howl went up like she was being eaten alive.

Was there a hatchet murderer under the house?

I looked at Lance, who was frozen to the spot, his eyes bugged.

Great bodyguarding instincts, Lance.

"Terry?" I shouted, jumping down into the hole after her. "What is it? What's the matter?"

When my eyes adjusted to the darkness, I saw her on her hands and knees in the mulchy dirt. The flashlight was lying on the ground where it had rolled, the light pointing away from her. I scuttled over on my knees. "Say something, for chrissakes. You're scaring me to death!"

She tossed a handful of confetti in my direction by way of an answer. I picked up a little spitball and unraveled it with my fingers. It was about a centimeter square and bore a presidential-looking nose in green ink.

"What the hell?"

Terry picked up the flashlight and pointed it toward a dark corner. A gray mama possum stared frozen into the beam like an inmate caught by the searchlight. On her back were several tiny pink hairless possums giving us their best *Who, me?* looks.

Ah, the natural world. How it put all our little human problems in perspective—

"Goddamned rodents! Where's my gun!" I yelled.

I didn't have a gun, but it was a persistent fantasy at times like this.

"Calm down," Terry said.

"They *ate* our nest egg?!"

"It's their nest now." She pointed the light toward a pile of debris in the corner, and there it was—a nice, cozy little bed made out of shredded greenbacks in the center of the ripped plastic bag. "And they're not rodents, they're marsupials. Like kangaroos."

"They're big nasty furballs with sharp little teeth! That makes 'em rats in *my* book! I *told* you we should put the money in the bank!"

She laughed, crawling toward me. "So we put it in the bank of Universal Karma. Lighten up."

"Lighten up? You get over there right now and see if there's anything left! They can't have chewed through every single bill."

"No way. I'm not digging through possum poop for some lousy money."

"This was *your* idea!"

She grabbed the sides of the floorboards and started to hoist herself back up into the house. Lance grabbed her under the arms and yanked her up in one swift movement, her feet disappearing into the room above as she sang:

"Instant karma's gonna get you . . ."

"I'll karma *you!* I'm gonna go Hannibal Lecter on your ass! You're gonna be a sister soufflé! Get back here, Terry. I'm counting to three, and if you're not back down here, so help me God . . . *One, two—*"

The boards clanked into place over my head.

A half hour later, I came out of the shower with a towel around my wet hair, the spiderwebs and possum urine scrubbed and scalded away. But I was still burning with the humiliation of digging through a pile of spit wads to find any surviving dollar bills. Lance and Terry sat at the table in the kitchen under the harsh lamplight wearing latex gloves, trying to piece together hundred- and fifty-dollar stubs with the intensity of a couple of retirees doing a jigsaw puzzle made out of money.

There were two fifties repaired with cellophane tape on the corner of the table.

"Did you match the serial numbers on the front of the bills?" I asked them.

Lance and Terry looked at each other.

"Dang," Lance said. He pushed his reading glasses up on his nose and peered at one of the repaired bills, checking the numbers against each other. "Yep, this one's a winner."

I flopped down on the couch. "Feeling better?" Terry said.

"No."

"Forgive me?"

"Not a chance."

"It's good for your soul."

"Up yours."

"Oooh, hostility. Bad for your soul."

"You know what would be good for my soul? For that phone

to ring with a paying job. You know, like we used to have . . . ?
Matrimonial clients, warehouse thieves, deadbeat dads? An
honest day's work, with an honest day's pay—"

The phone rang.

Lance and Terry whipped around in their chairs to stare at
the phone.

"She's scary," Lance whispered.

I grabbed up the receiver. "Hello?"

"Hello, dear. It's Reba."

It was our great-aunt, who'd recently moved to Malibu with
her new love, Eli Weintraub, my erstwhile mentor. They'd met
on our last case and fallen instantly in lust. Now Eli had taken
retirement and Reba had bought a beachfront house so the
two of them could walk arm-in-arm in the surf, eat fresh fish
by candlelight, and drop in occasionally on Reba's son, our
cousin Robert, who was recovering from alcoholism in a spectacular $10,000-a-week rehab center called New Horizons. The
place was famous for getting celebrities off booze and drugs and
keeping them clean and sober for up to as many as thirty
days—or as long as it took to get them through their court
dates.

"Hi, Reba, we just got back from Hawaii. What's up?"

"I have some bad news, I'm afraid."

I must have made a terrible face, because Terry started
yelling, "What's the matter? Is it Eli? Did she screw him to
death?"

Shut up, I mouthed. "What is it, Reba? What's wrong?"

"Well, apparently your cousin has gone missing from New
Horizons," she said, and I heard fear mingled with her tone of
disgust.

"He fell off the wagon?" I said, as Terry picked up the extension to listen in.

"Well, we don't really know. That is, the staff at the clinic doesn't know. He didn't take anything with him, only his flip-flops. He left his copy of the *Bhagavad Gita* in his room. And he's never without that these days, as you know."

Robert had gone on a quest for natural, spiritual highs when he decided to give up the booze, and he never went anywhere without the Hindu Bible under his arm. This didn't sound good.

"What does Eli say about it?"

"Nothing. He's left me."

"Left you?" Terry exclaimed. "You just moved in togeth—"

"That's hardly my biggest concern right now," Reba said archly.

"Well, what are you going to do?" Terry asked her.

"Would you be a couple of dears and come out to see me? I'd like to discuss giving you a job. I'll pay you, of course."

"Reba, don't be ridiculous," I said. "Robert's family. If there's anything we can do, we're happy to. But we won't take a di— *Owww!*"

Terry had stomped down hard on my toe.

"We'll be right out," she said. "Don't worry about a thing, Reba. We're on the case." She hung up the phone and gave me an exasperated look. "You want to buy groceries with taped-up fifties the rest of your life?"

"Excuse me if I have qualms about charging a family member for finding another family member. Excuse me if I think that might just get us into even more karmic muck."

"Will you relax? The timing is perfect. You gotta let the universe do its thing and provide for us, see?"

"Whatever you say, O great and wise freckled chick," I said, rolling my eyes toward Nirvana.

three

*W*e decided to change clothes before hitting the road. I was pleased to see Terry ditch the island-hopper look for her usual uniform of flared, low-rider jeans, a long-sleeved scoop-neck tee, and a dog collar around her slender neck. She topped it off with a motorcycle jacket in the exact same shade of hot pink as our Harley-Davidson Softail Deuce. She also swapped her rubber flip-flops for black leather riding boots with a high chunky heel, ornamental metal studs, and a fantail of short fringe on the side.

I was considerably more subdued in my tan capris, white peasant blouse, vintage black leather jacket, and white bike helmet. Seated on the back of the Harley, I looked like the California Highway Patrol officer who had Terry in custody (which wasn't too far from the truth).

We fed the dogs, assuring them we'd be back soon, then

Terry and I fired up the bike and took off down the 10 Freeway west. Traffic had eased, but it still took a full hour to get to the point where the 10 dead-ends into the Pacific Coast Highway. We hooked a right on PCH and headed north toward Malibu.

The highway travels the length of the bay from Santa Monica up through Zuma Beach, past the rocky promontory of Point Dume and beyond the Channel Islands, ultimately cutting through the Sierra Nevada Mountains to emerge at Hearst's Waterloo, the castle at San Simeon. Once you hit Malibu, there's a sign that promises *27 Miles of Scenic Beauty*, a sign announcing the population to be 13,000, and my personal favorite—a sign that says *Falling Rocks*.

I'd never actually seen a biker bonked on the noggin by stones rumbling down off the cliff, or seen a car flattened by a boulder. But I unconsciously hunched up my shoulders as we zipped past the rock face, certain that there was a landslide up there with my name on it that was even now preparing to hail down on me like a skull-denting meteor shower. Terry didn't worry about it, of course, and buzzed along mindlessly as if the warning signs were for suckers.

She had paid a fortune for the bike when we cashed in Dad's insurance money. With its eye-popping custom paint job, it looked like Barbie's midlife crisis after being dumped by Ken for a younger doll—one with even higher arches and pointier boobs. I'm sure it seemed like a good idea at the time, but at that point she was doing more than a little recreational coke. Thank goodness that was all ancient history, I thought, as we sailed past the glittering blue ocean.

But now we had other concerns: Cousin Robert was missing in action, and I wondered what could have happened to the fifty-year-old mama's boy. Until he stopped drinking, Robert could be counted on like the Earth's rotation. At ten A.M., he rose, poured some cognac into the coffee brought by Grizzie, Reba's grumpy Irish maid, and then began his daylong career of imbibing and slapping paint on a series of canvasses that rarely sold. Then, after a life-altering fall down the stairs, he decided he was wasting his life and swore off the sauce for good. He'd enrolled in the program at New Horizons, just up the road here in Malibu, drying out in a spartan room with only a grass mat, wooden cot, and beefcake picture of His Holiness the Dalai Lama hanging over a scented candle.

Terry turned the motorcycle left onto the one-car-wide shoulder in front of Reba's new redwood beach house. Our aunt was a Beverly Hills grande dame, a well-preserved, self-obsessed seventy-year-old who had married and buried five husbands within four city blocks without ever changing her zip code (need I say—*90210?*). Each husband had died richer than the last, and Reba had more money than God as a result. More than the entire GNP of Heaven, probably. She'd been a service industry unto herself, keeping an army of boutique owners, caterers, plastic surgeons, manicurists, and masseurs fat and happy. They'd shed bitter tears when she packed it in for the beach at Malibu, but she'd decided she needed a fresh start after two of her best canasta-playing buddies wound up dead during our last case.

It was our first trip to the new house. We'd been too busy tying up loose ends before our Hawaii trip to pay a visit.

Terry parked, and we hiked up the sand-sprinkled wooden stairs to the front door. The second story of the house was here at street level, the first story built directly on the sand below. A third, smaller section angled off toward the ocean with a skylight on top.

"Nice digs," Terry said, knocking.

"What'd you expect, a fixer-upper?"

Grizzie opened the door with a sour look on her florid face, a whisk broom in her hand. "Mind your feet," she said by way of greeting. She thrust the broom at Terry, who looked at me, perplexed.

"Sand," I said.

"Oh." Terry lifted her boots and whisked the sand away from each sole before setting foot inside the door. Then she handed the broom to me and I performed the same ritual.

"Blighted sand!" Grizzie said. "Trackin' itself in here like we was bleedin' cave dwellers. I tell ya, girls. I don't know how much more o' this I can take."

Grizzie obviously preferred Beverly Hills, where there are no untamed natural elements trailing into one's domicile. Just nice manicured lawns and the occasional circular advertising the services of a renowned plastic surgeon littering the front walk. Obviously, the sand was stuck in her craw as well as on the new floor.

"You'll get used to it, Griz," I assured her.

"Not likely! Then there's the gull droppin's, and the dampness, and bits of shell everywhere, and now a dead body on top o' everything!"

"Excuse me?" I said, blinking.

But Grizzie had already stomped off in the direction of the kitchen, muttering under her breath. Terry and I looked at each other, wondering if we'd heard her correctly.

"Darlings!" Reba trilled.

She breezed in wearing her beach attire—an African-themed caftan in bold yellows and reds, with a thick elastic band holding back the hennaed hair from her high-boned, patrician face. Gloria Swanson does Nairobi. "I'm so glad you're here! I've been at my wits' end."

"Hi, Reba," we said in tandem, receiving our air kisses. "What's up?"

"Well, it's been hell around here. Robert missing, and Eli leaving me because he's too bored at the beach, and—"

"And a dead body somewhere?" I inquired, just to test my hearing.

She made a little moue of distaste. "Let's have coffee first, before we jump right into the unpleasantness."

Unpleasantness? *Okay . . .*

Terry looked at me goggle-eyed. I shrugged back at her, then followed Reba as she scuffed on red leather slingbacks into the breakfast room. It was paneled with light wood and had a spectacular view of the ocean through a spotless plate-glass window. Grizzie plunked down a tray with ceramic cups, a milk jug, a thermos pitcher, and a bowl containing large brown lumps of natural sugar.

"Where's the silver service?" I asked. Reba had been using the same silver coffee service for as long as I could remember, buffed to a mirror sheen by Grizzie's chapped, red hands. Its absence seemed somehow sinister.

"Hmmph!" Grizzie said, before stomping back into the kitchen to prepare the muffins and mangoes that always accompanied the coffee.

"It's too 'heirloom' for the beach," Reba said. "We're much more relaxed out here."

"I know *I'm* relaxed. Aren't you?" Terry quipped.

I sighed and waited impatiently for Reba to come to the point. We were used to her going miles around "unpleasant" issues, but if there was a dead body somewhere in the vicinity, I wanted to know what the story was.

"As I was saying," Reba started to say, pouring the coffee with upraised pinkies, "Eli got bored. I should have known that such a vital, virile man would have difficulty adjusting to a life of leisure. I just didn't think about it. I was too blinded by love."

Eli Weintraub was smart and funny, and a peerless criminal attorney. But he had a stogie surgically attached to his bottom lip, suits that were a testament to the indestructibility of polyester, dating, as they did, from the mid-seventies, and he looked like a giant, pockmarked Teletubby, minus the head antennae. I loved Eli, too. But you'd almost *have* to be blind to be romantically attracted to him.

"Not enough challenge without his legal practice?" Terry asked.

"Precisely."

"Well, perhaps if you told him you'd found a *dead body* . . ." I suggested.

"Well, that's just the thing, dears." Reba waved a diamond-encrusted hand in the air. "I drag him to the beach, he gives up his practice, then I present him with a missing son and a dead body in my rug? I don't know how much strain a new relationship can be expected to endure—"

"WHAT BODY?" Terry yelled.

Reba's jaw flapped open at this rudeness. "Well, I was getting to that, missy, if you'll hold your horses."

Terry fell forward, sinking her head in her hands. I leaned back in my chair and took a sip of coffee. We'd have to play it Reba's way, however insane. She took a deep breath, smoothed out her caftan, and finally dove into the story with morbid zest.

"I went into the guest bedroom earlier, where I'd stored the rugs that Lenore left me in her will—"

We nodded.

"I wanted to see if any of them were suited to the new house, and I thought perhaps you girls would like one for your little cabin. You know, to dress it up a bit—"

Terry waved impatiently. "Stick to the body. Where was it?"

"I was *getting* to that," Reba huffed. "I noticed that one of the rugs—a Turkish dinner rug, actually—well, it was rather lumpy. So I took it by the corner and unrolled it, and what do you know? Out she came!"

"She?" we asked. "A girl?"

"A young woman. Somewhere in her twenties, with blond hair, bleached to within an inch of its life." She clapped a hand over her mouth. "Oh dear, that was insensitive, wasn't it?"

I rolled my eyes. "Reba, I don't think this woman's in a position to mind a catty remark. What else? Do you know what killed her?"

"Well, how would I know that?"

"Was there any obvious cause of death, like a bullet hole, stab wounds . . . ?"

"Oh my, yes."

"What was it?" Terry said.

"Well, the decapitation, I should think."

"Decapitation!" I shouted, and watched in alarm as Terry's face practically turned purple. "Why didn't you say anything about this when you called?"

"Well, you never know who could be listening in on a phone call, do you? I thought it more prudent to discuss this in person."

"All right," I said. "Please continue. So . . . the head was forcibly separated from the body?"

"Well, that's a reasonable assumption, isn't it?" she said. "There aren't too many people walking around headless, that I know of."

"So what you actually found was the head," Terry said.

"No."

"I thought you said she was a bottle blonde."

Reba pursed her lips in distaste. "Yes, but I wasn't referring to her *head* hair."

Oh dear God. Why did we ever come home?

How did the dead girl get there, who could she possibly be, had there been any strange persons lurking about the house . . . ? Reba had no answers, no ideas.

"And how long have the rugs been here?" Terry wanted to know.

"Oh, a couple of weeks," Reba said.

"And you just now noticed this 'lump'?"

"It wasn't there before, I assure you."

"No, it wouldn't have been," I said. "The body can't have been delivered in a rug two weeks ago. You'd have noticed the smell, no way around that." I finally thought to ask her, "You *have* called the police, haven't you?"

Reba leaned in and whispered, "I thought it best to keep this *en famille* for the moment."

"But . . . when did you find it?" Terry asked, her mouth agape.

"This morning."

Terry slapped her forehead. "You found the body this morning and you waited for us to get back from Hawaii? Reba, do you know how this looks?"

"How?" she asked, her eyes big and innocent.

"Bad," I said.

"Well, I don't see why the big rush. She's not going anywhere. . . . Anyway, it was closer to noon, now that I think of it."

Something was very wrong here. And I wasn't thinking only of the brutally murdered woman. It was Reba's reaction to it that was bothering me. Even for someone with her boundless capacity for denial, this was much too casual a response to such an outrageous occurrence.

Then it hit me. She'd been *afraid* to call the police. But why? Did she think someone in the household had had something to do with the heinous deed?

No. The idea was ridiculous.

We convinced Reba that the police had to be notified. And even though the last time I'd seen him I hadn't been too friendly to Detective John Boatwright of Beverly Hills Homicide, I decided to call him on the grounds that it would be best to report this to someone who knew us.

Okay, maybe "not too friendly" isn't the right way to describe what happened. He'd come over to take me out on a date, and there'd been a little case of mistaken identity wherein he stuck his tongue down Terry's throat. I called him a bastard, and Terry bashed him over the head with a bunch of flowers he'd brought for me, and then he left.

So what first date is perfect?

Still, I was pretty sure he'd give us the benefit of the doubt when it came to a dead body in our aunt's house. Whatever the idiosyncrasies of our family, I didn't think he'd suspect us all of some big plot to murder an anonymous blonde. Or whatever color her hair was.

Boatwright didn't answer his extension, so I tried his cell phone. He seemed genuinely happy to hear from me—he probably thought I was calling to apologize for the kiss snafu—but I got down to the new business right away.

"I was hoping you could help us with something," I said.

"I can't fix traffic tickets."

"Ha. I wish it was that simple."

"Okay, what is it?"

"Well, my aunt Reba left Beverly Hills and moved out to Malibu. She, uh, bought a house on the beach, and she's found . . . well, she's found a corpse in it."

A long silence. "You're kidding, right?"

"Um, no."

"By corpse, do you mean a human body? I mean, we're not talking about a dead seagull or something like that."

"No, it's a human body. One that, unfortunately, is missing its head. So I guess it's more of a torso, strictly speaking."

"Arms and legs intact?"

"I'm assuming. Didn't look. Didn't want to mix my DNA up with the scene, you know what I mean?"

"Then we'll call it a body for now. Male or female?"

"Female, twenties."

"And where did your aunt find this body?"

"In her spare bedroom."

He cleared his throat. "Where was it exactly?"

"Well, she'd had a bunch of Oriental rugs shipped to her by a Beverly Hills law firm—you remember that business with Lenore Richling?"

"Uh-huh."

"Anyway, the rugs had been housed in a storage facility, then shipped to Reba after the will was probated. And she started to roll them out to, you know, see if any of them were suited to her new beach lifestyle . . . because they might be too heirloom—"

"Too formal," Reba corrected me in the background. "Silver can be heirloom, not rugs."

"Sorry, uh, too *formal* for the beach. So she rolled out a Turkish dinner rug, and what do you know? Out tumbled a headless body!"

He sighed like Sisyphus looking up a big friggin' hill. "Look. If you're in Malibu, you need the sheriff's department. But if you want, I can make the call for you."

Uh-oh. The word "sheriff" conjured up someone with a pair of six-shooters and a ten-gallon Stetson who referred to a woman as "little lady." I wouldn't mind too much, but if someone called Terry "little lady," she'd probably end up back in the slammer for assaulting an officer.

"Can't you come, too?" I asked a little more timorously than I'd planned. "I mean, I know it's not your beat, but—"

"I wish I could, but I'm tied up at a triple homicide."

"Well, okay. If you think that's more *important* . . ." I heard another sigh, so I went into placating mode. "But it does make me feel better to know you're going to speak to them on our behalf. You will tell them we're not murderers, right?"

"I'll vouch for you not being a murderer, but I don't know about your sister. Listen, I don't have to tell you not to touch anything, do I?"

"No, uh-uh," I said. I knew the drill, and besides, dead-torso-touching was not high on my list of fun things to do. I gave him Reba's new address.

"Okay, bye," he said, like we'd just had a normal conversation, then hung up.

I let out my breath. "He's calling the sheriff for us," I announced.

"Well, I feel better already," Reba said. "That's a tremendous weight off my shoulders." Then she clapped a hand to her mouth again. "Oh my, that *was* insensitive, wasn't it?"

Terry was tempted to take a look at the ghoulish scene, but I dissuaded her from going into the bedroom on the strength of the DNA argument. I told her she didn't want her skin cells mingling with the dead girl's.

"Nobody's going to think we did this," she said.

"You never know. They can't find some other suspect, they might very well try to pin it on one of us. Everyone around here is still touchy about O.J. slipping through the cracks."

Then, as if it were "high tea" instead of a crime scene, Grizzie served some fresh coffee, along with English muffins and mangoes. This represented Reba's idea of the four essential food groups: protein (half and half), grain (refined flour), mangoes (fruit), and coffee beans (legumes). It was literally all we ever saw her eat, day or night. The performance of this ritual was comforting, but surreal at the same time. I couldn't believe it was happening with a dead body in the next room.

"Reba," I said, "before the sheriff's deputies get here, I think we should get a few things straight."

She smeared orange marmalade on a muffin. "What things, dear?"

"Well, for instance—shouldn't we tell Eli about all this? I mean, he *was* living here and you *are* his—" *Bitch* probably wasn't the word I wanted. "His *paramour.*"

Reba shrugged her bony shoulders and sniffed. "If he wants to know what's going on over here, he can jolly well call once in a while."

Terry looked at me, shaking her head.

"I have a couple of reasons for asking," I said with all the patience I could muster. "One, he's a criminal defense attorney, which might come in handy under the circumstances—"

Reba's eyes bugged. "Surely you don't mean to suggest—"

I put a soothing hand on hers. "I'm only suggesting that it's always a good idea to have a lawyer when . . . *bodies* . . . are found on the premises."

She gave me a *So what?* flick of her chin.

"Second, we have to think about Robert. His going missing from the rehab place just as a body shows up, well . . . it looks kinda funny."

"Ha-ha funny?" Reba said, cocking an eyebrow.

"Certainly *not* ha-ha funny."

"Then *suspicious* funny?"

I nodded.

"Well, I'm sure there's no connection, one with the other," Reba said, waving a butter knife dismissively.

"We're sure there isn't, either," Terry said, picking up on my solicitous tone, "but like Kerry was saying, you want to have your bases covered with the law. So . . . how was Robert doing with sobriety? Was that working out for him?"

Reba glared at Terry, and I swear I saw her pupils elongate like a furious mother cat's. "I won't even discuss it with you. I don't like what you're insinuating!"

Being solicitous was getting me nowhere, I realized. I leaned forward and enunciated harshly to make my point. "Reba, there's been a murder! We don't have time to be careful of everyone's feelings!"

She cowered from me, leaning back in the chair, her mouth a big round O. "Have you been taking assertiveness training?"

"No!"

"Well, you could have fooled me." She was instantly back in control, sitting up and nibbling on her muffin.

"The police are going to be a bit more assertive than I'm being now," I said. "So you might want to try being a little more forthcoming."

"She means cut the bullshit," Terry said.

"I *know* what forthcoming means, Ms. Potty Mouth. All right . . . what do you want to know?"

I steeled my ocular muscles to keep my eyes from spinning. "I want to know exactly when Robert went into the rehab program, exactly when he disappeared, and exactly who else has been in this house at any time besides you, Eli, Robert, and Grizzie."

Reba jabbed a berry-colored nail in the air. "Excellent point. It could have been someone I gave access to. Some nefarious someone with a body to hide. An evil plumber, for instance . . . or a serial killer disguised as the UPS man!"

I nodded encouragement. "Now you're thinking it through. That's really good. So you had a plumber and a UPS man here?"

"No," Reba said. "But the police won't necessarily know that, will they?"

Terry shook her head, sighing.

"Reba, I think it'd be best if we stuck to the truth for now," I said. "We're not trying to cover anything up, we're trying to figure out who the real killer is, okay? Now, who has actually been in the house?"

Reba tilted her head, considering it. "There've been a couple of people from the neighborhood who came by to welcome us, but they didn't come in . . . and a real estate agent who wanted to know if I cared to sell—"

"Right after you moved in?" Terry said. "That's a little odd, isn't it?"

"I don't think so. They're very aggressive out here. Apparently, there's always some movie or television person who has a little success and can't wait to blow it on a Malibu address and . . . Oh! That reminds me. There was an actress who came by also. Lovely girl, I must remember to ask who did her face— when I get to know her better, of course. One doesn't just walk up to a total stranger and say, 'Great face-lift! Who did it?'

because you're not supposed to know, you see. But of course, everyone *does*. . . ."

Sweet Jesus, how did you keep this woman focused?

"Who was the actress?" Terry said impatiently.

"Hmm, let me think. She has auburn hair, late forties, wonderful style . . . I know! She was in that television series about the pioneering gynecologist on the open plains. . . . What was the name of it?"

Terry frowned. "Gynecologist . . . ? You mean *Catherine James, Midwife*?"

"That's the one," Reba said, nodding. "So engaging. Very authentic portrayal of life in the Old West. But you know, I would have sworn they used the same infant over and over in the show . . . poor child must have been birthed a hundred times—"

"Reba . . . *focus*," I said.

Her head whipped back around to me. "Right. At any rate, that was the show, and her name was . . . Heather Granger! That's it—Heather Granger. She came around and asked if I would participate in her charity beach house tour."

"What's that?"

"Oh, you know, people come in buses to see how the other half lives, and you give them finger sandwiches and whatnot. They buy a ticket to the tour and the proceeds go to some children's fund or other . . ."

Maybe the fund for overworked infant actors.

"This is interesting," Terry said. "Did she come in the house?"

"Yes, she very much wanted to see it. I didn't see why I shouldn't show it to her."

"That's kind of forward for a total stranger," I said, "don't you think?"

"But she wasn't a total stranger, she was Catherine James, Midwife. One hardly expects a heroic pioneer woman to go stashing dead bodies in one's house, does one?"

"Don't underestimate actresses," I said. "They're killers. They have to be, to get by in that business. Did she see the rugs?"

"As a matter of fact, I did show them to her. I said that if they weren't suitable for this place, and after you girls had your pick, I might donate them to her charity."

"Did she take a particular interest in them?" Terry asked. "Did she take a close look at them or anything?"

Reba closed her eyes as she tried to remember. "You know, I think she *did* follow me into the room. She gave the rugs a quick once-over. You know, eyeballing them to gauge their value . . ."

Terry nodded at me. File this chick under "suspect," her expression said.

"Did she seem interested in your schedule?" Terry pressed her. "Like when you were out of the house or when you were home? Did she seem unusually interested in where the doors were, or whether you had an alarm system or anything?"

Reba shook her head, adamant. "I assure you, she did nothing to arouse suspicion. If she had, well . . . I'd have noticed, wouldn't I?"

I sincerely doubted it. If Heather Granger had walked into the house dragging the dead girl by the hand, Reba would still have been fixated on the actress's cosmetic surgery and her wardrobe.

Hmmm. What could a devious person do without necessarily arousing suspicion?

"Did she ask to use the bathroom or anything?" I asked.

Reba perked up at this. "Why, I do believe she did. Said

she'd been out for hours and needed to freshen up. . . . I directed her to the guest powder room. Why?"

"Is there a big window in the powder room?"

Reba's eyes popped. "Now that you mention it, there's a sliding glass door. She could have unlocked it and left herself a way to get back in!"

I got a thumbs-up from my hard-to-impress twin. "Good one," Terry said.

"No, it's out of the question," Reba said. "I simply can't believe that such a nice young woman could be involved in anything so horrible. . . . It's inconceivable."

"Nevertheless," I said, "I think you should mention it to the police."

"Very well," she conceded, "I'll mention it."

"Good. Now, when did Robert go into the rehab program?"

"About three weeks ago. He would have finished in another week, but he went missing two days ago."

"Did you call the police about this?" Terry asked her.

"No." Reba pierced a table crumb with her nail and flicked it onto her plate. "Naturally, I assumed he left to go on a toot. They say it happens. Faced with a life of sobriety stretching out endlessly in front of them, some of the patients leave the program and . . . Well, suffice it to say that I didn't want my son dragged home from some cocktail bar in chains."

"And he took nothing with him when he left?"

"No. All of his things were in his room. I went and collected them." She stood up and scurried over to the master bedroom, then came back out carrying a Louis Vuitton tote.

Terry unzipped the bag and brought out Robert's copy of the *Bhagavad Gita* and a smoking jacket, followed by several pairs of socks and some paisley silk boxers. "Of all times to be without latex gloves," she said, wrinkling her nose. Then she laughed and pulled out a cellophane package of Ding Dongs. "They let them eat Ding Dongs in the program?"

"I doubt that," I said. "I'm sure they're supposed to be developing good nutritional habits."

Reba scowled at the junk food. "I've never known my son to eat garbage like that."

"Yeah, but recovering alcoholics tend to crave sweets," Terry said. "Maybe Robert's been sneaking off campus to buy them." She dug in the bag again and pulled out a slick four-color brochure by the corner. It looked like an ad for a science fiction movie—a bright white light illuminating some kind of spaceship, with an otherworldly creature alighting from the craft.

"What the hell?" Terry grabbed a napkin from the serving tray and a coffee spoon, opening the brochure without touching it. The lurid red type said "Children of the Cosmos," and inside was a picture of a bald man covered in gold paint and draped in gold lamé who was billed as "Abaddon, Messenger of the Gods."

"Huh?" I said. "Who's this Abaddon person?"

"What makes you think he's a person?" Terry said.

I read aloud from the brochure: "'Abaddon communicates regularly with the alien intelligences who are the true Masters of the Earth.'"

"Uh-huh," Terry said. "Well, if they're running things down here, they could do a better job of it."

"That's strange." Reba peered at the brochure. "He's never been interested in this sort of nonsense before. Masters of the Earth, indeed."

Grizzie cleared away the coffee, making an extremely rare foray into the conversation. "Best not be judging these things without all the facts, missus," she said, then trundled away without further comment.

The rest of us looked at one another in shock.

Terry started to sing the *Twilight Zone* theme: *"Dee dee dee dee, dee dee dee dee . . ."*

Then the doorbell pealed out with the first bar of Beethoven's Fifth:

Duh duh duh DUH.

"The sheriff," Reba said urgently, rising from her chair. "I must go freshen my lipstick."

$\mathcal{D}$etective Thomas introduced himself, and I found that my tongue was stuck to the roof of my mouth like it was cemented there with Polident. What *was* my problem? I wondered, unable to peel my eyes off his muscular build and rugged jaw. Was I turning into some kind of law-enforcement fetishist? Fortunately, Terry did the talking and I only had to nod, while pondering whether there was some evolutionary basis for being drawn to men with weapons on their belts. Was it a vestigial hunter-gatherer thing, perhaps? Were semiautomatics perceived as handy for bringing down rampaging mastodons and warmongering Cro-Mags?

Or was I merely horny?

"'Scuse me, ma'am?" Detective Thomas said, looking right at me.

Damn, I said that out loud? "Uh, sorry?" I asked innocently.

Terry grinned. "You said something that sounded like 'corny.'"

"Oh, I'm sure it wasn't important—"

"No, I'm sure it was," she insisted. "Keep thinking, Kerry. It'll come back to you. Now, what rhymes with corny . . . *thorny*?"

"That's all right, ma'am," Detective Thomas said. "I'll talk to you after I have a look at the body. You ladies make yourselves comfortable here in the kitchen."

He headed toward the back of the house, followed by two crime-scene techs carrying what looked like large tool cases, and a coroner's assistant toting a medical bag. I winced, thinking about what was waiting for them in that room, but their faces were as calm and bored as those of office workers trooping off to the Xerox machine. It would take more than a headless girl to ruffle their feathers, I realized.

The sun was setting, casting an orange light over our faces as we sat around the breakfast table, speaking in whispers.

"Did Robert ever mention this Abaddon person to you?" I asked Reba. "Ever talk about the Children of the Cosmos?"

"Certainly not. He knows how I feel about those sorts of . . . New Age hucksters."

"So he wouldn't say anything to you if he'd developed an interest in it?"

"Well, it would certainly surprise me if he were interested. I raised him to have more common sense than that."

Terry looked at me. "Maybe he picked up the brochure at the rehab place."

I shook my head. "A reputable clinic wouldn't be pushing this sort of thing, even if it is in Malibu."

We waited in silence, gazing out at the ocean and watching as the sun melted into a shimmering golden puddle on top of the water. Twenty minutes later, Detective Thomas returned from the bedroom and removed his hat. He had thick, wavy brown hair and a craggy face that was a handsomer version of Lyle Lovett's. Tall and rangy, he was dressed in dark khakis, a tan sport coat, and a denim shirt with a gold knit tie. Brown lizard cowboy boots gave him a "Country Mouse goes to the Big City" look.

"May I?" he said, waving his hat at a chair.

Reba nodded, and he sat down, taking out a small spiral notebook and opening it to a blank page. He carefully noted the date, time, and all of our names, his handwriting small and neat.

He got right to the point, looking at Reba. "You found the body, ma'am?"

"Yes."

"This may sound obvious, but did you check the rest of the house for a head?"

Reba sat back, startled. "Why, no. I didn't."

"Why not?"

She made a *Search me* face. "I can't say. It . . . didn't occur to me. It was sufficiently horrible to find the body."

He made a note. "At what time did you find it?"

"Let me see," Reba said. "The local news was on . . . it must have been right around noon. I remember because I had just finished brunch, and they ran a story about a couple of redheaded twins who had foiled a hijacking at LAX, and of course that reminded me of the girls. 'What a coincidence,' I said to myself, 'I have two redheaded nieces who are flying today—'"

She stopped suddenly, her mouth hanging open, her eyes darting back and forth between Terry and me. Then she blinked and shook her head, as if dashing away a silly thought. Terry and I stayed silent, but I noticed Thomas giving us a curious frown.

"Anyway," Reba continued, "I thought of the girls, and how I'd like to give them one of the rugs. I went in to look at them, and . . . voilà."

"It's now eight o'clock, ma'am. Why did you wait so long to call the police?"

Reba cut her eyes to us. *Stop looking so shifty-eyed*, I beamed to her, but her lids fluttered as she tried to come up with an answer, with Thomas calmly studying her nervous reaction.

"Well, my nieces are private investigators," she said, "and I thought perhaps it would be best to wait until they got home to advise me."

He sat back in his chair, arms folded over his chest. "I don't understand. Why would you need someone to advise you to call the police when there's a dead body in your house? You look like a sensible lady."

Reba shifted in her seat. "Well, it's just that . . . I had other concerns. My son has gone missing from a rehab facility down the road on PCH and, well, with one thing and another, I don't suppose I was thinking too clearly. . . ."

Thomas leaned in. "A rehab facility?" He pronounced it like "An opium den?"

"Yes . . . uh . . . he had a wee drinking problem. Nothing too serious, just a little overindulgent, you know. But he seemed to think it was time he quit, so he checked into New Horizons and was doing very well by all accounts." She cleared her throat. "It's a purely voluntary program, I hasten to add."

"No need for haste, ma'am. We have all the time in the world," Thomas said with a grim smile. "Now, when did he leave the 'rehab facility'?"

Reba looked like a trapped animal. Even she was beginning to realize this didn't sound too good. "Two days ago?" she said with a forced lilt to her voice.

Thomas frowned. "And did you call the police about this?"

Reba's eyes rolled up toward the ceiling as if she were trying to remember. "No, I don't believe I did."

"Why not?"

"Why, I . . . I can't really say."

God, this was painful. Thomas was clearly making a connection between Robert's disappearance from New Horizons and the sudden appearance of the body in the house, and it seemed Reba could only dig herself in deeper with every utterance.

"Did you suspect your son of . . . *involvement* . . . with this situation?" Thomas asked.

Reba's whole body stiffened. "Certainly not!"

His voice went low and intimate. "See, ma'am, the trouble I'm having with all of this is your clear reluctance to bring in the authorities. And that naturally makes me think you have something to hide—"

I'd heard enough.

"Reba, ask for a lawyer," I said firmly.

But she wasn't listening. She was too flustered. "He's a good boy!" she blurted out. "He was never any trouble, even as a child! Oh, there was the occasional stolen cookie, the occasional broken window . . ." She dropped her voice. "Though he *did* rather enjoy pulling the wings off of insects, now that I think of it."

I said it louder. "Reba, ask for a lawyer."

"He doesn't even like girls, that I know of. . . . Not that he *dislikes* them. I mean, certainly not enough to . . . *you know*—"

"*Is there a friggin' lawyer in the house?*" I yelled.

Thomas angled his body, leaning his arm on the table so as to block Reba's view of me. I popped up behind him and sliced a finger across my throat to indicate to Reba she should shut the hell up.

"Has something against girls, has he?" Thomas said to her in a confidential tone.

"He may be many things," Reba said, "but my son is not a murderer!"

I was so caught up in the unfolding nightmare that I didn't even hear the front door opening. Suddenly, a basso profundo voice called out to Reba from the foyer.

"Hullo, Mumsy? Mumsy dear . . . ?"

It was Robert!

Terry, Reba, and I shot up from our chairs.

"Robert dear!" Reba cried. "Where the devil have you been?"

Robert stumbled into the breakfast room looking like a madman. His frizzy red hair stuck up like Eraserhead's. The orange stubble on his face gave him a grizzled pirate look. He wore Bermuda shorts and a muscle shirt, his beefy arms and legs covered in dirt, his grimy feet shod only in flip-flops. In his hand was a mesh bag that held an object the approximate size and shape of a bowling ball, with long blond hair trailing through the holes.

"I have no idea where I've been, Mums," Robert said. "It's all a blank."

A sheriff's deputy had followed him into the house, and I noted with mounting horror that the deputy had a gun aimed at Robert's back. I pointed to the object dangling from Robert's hand. "Hey, Robert," I said in a trembling voice, "um, what have you got there in the bag?"

He shrugged his chubby shoulders in bafflement. "Well, I'm not an expert on these matters, of course, but it seems to be a human head."

Reba collapsed to the floor in a dead faint.

Kerplunk.

The real trouble started when Reba regained consciousness to find Robert under arrest. The sheriff had no choice, really. When asked repeatedly whether he had anything to do with the murder, Robert could only answer, "Well, I don't recall doing it. You see, I've been in a bit of a fog."

They read him his Miranda rights, but they may as well have been speaking Japanese. Robert rambled on, hammering nails in his own coffin as he chatted away.

He'd awakened in a canyon, he said, completely disoriented. The head was on the ground next to him. Naturally, he thought to return it—if not to its rightful owner, who was no doubt beyond needing it—at least to someone who might be able to identify the poor creature. So he'd put it in a mesh bag he had with him and brought it here. Unfortunately, some of the girl's features appeared to have been eaten away by wild animals, he told us, so identifying her might prove to be a problem.

Reba's maternal instincts came into play as soon as she realized where all of this was heading.

"All right," she shrieked. "I admit it!"

Thomas looked over at her, clearly annoyed. "Admit what, ma'am?"

"I killed her! Killed her and decapitated her! I don't know *what* got into me, but there you have it. Guilty as charged!"

"You haven't been charged, ma'am. And I think you're making this up."

Reba dressed him down like a maître d' who'd botched her reservations. "Do you impugn my honesty, young man?"

Terry and I turned to each other helplessly.

"Yes, ma'am, I *am* impugning your honesty . . . though I'm

surprised it bothers you, being as how you just confessed to murder."

Now it was Robert who realized what was happening.

"She's lying!" he bellowed. "I remember now. I did it. I killed her and stuffed her body in the house . . . ?" He looked to me for help, but I rolled my eyes. "Somewhere . . . ? Pretty sure, yes. I killed her wantonly, then I snuck into the house and hid her body. . . . Leave Mumsy out of this, fellows! *I'm* the one you want!"

The sheriff's deputies shuffled their feet and pointed their guns—first at Reba, then at Robert.

I grabbed Thomas by the arm and dragged him into the kitchen. Flipping my hair in what I hoped was a fetching manner, I said, "Detective Thomas, you can't really believe this . . . this *comedy*?"

He gave me a fatalistic shrug. "I'm in a real peculiar spot, Ms. McAfee. See, I've got two people confessing to a murder, and both of 'em could have done it. I don't see as I have any choice but to arrest them."

"But that's absurd," I protested. "Okay, I'll grant you Robert doesn't have an alibi, but he's just a big teddy bear! He doesn't have a violent bone in his body . . . and the idea that Aunt Reba would do anything so pointlessly brutal and . . . and *messy* . . . defies all reason. Look at her!"

Thomas turned and looked at Reba, who was sitting on the couch in the living room, blue wrists thrust outward, begging to be cuffed.

"Take *me*!" she cried. "Take *me*!"

Thomas brought his gaze back to me, then leaned in and whispered, "She seems a bit touched, if you want my honest opinion."

I had to give him that. "Okay, but she's not *homicidal.*"

"Arrest me!" Reba warbled. "Throw me in the clink!"

Jesus, who was that? Susan Hayward in *I Want to Live*?

"Try to see it my way," Thomas said. "I've got a dead body, and I've got two suspects claiming responsibility for it. As a law-enforcement officer, I'd be derelict in my duty if I didn't go ahead and arrest them."

"Well, no more interrogation until I get them counsel," I said.

"They're adults, Ms. McAfee. Voting age. Hell, even retirement age in your aunt's case. . . . If they want a lawyer, they'll have to ask for it themselves."

"But they're obviously not in their right minds!"

"You're kind of making my point." He glanced back at his suspects. "Look, I've seen weirder. The son did it and the mother's some kind of accessory after the fact. Happens all the time with these sex killers. The overprotective mama's the reason they go off in the first place."

"You're *way* off base."

"Maybe. But it's my call to make. Now, you'll have to excuse me. I've got police work to do." He started back to the living room circus.

"Detective Thomas . . . ? Can I at least pack an overnight bag for them?"

He turned to me, shaking his head. "Sorry, miss. It's not summer camp."

I heard the clanking of metal as Reba was handcuffed.

"You have the right to remain silent . . ."

Fat chance.

"You have the right to an attorney. If you cannot afford an attorney, one will be appointed to you by the court . . ."

This can't be happening, I thought as they dragged her off the couch and toward the door, her hands shackled in front of her.

Apparently, they didn't think she was enough of a threat to cuff them behind her back. I couldn't conceive of her trying to scratch their eyes out in some desperate attempt at escape, but you never knew.

Only a few hours ago, the idea of Reba and Robert being arrested for a hideous murder would have been inconceivable, too.

five

"*H*oly shit," Terry said, leaning against the bike, her helmet slung alongside her hip. "What just happened?"

We were standing in the front drive, watching the squad car pull away with Reba and Robert handcuffed in the back seat. We'd been chased out of the house, which was now festooned with yellow crime-scene tape. Grizzie was downstairs in her beach-level apartment, packing her things. The investigators had tried to question her about the crime, but all they'd gotten was "Who do I look like? John bleedin' Walsh? I know nothin' about it! And I'll thank ye not to track in any more bleedin' sand!"

I wished that Reba had been that good at stonewalling. She'd be checking into a five-star hotel right now, instead of heading off to jail to rot away without any access to Lancôme makeup and skin-care products.

"Guess it's time to call Eli." I held out my hand for the cell phone.

Terry pulled it out of her jacket pocket and tossed it to me. "Be sure to mention that Reba found a dead body in her house and that Robert was walking around in a daze with the dead girl's head in a bag, and now they're about to be booked for murder."

"You think?" First I tried him at his Mid-Wilshire office, thinking he might be working late to make up for time lost at the beach. Sure enough, his ever-faithful secretary, Priscilla, answered the phone, her gum snapping audible before she even spoke. "Eli Weintraub's office."

"Hi, Priss. It's Kerry."

"Hi, stranger. Want to speak to the man?"

"Yeah. Is he available?"

"He's with a client. Don't know how long he'll be. Can I have him call you back?"

"Sure. Just tell him Aunt Reba and Cousin Robert have been arrested for murder. Ask him to call me on my cell phone as soon as possible."

A beat. "Sorry? We have a bad connection. . . ."

"REBA AND ROBERT HAVE BEEN ARRESTED FOR MURDER."

"Thank you. Hold, please," Priss said.

Eli came on the line within seconds, his voice raised to the level of a sonic boom. "Is this your idea of a joke?"

"I wish." I explained the difficult circumstances Reba and Robert found themselves in.

"Why didn't she call me?" he yelled. "Did she do it?"

"Of course not! How could you even ask?"

"Well, I've noticed she has a penchant for emasculation. Maybe decapitation isn't too much of a stretch."

Aha—the domestic troubles begin to surface.

I tried to sound sympathetic. "Eli, I realize that you two have had problems, but do you think you could put them aside for the moment and go see Reba and Robert at the Malibu sheriff's station? They desperately need representation."

I heard a long-suffering sigh. "Well, I did say I was missing the action—"

"Good man," I said quickly. "We'll meet you there."

If it weren't for the fact that Reba and Robert were housed there under suspicion of murder, the Los Angeles County sheriff's station would be an attractive place to visit. Facing the bay and set back from the Pacific Coast Highway, it was part of a modern, low-slung complex that included some municipal offices and a courthouse. A high, airily constructed arcade ran between the sheriff's department and the courts, framing the mountains beyond in its graceful arches. Tonight the floodlights sent up a halo around the arcade in the humid ocean air, reminding me of that spaceship we'd seen on the brochure from Robert's tote bag.

Gotta find out who those alien people are, I reminded myself.

We parked the bike in the lot and waited until Eli arrived in his gold Ford LTD with a white vinyl roof. He jumped out of the car, yanked the stogie off his lip, and enveloped us in a nuclear cloud of cigar smoke as he hugged us.

"This isn't some cheap ploy to get me back, is it?" he said.

I gave him a disgusted look. "I'll say what I told the sheriff's detective, Eli. She may be mental, but she's no murderer."

He shrugged. "You know her better than I do."

We crossed the small parking lot to the main building. Once we passed through security (where Terry was forced to peel off most of her outerwear, all of it containing metal studs of one form or another), we were ushered to a brightly lit waiting area. Then Eli was led down a corridor for separate meetings with his clients in the interrogation room.

"I'll need an ashtray." Eli's voice boomed off the tile floor as he and a young deputy disappeared down the hallway.

"There's no smoking, sir."

"Tell someone who gives a shit. Never mind, I'll use the floor."

Terry and I cooled our heels, flipping through back issues of *Law Enforcement Today* and *Neighborhood Watch Quarterly*. Hadn't these people ever heard of *US Weekly*? We read all about the most wanted Malibu miscreants on the bulletin board—check forgers and car thieves and a couple of pot purveyors. A pretty law-abiding community, all in all—until very recently.

Finally, Terry said, "I can't believe Eli asked if Reba did this to get him back."

"He was reacting out of disbelief, I guess. And who can blame him?"

"Well, the question is not whether *she* did it, but what was Robert doing during his blackout."

"You can't really think he had anything to do with it either," I said. "Do you?"

She looked away, refusing to meet my eyes.

"*Terry*, a little faith, please?"

She rested one of her boots on the edge of the chair and buffed it with her sleeve, her mouth set in a skeptical line.

"Anyway," I said, trying to bolster her waning loyalty, "even if he blacked out, he should at least be able to recall where he was before it happened. If he left New Horizons to go on a binge, as Reba suggested, he should remember making the decision and sneaking off, right? Somebody's bound to be able to place him somewhere for the last two days. We'll find him an alibi."

Before Terry could answer, Eli came back down the hallway, shaking his head and rolling his eyes.

I rushed to meet him. "What did she say?"

"She did it," he mumbled past his stogie, heading for the front door. Terry and I tagged along behind.

"What about Robert?" Terry demanded.

"*He* did it, too."

"Bullshit!" I said. "Let's hear some details. How'd they manage it? How'd they saw the head off? Where's all the blood?"

"That's completely beside the point."

"What *is* the point?"

He turned and faced us, and I noticed for the first time how exhausted he looked. "She said she had nothing to live for anyway now that I've left her, and she might as well sacrifice herself for her son."

I'd half expected something like this. "Eli, this breakup . . . was it supposed to be permanent?" I asked him.

"Hell no! I just wanted a little space. And I had to get back to work. I was going nuts without it. But . . . I love the woman, girls. More than I've ever loved anyone."

Well, that came as a relief. Maybe when Reba realized her relationship with Eli wasn't over, she'd be interested in her freedom again. "Did you tell her that?" I said.

He shook his head. "She was in no mood to listen. You know your aunt, girls. Maybe I couldn't hack retirement, but she can't live without drama. On some level, she's actually loving this."

We stood at the front door to the station.

"And Robert?" I said.

Eli frowned. "He could be in real trouble, since they got him with the goods and he can't or won't account for himself. The question is whether Reba will be charged with murder one, or as an accessory."

"But you'll defend him? You'll defend both of them?" I said, a hint of desperation creeping into my voice.

He patted me on the shoulder and sighed. "Of course. I'm gonna have to pull some new tricks outta my bag, though. Never had clients who were so eager to be convicted before. If they stick to their stories, the best I can do is plead them out."

"*If* they bring charges," I said, "which I doubt. The DA would look like an ass. Anybody with one eye in his head can see what this is—a mother and son covering for each other, and the real murderer is out there still."

"Between you and me, the DA *is* an ass, okay? But obviously, I'm gonna do whatever I can."

"Well, while you're doing your lawyer thing, we're gonna be out there looking for the real killer," I announced.

"Don't go rushing into anything, okay? Let 'em sleep on it. We'll see what a night behind bars does for them"—he yawned—"and what it does for me. I haven't had a decent night's sleep since I met your aunt, know what I'm saying? She's an animal. At least with her in custody, I can catch some quality z's."

Ewww. I didn't need the visual of Eli and Reba working their way through the *Kama Sutra* on a nightly basis.

Eli pushed through the doors and shuffled out into the parking lot. We followed him outside, then watched him pull away in the LTD, waving to him from a pool of dewy light and contemplating a future with our only surviving family members headed for lethal injection.

We decided to go back to Reba's house to check on Grizzie. She'd been typically stoic when they took Robert and Reba away, but I suspected she was shaken up. How could she not be? She'd worked for Reba for thirty years, longer than we'd been alive. We planned to invite her to stay with us until the whole thing blew over, and I hoped she had enough money in the bank to tide her over until her employers' release, because we were broke as kittens.

"I can't believe Reba's sticking to this ridiculous story," I grumbled, as we trudged down the stairs to Grizzie's apartment.

"Hey, twenty-four hours without coffee, muffins, and mangoes—she'll recant," Terry said, knocking on Grizzie's door. "Don't worry. It's much ado about nada."

Grizzie answered, standing in the doorway wearing a cardigan, a flowered skirt, and sensible walking shoes, her stockings rolled at the knee. She wore a straw hat on her head, and there was a tapestry carpetbag at her feet. She looked like Mary Poppins thirty years later, packing an extra fifty pounds thanks to too many spoonfuls of sugar.

"Me poor lasses," she said, waving us in.

"We know, mind our feet," Terry said, but Grizzie shocked her, stepping forward and enveloping her in a bear hug. She released Terry, then did the same to me.

"You'll be needin' a spot of tea," she said.

"Where're you going?" Terry pointed to the carpetbag. "We were going to invite you to stay with us."

"Thanks, but I got me another job."

"Already?" Terry asked in shock.

"A woman of my qualifications is always in demand," Grizzie said, reaching for a teakettle on the hot plate. "I've turned down more offers over the years than a three-breasted streetwalker. One phone call and I'm off to the races." She poured the tea into porcelain cups and we took the sugar cubes she offered, plopping them into the steaming Earl Grey.

"But . . . who will you be working for?" My mind was incapable of picturing Grizzie in any context other than Aunt Reba's household.

"A Beverly Hills lady, friend o' your aunt's. Mrs. Angela Pillsbury. She's been after me for ages to come 'n' work for her."

"Well, I guess it's a good thing," I said, and to my surprise felt a little tear stinging the corner of my eye.

"Can't stay here anyways, sheriff says. Got to be out o' the crime scene till they're done with it. No point in stayin' if I can't be cleaning the place. What would I do, sit on me duff watchin' Oprah? Not likely. I need me work."

That was true. I'd never seen another workhorse like Grizzie in my life, in any field. But this was like losing another member of the family. Grizzie must have seen the despair on my face, because she put a rough hand on my cheek.

"I'll always be near, lasses. Whenever ya want me, just give a call."

"Angela Pillsbury's a royal bitch," Terry said petulantly.

Grizzie's eyebrows went up. *And that would be something new?*

"And her grandkids are little princess bitches. They live at Neiman Marcus. They only go home to eat, sleep, and throw up."

Grizzie shrugged. "Ah, what d' I care? Only got two years before retirement, anyways."

"Retirement?" Terry and I said at once. The idea of Grizzie hanging up her Playtex gloves was inconceivable, like the stars retiring from the heavens.

"Forty years o' hard work is enough for one body," Grizzie said. "I'll take me million dollars and go back to Belfast. Buy me a pub and spend me golden years pullin' drafts and spinnin' yarns about Beverly bleedin' Hills."

What did she just say?

"Million dollars?" Terry gaped. "You . . . you have a million dollars stashed away?"

Grizzie gave her an affronted look. "Well, what d' ya think I've been doin' with me paychecks? Investments, lasses. Yer old Griselda's not stupid, y'know."

She took the teacups from us and rinsed them in the sink. Then she did a quick dusting of all the surfaces, checked that all of the electrical appliances were unplugged, and turned out the lights.

"Mind if I take a house key?" I asked, as Grizzie locked up the apartment.

She gave the whole bunch to me. "Aye. I'll not be needin' them."

"Do you have a ride?" Terry asked.

"They'll be comin' to collect me in five minutes." Grizzie picked up the bag and began tramping up the stairs to street level.

"We'll wait with you," Terry offered.

We stood in front of the house, and as the traffic whizzed past us on PCH, I suddenly remembered something Grizzie had said—something I'd forgotten to ask her about in all the hub-bub over the body.

"Grizzie, what were you referring to when we were talking about aliens? Remember, you said we shouldn't judge without all the facts?"

She nodded. "I was referring to the time when I was taken up in one o' the spaceships and had me a little tour."

My head jerked violently on my neck. *What?*

"Aye. It were many years ago now, back in Ireland. I don't talk about it much, bein' as how people treat ya like yer daft, but I know what I know. I was driving a country road outside Killarney, and there was a light like to strike me blind. And the next thing ya know, I'm rising up in the air, as light as you please—"

"Are you telling us you were abducted by aliens?" Terry said, gawking openly at her.

Grizzie huffed indignantly. "I'll thank ye not to be treatin' me like one of yer crackpots!"

"Sorry," Terry said sheepishly. "So then what happened?"

"Like I said, I had the tour. It was a fine-looking ship, all shimmery and transparent-like. The walls would disappear when ya wanted to walk through 'em."

I couldn't believe I was hearing this from Grizzie, of all people. Millionaire scullery maid and alien visitee. The hits just kept on coming.

"So, what did they look like?" I said, trying to keep the skepticism out of my voice. "The beings. Did you see them?"

"They were the Grays. Little people with big black eyes and reptilian skin. Charmin' little buggers, really. Probably where we got our legends about leprechauns."

"And did they . . . experiment on you?"

She gave me a frown. "Now yer gettin' personal, me lass."

Okay. Hard to know where the boundaries were when discussing alien abductions. I'd have to check with Miss Manners on that.

"Come on, Grizzie," Terry said. "This is a joke, right?"

"Have ye ever known me to joke?"

We'd never known her to do anything but sigh a lot and crank around the house, muttering under her breath like Popeye.

"No, but . . ."

"Well, there ye are."

A black Town Car stopped in the middle of the road and put on its blinker.

"Griz, one more question," I said. "Did you ever see Robert with a young blond woman?"

She spewed out a belly laugh. "Your cousin? With a young blonde? He's been keepin' company with Jack Daniel's so long, that thing o' his must have all the get-up-and-go of a garden slug. He's completely sexless, our Robbie."

The car made a U-turn into the gravel driveway in front of the house. A uniformed driver got out and held open the door for Grizzie. She blew us a kiss before clambering into the back seat, grunting audibly with the effort. Then the sleek black automobile whisked her away—away from the scene of the crime and into a life without us.

"Well," I said, letting out a sigh, "I guess we better get back and feed the dogs."

"Home again, home again—"

"Jiggedy friggin' jog."

six

*O*ur little cabin sits in a canyon that cuts through the hills separating Los Angeles from the San Fernando Valley, a half-mile up from Santa Monica Boulevard just off of Beverly Glen. The backyard butts right up against the canyon wall, which rises at a sixty-degree angle to a height of a hundred feet and is covered with vines and bushes, pine trees and scrub. It's home to a Disney cast of wildlife creatures: birds, bunnies, raccoons, deer. Sometimes I imagine them breaking into elaborate song-and-dance numbers while we're asleep at night.

But there's also the occasional coyote (cue the bad-guy music) that skulks through the canyon looking for bite-sized snacks like the baby bunnies or our pint-sized dogs, so we're always on the lookout for predators. When we arrived home, we let Muffy and Paquito out to do their business under a watchful eye, then they chased each other around the small yard for a few minutes, sniffed everything in sight, and were ready to go back inside, mission accomplished.

I took a pizza out of the freezer while Terry went online to do some research.

"Hey, c'mere," she eventually called from the office nook, which was around the corner from the breakfast nook. The builders of our house had been big on nooks. I suspected they were Keebler elves, judging by the dimensions of the house and their fondness for alcoves they could cram their little elf selves into.

I put the pizza in the oven, then went over to see what Terry was looking at. It was a fansite devoted to our chief suspect, Ms. Heather Granger. It showed a glamorous black-and-white publicity photo signed with a swooping feminine hand in lavender ink—*Forever, Heather*.

I laughed. "Well, she's had a longer career than most, but 'forever' might be pushing it."

"This is really interesting," Terry said.

"Her acting career is interesting?" I said, not bothering to disguise my skepticism. Years on a soap opera followed by years of prime-time dramas, then, if I remembered correctly, a stint on Home Shopping Network pitching a microwavable line of country crockery.

Terry shot me a look. "God, no. Not the acting stuff. I'm talking about her marital career."

We spent an hour searching the online archives of the *Malibu Times* and the *Los Angeles Times* and whatever tabloids we could find. And we made an interesting discovery.

The romantic lives of Heather Granger and a bunch of other actresses seemed to intersect over the years. The same beautiful faces showed up in the society pages over and over again, the women trading up as time went by—appearing on the arms of wealthier and more prominent men—until the women reached a certain age, at which point they fell off the pages altogether, their husbands having evidently chucked them for a new generation of babes on the first rungs of the social ladder. The babes would then stick around until they'd put in enough time for community property, and could get the rich old geezers settled in nice retirement homes before heading off to a life of day spas and ladies' lunches. Such are the dreams of the everyday trophy wife.

Heather Granger had had a very successful climb. Her face glowed from the pages as she hosted this or that charity gala, or opened up her splendid Mediterranean villa to the garden society, or slopped the occasional lunch in designer duds for the down-and-out (who grinned toothlessly into the camera as they snarfed up her charity fare).

She appeared to be absolutely indispensable to the social scene—until she wasn't. At some point a couple of years ago, she'd dropped completely out of sight.

"I never thought of it before," I said, "but there's a glass ceiling for trophy wives, too. Get to a certain age and you're put out to pasture. She probably got traded in for a shinier, less tarnished model."

Terry pushed back from the computer. "What do they do once they get to that age and they're dumped?"

"Lunch, shop, get cosmetic surgery . . . You don't go through a string of marriages like that without putting together a nice little retirement account."

"I'll bet she's not too fond of the bosomy little blondes coming up after her," Terry said pointedly.

It took me a moment to realize she was referring to the corpse. "How do you know our girl was bosomy?" I asked. "We didn't even see her."

"Safe bet, isn't it? A sure way into the heart of a certain kind of man. Cheap and easy and available on any street corner in LA. These days you can practically get a breast augmentation at the Jiffy Lube."

I peered at the screen. "Who was Heather's last husband?"

She clicked through some more pages. "Last hubby of record seems to be one Frank Steinmetz. Big movie producer. Look, here's a photo of them on the beach."

Heather was cuddled up in a cable-knit sweater next to a wizened dwarf of a man with a full head of silver hair. She bent her knees and leaned on his shoulder in an effort not to tower over him. The power couple was posed in front of a large boxy stucco house.

"Where's his house?" I wondered.

"Malibu." Terry looked closer. "Holy cow! I don't believe this. . . . Would you check out the house next door to theirs?"

I squinted at it. "Is that—?"

"It is! See the window there, the back porch, the skylight? Their house is right next door to Reba's!"

We contemplated this in stunned silence for a moment, trying to fathom what it meant.

"So our prime suspect lives next door, eh?" Terry said.

I held up a hand. "Wait. . . . If she lives next door, I think that makes her *less* likely to be a suspect. I mean, it's only natural to go around and knock on the doors in your own neighborhood if you're trying to put together one of those events, right? There's nothing particularly sinister about that."

"Hold the phone." Terry located another picture, snapped on

the red carpet of one of the awards shows. Mr. Frank Steinmetz had a very arresting young woman on his arm—a highly bleached blonde, about twenty years junior in age and twenty pounds lighter than Heather Granger appeared to be.

"A generic young blonde, just like our vic," I said. "Maybe Steinmetz dumped Heather for her. What's her name?"

"Her name is 'unidentified guest.' I guess the press doesn't work that hard at identifying the bimbo du jour."

"So maybe Heather took exception to Frank having a new girlfriend and decided to chop off her pretty little head. What we need to know is, who actually lives in the house next door to Reba? Is it a newly single Frank, or is it the former Mrs. Steinmetz?"

"Well, perhaps it's time for the colonoscopy," Terry suggested, referring to a particularly invasive kind of computer software that let you peer deeply into a person's private life, discovering their home address, unlisted phone number, medical prescriptions, history of DVD rentals, reading preferences, online sexual predilections, and credit report—all within a matter of minutes. This was not some arcane, semilegal PI stuff that got delivered to you in a paper bag. You could buy it on the Internet for $39.95.

"Okay, so it looks like Heather's got her own house up in Zuma Beach," Terry said. "And Frank Steinmetz is living in the house next door to Reba's."

I made a note of Heather's address. "See if you can find out who the blonde is," I said.

We did some more searching, looking for the nameless blonde. What we found was a *slew* of young blondes. Apparently, since his split with Heather, Frank Steinmetz had been going through them like mineral water.

His name had had a familiar ring to it from the start, and as we searched further we quickly realized why. We had in fact seen it on the big screen many, many times. His career as a producer spanned thirty years, spawning everything from teen sex romps and blaxploitation movies in the seventies, to action features, war epics, and the occasional teacup-rattling Oscar contender through the eighties and nineties. The movies kept getting bigger, the actors more bankable, the production costs rivaling the annual budgets of small nations.

But Frank didn't seem to be quite as active these days—probably losing ground to the young Turks. Even so, I reflected, the combined cost of the films he'd made would be somewhere in the billions of dollars, and a respectable chunk of that would have gone into his pocket as producer fees.

"Wow," I said. "I guess he can afford to squire around a few blondes."

Twenty minutes later, Terry had uncovered a whole other aspect of Frank's personality. She'd found a picture of him at Will Rogers State Park in a polo getup, holding a gigantic gold trophy. This linked to more pictures of Frank in various poses with gorgeous-looking horses, hoisting ribbons and awards and doffing his polo helmet, his arm slung around this big celebrity or that winsome babe. The man was so small he could have easily passed for a jockey.

"I say we go have a talk with Ms. Granger and Mr. Steinmetz," Terry said.

I nodded and yawned. *"Mañana, mañana . . ."*

"Well, of course *mañana*."

We turned off the computer and helped ourselves to pepperoni pizza, inhaling the whole thing in just fifteen minutes. Somehow during the day's activities—coping with terrorists, finding a dead, headless body, and visiting our relatives in jail—we'd worked up quite an appetite.

Afterward, I kissed the pups, who were happily snoozing on the couch, and went to bed—visions of overage trophy wives dancing in my head.

seven

$\mathcal{T}$he next morning after coffee and kibble, we left the house and headed back down to the beach. First we were going to New Horizons to speak to the staff, then to the Malibu jail for visiting hours, then up to Heather Granger's in Zuma Beach, before heading back down to Malibu to get a gander at Frank Steinmetz's house.

Gee, our dance card was full and it was only the first day back from vacation.

The main traffic was coming toward us, commuters from Malibu and Topanga slogging south on their way to work, but the happier traffic was headed north—rusty cars with surfboards strapped to the roof, SUVs full of little kids wearing water wings, cyclists and bare-armed bikers out to enjoy the cool, clear May weather.

We passed Pepperdine, a prestigious and very expensive private university sitting high on a hill facing the ocean, like an island fortress full of privileged young adults. A few doors down from Pepperdine was a sprawling compound set back from the road—a gated facility on an expanse of green lawn. A brass plate etched with "New Horizons" was embedded in the brick column anchoring the gate.

We pulled up to the guardhouse midway up the drive. The guard wore a gun on his belt, I noticed. I was also pleased to note that he didn't start my heart beating wildly. Of course, he was fifty and portly, but still, it was a relief to know that my new fetish was limited to *hunky* men with guns.

The guard leaned out the window, giving us a quick once-over. "Checking in, ladies?"

Terry gave him an indignant look. "Do we look like a couple of dope fiends to you?"

The guard drew back his chin.

"Don't answer that," I said, smacking her shoulder. "We're here about our cousin, Robert Price. We need to speak to the director."

"Do you have an appointment?"

"No, we have a family emergency," Terry said. "Our cousin disappeared from your fine institution, and we want to talk to someone about it.

"Names?"

"Kerry and Terry McAfee."

"Are you two twins?"

Some people just ask for it every time.

"Yes, now we are," Terry said, matter-of-fact. "We killed our sister because we were sick of hearing, *Hey, are you three triplets?* She's buried in the backyard."

The guard blinked once, then shrugged and called in to the

clinic. After a moment, he pushed a button and we heard the clunk of the release as the barrier lifted.

"Park in the driveway and go in the front door," he said, pointing.

Terry pulled past him with a little wave, and we circled around the drive to the front of the baronial brick building, parked, and made our way across the flagstone porch to a large white door.

"Substance abuse is a booming business," I said, casting an admiring eye around the property.

"Yeah, they get you coming and going. The alcohol companies and drug dealers on the way up, the rehab facilities on the way down."

Within seconds of ringing the buzzer, the door was opened by a young woman with dark hair in a China doll cut. She wore rectangular black glasses and a lightweight wool suit with low-heeled black pumps. I thought she would have been attractive if her hair and clothing weren't quite so severe. Also, the shoes weren't doing much for legs that might have been shapely, given the right footwear and skirt length.

"I'm Amanda Exeter," she said, thrusting a hand in my direction. "Executive assistant to the director." Terry and I took turns shaking. "I'm so sorry about your cousin," she said without a trace of sympathy. "Please come in."

The spacious lobby was empty. No patients lounging on the overstuffed couches in front of the fireplace or milling twitchingly about. They were probably in their rooms, brushing imaginary bugs off their skin, wrestling with hallucinated demons, or bashing their heads into the wall to take their minds off the cravings.

We walked to the conversation pit in front of the fireplace as Amanda prattled on. "Our contract explicitly states that participation in the program is strictly voluntary. We are not responsible for clients who choose to leave without notification. Of course, we try to make leaving the grounds as difficult as possible, to avoid patients . . . decamping without our knowledge. But every now and then someone gets through and experiences, well, a slip."

Terry gave a sardonic laugh. "He didn't slip, so much as *slide*, into a big pile of—"

"Yes," Amanda interrupted, giving her a curt smile. "We heard."

"You heard he's been booked for murder?" Terry could rarely resist zinging people, and this hyperprofessional drone was just the sort she loved to rattle.

"Yes," Amanda replied smoothly, as if she'd just been told that Cousin Robert had stubbed his big toe.

"Would it be possible to speak to the director?" I asked.

She glanced at her watch, then looked back up at me. "May I ask why?"

What was going on? We'd just told her that Robert had been arrested for murder, and here she was, acting like it was just an ordinary day and all of this was one giant inconvenience for her personally.

"We'd like to know more about what goes on here," I said. "We want to know what Cousin Robert was doing and how he was doing before the . . . incident."

Amanda clutched her appointment book to her chest. "I'm so sorry," she said with no discernible regret. "Mr. Peavey is talking to the police right now about the matter. It won't be possible for him to see you."

So the sheriff's merry men were already here.

"It's all right," I said. "We'll wait."

"I don't know how long he'll be. He had to postpone several appointments in order to deal with this situation." She clucked her tongue. "I'm afraid he's all backed up."

"I hear Ex-Lax is good for that," Terry deadpanned.

Amanda glared at her.

"Why don't we make an appointment?" I said, giving Amanda my *You must have heard my sister wrong* smile. "We'll come back when it's convenient for him. How's four o'clock?"

"Let . . . me . . . just . . . check," she said, the words popping out of her mouth like little pellets of disgust. While she consulted her date book, I looked around the lobby. It was done in soothing lavenders and soft greens, and had that loud, syrupy-sweet mental institution music piped in over loudspeakers that was like having cotton candy forcibly jammed into your ear canals. Still, I could feel the desperation underneath the surface calm. It seemed to me that the place was crawling with the heebie-jeebies of the absent patients.

"Five-thirty. Will that do?" Amanda handed Terry a business card. I peeked over her shoulder and saw the name "Wendell Peavey, Director." The logo was a baby-blue graphic that was supposed to evoke the beach and the vast ocean horizon.

"Fine," I said. "We'll see you then."

"Please call to confirm before coming," Amanda cautioned us. "There's really no way of knowing how this day is going to turn out."

I hoped her words weren't as prophetic as they sounded.

I made Terry stop at a drugstore on the way to the jail, where I bought Reba a small plastic atomizer of hair spray and the most expensive lipstick they had in her earth-tone palette— Luscious Kumquat. I knew she had to be beside herself without a bucket of beauty products to slather on herself. I put them in my jacket pocket, figuring it would be easy to get these harmless objects past the metal detector at the jail. But it was not to be.

I tossed my purse on the X-ray conveyor belt, then walked through the metal detector, setting off the alarm. The deputy wanded me, made me take off the jacket, then wanded it, too. He pulled the lipstick and hair spray out of my pockets, tossing them into a plastic tray.

"These are potential weapons, miss."

"Please, Officer," I said. "They're for my aunt. She's got to be feeling grungy after being here all night without any toiletries."

"Shoulda thought about that before she murdered somebody."

"Thanks for the big fat presumption of innocence," Terry snapped. "Can we see her now?"

"Sorry, only one visitor per inmate."

I turned to Terry. "That's okay. You go see Robert, I'll see Reba."

"Sorry, only one visit per visit."

"What?" we said.

"That's the rules."

"But we've got two relatives in here," I begged.

"Charming family," he said.

Terry plopped down on a Naugahyde couch in the waiting area. "That's okay. You go ahead. I'll wait."

Another deputy nodded for me to follow him down the hallway. I signed a visitors' log, showed my ID and turned over my purse, and was staunchly forbidden to touch or to pass anything to the inmate. Then I was ushered into the visiting room, where I sat at a long table separated by glass partitions, just like you see in the movies.

After a few minutes, Reba was led into the room. She was

swallowed by the prison jumpsuit, which looked like a giant orange parachute belted with chains—the best fit they could get, probably, there not being too many felons who stood five foot one and weighed ninety pounds soaking wet. I noticed that her hair had held up pretty well overnight, but she was hiding her face in her hands.

It was just as I'd thought. Being caught without her makeup on was worse than being caught red-handed with a headless corpse.

She sat down, turned from me, and picked up the phone with cuffed hands.

"How you doing, Reba?"

A sniff, followed by the muffled voice. "Oh, about as well as could be expected for a *caged animal.*"

We couldn't have a conversation this way.

"Reba," I said. "Turn and face me. I couldn't care less what you look like right now."

She turned around slowly, and I did a double take. She was wearing eyeliner, eyebrow pencil, and lip liner. Where did she get them?

"It's tattooed," she confessed, seeing my surprise. "I feel so silly and vain. I did it when Eli moved in. I didn't want him to wake up screaming when he saw me au naturel."

I swallowed hard to keep from laughing. "Oh, that must have been painful, huh? The things we do for love . . ."

"Might have saved myself the pain," she said bitterly. "The man doesn't love me, doesn't love me at all!"

"Reba," I said, frustrated that she seemed to be ignoring the slightly more pressing issue of the murder charge, "Eli loves you. He told me so."

Her face brightened like a kid with a Tootsie Pop. "He did?" she said, gripping the phone with both hands.

"Of course, and he's not going to let you go down for this thing."

"He still loves me," she cooed.

"Yes, and you need to get out of here, for his sake as well as yours. Have you reconsidered your confession?"

She pressed her lips together. "No, absolutely not."

"Look, it's not going to do any good for you to make a false statement, Reba. You might even aid the real killer by keeping the focus on you and Robert."

She sank forward on the counter. "I don't see that I have any choice. Robert's the most obvious suspect, and unless I divert attention from him, he'll be sent up the river. Anyway, the cat's already out of the bag, so to speak."

"Listen, I'm no lawyer, but it seems to me that there's a lot of gray area here. Eli could argue that the confessions were coerced. I was asking for an attorney on your behalf, and you made the statements without benefit of counsel. With a little luck and the right judge, we can get your confessions thrown out. Then they'll only have the body on the premises and no motive whatsoever."

"But there's still Robert with the head. And no memory of his whereabouts."

"Reba, I understand your wanting to protect him, but—"

She threw back her head, wailing, "I bore him in my womb!"

Jesus.

"Yes, Reba, I understand."

"You're too young to understand! He's my entire legacy. My only child. It's a mother's heavenly duty to protect her child!"

I closed my eyes so she couldn't see them rolling to the back of my head.

"Reba, all I can say is that Eli will do what he can, and Terry and I are out looking for the real murderer right now. Please, I'm begging you to take back your confession."

A theatrical sigh. "Bless you, dear. Bless your hard little head for thinking you can help me. But I'm afraid it's my destiny to die for my only son."

She placed the phone back in its cradle and stood, signaling to the matron that she was ready to go. She gave me a brave little smile, waving her cuffed hands, then disappeared through the door.

I rubbed at the pain blossoming in my forehead, then noticed the guard looking at me. I hung up the phone and walked directly to him.

"Listen," I said, sidling up beside him and giving him my most disarming smile, "I know it's against the rules, but could I have another visit? See, both my aunt and my cousin are in here for the same murder, which of course they didn't do . . ."

He gave me a look that said *You gotta be kidding me.*

"Anyway, I need to talk to him, too. Can you make an exception? It's kind of an unusual family—I mean, family situation." I tilted my head and batted my eyelashes ever so slightly.

He relented. "Wait here a second. I'll check it out with the sergeant."

After a few minutes, he came back and waved to me. I smiled and followed him down a harshly lit corridor to the men's ward, then entered another waiting room. I sat down at another table, surreptitiously eyeing the other prisoners, who were conferring with their loved ones or lawyers in low tones. Most of them looked like refugees from the Jerry Springer show—missing teeth, scraggly hair, crude tattoos. The door behind the prisoners opened and Robert was ushered in, making the other inmates look like *GQ* models.

His weed-whacked red mop was jutting from his scalp. His freckles floated on pasty skin, his orange, stubbly beard set off by the tangerine-colored jumpsuit. His champagne gut strained against its middle, threatening to split the seams. I hated to admit it, but he looked every bit the mad murderer of Malibu.

I swallowed my surprise and mustered a supportive smile as he plopped down across from me and picked up the phone.

"Hi, doll. How's your better half?"

"She's fine. We're both fine. How's it going?"

He shrugged. "Wish I knew how I got here."

"Robert, you have to stop saying you committed this murder."

"Well, my dear little Nancy Drew, I don't know that I *didn't*."

"Well, *I* know you didn't, Robert. You're not capable of such brutality."

He clutched at the phone, his eyes tearing up. "I've lived a dissolute, disreputable life, Kerry. One of selfishness and self-indulgence. And Mumsy's always stood by me. I need to stand by her now, in this her moment of crisis."

"Mumsy's *not* going down for this," I assured him. "Don't you worry about her. Nobody's going down for anything if you'll just tell the truth about the situation."

"The truth shall be known *in the end*," he said with a tone of great import.

What was this? A suicide threat?

"Robert, are you thinking of doing something crazy? 'Cause if I have to, I'll have you put under a suicide watch—"

He dismissed my fears with a wave of his big paw. "No, of course not. I'm merely going to go on a fast."

"A hunger strike?"

"An effort at self-purification, my dear. Believe me, it's long overdue. I plan to meditate and fast until the truth of the matter presents itself to me. Then, if I did the heinous deed, I'll take my punishment."

"Well, it *would* be helpful if you could remember where you were."

"That's exactly what I intend to find out."

"Robert, does the name 'Abaddon' mean anything to you? Or 'The Children of the Cosmos'?"

He scrunched up his nose. "Is this some newfangled band you kids are into? Because, you know, I'm a Cole Porter man all the way."

"No, no. You had their brochure in your bag. The one you had at New Horizons."

He shook his head and the Don King mass of hair did the wave up on top. "Can't imagine how it got there."

"And you don't remember anything about the day you went missing? You didn't decide to go out drinking or anything like that?"

He looked insulted. "Certainly not."

"Okay. I had to ask."

"Well, it's back to the cellblock with your old cousin. Thanks for the visit, my dear. I'll be much trimmer next time you see me," he added with a wink. "A slender stalk of a boy."

Yeah, I thought, *I'll be holding my breath for that one.*

As we headed back out to the parking lot, I filled Terry in on the visits.

"Reba's determined to sacrifice herself for her only child, and Robert's atoning for years of being a drunk by taking the blame. Plus, he's going to go on a hunger strike."

She sighed. "What do we do?"

"Let's call Eli and get an update."

I took the cell phone and reached him at his office.

"I can't talk them out of these confessions," he said. "And so far it's not looking good. I spoke to the prosecutor, a real hard-on who thinks he's got an open-and-shut case. Prima facie. He won't even talk plea bargain."

"He can't really believe that."

"Oh no? He's going to the grand jury today to get an indictment."

"What!"

"Relax. I've got a plan."

"Okay, what's the plan?" I said, trying to control my panic.

"If I enter a not-guilty plea, Reba will go batshit in the courtroom, okay? And that's how I start laying the groundwork for mental incompetence."

"Mental incompetence?" I said, turning it over in my mind. "That could work, that could work . . ."

"Right. I'll establish that she's too crackers to participate in her own defense, which is her constitutional right. Same for Robert. They'll see Reba wigging out, then they'll look at Robert and say, 'Well, the apple doesn't fall far from the tree.' We'll have the obligatory evaluations by the shrinks, judicial review, maybe even a jury trial on the competence issue—all of which will buy us time."

"Buy us time?" I said hopefully. "Does that mean you think we can solve this case before it's too late?"

There was an uncomfortable silence. "Anything could happen. My job is to drag things out till it does."

That didn't sound too positive.

"Eli, level with me. If it goes to trial, you'll plead not guilty by reason of insanity?"

"Probably. Depends on the evidence."

"That's a tough defense, isn't it?"

"One of the toughest."

"And if they're found not guilty by reason of insanity . . . they'll spend the rest of their lives in mental institutions, strapped into straitjackets, bouncing off rubber walls?"

Another silence, punctuated by cigar-wheezing.

"Eli . . . ?"

"It's my only option at the moment," he said quietly. "Let's go with the plan and hope for the best."

The best was not sounding too good, I thought, as I shut the phone. Still, I'd rather be visiting my aunt and cousin at the funny farm than leaving flowers on their graves. I filled Terry in, doing nothing to hide my dismay.

"Perk up," she said. "It's early days yet."

"Yeah, I guess so."

"Let's go talk to this Heather person. See what the former trophy babe has to say for herself."

"Okay," I said, sighing. "Let's roll."

And we hopped on the motorcycle, taking off for points north.

eight

Zuma Beach is a rustic enclave of unremarkable houses worth millions of dollars because of their scenic location alongside the Pacific Ocean. We got there in fifteen minutes, pulled off the main road, and went up a hill until we came to a barely paved street with gravel shoulders and a fantastic view of the waves crashing below.

Heather Granger lived in a rambling white ranch house with mullioned windows and a long front porch. Wind chimes hung from the roof, swaying in the ocean breeze and tinkling in a thousand different tones. It sounded like the sort of music you'd hear during a massage or hypnotherapy session. Pleasant for an hour or so, but after that it might send you on a shooting spree.

The house was surrounded by an impeccably landscaped, lush green lawn that sloped down to a horse paddock in the back. At the edge of the property were stables and a fenced-in ring, complete with barrels arranged for racing.

The door was opened by Heather herself, instantly recognizable from the online pictures we'd found, not to mention the hours of reruns wherein she tended to the birth and rebirth of that lone baby on the open plains. Her long auburn hair was perfectly styled, and she wore a long, flouncy Indian skirt, a beaded necklace, and dangling crystal earrings. If it weren't for the exquisite makeup job, I'd have taken her for a Berkeley throwback. She was striking, if a decade or two beyond her prime.

"Oh, hello," she said, looking surprised. "I was expecting someone else. Can I help you?"

"Ms. Heather Granger?" I asked.

"Yes?" She smiled in embarrassment. "I'm sorry—are you new at EquiSpa?"

"EquiSpa?"

"The horse farm. I've hired someone from there. I'm preparing some horses for sale."

"We're Kerry and Terry McAfee," I said, offering her my hand. She had a firm grip, with an outdoorsy roughness to her palm. "Reba Price-Slatherton is our great-aunt."

"Ohhh." She took my hand in both of hers, overcome by sympathy. "I heard, I'm so *sorry*."

"That's strange," Terry said, eyeing her suspiciously. "How'd you hear so quick?"

One day I was going to teach her manners, I thought. Or at least subtlety. She was always nailing people prematurely, and sometimes it cost us goodwill too early in the game.

"It's a very small community," Heather said, her laughter tinkling like the chimes above her head. She gave Terry's hand a normal shake, forgoing the two-handed method.

"Well," I said, taking a deep breath, "as you seem to know,

both our aunt and our cousin have been arrested for murder. We're looking into the matter, as it all comes as quite a shock. Obviously, we don't believe they're guilty—"

"Oh, I'm sure they're not," Heather assured us, raising her perfectly shaped eyebrows. "But I was just on my way out—"

"You have to wait for the horse person, don't you?" Terry asked.

Heather's mask of ageless charm vanished for just a second as her deep-brown eyes took in Terry with an appraising look.

"Yes, as a matter of fact, I do." In a flash, she was smiling and gracious again. She gestured to the hallway behind her. "Why don't you come in? Would you like some tea?"

We made our way into the living room and took a seat on ottomans upholstered in Middle Eastern kilims, clustered around a large brick fireplace. A stern Asian woman brought us tea in ceramic mugs.

"Thank you, Ming," Heather said, then turned to us. "Now, what would you like to know? How can I be of help?"

I breathed in the warm jasmine fragrance wafting up from my mug. "We were wondering about this tour of yours, the one you approached our aunt about."

"Yes, the 'Beach House Extravaganza.' I've been involved with it for three years now. A very successful fund-raiser."

"What sort of fund-raiser is it?" Terry asked. "Something for children?"

"Yes, the Children of the Cosmos."

I almost dropped my mug on the floor. Terry looked at me with a stunned expression. "You mean those alien people?" she said.

Heather looked displeased. *"Alien people . . . ?"*

Mental note: Check with Miss Manners on the politically correct term for extraterrestrial whackjobs.

"Oh no, we didn't mean . . ." I tried to save the situation, hoping she'd overlook Terry's gaffe if we affected a genuine fascination with the subject. "A friend was telling us about them . . . it sounded very interesting. They're the ones who believe we're not alone in the universe, right?"

"Yes, that's right. It's an organization devoted to spreading the word about our true origins. Our place in the cosmos, as it were. We humans are rather insignificant in the scheme of things, you know."

"This is the group you're raising money for?" Terry said. "I thought you were running a charity."

Heather laughed and poured some honey into her tea. "It's hardly a charity. But it is a worthy cause."

"There's somebody named 'Abu Dhabi' or something, right?"

"Abaddon, messenger of the gods," Heather corrected her.

"What's his story?" I asked, shooting Terry a sideways look.

Heather's posture shifted, suggesting that she was having second thoughts about deciding to talk to us at all. "His *story* is that he has evidence of our having descended from 'visitors.'"

"What sort of evidence?" Terry asked, doing nothing to hide her disdain for the subject.

"Well, he's been visited himself on many occasions, usually corresponding to the phases of the moon or in conjunction with large-scale earth events, like earthquakes, volcanic eruptions, or tsunamis—" She gave us a patronizing smile. "I can see you're skeptical, but that's all right . . . it's all part of the plan."

"What plan?" I said.

"Let me put it this way: Many are abducted, few are chosen."

I bit my lip to keep from laughing. "So Abaddon was enlisted for some special purpose by these . . . visitors from outer space?"

"Yes." Heather straightened her spine, her eyes taking on the feverish glint of a zealot as the words tumbled excitedly from her mouth. "To prepare us for the day when our ancestors return for us. To stop our unchecked progress toward self-annihilation . . . to join with us in the ongoing process of evolution . . ."

"Do you tell the people you approach about this tour what the money goes for?" I asked. This was precisely the sort of "flaky, New Age" philosophy that Reba abhorred. I found it hard to believe that she would give Heather the time of day if this was what she was promoting. "Because our aunt is not usually interested in"—I scanned my brain for an inoffensive synonym for *crackpot*—"organizations with this kind of agenda."

"Of course, I *tried* to tell your aunt about it," Heather said. "But she said as long as it was a reputable organization, she didn't need the details."

Had to admit that sounded like Reba.

"What type of people belong to the group?" Terry asked her.

"Oh, it's a very broad range. Young, old, male, female. It's really impossible to name a *type* of person. Anyone who's interested in the truth."

Terry tapped her nails on the side of her mug. "Not missing any members, are you?"

"Missing any . . . ?" Heather said, her hand slipping up to tug on a crystal earring. "Oh, you're talking about . . . Has the girl been identified yet?"

"Not that we know of," Terry said. "Just asking."

Heather's eyes dropped to her high-heeled sandals, studying the beige leather straps. I wondered if she was running over the roster in her head to determine if anyone was in fact missing from the group.

"Would you happen to know if our cousin Robert was ever approached by your organization?" I asked her.

Heather lifted her eyes and shook her head. "Sorry, I'm in fund-raising, not recruiting."

"Recruiting, huh?" Terry said, her mouth twisting cynically. "Sounds like a cult to me."

That sealed it. Heather's smile evaporated, and she set her mug down on the glass coffee table with a clank. "A lot of people try to paint us with that brush," she said coldly. "But there's no coercion whatsoever. Membership and attendance at meetings are purely voluntary."

"What about donations?" Terry said, deliberately pushing her buttons. "Are *they* voluntary, too? I bet it costs a pretty penny to get to the truth, doesn't it?"

Just then the doorbell rang and Heather jumped to her feet. "Thank you so much for coming by," she said, dismissing us. She grabbed my arm and began pushing me toward the door with surprising force. "I do hope things work out for your family."

I jerked my arm away and put my hand to the stinging spot where she'd gripped it. "Take it easy," I said. "We're leaving."

Heather was taken aback, as if she hadn't realized she was handling me so roughly. "I'm so sorry. I'm in a bit of a rush. Please do give my regards to your aunt," she said apologetically.

Terry made a face. "Yeah, we'll be sure to do that, next visitors' day at the jail."

Heather reached for the door handle. I put a hand on the door to prevent her from opening it. "We'd like to speak to Abaddon," I said. "Can you tell us how to get in touch with him?"

She gave me a pitying look, like I was a sad little earthling who understood nothing of the man's greatness. "You don't get in touch with him—he gets in touch with you."

"Well, then, will you tell him we're looking for him?" Terry said.

Heather laughed. "Heavens, no."

"Then how's he going to know we want to talk to him?"

She shrugged her shoulders. "How does he know everything?" she said with complete seriousness. I removed my hand from the door, and she swung it open to let us out.

On the front porch stood a woman about our age, her light blond hair cut short and shaggy. She was tall and willowy—six feet, at least—weighing in at about a hundred fifteen pounds. She hung her pretty, childlike face as if she were embarrassed about her height, looking out from underneath her feathered bangs with large brown eyes.

Terry's jaw dropped, and I thought I could smell ozone from the thunderbolt that had just struck my sister.

"Hi, I'm Twink," said the coltish girl with the mile-high legs, her hands thrust into the back pockets of her jeans. "From EquiSpa?"

"Yes, dear. Please come in," Heather said.

We nodded to the girl as we stepped off the porch, Terry's romantic sensors beeping like the EKG of a heart attack victim. As we headed down the walk, she peered over her shoulder, hoping to get the rear view, but the woman improbably named Twink had disappeared into the house.

Her orange Toyota was parked in front of our bike. It bore an *EquiSpa* sticker on the back windshield, with a graphic of a horse in a rearing posture, its hooves pawing the air.

Terry shook her head as she mounted the bike. "Was she cute or *what*?" Her freckled cheeks were flushed.

"Yeah, pretty cute." I swung my leg up and sat down behind her.

"Definitely have to work on that name, though." She lowered the helmet down over her two long braids.

"Yeah," I agreed, thinking this could be trouble, but with an upside. Maybe it would put an end to the talk of spending the rest of her life on the island with Lailannii.

We'd decided to stop somewhere to grab a bite and mull over everything we'd heard thus far. Terry pulled into the lot of a beachfront restaurant in Malibu called the Pier View, parking next to a school of hogs that were huddled in the corner. The place was apparently a watering hole for the packs of bikers who enjoyed rumbling up and down the PCH on their muscle machines, simulating major earthquakes.

Inside were the hog owners themselves, all black leather and tattooed muscle. They seemed determined to ignore the incredible natural beauty surrounding them, drinking beer and playing pool in the dark. One huge guy had an inch-wide strip of short, bristly hair that was perfectly aligned with a Hitler mustache under his nose, and continued in a matching strip on his chin. It looked like his head had been Velcroed.

As we headed through the bar toward the outdoor deck, one of the bikers scuffed over in flip-flops, his greasy, sandy-blond hair falling to his shoulders. He pulled it back into a ponytail as he approached.

"'Lo, ladies. Help you?"

He held out a couple of menus, and it hit me that he was our waiter. Life here at the beach was entirely too laid back for me. I like my food handlers shod and preferably shorn.

"We'll just have some iced tea," I told him.

"And supernachos," Terry added, following me to the door.

"I hope you have cash," I whispered to her.

"I've got one of the taped-up fifties. Hopefully, they'll take it."

We sat down at one of the outdoor wooden tables. The sun was at high noon, and its rays bounced off the waves and the sand and the white walls of the deck, searing my retinas even through the polarized blue lenses of my Oakleys. Sandpipers hopped along the water's edge, pecking at crabs. Gulls swooped and dived, looking for fish, while a few of them strutted along the wooden rail of the deck, sizing us up as our potential as french fry donors.

"Okay, time to make some notes," I said, pulling my trusty steno pad out of my faux Balenciaga shoulder bag. I had developed a habit of diagramming our cases, with the core question at the center of a radial graph, and lines jutting out to the sides representing the different participants and tangential issues. It helped me think more clearly, but it drove Terry crazy.

She pulled her shades down on the bridge of her nose so I could see her eyes rolling. She hated the very sight of the steno pad, because it reminded her of school—a twelve-year ordeal that had been more torturous for her than the three-year stint in Sybil Brand prison for women.

"Look, don't give me a hard time about this," I said. "We solved our last case precisely because I diagrammed it."

"We didn't solve jack! We had some luck. Mainly, we kept walking right past the real killer, while you were spinning paranoid fantasies from your little diagram."

"Shut up," I said. "I'm the boss of you." Which was true, although I didn't usually pull rank. I scribbled away on the pad for a few moments. "Okay, here's what we've got . . ."

At the center: "Murder—young female victim, bleached blonde, unidentified."

On the radiating lines: "Aunt Reba—in possession of the body of the victim. Cousin Robert—returned from a mysterious sojourn with the head of the victim in a net beach bag. Heather Granger—the only unknown person admitted to the house in recent days, involved with a crackpot cult. And Heather Granger's ex-husband, Frank Steinmetz—who lives next door to Reba. Seen with multiple young blondes on his arm."

I stopped and admired my graph. "That pretty well sums it up, doesn't it?"

She grabbed the pad excitedly. "Omigod, you got it!"

"What?"

"It was Colonel Mustard in the library with a pickax!"

I glared at her. "Drop dead."

"With or without my head?"

"You could help, you know," I said testily. "Put some actual thought into the case for a change, instead of crashing around like a blindfolded bull."

"I've given it plenty of thought already." Terry reached into her pocket and pulled out her tube of Cherry Burst lip balm.

"Then thrill me with your acumen."

"Well, it looks like the Cosmos Kids were coming at Reba and Robert from two different angles." She applied a glistening layer across her lips, then grabbed the pen and drew arcs between Heather and the two of them.

"What would they want with Reba and Robert?" I asked.

"Moron. They're very, very rich."

"Yeah, but they don't go in for that kind of stuff."

"Are you totally naive? They don't have to at first—all they have to do is get them in the door. These cult people are experts at mind control. They weasel their way into your life little by little, and the next thing you know you're handing over all your worldly goods to them." She did a little impersonation of Heather: *"There's no coercion involved. . . ."* Bullshit. They coerce your brain cells."

"But Heather sure isn't hurting for worldly goods," I said, stating the obvious. "Maybe it's not a cult after all. Her life looks pretty normal to me."

"You don't have to wear saffron robes and bang on tambourines at the airport to be brainwashed."

"But Robert denies being approached by them."

"So they stuck their brochure in his bag when he wasn't looking, as a first step. He's a perfect target—he's in a very vulnerable place right now, giving up alcohol and reevaluating his life. He's never worked, has no particular belief system. He'd be a prime target for some loony fringe group."

"But Reba would cut him off without a dime if he got involved with people like that," I countered. "Then he'd be worth nothing." A lightbulb went on over my head. "Unless . . . Reba was implicated in a murder and got locked away, giving Robert control of her estate!"

"But Robert's also been implicated. He had the girl's head, for God's sake."

"You're right," I said, disappointed. "That doesn't work."

We sat in silence for a second.

Terry looked up at the sun, shading her eyes with her hand. "So Heather's selling the horses," she mused. "Is that to raise money for the Cosmeteers?"

"From all those pictures, it looked like Frank was the one who was big on horses. Could she be selling his polo ponies? Got them in a divorce settlement or something?"

Terry nodded. "Maybe it's worth a trip to this EquiSpa place to see if we can get a line on Frank and Heather there."

Our waiter arrived with the iced teas and a big, greasy plate of nachos with all the trimmings: cheddar cheese, refried beans, guacamole, onions, jalapeños. My mouth began to water like Niagara Falls.

"On the house," he said, winking at Terry. "We like to have pretty ladies on the balcony. Good for business."

"Thanks," she said, bowing her head and blushing. Terry was an ambidextrous flirter who could pretty much pique the interest of anyone—male or female—who happened across her path. And while she was truly a girl's girl, she didn't hesitate to work her charms on men whenever it served her purpose. They were drawn to her like the proverbial moths to a flame, which never ceased to bug the hell out of me. Here we were, indentical practically down to the last freckle, and somehow she attracted all the attention.

But in this case, since she'd saved us our last fifty, I swallowed my irritation.

The waiter actually tripped on the runner of the sliding glass door as he turned around, so smitten was he with Terry. He caught himself and glanced back over his shoulder, embarrassed by his clumsiness.

"Oh, sir?" I called to him. "Do you have the Yellow Pages for Malibu?" I wanted to look up the phone number and address for EquiSpa.

"Sure, I'll get it for you." He went back inside, giving Terry one last, lovelorn glance.

"Good work, you heartless tease," I said when he was out of sight. "Free food for false hopes."

"Nothing to it," she said, switching off the charm and getting back down to business.

I jammed a cheese-laden chip into my mouth, the tangy bite from the jalapeños zinging my salivary glands. Just then the guy with the Velcro head came to the doorway and peered out at us, looking pissed.

"Help you?" Terry asked through a mouthful of chips.

He came out onto the deck and hulked drunkenly over our table, reeking of stale beer and sweat. He had a lightning bolt tattooed across his right cheek, and the biceps bulging out of his black leather vest were tattooed with tangles of venomous snakes. He might have been the real thing, instead of the weekend-warrior types you sometimes see—accountants and lawyers who hop on a hog in leather and are born to be wild for the forty-eight hours between Friday and Sunday nights.

The biker's lips curled up in a snarl. "That your"—he pretended to gag—"*pink Harley* out there?"

I started up from my seat. "Yes, are we blocking you?"

He put a big hand on my collarbone and pushed me back down into the chair. I landed hard, sending a shock up my spine.

"Hey!" I yelled, more surprised than hurt. I looked over and saw that Terry's eyes were bugging out of her head.

"I just wanted to see what kind of . . . *assholes* . . . would desecrate a Harley by painting it"—he hocked up some phlegm, spitting it past us over the railing onto the sand below—"*pink.*"

Terry's chair scraped across the wooden deck. She was instantly on her feet, chin thrust out. "We're the assholes," she said, her hands clenched into fists. "What are you going to do about it?"

He gave her a sneer, flexing the muscles on his chest and arms. He shifted back and forth for a moment, looking at Terry, then at me, then back at Terry. I couldn't tell if he was trying to intimidate us or merely trying to decide what to say next. "Just wanted to let you know that we don't like *assholes* around here," he finally growled.

Terry continued to glare at him as he turned and swaggered back toward the restaurant.

Whew. I felt the knot in my stomach unclench and I reached for a grateful sip of iced tea. "Holy shit, can you believe that guy?" I whispered, as I watched him head for the door. "I was afraid things were going to get physica—"

That was when the supernacho sailed through the air and splatted on the back of the biker's head.

"Terry, no!"

The biker spun around, and I watched in horror as another supernacho with guacamole hit him right in the eye. He stood there for a moment, stunned, then wiped off the green gunk and *roared* across the deck, charging like an enraged rhino.

Terry stood her ground. "Bring it on!" she screamed, fists next to her face and her body in a boxer's hunch.

Well, this is the end of an interesting life, I thought, as the biker barreled toward us with murder in his beer-reddened eyes.

He hurled himself at Terry. She sidestepped at the last second, and the man crashed into the railing at waist level, then toppled forward screaming, arms and legs flailing, as he plunged headfirst off the deck. Gulls shot up into the air, squawking their bird brains out.

"Yahhhhhhhhh!" the biker screamed.

Then silence.

I gasped and leaned over the rail to assess the damage. The biker lay motionless, sprawled on the soft sand below.

"Great!" I wailed at Terry. "You killed him!"

She shook her head. "No, I didn't. Look."

His arms and legs twitched. Then he lifted his face out of the sand and started to pull himself up to his knees—

Time to go. I snatched up my jacket and turned to see that a crowd had gathered at the door. Were they going to turn into an angry mob because Terry had assaulted one of their own?

Terry jammed her helmet onto her head. "Let's book!" She popped another nacho into her mouth and shoved her way through the phalanx of leather-clad brutes, who made no move to stop us. Instead, they whistled and clapped, yelling, "Way to go! Fucking A! You rock!" like we were departing championship wrestlers.

The ponytail guy thrust the Yellow Pages at us as we passed. "Thanks!" I said, grabbing it, then we tore out into the parking lot and jumped on the controversial Harley in question. "Can we paint it a different color now?" I shouted.

"No way!" she yelled back, amping the throttle and blasting out of the parking lot. As we streamed into the traffic on the PCH, we left a cluster of cheering bikers in our wake.

nine

*W*hen we were a safe distance from the restaurant and our adrenaline gauges were back in the black, Terry pulled over onto the side of the road. We stood for a while, breathing deeply and letting the ocean breeze wash away the rest of the tension. We also took the opportunity to look up EquiSpa in the Yellow Pages, and found a half-page ad promising, *The ultimate in equine care.*

Sounded a little hoity-toity for a horse farm, but what did we know?

We found the turnoff halfway between Malibu and Zuma, traveling up a narrow road past green hills surrounded by wooden fences. The land roamed easily out here. Wide-open space—no teeming masses, no cookie-cutter houses, no blanket of smog—and the air carried the scent of orange blossoms. Hard to believe we were just miles away from the armpit of the LA basin, downtown.

Eventually, we came to a large sign in iron scrollwork that said *EquiSpa*, arching over what looked like the entrance to South-fork. I got out and opened the gate, and Terry bumped over the cattle guards onto the gravel road. I closed the gate again, hopped back on the bike, and we rode for another two hundred yards up to the main building, a two-story replica of an English coach house. There was a row of stables down the road to our right, and trainers working their horses in a ring behind the house. Terry parked next to a shiny red GMC pickup truck loaded with horse gear, and we headed up the walk.

We stepped through the open front door into a brick entry hall that was hung with old-fashioned harnesses and saddles, antique bridles, and rusted spurs. We followed the hall into the main lobby, where a sleek young woman with a long dark braid sat behind a concierge desk. Her attire was horsey but expensive—very Ralph Lauren—her cowboy boots two-toned leather in tan and burnished brown.

She looked up from some paperwork. "Hello, I'm Jeanie. Can I help you?"

I held out my hand. "Kerry McAfee."

Terry held out hers. "Terry. We're going on vacation, and we're looking to board some horses. Could we have a look around?"

Jeanie gave us a curious look. "*Problem* horses?"

Terry glanced over at me. "No, good horses. No trouble at all. They'll be good as can be—"

"We're not an ordinary stables," Jeanie said. "We specialize in horses who are experiencing problems."

"Oh," I said. "What kind of problems?"

"Injuries mostly, or various forms of behavioral problems—stress brought on by overwork, self-esteem issues. Things like that."

Self-esteem issues? For a horse?

"How would we know if a horse is having self-esteem issues?" Terry asked her. "What are the signs?"

"Oh, it runs the gamut, from polo ponies that don't put their all into the match, to show horses who don't put their best hoof forward, so to speak, in competitions."

Terry looked at me, and I could almost hear her mental gears whirring to put the lies in motion. "Now that you mention it, we do have one horse that's a problem. Hard to ride—"

"Bridle shy?" Jeanie said.

"That's it, bridle shy," Terry said. "He's an Arabian stallion," she added for good measure.

"Excellent," Jeanie said, happy to diagnose a horse neurosis at last. "Then you've come to the right place. Let me give you the tour. That'll give you a better idea of what we do here."

She led us through the house, the wooden floors covered with expensive Orientals and dressed with potted palms and antique furniture. We went out through a set of French doors onto a sheltered back patio, where a porch swing moved in the breeze.

We crossed the yard and stopped by the dirt ring, where we watched a beautiful brown Thoroughbred and a smaller, wilder-looking horse running along the fence. They threw their heads as they ran, tossing their manes, bucking and snorting. The smaller gray horse nipped the large horse and got a playful bite in return. Their mouths were open, showing their teeth, and I would almost swear they were laughing.

Then the gray horse stopped and threw himself to the ground, rolling in the dirt like a dog. The brown horse trotted away from him, but looked back over her shoulder as if she were contemplating a roll in the dirt herself. Then she slowed to a walk instead, and when she got to the opposite side of the ring, rubbed her neck against a wooden post.

"She's too dignified to roll in the dirt," Jeanie explained.

"Excuse me?" I said.

"That's the problem with a lot of these horses. They have a certain image of themselves and they can't cut loose. That's why we have Misty in there running around with Gabriel. He's a wild mustang who was rescued out in Nevada with a simple fracture in his hind leg. We're hoping that he'll help Misty get in touch with her inner filly. She's been depressed for months."

Terry laughed. "If she's depressed, why don't you just give her Prozac?"

It was intended as a joke, but Jeanie nodded in earnest. "Oh, she's on a regular course of Prozac, but you can't count on pharmaceuticals entirely. She needs to rediscover the joy of living. Come on, I'll show you the stables."

We left Misty contemplating getting down and dirty. I sincerely hoped she'd manage it. I myself could identify with someone who was too uptight for a life-affirming roll on her back.

We went down the hill to the stables, which had New Age music emanating from within. We walked into the cool dark interior, and I inhaled the scent of alfalfa, like a newly mown lawn. The celestial sounds that were piped in made me think of the mind-numbing music playing in the lobby of New Horizons, as well as the chimes tinkling on Heather's porch. All of Malibu seemed to have the same spaced-out sound track, like Muzak from Mars.

The floor of the stables was immaculate. Hard-packed dirt with the occasional scrap of hay. Again, I noticed the absence of that distinctive horsey smell so common on farms and at petting zoos. In fact, I thought I was picking up the scent of eucalyptus.

Jeanie went to the first stall, which contained a black mare whose nose was covered with a soft leather mask, with big holes for her nostrils. She stroked the horse's forelock while pointing to the padded stall walls. "This is Penelope. She has a problem with self-mutilation. Rubs her nose raw on the wood when confined. We've got her on Zoloft, and obviously the mask and the padding prevent her from doing too much damage to her face—"

"Wow. A self-mutilating horse. Who'd have thought?" I said. "So all of these horses are on antidepressants?"

Jeanie nodded. "A lot of them. It's very good therapy for these sorts of psychogenic problems. Penelope's also undergoing acupuncture treatments and psychotherapy, and she's making terrific progress—aren't you, girl?"

She got a loud snort in response. Penelope hitched her head and backed up in her stall, turning herself around to face the back wall. "She suffers from social phobias as well," Jeanie whispered.

"You said psychotherapy," Terry said, obviously straining to keep a straight face. "Exactly how does that work?"

Jeanie laughed. "I know what you're thinking. A horse is a horse, of course, of course, and no one can talk to a horse, of course."

"Yeah, I was kind of thinking that."

"We have an animal psychologist on staff who specializes in making a psychic connection with the patients in order to deal with their issues. Penelope, for instance, developed performance anxiety when her guardian—we never use the word 'owner'—forced her into showing when she was too young. The doctor's working on giving Penelope back her self-worth, convincing her that her value as a horse isn't tied to her looks or her performance."

"Do they like this music?" I said, wondering what it was. Yanni plays love songs from *The Tibetan Book of the Dead*?

"They do," Jeanie assured me. "It's scientifically designed to produce alpha waves, or a state of relaxation in their brains. It's soothing to them and makes them more susceptible to therapy."

Jeanie walked over to an elaborate built-in stereo system near the front door. She turned the volume down on the music channel, revealing a murmuring man's voice underneath. "Good girl . . . Excellent stance . . . You're such a beautiful horse . . . What gorgeous flanks . . . You have such a shiny coat . . . !"

Terry and I stared at Jeanie. "Subliminal reinforcement," she said, winking. "Works wonders for their self-esteem."

"What does all of this cost?" I asked her.

"Boarding and food, which is all certified organic oats, hay, and alfalfa, comes to just three thousand dollars a week. The doctor visits, massages, acupuncture, and various other therapies are extra, of course. They run about three hundred and fifty dollars an hour."

We nodded, as if this were right in line with our budget instead of our estimate of a sheikh's weekly take. Jeanie wandered over to another stall. "This is Brandy. She has an eating disorder."

"An eating disorder?" Terry asked. "She looks fit to me."

"Well, we've been exercising her a lot. She was rather porky, though, weren't you, darling?" She rubbed Brandy's white nose. "And being all white, well . . . it's hard to hide those extra pounds," she whispered. "Dark horses can get away with more."

I looked into Brandy's stall and saw several floor-length mirrors attached to the walls. "The doctor feels that if Brandy is forced to see herself as others do, she'll be less inclined to overeat. And, of course, we've got her on a strict diet of high-protein grasses and oats with organic carrots as a special treat."

And so it went. Listening to the psychological woes of a

bunch of animals, as if they were the emotionally scarred children of horse divorce.

"This is God's way of telling you that you have too much money," I whispered to Terry as we left the stables.

"I know. If this is what these people do to their horses, can you imagine what they do to their kids?"

Next was a tour of the steam bath stalls inside the hydrotherapy building, and a look at the "hydraciser," which was a water-filled tub with a treadmill on the bottom. An injured horse could thus exercise torn muscles while being buoyed by the water. Then we were shown the "friends therapy" paddock, where horses were paired with a bird, a dog, or a bunny rabbit so they could experience the companionship and emotional support of their furry or feathered counterparts in the animal kingdom.

Our minds were still reeling from the tour as Jeanie led us back into the main building.

"Shall we start the paperwork?" she asked, sitting down at her desk.

Terry looked at me. "Oh, uh, we'll need to discuss it first."

Jeanie handed us each a brochure. "The sooner you get your horse in our care, the sooner the healing can begin. In here you'll find testimonials from people who swear by our service. Horses that were thought beyond help are now well-integrated, functioning members of the equine community."

I tapped the brochure on the back of my hand. "I'm sure. We really appreciate the tour. Tell me, if we wanted to leave our horses at home and hire one of your people to take care of them while we're gone . . . ?" I opened the brochure to a page with photographs of the staff.

"Oh, I hope you won't raid our staff," Jeanie said. "We've lost two trainers in the last week, and I don't think we can afford to lose any more. Qualified stable help is so hard to find."

As opposed to psychic horse shrinks, who appear to be plentiful.

"Really?" Terry said casually, opening up her own brochure. "Who's not here anymore?"

Inside, I saw Twink's photograph above her full name—*Twinkle Starr.* She was listed as a trainer and assistant stable manager. I pointed to her picture. "Is this the girl's real name?"

"Yes," Jeanie said with a little edge in her voice. "She's one of the ones we've lost. She went to work for one of our former clients."

"Heather Granger?"

"Uh-huh." She squinted at me. "How did you know that?"

"Oh, you know how small the horse world is," I said.

"Yes." She looked suddenly suspicious. "Where did *you* say you live?"

"Paso Robles," Terry said smoothly. "We could board the horses there, of course, but we've heard such great things about *you.*"

Jeanie then gave us what may have been a test, pointing to a wholesome-looking brunette in the brochure. "Do you know Becky Madrigal? She was from that area. Somewhere up there in wine country, anyway."

Terry peered at the photograph. "She *does* look familiar."

"Why do you say 'was'?" I asked Jeanie.

"She left us to pursue a singing career. Apparently, she's going to try her luck in Branson, Missouri."

"Good for her," Terry said. "Gotta follow your dreams."

Jeanie gave a little snort of derision. "It helps if you can sing." We waited for an explanation, and she blushed in embarrassment. "Sorry, that was tacky. But I've heard the girl singing in the stables. She should have stuck to grooming horses."

"Well, you never know. Willie Nelson's huge, and he can't sing," Terry said.

Jeanie shrugged. "I guess you're right."

We thanked her for her time, then started making our way to the front door. "I'll look forward to hearing from you," she said with a sales-pitchy smile and a wave.

When we were outside, I read to Terry from the brochure:

"'As a yearling, Thunder began experiencing nightmares. He'd kick at his stall door and whinny all night. Dr. Genevieve Forster's therapy helped him to realize that he was in a "safe place," that his demons weren't real. The nightmares have stopped completely! I can't thank EquiSpa enough for giving me back my Thunder.'"

"Prozac, can you believe it?" Terry said, rolling her eyes. "Who wants a slap-happy horse? And subliminal therapy! I tell ya, Malibu makes Beverly Hills look like a bastion of normalcy."

"So," I said, "it looks like our friend Frank must have boarded his polo ponies here at one time. And now Heather's hired one of their hands to help her dispose of the horses."

"Yeah, but what does it get us? I feel like we're grasping at straws."

"Gotta grasp something," I said, as we piled back on the bike. "Like you said, it's early days."

We pulled out of the driveway and were a half-mile away from the stables when a large white van rumbled past us. I squinted through the dust cloud it had kicked up, catching sight of the side panel. It bore a cartoon character of a man shoveling food into his smiling mouth with a fork. Underneath the graphic in large crayony letters were the words *Hungry Boys Catering*.

A catering company, on its way to a health spa for horses?

I wondered if they served alfalfa cubes to their clients on little paper doilies.

It was getting close to five-thirty, so we headed back to New Horizons for our appointment with the director. We found a different guard manning the entrance.

"We're Kerry and Terry McAfee," I said to him. "We have an appointment with Mr. Peavey."

"Just a moment," the guard said. He nodded as he spoke on the phone, then stuck his head back out the window. "Mr. Peavey is unavailable. Ms. Exeter suggests you call tomorrow morning."

Terry turned to me. "This is pissing me off."

"Well, what do you want to do? Crash through the gate and bust down the door?"

She waggled her eyebrows with an impish smile.

"Forget it," I said.

"Okay. I'm hungry anyway."

"No more restaurants!" I groaned.

"Chill," she said. "We'll scrounge something at Reba's."

The guard was still looking at us, waiting for some kind of response.

"Okay, thank you," I said, and waved to him. We'd do as we were told. No sense in antagonizing the man.

"We'll be back," Terry said in a thick gubernatorial accent, then she wheeled the bike around and we headed back down PCH to Reba's house.

ten

R eba's house was still ringed with crime-scene tape, legally off-limits. Terry cut the engine in the drive and we pulled off our helmets.

"Well?" I said.

"Well, what?"

"It says in plain English—*Do Not Cross*."

"*Qué es eso*, Do Not Cross? *No hablo inglés.*"

"*Terry* . . ."

"So what are they gonna do? Arrest us?"

"Maybe."

"What is it, a misdemeanor?"

"In your case, probably a second strike. Two-thirds of the way to a life sentence."

"Fuggetaboutit," she said. "This isn't a crime scene, it's a body dump. They'd know that if they had half a brain."

I turned over the possibility of our getting caught and decided it was minimal. It had been close to twenty-four hours since they'd responded to Boatwright's call. In a murder case, evidence is collected as quickly as possible to avoid crime-scene contamination, so it was doubtful they'd be coming back anytime soon. Besides, the sheriff's department was pretty sure they had their man.

Or rather, their man and their woman.

We ducked under the tape. I cut through the sticker seal warning of dire consequences for entering, and unlocked the door. Terry and I slipped inside.

The blinds had been dropped over the large picture window. I pushed the door closed behind me, but not all the way. I wasn't sure I wanted to stay.

"Dark in here," Terry said.

The house was ominously still. And though the body was no longer here, the knowledge that it had been made the skin on my forearms do a little tap dance.

"Let's check out the spare bedroom," Terry whispered. I hesitated, and she yanked me forward. "Come on, sissy girl."

We tiptoed down the hallway to the right, Terry in the lead. She turned the knob on the guest bedroom door and pushed it open. . . .

The rugs were gone, taken into evidence. I went a few steps inside to show her how brave I was, peering at the bleached oak floorboards. They had probably used Luminol to determine where the blood was distributed, if any—but that would have evaporated long ago. No blood was visible anywhere.

Had the body been drained before it was transported? Or had enough time passed between the murder and transportation of the body that the blood had coagulated, resulting in a lack of spillage?

"No blood," I said. "That suggests the girl was killed elsewhere and brought here afterwards."

"Yeah, but their theory allows for that. Robert killed her in the canyon, brought her here, then wandered around with the head for a couple of days for his own sick reasons."

I sighed. "Right. Let's check out the powder room."

We crept into the guest bathroom. As Reba had said, there was a large sliding door of pebbled glass inside. The door handle still bore evidence of fingerprint dust. I gave it a push.

"Locked," I whispered.

"But was it locked before the police got here?"

I shrugged. "Maybe yes, maybe no. Too bad we didn't check it out before."

But we hadn't wanted to do any crime-scene contamination ourselves. We couldn't have known then that such information might be vital to exonerating our relatives. I'd have to remember to ask John Boatwright—he of the aborted first date—to suss out that information. As a police detective, he'd have a better chance of getting the scuttlebutt on the investigation, even if it was in a different jurisdiction from his.

I unlocked the door and slid it open, realizing that it would indeed have been very easy for someone to drag a body in through the door while the household slept. I thought of Heather and wondered if she could have purposefully left the door open for someone to sneak in.

But why this particular house, especially when there was a whole beach available for dumping the body without such a high risk of being caught?

"Why this house?" I whispered.

"Why are we whispering?" Terry whispered.

"I was just wondering, why this house?" I said at a normal

volume. "Somebody obviously wanted to frame Reba and Robert for the crime, but why *them*?"

"An excellent question," a man's voice said.

Terry and I screamed and jumped into each other's arms. Detective Thomas stepped into the doorway, flashlight in hand.

"Shit!" Terry said, pushing me away. "You scared us!"

"Sorry, but you know you're not supposed to be in here."

"So that entitles you to give us a heart attack?"

He laughed. "You know, somehow I thought I'd be seeing you two again."

"How'd you get in?" I asked him.

"Front door, just like you."

"And you're here because . . . ?"

He looked at me and said nothing.

Terry broke into a smile, nodding her head. "'Cause you know this case is a bunch of crap."

He took a second to respond, looking around the room. "The DA doesn't think so."

"But you do?" I asked hopefully.

He shook his head. "I'm not saying anything on the record."

"By the way, was this sliding door locked when you guys did your investigation?" Terry asked. "You know, it could have been left open on purpose, so someone could come back later and hide the body."

"Yeah, it was unlocked."

Terry high-fived me. "Get any prints?"

"Not a one."

"Oh," we said, disappointed.

Thomas clicked off his flashlight and turned around, and then we followed him down the hallway into the breakfast area. He separated the slats of the picture window to look outside.

"So . . . off the record," I said. "You think this case stinks, right?"

He sat at the breakfast table, placing his sheriff's hat in front of him with a sigh and rubbing the imprint from the hatband on his forehead. "The captain's with the DA on this."

"Then why *are* you here?" Terry asked.

He pointed to his gut. "It's not lying still. Won't let me eat. I get grouchy when I don't eat."

Well, that was good news. The lead detective wasn't satisfied with his arrest. On the other hand, the mention of the district attorney was a reminder that local politics can be a scary thing when inserted into an investigation.

"We've been doing some poking around on our own," I said. "And we've learned some interesting things."

"By all means, fill me in."

Unfortunately, all we had was a mishmash of vague suspicions and unconnected happenings. But as I laid them all out, I saw Thomas perk up at the mention of Frank Steinmetz.

"Apparently, he has a thing for young blondes," I said. "Just like the girl who was murdered. Since he broke up with his wife, he's always got one on his arm."

"Yeah, I thought of Steinmetz, too, since he lives right next door. But he's been out of the country for the last two weeks. In Spain, on some kind of movie scout. We just got to him this morning, and his passport confirms it."

"But he's got tons of money," Terry said. "He could have paid to have it done. And doing it while he's out of town makes the most sense."

"Okay, but why stash the body here?" Thomas said. "Isn't it a little close for comfort? Why risk breaking and entering his neighbor's house when he could have had the corpse dumped in a canyon?"

"Well, it worked, didn't it?" I said. "Someone else *has* been arrested for the crime. And the head *was* thrown in a canyon, if you believe our cousin Robert."

Thomas nodded, pondering this.

"Has the victim been identified yet?" Terry asked him.

"Yes. Her sister had reported her missing. We called her in and she was able to provide an identification."

"Oh God," Terry and I said together, as we imagined the horror of IDing a sister by her detached head. In our case, however, it wouldn't be necessary. You'd only have to look at the surviving sister to know you had a match.

But wait a minute—

"I thought her face had been devoured by wild animals," I said. "How did the sister identify her?"

"Height, weight, general physique. Plus, she had a distinctive tattoo. A dragon on her left hip."

"You couldn't match her fingerprints?" Terry said.

"Didn't get any matches locally. The girl's a recent transplant from Philadelphia, with no California driver's license and no criminal record. Before the sister came in, we sent the prints out to AFIS at Quantico for a national search, but the results won't be back for a couple of weeks."

"How about dental records?" I said.

"That would have been our next step if the sister hadn't come forward."

"So who was she?"

"Actress, name of Candy Starr."

"Porno?" Terry said.

He laughed. "No, that's her given name."

The letters flashed in neon in front of my eyes. "Wait. Starr with two *R*s? S-T-A-R-R?"

"Yeah. Why?"

I grabbed the EquiSpa brochure out of my jacket pocket and flipped it open on the table. "Is the sister's name Twinkle?"

"Yep, believe it or not."

I pointed to the willowy blonde we'd seen at Heather's, the one who'd made Terry's blood pressure rise. "Is this her?"

He looked down at the photo, frowning. "Where'd you get this?"

"We saw this girl at the home of Heather Granger, the ex-wife of our buddy Frank Steinmetz, according to online reports. There's your connection between the dead girl and Mr. Steinmetz."

"Pretty loose connection."

"Yeah, but it's interesting," Terry said.

"What do you know about a group called the Children of the Cosmos?" I asked him.

"Those flakes?" He grimaced. "They've been very active out here for a few years now. We've had some complaints, even had the feds looking into them, but they're real clever. Got themselves lawyered up for filing defamation suits, and they're working right now to get classified as a religion for the tax breaks."

"A religion?" Terry said. "Are you telling me any wacko can walk in off the streets, have his cult classified as a religion, and get tax breaks?"

"If you've got enough money and enough lawyers, yeah."

"They have a lot of money?"

Thomas shrugged. "Their followers tend to be very rich. What I call 'floaters,' people with lots of money and leisure time, no real roots in anything. They're looking for something meaningful in their lives. But the organization is hidden behind a bunch of dummy corporations, so it's hard to trace exactly where the money comes from—"

"And where it goes," I added, and he nodded.

"So what it amounts to is that they're a bunch of scam artists," Terry concluded.

"That's what I think, but just try proving it."

"Well, Heather Granger is one of them," I told him. "She approached Reba about the group, and she used *that* bathroom while she was in the house. No one else uses it, so she could have easily left the door open."

Thomas shook his head. "Unfortunately, it's all too vague to take to the DA."

"So what are you saying?" Terry said. "You're just going to ignore all of this and let them go ahead with prosecuting the wrong people?"

He winced at the accusation. "Look, I'm sorry. My hands are tied."

Terry and I exchanged dismayed looks.

"Don't you take some kind of oath to uphold the law?" she said.

As usual, she'd pushed too hard. Thomas stood up and plunked the cowboy hat on his head, giving us a rueful smile. "Off the record," he said, heading for the door, "I wish you luck."

"How much time do we have?" I called to him.

"The district attorney got his indictment today, arraignment's tomorrow."

Terry and I sank back in our chairs. "What's the hurry?" she said.

"If the suspects are being held in custody, they have to arraign them within forty-eight hours."

"Look," she said, "we're wasting a lot of time right now, commuting from LA. If we're going to keep investigating, we need to be here at the beach."

"So?" he said.

"So we need to stay here in the house. Are you done with it? I mean, can you get the crime-scene tape taken down?"

"Done. Although I'm not sure it's a great idea for you to be hanging out here."

A chill skittered up my spine. "You think whoever did this might come back and do it again?"

He gave me a *Who knows?* look. "At any rate, I'm sorry to say you're on your own. I can't be seen as undermining the DA."

And with that disheartening pronouncement, he was out the door.

I crossed the living room, kneeled on Reba's rust-colored ultrasuede couch, and peered out the front window to watch Thomas climb into his department-issue SUV. He must have arrived just after we did and seen our motorcycle out front. Or maybe he'd been staking out the place and actually saw us break in. I watched him pick up the radio and speak to someone, then he started up his engine and took off on PCH.

"Schmuck," Terry said, joining me at the window.

"And to think I was attracted to him," I said.

She looked at me, shaking her head. "These days you're attracted to anything with a pulse and a package."

"And a piece."

"*What?*"

I nodded. "It's evolutionary, I've decided. Survival of the best armed. Probably to do with the state of the world these days."

She put a hand to my forehead, feeling for fever. "You've been doing this too long. It's affecting your brain. You're a California girl! You've always been Ms. Anti-gun."

"Well, now I think they're kind of sexy."

"And you've always had a very low sex drive."

"What do you know about my sex drive?" I scowled. "Just because I don't act on it doesn't mean I don't have one."

"Well, for God's sake don't act on it now. Now is not a good time to unleash the beast."

"Don't worry. The beast is leashed, muzzled, tied to a stake, and surrounded by an electrified fence. Look, if we're gonna move in here, let's make it easy on ourselves. We'll take Reba's Mercedes so we can haul the dogs and some clothes all at once."

"Righty-o," she said.

Twenty minutes later, we'd scarfed down some microwaved mini-quiches we found in the freezer, fired up Reba's Mercedes SL with the mint-green exterior and white leather interior, and with Barbra Streisand bellowing show tunes from the CD player, we headed back across town to Beverly Glen.

eleven

"Oh, no," Terry said as we approached our house.

A *Live at Five* news van was parked outside. It didn't immediately occur to me what this meant. "What, did we have another break-in or something?" I asked, confused.

"No, they found us . . . the Smith twins!"

"Damn!" I slid down in my seat. "What do we do now?"

"We can't go in." Terry burned rubber away from the house. "If we do, not only will they bug us for a statement, they'll follow us out to the beach, and there goes our investigation. They'll be trailing behind us everywhere we go."

"I *knew* this thing was going to be trouble. Can't a person do a good deed without being pursued by a rabid pack of newshounds?" I groaned in frustration, then an idea occurred to me. "Hey, wait a minute. . . . Lance!"

"Huh?"

"He's still got the key, doesn't he?"

"They'd follow him, too."

"Maybe he can give them the slip and grab the doggies and some clothes, and then we can arrange a secret rendezvous."

She nodded. "Okay. Give him a try."

She handed me the cell phone and I scrolled down for his number. He answered on the second ring. "Hey, dude, it's Kerry. Can you do us a favor?"

"Can I refuse a favor to one to whom I owe my very existence?"

Such an actor.

"Lance, you owe us nothing. But I'd be very grateful if you could help us out with something."

"Speak and it shall be done."

"Look, there's a news van outside our house. We think they're onto us—you know, the Smith twins."

"Bastards!"

"Yeah, well . . . we can't risk being followed right now. Could you go by the house and get the pups and their stuff, and maybe some clothes for me and Terry, and bring everything out to us in Malibu?"

"Sure. Any special kind of clothes?"

"You know, jeans, T-shirts, a sweater or two . . ."

He lowered his voice into the Barry White range. "Unmentionables?"

"Yeah, those, too."

"Gonna be needing your black belts?"

"If you can find any black belts in our underwear drawer, bring 'em along."

"Sounds kink-*ay*."

"Make sure you're not followed, okay?"

"Count on it, babe."

I gave him the address and hung up, laughing. "He's really into this," I told Terry. Then I happened to glance in the side-view mirror. "Oh my God."

"What?"

"Look! The news van. It's back there!" I could see its satellite dish poking up several cars behind us.

"Shit on a stick!" Terry said.

She stepped on the gas and zoomed alongside the SUV in front of us, passing it illegally. The driver laid on his horn, and I turned around to see him giving us the finger. He roared up on our bumper so we could feel the full force of his road rage. Either that, or he was going to shoot out our rear windshield. You never knew in LA.

"Ter, we're not on the motorcycle now," I reminded her, gripping my armrest. "Do you think you could take it a little easi—?"

She floored it around a Ford Escort, barely missing an oncoming Audi. The driver of the Escort was gesturing and cursing when the original SUV came barreling around his side, attempting to cut in between us and the Escort so he could continue to signal his displeasure. But suddenly there was a squealing of brakes and a crunching of metal as the Ford Escort rammed him from behind.

Both vehicles screeched to a stop in the middle of the winding canyon road, horns blaring like air-raid sirens.

I turned and saw the drivers jumping out of their cars. Then, after a few seconds, the news van came screaming around a blind curve. Not prepared for the pileup, it slammed into the Escort, which slammed into the already smashed SUV, propelling it over the yellow line and into the path of an oncoming Hummer, which smashed the hell out of its previously uninjured front end, and was in turn rear-ended by a Jeep, which crumpled like a Japanese lantern on the Hummer's back fender.

The satellite dish from the news van went sailing through the air, reentering the earth's atmosphere ten feet behind us, crashing to the road in a spray of high-tech debris.

I sank back in my seat, breathing heavily, and looked over at Terry, who was as chill as a dry martini. "Who taught you to drive?" I yelled. *"Satan?"*

She winked at me. "I aced the exam."

I took one last look at the pileup in the side mirror and, not for the first time, I was really glad Terry was on *my* team.

Detective Thomas had made good on his word. By the time we got back to Reba's, the crime-scene tape had been removed. We had no hesitation about letting ourselves into the house this time, except for the obvious one—another possible visit from the killer. I tried not to dwell on that idea, especially now that the sun was going down.

"Should we go check out Frank's place?" I asked Terry.

"No time like the present," she replied.

We stepped out onto the wooden deck that ran the length of the second story, looking over at the houses to the left and right, tightly packed together on this prime beachfront property. From our vantage point, we could lean on the railing and angle our necks like flamingos, seeing straight down into Steinmetz's back terrace. It was paved with terra cotta tiles and had a privacy wall in translucent panes that blocked the view from the beach.

Two people were seated beneath a blue-and-white-striped umbrella, a man and a woman. We could see portions of their arms and legs. She had long, lovely limbs; he had skinny legs with knobby knees, dark blue veins stippling his calves.

"Let's take a closer look," Terry whispered.

We walked along the wooden deck, then down the stairs to the soft, still-warm sand. The beach was deserted. Technically, it wasn't a private beach, the coastal commission had decreed it public, but there were few people who had the nerve to drive here, haul out their beach paraphernalia, and hike through somebody's five-million-dollar property to catch some rays.

Still, the residents of Malibu were always being forced to unlock fences, remove walls built into easements, and generally make the beach accessible to Joe Citizen. It was a source of constant conflict with the owners of these fabulous houses, most of whom leaned conspicuously left in politics, supported all sorts of liberal causes, and lent their names to charities designed to help those less fortunate. They just didn't want those less fortunate darkening their picture windows and littering their beaches. And for the most part, the riffraff was content to hang out on the beaches at Santa Monica and Venice instead.

Terry and I rolled up our jeans, dumped our boots on the stairs, and headed down toward the water. We let our feet sink deep in the wet sand, pulling them out again with a satisfying sucking sound, then wandered up to the area in front of Frank's house. In addition to the walled-in patio at beach level, there was an upstairs deck for drinks by sunset. A door with frosted glass prevented us from seeing into the terrace.

"Let's get closer and see if we can hear anything," Terry said.

We made our way along the small pathway between the two properties, sticking close to the wall surrounding Frank's patio. We could hear a conversation between the man and woman, and it didn't sound friendly. We hunkered down next to the wall to listen, and what we heard next made our breath catch in our throats.

"You son of a bitch!" the woman shouted. A seagull squawked in response, then both sounds died out, leaving only the noise of crashing waves.

The man said something low. Something we couldn't make out.

The woman again: "You bastard! You *killed* her!"

Terry and I looked at each other, agog. Someone was accusing our suspect of murder? How convenient.

A woman with long blond hair came barreling out of the walled-in terrace onto the sand, waving her arms, apparently hysterical. She wore a thin cotton blouse and a thong bikini bottom.

"Killer! Murderer!" she cried, then ran toward the water and threw herself into the surf, where she thrashed around in the waves, sobbing. She looked like a page from the *Sports Illustrated* swimsuit issue—the setting sun glinting off her straw-colored hair, her wet cotton blouse molded to her voluminous, heaving breasts.

Frank walked slowly out from the terrace, clapping his hands.

"Brilliant!" he said.

The girl looked up from her tragic pose and smiled, the tears evaporating like yesterday's reality show. "Really?" she said, jumping to her feet.

He continued to applaud as she ran back to him, now only a few feet away from our hiding place. "Truly, it was brilliant."

She stood before him with her head bowed, then looked up under her wet lashes with a coy smile. "Does this mean I have the part?"

He massaged his chin stubble, frowning.

"Unfortunately, you're just not right," he said. "Too tall, too thin."

The girl's face hardened instantly. "Lots of actresses are tall and thin," she countered, her voice tense. "Nicole Kidman is no dwarf."

His hands went out to the side as he shrugged. "Okay, I was trying to let you down easily. You're a great lay, babe, I mean that. But you just don't have *it*—"

It happened so fast, he didn't even have time to react.

She sprang at him, shrieking like a wild monkey, pummeling his chest with her hands. He grabbed her by the wrists and tried to stop the onslaught, but she broke free and scratched at his face with her long pink nails. Bright streaks of red appeared as he fell back on the sand, howling, covering his face. He rolled over onto his stomach in an attempt to save himself from further attack. She put her foot to the back of his head and thrust it down with such force that the sand began to fill his ears. His arms flailed desperately.

"Well, you're a lousy lay!" she screamed at him, finally letting her foot off his head. He jerked up, spitting out sand and gasping for breath.

"You're crazy!" he yelled, scuttling backward on the sand on his hands and feet.

She exploded with laughter. "No, I'm just *acting* crazy. See? I'm pretty damn good." She kicked more sand in his face, then turned and ran down the beach, head down and arms pumping.

Frank picked himself up slowly, looking around to see if anyone had witnessed his humiliation. Then he walked back to the patio, brushing the sand off his face and shaking it out of his hair.

"Fucking actresses," he grumbled.

* * *

We snuck back to Reba's house, half giggling, half horrified.

"Oh my God," I said when we were safely inside.

"You can say that twice," Terry agreed.

"Omigodomigod."

"He really has a way with women, huh? He's lucky he walked away with his balls intact."

"I could use a drink after witnessing that scene," I said. "How about you?"

"Yeah, but there won't be any alcohol here, because of Robert."

I opened the refrigerator and found an open bottle of chardonnay. "Guess again, babe."

"Whoa. Real supportive, Reba," she said, but reached up into the cabinet and brought down two blue Mexican wine goblets anyway.

"Blue glasses—where's the leaded crystal?" I said, as she set them on the table.

"Did you forget?" Terry asked. "We're much more relaxed down here." She poured the wine. "To relaxation."

I clinked her glass. "To ambitious blondes."

She shook her head in disbelief. "She was a beast, wasn't she?"

"Yeah, but you heard—first he took her to bed, and then he told her she was a no-talent."

"I know, but *jeez*, take your rejection, honey. It's all part of the game. You know, this makes me wonder . . ."

"What?"

"Well, maybe Frank really plays 'em before he dumps them, strings 'em along promising fame and fortune while taking them for all the booty he can. Maybe he has a sadistic streak, gets a cruel kick out of using them and then saying sayonara. And if this girl went psycho on him, maybe some other little actress did the same thing and he had to conk her over the head in self-defense. And then maybe he chopped *off* her head to make it look like some crazed sex killer did it."

"Possible, but . . . provable?"

"We've got to get into Frank's house somehow to find some evidence."

I raised my eyebrows. "Well, if we're all so relaxed down here, maybe he won't mind if a couple of babes drop in from the beach to say hello. A couple of potential conquests?"

She nodded, grinning. "Are we gonna tell him we live at the crime scene, or are we gonna make like mermaids who wandered in from the surf?"

"Good question," I said. "We don't want to put him on guard. Let me think on that one."

The doorbell rang, and Terry jumped up to answer it. Lance was standing outside with a duffel bag on his shoulder, holding the dogs in their travel pouches—a blue vinyl *Hello Kitty* backpack for Paquito, a *Josie and the Pussycats* backpack in pink for Muffy. When we took them for rides, we strapped them to our backs in these ultramod dog carriers. Motorcycling was their most favorite activity, after eating and snoozing.

"I don't know what happened," Lance began, handing one dog to each of us and setting down the duffel and a large bag of dog food. "But there were no reporters at your house when I got there. Traffic was backed up like crazy, though. I had to park on the other side of Greendale and hike up to your house."

I shook my head. "LA, huh?"

"Probably some idiot tried to pass on Beverly Glen and caused the pileup," he theorized.

"Reckless drivers," Terry said, shaking her head in disgust. "They should be shot."

We set the dogs on the floor, and they immediately scampered over to the door to the closed guest bedroom, scratching at the wood and whimpering. I followed them, swooping them up in my arms while they wriggled in protest.

"No, honeys, you don't want to go in there," I told them.

"Let them go," Terry said. "It's their whole purpose in life—smell and be smelled. If it's dead, it's that much more interesting."

"*Ewww*," I said, feeling nauseated at the thought.

Lance frowned at me. "Something's dead?"

"Yeah, there was a corpse in there. A beheaded girl. That's why I don't want them sniffing around."

His eyes bugged. "A beheaded girl?" His Adam's apple pounded up and down like the bell on a carnival strongman machine.

"That's why we're here," Terry explained. "We're trying to figure out who killed her, because our aunt and cousin have been booked for the murder."

Lance fidgeted and started to make his way toward the door. "You know, I just remembered. I've got an audition. Underwear commercial. Big buckeroonies." He practically leaped across the room, like a ballerina with a severe pituitary problem. "You need anything else, just give me a holler, okay?"

The door slammed and he was gone.

"Guess we can't count on him coming to our rescue," Terry said.

"Don't worry, we've got guard dogs." I set their combined fifteen pounds of ferocity on the floor. Terry opened the door to the guest bedroom, and they dashed in and did their reconnaissance, madly sniffing the floor where the body had been.

"Well, at least we know we've got corpse radar when we need it," Terry said.

"You gonna volunteer to sleep in here?" I asked her.

"Oh yeah. I'll sleep in here when hell hosts the winter Olympics."

"Hey, let's take a look at Robert's room. We haven't done that. We might find some kind of clue."

"Right."

We went down the hallway past the large master bedroom, then up the stairs that led to the third level of the house. Robert's room had a wall of glass facing the ocean, tall ceilings of bleached wood, and a large overhead skylight. During the daytime, the room must be brilliant with light.

Paintings leaned against the walls in various stages of completion. Robert's style was a harshly abstractionist one, with large splotches of black paint mingling with bright red and dark greens on canvases that were deliberately ripped in places, leaving gaping holes that were then sewn together with rough twine. The holes were a violent motif that ran through all of the paintings. It looked like a critic had expressed his opinion of their artistic merit with a butcher knife.

I had to admit, they were kind of dark and disturbing.

"No wonder he never sells anything," Terry said. "Those sewn-up holes remind me of the tribal practices where they stitch up the woman's—"

"Don't say it!" I yelled, crossing my legs.

"Sorry."

"You think there's hostility toward women in these paintings?"

She shrugged. "We'd better not overthink it."

The queen-sized bed was covered in gauzy batik material, piled with those colorful Indian pillows with little mirrors embroidered onto them. There was a floor-to-ceiling closet on one side of the room. Terry walked over to open one of the sliding doors. I tensed reflexively, clenching my eyes shut, though I wasn't sure what I expected to see. If there were any more bodies lying around, surely the police would have found them.

When Terry didn't cry out in horror, I opened my eyes and joined her in front of the closet. It contained nothing in the rotting-cadaver department. Only a few articles of clothing on hangers—smoking jackets and silk pajamas, mostly, Robert's uniform of choice—and paint supplies stacked on the floor.

"Check it out," Terry said, laughing. She pointed to a large box full of Ding Dongs in the corner. "He's all set for a major earthquake."

"So maybe he's hooked on these, and snuck out of rehab to buy them," I said, recalling the Ding Dongs in Robert's bag. "And then maybe he went into some kind of diabetic shock and passed out. And somebody planted the head on him while he was unconscious."

Terry rolled her eyes. "If we're going to spin theories, let's at least spin one that sounds a little plausible."

"You got a better one?"

"I hate to say it, but the most plausible scenario is that he did it."

"There you go again!"

"I'm just saying . . . Look, Kerry, he's a drunk and we all know it. He disappears for two days, then shows up all grungy and toting the head around with no 'idea' how he got it. The body's in his own house, and let's not forget, he *has* confessed. I think we have to at least consider the possibility he's guilty."

I stood there, shaking my head. "Do me a favor. If I'm ever accused of a crime, don't be a character witness for me."

"Hey, facts are facts."

"And that's all they are. We have to go beyond the facts and find the truth. You can't lose faith, Ter. This is *family* we're talking about here. And it's not like we have any to spare."

She nodded. "True."

"Look, let's go check out the neighborhood around New Horizons and see if we can find the place where he bought his snacks. We might find a witness who remembers seeing him wandering around. Maybe we can place him somewhere during his missing days."

"All right," she sighed. "First thing in the morning."

We spent the evening trading places on the deck, scoping out Frank's house. Terry was on duty at eleven o'clock, when I heard a car door slam. I rushed to the windows at the front of the house, straining my eyes to see who was paying Frank a late-night visit. A tall, stunning blond woman exited a BMW wearing a long fur coat and stiletto heels.

It was chilly at night here at the beach, but there was certainly no need to drape yourself in animal pelts like Nanook of the North. She was probably some kind of escort or call girl— nude underneath the fur coat, or at least scantily clad. After this evening's earlier fiasco, you'd think he'd want a little hiatus from blondes. But this Frank clearly had the appetite of a man twice his size and half his age.

The woman rang the bell, and after a few moments the door opened. She slinked inside. I waited for a few minutes, then went out onto the deck to tell Terry what I'd seen, and that I thought we should call it a night. I figured the furry blonde would keep Frank busy into the wee hours, and all the activity would be of the behind-closed-doors variety.

Terry was staring at the waves, hypnotized by their rhythmic crashing.

"Ter . . . ?"

It took a moment for her to acknowledge me. "Yeah?" she said dreamily.

"I think we can call it quits. Frank just got a visit from a tall blonde in a fur coat."

She chuckled. "Mink?"

"Who knows from dead-animal skins? It could have been muskrat."

She yawned and stretched. "The man's insatiable."

"I wonder why the police aren't more interested in him, don't you?"

"Thomas said he had an alibi."

"Even so."

"Maybe he's got a lot of pull with them. Big producer, major contributor to the sheriff's campaign . . ."

"Well, anyway, I don't think we're going to do much good staring at his house while they play hide the salami."

"Okay," she said. "Tomorrow we'll pop in for a cocktail."

"All right. I'm gonna hit the hay."

I headed directly for the master bedroom. I didn't want to negotiate with Terry for it. I was pulling on lacy yellow pajamas when she appeared in the doorway.

"You taking this room?"

"Yep." I pulled down the covers and slipped in next to the sleeping dogs (clever little buggers, they'd already sussed out the best bed). "Why don't you take Robert's studio?"

"Fine. I'll sleep with the sutured genitalia. You taking both pups, too?"

"Look at them, so cute all curled up together. It'd be a shame to separate them." Paquito and Muffy were sound asleep, their butts jammed together for warmth.

"Yeah, okay. *Pig,*" Terry said, walking out of the room. "Sweet dreams."

"You, too." I turned out the light and nestled into Reba's silk pillowcases, eager to forget all about Frank and his call girl and commence my sweet dreaming.

The horses were whinnying, obviously upset. They snorted and stomped in their stalls. I became concerned for them.

"What's the matter, horsies?"

I heard Willie Nelson singing "Blue Skies."

It wasn't their usual soothing music, I realized. That must have been why they were agitated. And the channel wasn't coming in clearly. It was producing a high-pitched electronic noise that was offending their highly tuned senses.

"It's okay, I'll fix the music," I told them.

I went to the stereo system as I'd seen Jeanie do and turned the knob. The music disappeared, and a man's voice could be heard on the other channel. He spoke in a low, murmuring voice:

"You're a dead girl . . . You're dead . . . You're a dead girl . . . You're dead . . . You're a dead girl . . . You're dead . . ."

God, what was this?

I spun the knob around and around, trying to shut out the horrible voice. But the volume went up instead to an insanely high decibel level. And now it sounded like an old phonograph record that was skipping on the one word:

"DEAD . . . (hic) . . . DEAD . . . (hic) . . . DEAD . . ."

The horses kicked up a fury, whinnying pitifully and pounding their hooves. Poor things, I had to let them out of there before they hurt themselves. I ran from stall to stall, throwing open the doors.

But the stalls were empty.

"*DEAD* . . . (hic) . . . *DEAD* . . . (hic) . . . *DEAD* . . ."

The voice was deafening. Vibrating through my body like a thousand pounding drums. My skull was about to explode.

I had to get out of the stables. I started to run, but no matter how fast I went, the space opened up in front of me continuously. Stalls stretching out forever in an endless line of crude wooden doors. In microscopic detail, I could see the splinters sticking out of them like sharpened bamboo shoots, about to impale my body.

"Let me out!" I tried to scream, but I had no voice.

Then, suddenly, it was all gone. The stables, the threatening voice . . . *poof.*

It was dark. I heard a woman crooning behind me.

I turned to look. It was Candy. Her blond hair was ragged with long dark roots, and she was dressed in a black sequined gown that was ripped as if slashed, the holes in the fabric crudely repaired with twine. She sat on a stool in a spotlight, radiating a sad, punk kind of glamour.

"*I'm through with love,*" she sang in a reedy voice, "*I'll never fall again . . .*"

Where were we, in a nightclub? I looked around at the empty tables. It was just she and I, alone. A private concert.

"*Said adieu to love, don't ever call again . . .*"

I looked back at Candy. She reminded me of a waifish, beat-up Marlene Dietrich. I listened to her for a minute, moved by the pathos in her singing, then it suddenly occurred to me. . . . She was here, singing . . . she wasn't dead . . . there had been no murder. *It had all been a terrible mistake!*

"Candy," I cried out. "You're alive! You're alive . . . !"

She stopped and squinted out into the darkness to see who had yelled so rudely. Then she sighed, cupped her hands on her jaw, ripped the head off her neck, and threw it in my direction.

It sailed toward me with its eyes glinting, the shiny, blood-red lips parted in a smile. . . .

I woke up to the sound of my own screaming.

The dogs barking.

The pounding of Terry's feet on the stairs.

She slid around the corner on her socks, eyes as big as dinner plates. "Ker, what happened? Are you okay?"

I was hyperventilating and my shirt was drenched in sweat.

"I'm sorry," I said, panting. "I had a nightmare."

Terry blew out a breath. "You scared me half to death!"

"I scared myself half to death. I had the most horrible dream about a headless girl. About Candy."

Terry sat on the bed, patting my leg. "Shhh . . . It's okay now. Everything's okay. Shhh." Muffy licked my elbow.

When I got ahold of myself, I told her about my dream. "What do you think it means?" I asked her.

"What does it mean? It means no more Stephen King books for you."

"But it felt like I was supposed to get something from it. . . ."

She pooh-poohed this idea. "It was just a nightmare brought on by sleeping in the same house where the body was."

"I guess so," I said, but the nagging feeling wouldn't go away. I was convinced that there was a message about the case inside the terrifying imagery that my mind had conjured up as I slept. But as the minutes went by and I came more fully awake, the dream slipped away into the vapor. The meaning, if any, fading along with the ghastly sideshow.

Terry was probably right. It was just a horror flick of my own invention.

We chatted for another ten minutes, and when she was finally convinced that I was okay, she went back off to sleep in Robert's loft.

I pulled the pups closer and stared at the ceiling, not sure I wanted to sleep ever again.

twelve

*M*orning, at last.

I'd awakened a minimum of five times during the night in a cold sweat, terrified of having another dream. Sleep-deprived though I was, I was happier to be alive than I'd been in a long time. It was impossible to cling to the night terrors with the warm Malibu sunshine pouring in the windows of Reba's bedroom.

I leaped out of bed along with the dogs, who were eager to start their day. They appeared fully rested, with no disturbing thoughts in their tiny brains. Whatever nightmares they'd had about being browbeaten by cats or outrun by bunnies or mocked by giant, empty kibble bowls had vanished with the sun.

"Come on," I said joyfully. "Let's fetch the paper!"

Muffy and Paquito couldn't actually fetch the *Los Angeles Times*. It's a large paper that's delivered flat. If they ever actually tried to get it in their tiny mouths and drag it into the house, it would end up looking like the possum litter.

But they lead a very active fantasy life, our dogs. They didn't need to actually grip the paper in their teeth to believe they were helping me fetch it. They just had to trot out with me to the front walk, wagging their little butts and sniffing the paper for any "pee-mails" they'd received on the World Wide Woof.

"I wasn't aware you knew anybody on this side of town," I said to Paquito, who was working furiously on the front page, sniffing so hard I thought his itty-bitty lungs would implode. "Making some new friends?"

I picked up the paper, yawning, and started back into the house, turning it over in my hands. I glanced at the front page and gasped when I saw the bottom right corner. There in the listings for the various sections was the heading "Smith Twins Strike Again?"

The dogs jumped all over my feet, distressed. *What'sa matter? What'sa matter?* they whimpered. I quickly bent down to reassure them.

"It's okay, honeys. Mommy just got a little shock to the system. Come on, let's go inside."

I put food in their bowls and they munched away, calm again after my shake-up. Terry was still asleep up in Robert's studio. The coffee had brewed, and I decided to get some into my bloodstream before I tried to assimilate the article.

"It's probably somebody else," I told the dogs. "A lot of people use the name Smith. I mean, actually *have* the name Smith . . ."

I pulled out the California section and laid it on the table in the breakfast room, gulping down coffee as I read.

MALIBU—*The mysterious twin avengers of Flight 222 have struck again.*

It was us! My heart began pounding out a salsa beat as I read on:

Anonymous do-gooders, described as redheaded female twins in their twenties, have moved from Yemeni hijackers to bully bikers. The latest episode of vigilante justice occurred at a popular beachfront restaurant, Malibu's Pier View Café.

A witness to the event was one William "Fat Boy" Schwartz, a local resident and a regular of the restaurant who had also been a passenger on the now legendary Flight 222 from Honolulu. Attempted terrorists on that flight were also subdued by the mysterious redheaded twins.

"It was definitely the same chicks, man," he said, referring to two women who were involved in the incident at the Pier View. "I recognized their style. It was like watching the Powerpuff Girls in a Tarantino movie."

There was a photograph of Fat Boy on his hog. He was easily a four-hundred-pounder, his ample flesh oozing over the sides of his bike and straining against a size XXXXXL T-shirt. I didn't see how I could have missed him at the restaurant *or* on the plane.

Fat Boy reported that the twins were eating nachos, minding their own business on the deck, when they were accosted by a man who had been consuming beer since the restaurant had opened for business.

"He went out and tried to pick a fight. Some guys can't stand seeing chicks on a Harley, I guess. And theirs is painted pink,

which really p—ed him off. And he started whaling on them, and one of them picked him up and threw him right off the deck. I mean, here's this skinny little flat-chested chick, and she just picks him up and throws him over her head . . ."

HEY!

Why did everyone in the free world feel the need to report to the press that Terry and I are flat-chested? Was this a matter of international import or something?

Well, I supposed we had bigger problems now. We were becoming vigilante celebrities—anonymous outlaws. I skipped over most of the rest of the article to get to the dreaded conclusion. Were we wanted for assault?

The Smith twins, so named because they wore WH Smith bags over their heads to avoid publicity after the terrorist incident, were caught on this occasion without their headgear. Even so, descriptions of the women remain vague. Witnesses say the twins simply moved too fast—they were a blur of motion.

"Hey, people have a right to defend themselves, right?" Fat Boy asked, causing the entire restaurant to break out into applause.

The biker who was thrown from the balcony apparently walked away from the fall. A cocktail waitress called Emergency Medical Services, but the alleged victim was gone by the time they arrived.

No one present was able to provide the name of the man involved in the incident. And the identity of the "Smith twins," as they are becoming known, is still a mystery.

Who were those bagged women?

All that is known for sure is that they mete out their particular brand of justice from the back of a pink Harley-Davidson.

I felt momentary relief. Velcro Head wasn't identified, probably because of a biker code of ethics against informing. And witnesses had declined to describe us, probably for much the same reason. But interest in who we were was heating up, and the *Live at Five* people knew where we lived. Now, to top it off, a description of the bike had been published.

¡Ay, Caramba!

Jerry and I had coffee on the deck, Muffy and Paquito snoozing happily at our feet. I handed her the paper, and she quickly scanned the coverage of the Smith twins.

"I love the bit about the Powerpuff Girls," she said cheerily. "Hey, maybe we *should* approach Tarantino about our life story. They don't actually have to use twins in the movies, you know. They could have one actress play both parts and then use editing to—"

"Hello!"

"What?"

"When you get your head out of your own starstruck butt, you might want to think about what this means for us."

"Huh?"

"We need credibility in this investigation so we can get Reba and Robert off death row!"

She waved a dismissive hand. "They're not on death row. Quit exaggerating."

"They're not far from it! And if you keep getting into food fights with homicidal maniacs, we could end up in prison right beside them."

She stuck out her lower lip. "I was provoked."

"Yeah. Fortunately, you weren't driving a lethal weapon when you were provoked, or the guy would have been a grease spot on PCH. You gotta get your anger under control, Ter."

"Okay, but tell me something," she said. "How come everyone talks about how flat-chested we are? Is that against the law or something?"

"The laws of nature, maybe," I said sulkily.

"Well, I think we're just fine."

"I have to admit, I've always felt a little ripped off. . . . I mean, I'd like to wear Agent Provocateur as much as the next girl. Couldn't they spare enough boob material for a B cup, at least? Who hogged it all, Pamela Anderson?"

Terry glanced down at the paper. "She and Fat Boy Schwartz, looks like."

The sun suddenly moved behind a bank of clouds, taking whatever was left of my sunny mood with it.

"Come on," she said, finishing her coffee. "Time to go track Robert's movements around the neighborhood. A little old-fashioned detective work will perk you up."

"Think we should use Reba's car for a while? I mean, just until things cool down a bit? We're kind of conspicuous on the bike."

She gave me a disgusted look. "Hey, it's not like we're friggin' Elvis, okay? I'm not changing my way of life over this whole thing."

"You're right," I said, suddenly indignant over our treatment in the press, our unsought new celebrity status. "We don't change our way of life."

"Damn straight," she said, pumping a fist.

We found a framed photograph of Robert on Reba's dresser. Ten years younger, but only a little thinner, posed in front of a work in progress. Red-bearded, wiry-haired, covered in splotches of paint, looking like Long John Silver trying to pass himself off as Pablo Picasso. We planned to show it around the neighborhood, convinced that no one who'd ever actually laid eyes on our cousin would be likely to forget it.

About a quarter-mile down from New Horizons, there was a wooden shack of a storefront that looked like it had been there since Frankie and Annette were shaking their booties on the beach. It was covered with wild designs in fluorescent pinks, oranges, and greens, and cartoon surfers sporting big shiny lips, their long blond hair streaming out behind them as they rode the curls.

I tapped Terry on the shoulder, pointing, and she angled into the parking lot. The hand-painted sign over the door said *Malibu Beachwear.*

We entered to the sound of tinkling bells and the stench of heavy incense. The incense masked a more pungent, peppery odor that I associated with people who say "man" a lot. As in, *Hey, man, anything left in that roach, man?*

"Morning, ladies. Can I help you?"

I turned to the voice and was immediately transported back in time by about thirty years. Before me was an elfin creature with a long gray beard brushing his very brown, rounded belly. His hair trailed down his back in a yard-long braid, and he wore an open flowered shirt over lemon-yellow drawstring shorts. His face was so tanned it could have been used for a pair of Weejuns, with white lines radiating out from his bloodshot blue eyes, indicating he did a lot of smiling or squinting in the sun—more likely smiling. He was a sixty-year-old beachcomber with the mellow demeanor of a lifetime stoner.

"Hi," I said to him.

"Bunga," he said, extending his hand.

I blinked. "Pardon?"

"My name. Short for Cowabunga."

"Oh." I stifled a laugh and shook his hand. "Hi, Bunga. I'm Kerry McAfee, and this is my sister Terry—"

"Whoa!" He dropped my hand, and I wondered what the trouble could be. "You don't look anything like your pictures," he said, peering into our faces intently.

Terry and I frowned at each other.

"Huh?" we said.

He pointed to a TV behind the counter. A local newscaster filled the screen, with the words *Breaking News* flashing in the corner. When I saw the photographs in the background, my knees practically gave way. I grabbed a hold of Terry's arm.

"Turn up the volume!" she yelled at Bunga.

He punched the volume button on a remote.

". . . local girls, graduates of Burbank High School . . ." the announcer said, as a candid photo of me, lifted from our high school yearbook, filled up the screen.

I was seated next to a chessboard with a stupid grin on my face, holding up a blue ribbon. My hair was cut chin-length, my bangs curling up from my forehead, making me look like a chess-playing poodle.

". . . where Kerry McAfee was class president and chairman of the local branch of Junior Achievers, as well as secretary of the chess club . . ."

I groaned in pain, but Terry started howling with laughter.

They zoomed in on her picture next. She was dressed in her basketball uniform, her hair styled in a bright orange Mohawk that made her look like a rooster with its claw caught in a socket. She was smoking a cigarette with one hand, shooting the cameraman the finger with the other, sending out death rays with her scowl.

". . . and Terry McAfee, a star center, who was suspended

from the basketball team for bad behavior just before the finals, possibly costing her school the championship . . ."

Terry banged her fist on the counter. "That was a bullshit charge! That joint was *planted* in my locker!"

The newscaster's earnest face came back on the screen. "Not a very auspicious start for a future national heroine—"

I grabbed the remote control, clicked off the TV, then bashed myself with the remote on the forehead. "Shit!"

Terry started chuckling again. "Did you *see* yourself?" she asked me. "You looked like a total dweeb!"

"Oh, and you look so great, Ms. *Sid Vicious*? I can't believe they're broadcasting our high school pictures!"

"Well, you were the one who wouldn't let them take our picture at the airport! Here's your payback."

"Perfect. Just perfect. We're a *News Five* exclusive!"

Bunga looked us up and down. "Haven't filled out much since high school, have you?"

I spun around. "We *like* being flat-chested, thank you very much!"

He held up his hands in self-defense. "Whoa, there, chill. It's okay with me. You're just as God made ya."

I was starting to hyperventilate, my breath coming in rapid bursts. Terry looked at me, concerned. "Maybe you should breathe into a paper bag—"

"No more bags on the head!" I screamed.

She patted me on the back. "Easy . . . easy . . ." she said, walking me over to a rattan chair next to the counter.

"Our lives are no longer our own," I whined, sinking into the chair. "It's like a bad dream where we went to bed normal people and woke up as contestants on *Celebrity Boxing*, with no idea how we got there—"

"I'm telling you," Terry said. "It'll be over so fast it'll make your head spin. Nobody cares what happened last week. They'll be on to the next big thing in no time, you'll see."

I saw Bunga looking at me sympathetically. I leaned over, my elbows on my knees, and tried to steady my breathing. "Tell him why we're here," I said to Terry.

"Right," she said, turning to Bunga. "Actually, we're investigating a matter, and—"

"You the law, man?"

"No, we're private investigators. And don't worry, we're not interested in you. Did you hear about the girl who was found decapitated in a house down the road?"

"Dude, I sure did. A horrible example of man's inhumanity to babe. You're investigating it?"

"Yes. Our cousin has been wrongly accused of the crime." She handed him Robert's photograph. "Have you ever seen this man?"

Bunga looked at the photo and stumbled backward. "*No way. Not Roberto, man. The dude's a beautiful human being. He wouldn't kill anybody!*"

"You know him?"

"He used to sneak out of that fascist enclave up the road and we'd hang for hours. I'd smoke and he'd eat Ding Dongs and we'd rap philosophy. The dude's a major thinker, a very evolved human being."

"He came here to eat Ding Dongs?" I said, giving Terry a triumphant look.

"Cleaned me out, dude. I used to call him King Dong."

I took a quick look around the store, noting the surfboards, bright-colored shirts and shorts, leopard-skin bikinis, sex wax, and snack foods. On a wall near the cash register, something else caught my eye—a hook holding a bunch of multicolored mesh bags like the one Robert was carrying on that fateful night.

"How often did you guys hang?" Terry asked Bunga.

"Oh, he came by almost every night. But I haven't seen him for a couple of days now."

"What did you talk about?"

"The meaning of life, the origins of the universe . . ." Stoner talk. "The existence of aliens . . ."

Terry shot me a look that said, *What is up with everybody and aliens out here?*

"He doesn't believe in them, does he?" I said to Bunga. "I mean, as far as I knew he didn't."

"Dude, he's *seen* them. After we got to know each other, we'd go out at night in the canyon back there and watch 'em. You should try it sometime. They're all over the place. Some nights it's like the Fourth of July!"

"You've actually seen . . . alien aircraft?" I said, wondering how much these sightings had to do with his smoking habits.

"All the time, man. They're totally out there . . . *woo-hoo!*" He wiggled his fingers and did a little dance.

"Robert did say he woke up in a canyon," Terry said, looking at me. "Can you tell us where this canyon is?" she asked him.

"Right behind the store. I own all the land back there. But I'm going to sell it to a conservancy, 'cause I'm gonna retire soon and I don't want some developer to come along and turn it into a condo cemetery."

"And that's where you and Robert went to watch for UFOs?" I asked.

"Yeah. On several occasions."

"Do you mind if we go take a look?"

"Sure, help yourselves. I'd go with you, but I can't close the store right now. Tourist season."

"That's okay," Terry said. "We can go on our own."

"I'm telling you, man, if they've arrested that beautiful soul, it's a travesty," Bunga said, hanging his head. "A complete miscarriage of justice."

"Yeah," I said. "We think so, too."

"Hey, but if anybody can save him, the Wonderwomen of Flight 222 can!" he said, beaming.

I soon regretted hiking into the canyon by ourselves. It didn't seem like the most prudent idea to be trekking alone into the wild, even if we were alleged Wonderwomen. It was dark and overgrown. Blair Witch territory. Charlie Manson land.

Some of the canyons around Los Angeles are broad swaths cut out of the mountains, with major roads traveling through them, like Topanga Canyon Road or our own street, Beverly Glen Boulevard. But some of them are rabbit holes into the unknown and the uncivilized, home to wild animals and hideouts for drug dealers and psycho-killers lying in wait. They're ideal dumping grounds for unwanted trash and inconvenient bodies, and only the severely brain-damaged would venture very far into them.

Color us brain-damaged.

After a hundred yards or so, there was a sign that said *End of County Maintained Road.*

"Oh, that's reassuring," I said. "Even the county road crews won't go past this point. Their insurance probably doesn't cover getting murdered by serial killers."

"God, you are such a wimp, sometimes I can't believe we

share the same DNA," Terry said, waving her arms expansively. "Can't you enjoy being out in nature?"

"Yeah, nature's good," I said. *Nature, who gave us poisonous snakes and giant spiders and larvae springing to life on dead flesh in the form of maggots.* "I love nature."

My breath got shorter as the canyon got steeper. On the left, a rock wall rose at a sharp angle, brush and scraggly pines clutching its side like the skeletons of shipwreck victims clinging to a capsized lifeboat. On the right was a chasm that dropped into total nothingness.

I remembered what somebody had said about those chasms—*Don't worry about getting lost in one, you'd starve to death before you hit bottom.*

We hiked for another fifteen minutes, following the winding road in silence. Finally, Terry said, "I'll bet you anything this is the canyon Robert found himself in."

"Yeah, with a dead girl's head," I said with a shiver.

I was trying to banish that image from my mind, when a dry wind kicked up, blowing dust and grit into my eyes. And then I heard something that froze my blood in my veins—

An earsplitting scream.

My legs catapulted me to the side of the road before I had time to think about it. I rolled into a gravel-filled ditch, then heard another high-pitched, agony-filled cry.

Someone was being tortured or murdered!

I looked up from the ditch and saw Terry running in the direction of the noise.

"Terry, no!" I yelled.

But she'd already disappeared around a corner. I put my hands over my ears to shut out the sound of human anguish and squinched my eyes shut. I was still balled up, head tucked, when I heard Terry running back down the road a minute later. I removed my hands from my eyes and saw to my surprise that . . .

She was laughing. She held out a hand to me. "Come here, you've got to see this."

"Are you crazy?" I hissed. "You want to walk right into a murder scene?"

She grabbed my arm and yanked me out of the ditch. "It's not a murderer, it's a bird."

"What?" I said, brushing burrs and dust off my butt. "What kind of bird sounds like someone's slicing its throat?"

She waved me forward, and I had to jog to catch up with her. We rounded the corner into a clearing, where we saw the cement foundation of a crumbling stone house. Portions of its walls were still standing, but the piles of rocks at their sides spoke of years of neglect and dozens of earthquakes.

There in the middle of the floor stood a peacock on a pile of rubble, glimmering blue and gold tail feathers fanned out behind him. He dared us to set foot in his habitat, standing his ground like a gorgeous, cranky king of the heap.

He screamed again. I covered my ears.

"Jesus, what a sound!" It was even worse close up.

"I know, it's horrible," Terry said, then she suddenly made a run at the peacock, shooing him away. He took one look at her, folded his tail feathers, and fled.

"Leave him alone," I said. "It's his house."

"He'd never let us poke around," she said. "And something tells me this is just what we're looking for."

I followed her into the rubble. She pointed to a pile of cellophane wrappers and pieces of chemically preserved chocolate cake, guaranteed not to decompose until the year 2025. "This is it. Robert and Bunga's hideout."

We spent a few moments rummaging around through the debris on the floor. I turned over a large rock and found a marijuana pipe and a small Baggie full of dried leaves. There was a thick candle that had burned down into an oily puddle, and a couple of army blankets folded against the wall.

"So this is where they did their UFO watching," I said. "They came up here and camped on the floor, looking out through the missing roof."

"Yeah, and these are their matinee treats. Ding Dongs and a bag of weed."

I looked up at the cloudless blue sky, now visible in the clearing. "I bet it's dark as pitch out here at night. You can probably see millions of stars."

"And millions of space travelers," Terry added.

"Oh, give me a break. They're probably shooting stars. Robert wouldn't know the difference, and whatever Bunga sees is filtered through his resin-coated brain."

Terry walked the perimeter of the small house, thinking out loud. "So what if they came out here late one night and Bunga got Robert stoned. Robert's not used to it—it's not his drug of choice—and maybe it hit him hard. He passed out and woke up two days later. Meanwhile, the murderer tossed the girl's head out here, thinking the animals would get to it, and a coyote dragged it up here because he smelled the chocolate cake. When Robert came to, there it was."

"Interesting theory, but two whole days? Just because he got stoned?"

She shrugged. "Maybe it was spiked with pixie dust, maybe that's why they're seeing UFOs. . . . Could have been anything."

"Let's go get Bunga to fess up," I said. "If it turns out he gave Robert drugs and left him out here, it might be just the break we need. At least it's some kind of alibi."

"Okay, let's go."

Thank God we were going back down. I didn't think I had the nerve to push even farther into the canyon. When we got to the road, I started running downhill, my Pumas pounding the loose dirt.

"Last one to PCH is a rotten egg!" I yelled, then came around the corner to find myself face-to-face with an eighty-pound coyote hulking in the middle of the road.

I dug my heels into the dirt, screeching to a stop as my mouth flew open, my heart thudding against my rib cage.

The coyote looked at me, unmoving. He was clearly sizing me up for a meal, his tongue dripping from his mouth. Then he inched toward me, his head ducked and his yellow eyes locked on mine, just as Terry's footsteps came around the corner.

"Hey, wait up!" she yelled.

The coyote glanced in her direction and stopped in his tracks.

"Terry," I shouted, not daring even to wave my arm for fear the beast would take it as a threat and attack.

I heard her slam to a stop.

We stood there in a tableau of indecision. The coyote in front of me, Terry behind me. No one making a move.

"Kerry, stay calm," she whispered to me. "He won't attack you alone. They only attack in packs—"

And right on cue, two more devil dogs rounded the corner. They came up behind the first one in wing formation, golden eyes glinting.

Nature. Gotta love it.

"Terry . . . what the hell do I *do*?"

"Don't move," she said. "And don't look directly into their eyes. They'll take it as a challenge. Look down at the ground."

I looked down and saw spots in front of my eyes. My legs were tingling and my head felt like a Mylar balloon. I was sure I was going to faint.

Then Terry suddenly screeched at the top of her lungs, running behind me. I turned and saw her tearing past me, zinging a handful of rocks at the coyotes, showering them with stones.

The rocks glanced off their heads and backs and sent them scrambling, yelping in pain and surprise. They spun around and leaped over the ditch, running down the other side of the canyon and out of sight with their tails between their legs.

"Come on!" Terry grabbed me by the jacket, pulling me along the road. "Let's get out of here before they come back with a representative of PETA!"

I stumbled forward on legs that didn't want to support my weight, down the hill for ten minutes of lung-searing, muscle-cramping, fear-driven sprinting. Finally, we found ourselves near the mouth of the canyon at the sign that said *End of County Maintained Road.* I almost burst into tears when we staggered down to Pacific Coast Highway and I could see the ocean again.

"Damn, that was close!" I had barely enough air to say it.

But Terry wasn't close to tears. She was positively exhilarated. She grinned and held up her hand for a high five.

I didn't return it. "You sick fucking thrill junkie! I can't believe we share the same DNA, either! I want it back!"

She leaned over with her hands on her knees, catching her breath. "You ever think about the first settlers out here? They dealt with stuff like that every day. You would have lasted about five minutes as a pioneer woman."

"*If* I was insane or desperate enough to leave Boston, which I would never do. Nice, civilized Boston, with colonial architecture and English furniture and opera carriages—"

"Come on," she said, laughing, "let's go see nice, civilized Bunga."

He was selling Solarcaine at fifteen dollars a bottle to some chunky folks in shorts and flip-flops whose skin was a deep pomegranate color. A shameless case of tourist gouging. No wonder he could retire, at those prices.

After the tourists left, Bunga confirmed that the broken-down house we had seen was his and Robert's hangout. But he vehemently denied giving Robert any drugs.

"It's nothing to us if you did," I said. "Really, you can tell us. It might help his case."

"I'd tell you if I did, but he was firm—no more mind-altering substances. He was serious about getting clean. Said his body was his temple, man."

"Yeah," Terry said, rolling her eyes, "the Temple of the Most Holy Ding Dong."

We gave Bunga our business card and left.

Outside, Terry tried calling New Horizons again to make an appointment with Mr. Peavey. Again, she got the brush-off.

"Okay, make a note of this, Ms. Exeter," she said, the blood rising on her neck. "We're going to be there tomorrow morning at nine o'clock, and he *will* see us. Or he's going to be very sorry!"

She hung up and fumed at me. "I may have to smack that Exeter woman when I see her."

"No."

"Yes."

"Smack a pillow instead."

"The pillow doesn't deserve it. She does."

"Promise me you won't."

She looked away, sighing. "Okay, I promise."

"Thanks."

"As long as she doesn't piss me off again."

Oh boy.

thirteen

*W*e spent the better part of that afternoon staking out Frank's house. Terry and I again took turns on the deck, pretending to read Reba's *Sex After Sixty* magazine, while waiting for our opportunity to "drop in." Near sunset, Terry came running into the kitchen where I was munching a chicken salad sandwich.

"Hey," she said, grinning. "Looks like Frank's having a little hoedown next door."

"Really?" I ran outside to look.

Sure enough, there were tiki torches flaming along the perimeter of the terrace, and smoke rising from a barbecue grill. A bartender was arranging glasses on a portable bar in the corner.

"Perfect," I said, rubbing my hands together. "We can tell him that we saw a party going on and decided to come on over."

I dug through the clothes that Lance had brought to find suitable party attire, but there was nothing except our usual street clothes—jeans, Juicy Couture tanks, and the occasional hooded pullover.

"Hmm. We might want something a little more alluring. . . ." I wandered into Reba's closet to see if she had a slinky black sheath or something.

"I'm plenty alluring right now," Terry said with a look of disdain, rolling up her jeans to midcalf length and undoing her braids so that her kinky red hair tumbled down around her shoulders. "But you knock yourself out."

I found exactly what I was looking for—a black dress of ribbed Lycra with spaghetti straps. I took a shower, then squeezed into the tiny dress, stretching it almost to the breaking point over my hips. Although it probably came to Reba's knees, on me it covered only the upper third of my thighs.

I dug through Reba's shoes and found some elegant black Chanel sandals, but there was no way her size-six shoes were going on my size-eight feet.

So I decided to wear flip-flops. A cocktail dress and flip-flops. This is the beach, right? I slapped on some mascara and eyeliner and painted my toenails purple. I teased up my hair, then borrowed some diamond stud earrings from the little mother-of-pearl tray on Reba's dresser.

Terry came into the room looking exactly as she had before I started my makeover. "You're going like that?" I said, putting on some lipstick.

She looked in the mirror and nodded, comparing herself to me.

"We look like a before-and-after picture," I said.

"Yeah: Before, normal. After, Malibu beach whore."

I stuck my tongue out at her. "We'll see who picks up the most producers."

"You know perfectly well our best bet is to come on like a sister act. We play it like we're into threesomes, and watch the information tumble out of those old guys."

"What makes you think they're gonna be old?" I asked her.

She gave me a shrug. "Just a hunch."

I grabbed Reba's black pashmina, then we locked up the house and headed over to Frank's. The door to the courtyard was open, and inside it was teeming with beautiful people, all milling about with drinks in their hands. The men were mostly in their forties and fifties, and they were surrounded by hot young women in their twenties, dressed to slaughter.

"Perfect," Terry whispered. "Nobody even saw us come in."

We bellied up to the bar. I ordered a glass of white wine and Terry accepted a beer from the white-sleeved bartender. I took a sip as we scoped out the scene.

"There's somebody eyeing us from over there by the fence," Terry said.

He was a fifty-something guy with wet lips, lecherous eyes, and the shiny red face of a morning drinker. Terry nodded at me, and we sauntered over to talk to him. Once again, Terry's inner flirt took over.

"Hi, we're Terry and Kerry," she purred. "Are you alone?"

He smiled and raked his bloodshot eyes over us. Terry was right. He was definitely one of those "Can I double my pleasure, double my fun?" kind of assholes.

"I'm Gerald." There was the tiniest bit of condescension in his voice. "I'm the richest guy here, in case you haven't been told."

This threw us for a second, but Terry plunged right back in. "Who do you know here . . . ? Frank?"

He gave her a long look. "It's more like . . . who *don't* I know? As in—who haven't I been married to? Let's see, there's my first ex, Melody . . ." He pointed to a blonde with a tan and blindingly white smile on the arm of a man dressed entirely in black: black jacket, turtleneck, jeans, and cowboy boots. "And my second ex-wife is over there." He pointed to a skinny woman with a creamy complexion and long brown hair cascading down her back. She wore a shiny gold dress that fit her body like a snakeskin; then, as if the snake had swallowed a couple of soccer balls that were still lodged in its throat, two enormous mounds bulged at the top, straining her flesh as much as the fabric of the dress.

"She didn't have those bad boys when she was with me. They were a wedding gift from her new husband." He pointed into the living room. "And number three just sashayed into the house with a producer, probably looking for something to anesthetize her new nose."

"You sound pretty bitter," I said. "Why do you keep getting married?"

He shrugged and pulled a vial of coke out of his pocket, offering it to us. "Horniness springs eternal?"

"No, thanks," I said, pushing the coke away. He shrugged, poured some onto the back of his hand, and sniffed it up, then tucked the vial back into his pocket.

"I'm just trying to give you the lay of the land. You're cute, but you don't have a prayer here."

Terry and I looked at each other with raised eyebrows. Okay, we weren't sporting 48DDs, but we'd been known to turn a head or two in our time. "You have no genealogy," he offered by way of explanation. "No lineage." This assertion really seemed to crack him up. He chuckled and grabbed his champagne glass from the table, taking a big gulp.

"What do you mean?" Terry said.

He leaned in and lowered his voice, eyes shining with malice. "See, this is a real tight community. You can't just walk in off the street. Or off the beach, as it were. You have to have already slept with someone to get in. Your lineage is who you've been with."

"Let me get this straight," Terry said. "You're saying people in this crowd prefer used goods?"

Gerald snickered. "It's more like having a pedigree. Certain husbands or boyfriends get you points. Like, if you've ever been with Mick Jagger—major points. Or any one of a number of A-list actors. Jack Nicholson, for instance. It's all about money and/or fame. The guys you've been with have to have had lots of either, or some of both. Then a guy can tell himself, 'Wow. Mick Jagger slept here.' And trust me, he's more interested in sleeping with Mick Jagger than with the babe he's actually with. Kind of like sleeping in a bed and breakfast where George Washington laid his wig."

Terry shook her head slowly. "That is possibly the most disgusting thing I've ever heard."

He grinned. "Hey, if you can think of a better way to distinguish between all the chicks who show up here—most of 'em looking like they just got off the same surgeon's table—I'd like to know about it." He rolled his eyes. "I should be looking for 'personality' or 'character'? Ha. It's all about *who ya know, who you've blown.* And unless I miss my bet, you girls got no lineage, so you might as well give it up."

I couldn't tell if he was kidding or not. "Are you serious?"

"Deadly. Anyway, you can't go husband shopping as a pair. Nobody can marry the two of you. This isn't Provo, Utah, you know." Another fit of chuckling accompanied this witticism.

Terry was getting steamed. "We're not husband shopping," she said. "If you must know, we're working with law enforcement, looking for a murderer."

Gerald choked on his Champagne, then reached into his

pocket, grabbed the vial of coke, and threw it back over his shoulder, clearing the fence.

Terry smirked, pleased at his reaction. "I didn't say *we* were law enforcement, but if we were, that little stunt wouldn't get you anything. Why don't you tell us what you know about Candy Starr's death, Gerald, and we'll forget what we saw."

He began to stammer. "I—I know what you know, probably. Some twisto cut her head off and stuffed her body next door."

"That's interesting. Her identity hasn't been released to the public yet. How do you know so much?"

"Word's out about her," he said, chin quivering. "She was . . . she was kind of on the circuit, you know?"

"Oh yeah? What was her 'lineage'? How did she get in the group?"

"She was different. She'd do things that the regular gals wouldn't do. She was very . . . accommodating."

Terry reached out to clink her beer on Gerald's glass. He jerked back, like he feared she was going to bash him on the nose with it. "One more question," Terry said. "Did she ever 'accommodate' Frank?"

He swallowed and his eyes moved past us, focusing on someone behind my back. I turned and saw myself looking down into the face of Mr. Frank Steinmetz himself, his cheeks still bearing the claw marks from yesterday evening.

He couldn't have been more than five feet four, but I had to admit that he gave off an aura of power in spite of his short stature. One of the Mighty Morphin' Midgets that seemed to run Hollywood. He was dressed simply but expensively in a purple cashmere sweater, pressed blue jeans, and white buckskin loafers, a gold Rolex on his bony wrist.

"Hello," Frank said to us. "So glad you could make it. Come, let's have a private word in my office." His face was impossible to read. Was he interested? Curious? Homicidal?

I looked at Terry for a cue. "Sure. Love to," she said lightly, smiling at him.

He ushered us toward the back door of the house. I tried to mimic Terry's air of confidence as she strutted forward, but inside was a different story. Inside, my intestines were turning to mush.

We strolled through the spacious living room past guests who were chatting, drinking, and making out. He wouldn't kill us in front of all these witnesses, would he?

Frank opened a door off the living room, motioning us into his study. Like the rest of the house, it was decorated in a macho version of Danish modern. Black leather sofa and desk chair, teak desk covered with an assortment of high-tech chrome gadgets, a wafer-thin notebook computer.

The white walls were hung with a Who's Who gallery of photographs. Frank with Warren Beatty, Frank with Julia Roberts, Frank with former president Bill Clinton. Frank hob-nobbing with anyone who was anyone. No wonder he was a cocky little shit.

He waved us over to the sofa. We sat, and I yanked my skirt down on my thighs, crossing my legs to avoid giving him a Sharon Stone shot. Frank parked himself behind the desk and leaned back in the chair, bracing a foot on the crossbar. His face was craggy and arrogant, with a mop of wavy gray hair. The thick black eyebrows over his prominent nose had been plucked to avoid a unibrow—his only apparent concession to vanity.

I had to hand it to him. Unlike a lot of people in this town, he was letting himself age naturally. The skin on his neck was chickeny, the furrows deep around his eyes. No hair plugs, no face work, and his teeth were uncapped. He obviously relied on something other than boyish good looks to maintain his wealth and power.

"Now, ladies," he said genially, "you were not invited here. Want to tell me who you are and what you're up to?"

Terry shrugged. "We saw the party and thought we'd crash it. We didn't think it was any big deal."

He smiled, but it was all bottom teeth, like a shark's. "You want to give me a straight answer? Or you want me to call the police and have you arrested for trespassing?"

Terry huffed indignantly. "Go ahead. If you think it's a crime to try to meet some guys and score a free drink."

"Ah, but Terry," he said, "my information is that you don't like guys."

His information? And how did he know our names?

He chuckled at our surprise. "Who were you hoping to meet when you were spying yesterday? Not me, I hope. You're not my type. I prefer very loose, very blond, very bodacious women."

Terry called his bluff. "Disposable women?"

He glared at her with marble-hard eyes. "Sure, but I don't dispose of them by cutting off their empty little heads," he said, the smiling shark again. "I divorce them, I dump them, sometimes I even buy them off. I don't need to kill them. That's why you're here, isn't it? You think I had something to do with the murder?"

"Did you?" I said, causing him to laugh. A hoarse smoker's laugh.

"No, sweetheart."

"Well," I said, standing up, "that's all we needed to know. . . . *Buh-bye*."

"Sit down," he commanded.

I plopped back down on the couch, helpless to resist his authority.

He leaned back in his chair, regarding us calmly. "Who are you working for?"

We gave him a blank look in return. He picked up the phone and started to punch in numbers.

"Our great-aunt," I said quickly. "She lives next door."

He nodded and hung up the phone as if he'd already known.

"Why'd you ask, if you knew?" Terry said.

"I wanted to see if I'd get a straight answer," he said. "Now I know that if I want a straight answer, I go to your sister."

Terry jumped up from the couch. "That's it, we're outta here," she said, pulling on my arm. "Go fuck yourself, short stuff."

I dearly wanted to haul ass out of there, but I knew that if at all possible, we had to get more information from him before we made our escape. This might be our only chance. When I hesitated, Frank looked back and forth between Terry and me.

"Your sister doesn't want to leave, Terry. Your sister's very intelligent. She knows better than to walk out on Frank Steinmetz."

Terry's face broke into a sardonic grin. "Research has shown that people who talk about themselves in the third person, Frank Steinmetz, have very small dicks."

Frank leaned farther back in his chair, and his eyes glittered under the furry brows. "Do you know who I am?"

"You make movies. Big whoop," Terry said with all the disdain she could put in her voice. "Most of 'em I wouldn't go see for free." She waved to the pictures around the room. "You have big-name pals. So what? You still have a little dick."

After a heart-stopping few moments, Frank pulled open a drawer at his side. My gut clenched, sure he was going to pull out a gun and shoot my sister in the mouth. Instead, he motioned her forward.

"C'mere, Terry. I want to show you something."

She stared at him, unmoving.

"Terry, I told you I don't kill women. I don't even hurt them. I let them hurt *me*, if you get my meaning."

She gave me a puzzled look, then stepped forward and peered into the drawer. I got up to join her. Inside was a mini DV tape labeled "copy," a stack of bills bound with a rubber band, and a small cell phone in the otherwise empty drawer.

"What is this?" Terry said.

"This," he said, pointing to the tape, "is the record of an indiscretion."

"Yours?" I said.

He nodded.

"Are you going to show it to us?"

"If you insist."

"Why would we?" Terry said.

"I want you to find the SOB who tried to blackmail me with it."

"Blackmail?" I repeated dumbly. "Who's blackmailing you?"

Frank sighed and gave me an irritated look. One that said he was reconsidering his assessment of me. Terry quickly came to my rescue.

"I don't get it," she said, frowning. "You want us to work for you after I called you names?"

He gave a short laugh. "Had to see if you lived up to your reputation. Now I can believe you brought down the terrorists on that plane."

I sighed inwardly. "But you must have someone else who can take care of this for you," I said, not wanting the complication of Frank's little job in our lives. We had enough on our plate as it was. "You have resources—"

"Can't use 'em," Frank said. "You'll have to trust that I have my reasons. You'll be well compensated. Money, as the man said, is no object."

"Yeah, but conflict of interest *is* an object," I said. "We can't work for you."

"Why not?" His scowl conveyed, *Nobody says no to Frank Steinmetz.*

"Because you might be the one who killed that girl and stuffed her in our aunt's house."

"And if you did, we gonna nail your ass, muthafucka," Terry added with a gangsta accent.

Jesus, where had *that* come from?

Frank brushed away the threat with a wave of his hand. "Don't waste your time on me. I didn't do it. We have a confluence of interests here, not a conflict."

"How so?" I said.

Frank sighed. "I can see I have to show you the tape."

He plugged it into a small video player. "Ladies," he said, flourishing the remote with a showman's flair, "I give you Miss Candy Starr."

Instantly, the image of Frank was splayed across the screen of his fifty-six-inch TV—and in a very compromising position indeed.

He was on all fours, nude except for a push-up bra, one of those hard-packed rubber balls between his teeth. His lips were smeared with red lipstick, the tears streaming from his eyes causing his mascara to run in streaks and his false eyelashes to come unglued. A blond woman in a black mask and deluxe dominatrix getup—leather thong, wire bustier, spike-heel thigh boots—whipped Frank's hairy backside with a riding crop, while pointedly informing him that he'd been a *very, very bad boy.*

He punched the button on the remote and the excruciating spectacle disappeared. But the ghost of the image hung there, crowding the space like dirty laundry hung out to dry.

I had no idea what to say. I was incapable of speaking or meeting Frank's eyes. Fortunately, he picked up the conversational ball again, so to speak.

"Now you know why I can't go to my regulars with this. I deal with some very heavy people when it comes to financing my movies. Very macho—very *Italian*—if you know what I mean. I can't do business with them if they have this image of me in their heads. I'm hoping you're as discreet as you are ballsy, and that you'll have a little sympathy for an old man looking for some cheap thrills in his waning years."

We stood there for a moment, speechless.

"I'm very sorry," Terry said to him finally. "It appears that I unfairly maligned your shlong."

Frank let out a bitter chuckle.

"So," I said, "somebody's trying to sell you the original video, with the murdered girl in the starring role."

"Wrong. First they tried to sell me the tape when she was still alive. I refused to pay. I was hoping they'd lose their nerve. . . . Then the girl ended up dead. What worries me is that I haven't heard from them since."

Terry and I exchanged frowns. "But it's worth even more now," I said to him. "I mean, from the point of view of a blackmailer. It could implicate you in her murder."

"Right," Frank said.

"So what does this mean?" Terry looked at me for an answer.

Frank said, "Either they're sweating me, or—"

"Or they've brought in another party," I filled in, "who might be in a better position to help them exploit it. Someone who didn't mind killing to increase the tape's value. First they get the proof of your connection to her, *then* they murder Candy."

"I told you she was intelligent," Frank said to Terry. He

pointed to the money in the drawer. "This is untraceable to me. It's twenty thousand dollars."

"How much did they ask for last time?" I said.

"Two hundred fifty thousand."

"And you think you can buy them off with less than ten percent?"

"No, the money's your fee. You're not gonna negotiate with these people. I'll do that. *If* they call again, and *if* I decide to pay, you'll make the drop."

The drop? This was sounding more sinister by the minute.

"But how do you know they won't hit you up for even more? Or keep the original tape and pass off a copy on you?" Terry said. "They could string you out forever—"

He held up a manicured hand. "You don't concern yourself with that. They won't string me out forever. You just see what you can find out about who sent it."

I had no idea how we were going to do that. I was tempted to come clean and explain our usual MO—bumbling around until we got lucky—but hesitated for two reasons: Number one, twenty thousand dollars is a lot of money; number two, we'd seen him on the tape. If we refused to help him out, he might doubt our discretion going forward and do something to ensure it. Like sealing our lips forever in a lead-sealed coffin.

Whatever the case, I was fairly certain he was on the up-and-up on one thing. He hadn't killed Candy.

Terry solved my dilemma with typical alacrity. Her hand darted out and grabbed the money like a lizard's tongue snapping up a fly. She riffled the dollars under her nose, taking a deep whiff, then stuck them in the waistband of her jeans.

"We're on it," she said.

Frank nodded as if he never expected anything else. He pointed to the tiny phone and battery charger. "Take that. If I need to reach you, I'll call you on it. Needless to say, I expect twenty-four-hour access to you."

I picked up the cell phone. "Mr. Steinmetz—"

"Frank."

"Okay, Frank. Your 'macho' business associates. You don't think they could be behind this?"

He shook his head. "They make plenty off of me through our movie deals. They'd have no incentive to rip me off for a lousy two hundred and fifty thousand."

"What are your thoughts about your ex-wife?"

"Which one? Heather?"

I nodded.

"I think she's the biggest cunt I ever married. See, there's your proof I'm no killer. If I was, she'd be dead."

"Did you know she's selling your horses?"

"What?" Fury clouded his dark eyes, and he snatched up a brass letter opener from his desk and stabbed the leather blotter with it. The knife hung there for a second, then teetered and fell on the glass desktop with a clang. "Bitch!"

"You didn't know," Terry said.

He fought to get his breath under control. "I should have expected something like this. The horses were in her name for tax purposes." He rocked back in his chair, rubbing his chin. "She knows how much I love those animals. I guess I should be glad she's not grinding them into hamburger meat and delivering them to me in frozen patties. Well, she's gonna pay for this little stunt. As of this minute, the settlement negotiations are *off.*"

"Your divorce isn't final?"

"Her lawyer's been hanging me up for over a year."

"She's been hanging you up?" I said. "Do you think she might be hanging you up so she can pull a blackmail scam on you? Do a little better in the settlement?"

He looked at me steadily, beady eyes doing the math. "She could be. A man with my life—I don't put nothing past nobody."

Interesting how he slipped into cruder speech when confronted with the unexpected. His smooth exterior cracking with little hairline fractures.

"You think she's capable of murder?" Terry asked.

He considered it, his mouth twisted in a half-smile. "I think God never made a more mercenary female."

"Do you know about her alien club?"

"Yeah, I know all about those fruitcakes. She's been funneling my money to them for years, but I can't take her to court for it. Community property," he said with a sneer. "Buncha crapola."

"At the moment, she's our favorite candidate for the murderer," I said. "We think she paid a visit to our aunt and conspired to leave a door open before the body appeared."

He got a hopeful look, straightening in his chair. "If you can nail that bitch for this, I swear—I'll make you stars of the silver screen."

"No, thanks," I said. "We prefer obscurity."

"It's an empty offer, anyway," he said, shrugging. "Works on most of the broads, though. Listen, don't come back here. Don't call. If you have information for me, hang a towel over your deck. I'll call you on the mobile."

"All right." I reached out to shake his hand. He looked down at mine but didn't take it. For some reason, he didn't want to touch me. Or maybe he thought the gesture inappropriate under the circumstances. I withdrew my hand and followed Terry to the door.

"Girls?" Frank said.

We turned to look at him.

"Never bleach your hair."

Terry gave him a salute and we let ourselves out, wondering what the hell that was supposed to mean. Was he warning us of a health hazard caused by bleach seeping into the scalp? Or was it his way of cautioning us against horny old goats like him?

Probably the latter. From what we'd seen, blondes of Frank Steinmetz's acquaintance definitely did *not* have more fun.

We crossed the patio past the drunk and coked-up guests, and I noted that Gerald had disappeared. Probably out there on his hands and knees making like a crab, burrowing through the sand for his party candy.

When we got back to the house, there was a message from Eli. The arraignment was scheduled for the next morning at eleven o'clock.

"Should we go?" I asked Terry, as I peeled off the clingy dress.

"We told New Horizons we'd be there at nine."

"We could probably do both."

"Yeah, but it's more important to see Peavey. We know what's gonna happen at the arraignment: *How does your client plead? Blah blah. Bail set at blah blah.* Boom—you're out of there."

"Yeah, but it'd be nice to be there for moral support."

"Let's see how it goes with Peavey, okay? Maybe one of us can make it."

I flopped on the bed, leaning against the headboard. "Listen, I'm not feeling so good about our new client."

"Why not?"

I whispered, as if Frank could hear us through the walls of the house and yards of open space. "He runs with mobsters. He thinks he is a mobster. What happens if we don't deliver for him?"

She shrugged. "Don't be a pessimist."

"Okay, then what happens if we *do* deliver the blackmailer? Is he gonna wipe him out?"

She gave me a *you worrywart* look. "We get information for our clients, period. We're not responsible for what they do with it."

"But he implied that he may not pay. That leaves only one alternative—"

"He says he doesn't kill people."

"How charming of you to take him at his word. Anyway, he says he doesn't kill the women he uses and abuses. He didn't say what he would do with a blackmailer. In fact, he implied he *might* kill him."

"Or *her*."

"Right. Which brings me to my second point."

"What?"

"If the blackmailer killed Candy, and if Frank whacks said blackmailer, then we have no murder suspect to bring to the police. Robert and Reba are convicted of the crime."

"Oh," she said, scrunching her brow. "I see what you mean. Why didn't you say something before?"

"I was too intimidated to *think* it before."

"I guess we're a tiny bit screwed here."

"Not to mention, the tape is exculpatory evidence that could potentially put Robert and Reba in the clear. But if we told the police about it, we'd probably end up chained to the bottom of a pier piling."

"Yikes."

"Unless . . ."

"Unless?"

"We can find the killer, turn him or her over to the police, *and* assure Frank that we've got the video master. That no copies are gonna show up anywhere else."

"Okay, how do we do that?"

"Terry, if I knew how we were gonna do it, I wouldn't be experiencing heart palpitations!"

"Then I guess we continue to wing it."

"Sure," I said. "Wing it."

Like a couple of smart missiles they forgot to program before shooting 'em out of the cannon.

fourteen

ext morning, the guard at the New Horizons gate announced us and lifted the barrier. We were expected. Amanda Exeter met us at the front door. Same suit, different day.

"Mr. Peavey is waiting for you," she said.

"Good thing," Terry muttered.

Amanda turned on her sensible heel and led us down a lavender-carpeted hallway to a large office with a smaller ante-room, passing by her own immaculate desk as we went. The outbox held a stack of memos with perfectly aligned edges. There was nothing in the inbox—a testament to Amanda's hyperefficiency. A brass nameplate with "Amanda Exeter, Executive Assistant" was balanced precisely on the edge of the desk. She'd probably received it at birth instead of a teething ring. If anyone was born to this job, it was our Ms. Exeter.

She opened the inside door, which bore yet another brass

plaque with the title "Director," and we entered a plush, eggshell-colored office.

Wendell Peavey stood up behind his desk and held out a smooth pink hand. He was tall and sleek, with the well-nourished contours of an otter. Small round tortoiseshell glasses, black bangs slicked down in a swoop on his forehead, the long ends of his hair curling at the back of his collar.

"Wendell Peavey," he said, pressing our hands. "This business with your cousin—what a shock. Won't you sit down?"

Terry sat down and slung one of her biker boots across her knee. "It was a shock two days ago," she said. "Now it's old news."

Peavey looked down and cleared his throat. "Yes, well, I suppose one adjusts to even the worst of, uh . . . uh . . ." he said, trailing off.

I parked myself on the leather chair next to Terry's. Peavey sat back down behind the desk and proceeded to wring his hands. "Mr. Price was making very good progress. He was responsive to group therapy and participating in the activities and doing just fine. The recent developments are naturally very distressing. What else can I tell you?"

I got out my wallet and flipped it open to reveal my investigator's license. "We're here as family, but also as licensed investigators. Any help you can give us would be greatly appreciated."

"Of course, whatever I can do. Without breaching confidentiality, of course."

"I don't think confidentiality's a problem under the circumstances, do you?" Terry said.

"Well, it's always a consideration when one is dealing with matters of psychiatric health. . . . We have both a legal and an ethical obligation to preserve the sanctity of—"

"You mentioned activities," I said, cutting into his stream of unconsciousness. "Were there any religious activities here at the facility?"

He blinked. "There's a chapel, of course, but attendance isn't compulsory. Is that what you mean?"

"She means any nontraditional religious activities," Terry said. "Like people who believe in aliens . . . ?"

He made a face of pure disgust. "You're referring to the Children of the Cosmos. I assure you, every effort has been made to keep those people away from here. The sheriff's department has been notified of their completely inappropriate behavior, and we are doing everything that we possibly—"

"Hold it," Terry said. "What inappropriate behavior?"

He clamped his mouth shut, as if there were a tiny lawyer sitting on his shoulder whispering in his ear, *Liability! Liability!*

"I'm sorry. I've been advised not to say more on the subject."

"Just a goddamned minute." Terry slid forward to the edge of her seat, leaning one arm along the side of the desk. Peavey sank back, gripping the arms of his executive chair. "Are you telling me that these people are *active* here at New Horizons? You let them operate under your nose?"

Peavey's head shook back and forth, his jowls quivering. "Not intentionally, of course. We would never—" He took a breath, then confessed, "We've had a problem with infiltration."

"Infiltration?" Terry said. "What is this, the CIA?"

"I—I really can't say anything more on the subject."

"Mr. Peavey," I said, reassuring him with a gentle voice. "Our cousin was enrolled here at this facility, and you say he was doing well. But we happen to know that he was approached by this bogus cult just before he was found toting around a human head in a complete daze. He's being arraigned on murder charges today, and unless you want to be dragged into the trial, which will probably become a three-ring circus on Court TV because of the sensational nature of the crime and the glamorous location of your facility, I'd suggest you do everything in your power to help us absolve him of this crime so that it doesn't go to trial at all."

"My counsel is concerned about our accountability—" he whimpered.

"As he fucking should be!" Terry said.

"She," a voice behind us said. We turned and met the steady gaze of a fifty-year-old woman with shoulder-length ash-blond hair, dressed in a linen jacket, jeans, and pearls. She had high cheekbones and clear green eyes, and was as attractive as someone can be whose whole demeanor said, *I eat people like you for breakfast.*

"I'm Shannon Voss. Vice President of Legal Affairs. How can I be of help?"

"You can help us by telling us what these alien nuts have been up to around here," Terry said. "There's been a murder!"

The Voss woman gave Terry a tight smile. "Thanks, Wendell," she said to Peavey. "I'll take it from here."

She motioned for us to come with her. Peavey sighed and went limp in his chair. In the buck-passing tradition of corporate weasels everywhere, he was only too happy to have this ball-breaking woman take us off his hands.

We followed Shannon down the hallway to a corner office that was larger and more luxurious than the director's. Though her title was vice president, her view of the ocean said that she was the one to reckon with at New Horizons.

A young male assistant brought us bottled water before ducking back out of the office. "Thank you, Tad," Shannon said to him, situating herself in the center of a U-shaped leather sectional, her arms slung casually across the back of the couch. We perched on the corners, facing her.

"As Mr. Peavey was saying, it's come to our attention that an unscrupulous band of cultists has been using our program to gain access to our clients."

"The Children of the Cosmos," I said, and she nodded.

"We found one of their brochures in our cousin's overnight bag," Terry said. "We thought it was a strange thing to bring home from a rehab center."

"May I see it?"

"We don't have it with us," I said. "How did you find out this was going on?"

"We've had some complaints."

"From people who were approached by them?"

"Actually, no. From family members. Their loved ones participate in our program, and then they're suddenly enamored of this group, insisting on giving them all their money. We have no idea how they're recruited, and it's only the timing that's clued us in. When they arrive, they have no ties to any cult. When they leave, they're card-carrying members. But any time we ask about it in the patient population, we get nothing but blank stares or denials."

"But why here?" I said. "Why not sell flowers on the street corner like any other self-respecting cult?"

Shannon took a deep breath and let it out again. "People who come here are at a crossroads. They've depended on drugs and alcohol for years to cope with life, but their coping mechanisms have turned against them, ruining their health, relationships, careers. It should be obvious from the location and the facilities that this is not an inexpensive program. But your cousin was here, so you know about the fees—"

"Ten thousand dollars per week," I said.

She nodded again.

"Our aunt and cousin are in the money," Terry said. "We're not. But we're not impressed by it, either."

"I wasn't trying to impress you," Shannon said evenly. "I'm making a point. Our clients are vulnerable and rich. Many of them are celebrities, past and present, with nice residual checks coming in from their movies or TV series. We think these Cosmos people have sent their members to us claiming to be in need of treatment, when what they really intend to do is suck other patients into their doomsday cult."

"Doomsday?" Terry said. "They're Kool-Aid freaks?"

"Actually, we don't know what their endgame is, we only know that they require lots and lots of money to spread their gospel. And although we're not sure of this, we suspect that they've infiltrated treatment centers in other parts of the city, as well."

"How do they go about the recruitment, do you know?" I asked her.

"I assume directly."

"They just walk up and start blabbing about the cult? Why wouldn't people just tell them to bug off?"

She shrugged. "Apparently, what they're offering appeals to some people."

"But it wouldn't appeal to everyone. Why wouldn't the ones who don't go for it tell you what's going on?"

"Perhaps they threaten them. That's part of the problem. We really don't know. Or maybe they're expert at sniffing out the most susceptible members of the patient population."

"We know what they're about, sort of—they believe we're descended from aliens," Terry said. "But beyond that, I don't see what they offer people."

Shannon gave a snort of laughter. "What do all religions

offer? Immortality, preceded by a purposeful existence. A reason for being. Many of our clients come here looking for just that. Of course, all *we* can offer them is the usual 'higher power' crap—" She caught herself. "I didn't mean, uh . . . I'm an atheist, actually," she offered by way of apology.

"We don't really know where we stand on that particular issue," I said. "Although I did have a near-death experience recently."

"Really?" Shannon said, her eyes going wary.

"Yeah, with the white light and everything. I went to a place that looked like Heaven, but as soon as I mentioned *her* name"—I cast my eyes to Terry—"I got thrown right back out on my ass."

Shannon burst out laughing. I was pleasantly surprised to see her disarmed by humor. Maybe she wasn't such a tough nut after all.

"Our cousin Robert also denies being approached by the cult," Terry said. "*And* he denies knowing where he was when the girl was killed. I can't help thinking there's a connection somewhere."

"Yes." Shannon fingered her pearls thoughtfully. "You know, you girls might be just what I need to get to the bottom of this. Did I hear that you're private investigators?"

If she did, she either had some sort of eavesdropping device in Wendell's office or Superman's ears. But I decided not to press the issue.

"Yes," I told her.

"I'd be interested in hiring you. What are your fees?"

"Oh, uh—" I looked over at Terry. "We'll need a minute to discuss it."

"Fine, take your time," Shannon said, patting the back of the couch. "I'll be here."

Terry and I left the office wing and wandered into the lobby for a private confab. The mind-numbing music was much louder out here. Aggressive in its very blandness—no rhythm, melody, passion—so intrusive you couldn't hear your own thoughts, which may have been the whole idea.

"This is perfect," Terry said in a whisper. "I can't believe we're actually being invited inside to investigate. What a break."

"I don't think we should do this, Terry. We're already on too many tracks with this investigation."

"But it fits right in!"

"I'm not as convinced as you. After talking to Steinmetz, I really doubt this cult has anything to do with the case. It's more of a side issue."

"But check it out: The Cosmos Kids are operating here. Heather is one of them. Heather may be involved with Frank's blackmail. Hence, a connection to the murder. Not to mention Robert's possible contact with the cult."

I sighed. "How are we supposed to keep all this straight, let alone find the murderer?"

"We stumble around until we trip over something, as usual."

"But we can't take a week off in the middle of everything to poke around here. What are we gonna do, interview the patients one by one?"

Terry thought about it a second. "Hey, I've got an idea. A way we can keep investigating Heather, while getting a line on the Cosmos Kids here at the facility."

"How?"

"One of us checks in as a patient, making herself out to be a rich, troubled kid, right? Then we see who comes calling. Meanwhile, the other one keeps working on the outside."

"All right. Who checks in, you?"

"I was thinking *you*."

"Oh, I see. You're just the idea person. I do the actual dirty work, is that it?"

"You're subtler than I am."

"Yeah, but you're the former druggie. And a great liar. You'd be more convincing."

"I can't. I'd go crazy in here. This music makes me want to strangle someone!"

"Well, I'd go crazy, too! I'd rather have my frontal lobe pulled out through my nostril than listen to this *Cuckoo's Nest* crap all day long!"

We stared each other down. Finally, I blinked. "Forget it. Let them find their own cult people."

She gave me a frustrated look, then the light came on again. "I know!"

"What?"

"We pull a Hayley Mills."

"Oh," I said, nodding. "Not a bad idea. The old two-for-one?"

"And one-for-two."

I grinned. "Let's go run it past Shannon."

And in a matter of minutes, we were on the New Horizons gravy train at three hundred dollars a day, going undercover in pursuit of alleged alien abductees.

We checked Jerry into the facility under the false persona of "Faith Anderson," recovering heroin addict. The plan was to have her on duty for twenty-four hours, after which I would relieve her, having been debriefed before becoming Faith for the next twenty-four hours, and so on. While off duty from the clinic, each of us would continue the investigation into other aspects of the case.

Shannon told Terry she'd provide her with whatever she needed in the way of toiletries and clothing, then took her away to her room alone. We couldn't be seen together again on the grounds, since we planned to present ourselves as a single person rather than as a split-cell pair.

Terry would keep her cell phone with the ringer turned off so that I could reach her whenever necessary. She'd move among the patients, take part in the activities, go to group therapy and all that, trying to determine how the Cosmeteers were operating. I would hang on to Frank's mobile phone and pursue Heather on the outside.

Although it had seemed like a good idea at first, even kind of a lark, I found it unsettling to leave Terry there at New Horizons, confronting God only knew what loony tunes by herself. Being separated from my highly annoying sister always produced a low-level hum of anxiety. If you don't have a twin, it might be hard to imagine the bond you have with the other half of your accident of birth. When she's not there, it's like looking in the mirror and seeing no reflection.

"Watch yourself," I'd said to her.

"Don't worry. I know my way around addicts."

Yeah, but did she know her way around mind-controlling cultists? I wasn't an expert myself, but one thing I did know—the people who seemed least likely to fall for the lure of false prophets, the ones who prided themselves on their individuality and strong-mindedness, were often the best targets for those who knew how to manipulate the human psyche.

I looked at my watch as I got on the bike. I just had time to make it to the arraignment.

Terry usually performed the driving duties, and I had to

admit that I wasn't all that comfortable up front. Having this much lethal power between my legs reminded me of Slim Pickins astride the H-bomb in the last scene of *Dr. Strangelove*.

I turned the key, released the throttle, and the beast came to life.

Yee-haw! Let's go kill us some Russkies! Slim's voice echoed in my head, loud and clear.

fifteen

$\mathcal{I}$ slipped into the back of the courtroom, which was two-thirds full. Local curiosity seekers and trial junkies, mostly. A few journalists scribbling away on their pads. Fortunately, there were no television cameras or on-air Court TV types.

Eli was standing at the defense table, Robert and Reba seated to his left. Reba was well coiffed, but Robert's hair had been slicked down with pomade, sticking out in the back like an oily duck's ass.

The Honorable Jay Ratliff sat tall in his chair. He had salt-and-pepper hair, black-framed glasses, and a strong no-nonsense nose.

"In the case of *The people vs. Reba Price-Slatherton and Robert Somerset Price*, it is charged that on or about May 14 of 2003, Ms. Price-Slatherton and Mr. Price did commit murder in the first degree, in violation of Section 187 of the California Penal

Code, in that the defendants did willfully, unlawfully, and feloniously and with malice aforethought murder Candace Evelyn Starr, a human being."

Ratliff looked at Reba. "As to the charge against Reba Price-Slatherton, how does the defendant plead?"

"Not guilty," Eli boomed in his stentorian courtroom voice.

Reba jumped to her feet. "I object!"

The judge's eyebrows jumped up to his scalp.

"You are not in accord with the plea as entered?" he asked Reba.

I sank my head into my hands, then forced myself to look back up through my fingers. Eli was having a forceful, whispered conversation with Reba. After several moments of haggling, Reba apparently consented to the plea, nodding her head.

Thank God.

"Very well, I will agree," she said. "Not guilty."

"Thank you," said the judge.

"Under protest," she murmured as she sat back down.

"What was that?" said the court reporter.

Reba gave the court reporter an imperious look. "None of your business, young lady."

The judge leaned over his bench. "Ms. Price-Slatherton, you are speaking to the court stenographer. It is her *business* to record everything that is said in this courtroom *for the record.* Do you understand?"

"Oh. Beg pardon," Reba said, chastened.

"Thank you," said Judge Ratliff.

"Your Honor," Eli said. "We would like to request bail."

Deputy District Attorney Harlon Pinchbeck popped up to address the judge. He was a malevolent-looking beanpole—skinny neck, sloping shoulders, ballooning pants belted just below the ribs. "Your Honor, the people object to bail for this defendant. We believe she poses a flight risk. She's extremely wealthy, with bank accounts in Monaco and Grand Cayman. She also owns property in Paris, France, and in Costa Rica. Due to the severity of the crime, the horrible brutality of this premeditated butchery—"

"Your Honor, I object!" Reba cried again, jumping to her feet. "The place in Paris is just a little pied-à-terre. I could hardly think of spending the rest of my life in such a confined space."

The judge gave Eli an irritated look, then turned to address Reba. "Madam, you are represented by counsel. Sit down and be quiet. I hope you realize that you are facing a long stretch in a very confined space, indeed."

Reba sat down, an annoyed little tilt to her head. "Very well, Your Honor."

"I apologize for my client, Judge," Eli said. "She's mentally unstable, which is why—"

Reba was on her feet again. "I object! He's the unstable one, running out on a commitment without so much as a how-do-you-do!"

CRACK . . . CRACK . . . went the judge's gavel. "Counsel, please control your client!"

If I could have melted into a puddle, dripped through the cracks in the linoleum, seeped into the sewers, and run out into the oblivion of the ocean at that moment, I would have done so gladly.

"I'm sorry, Your Honor," Eli said. "As should be evident, my client is in dire need of psychiatric care."

"Why, you horrible, horrible man!" Reba pounded on Eli's arm with her little fists. "And to think I freely gave you my *body*!"

CRACK . . . CRACK. "I'm going to have your client removed from the courtroom, counsel."

Drip . . . drop . . . drip . . . drop . . .

"I understand, Your Honor," Eli said.

"Bailiffs, remove the defendant at once!" the judge ordered.

"Why, you beasts! Unhand me! Let me go!"

I could not believe my eyes. My great-aunt was being hauled away by two armed deputies, kicking and screaming and clawing at them like a harpy on PCP.

And I thought I'd had nightmares last night.

"I'll not stand for this! Do you know who I am?" She writhed around in their grip, the shellacked coif never budging an inch despite all her thrashing. "Why, I could buy and sell all of you!"

Then *boom*. She was through the side door and out of sight.

I looked over and saw Pinchbeck shaking his head, staring at the space where Reba had been, completely stunned.

The judge gave Eli a stern look. "Counsel, you must know that a defendant *non compos mentis* cannot enter into a bond agreement."

"I do, Your Honor," Eli said. "Under the circumstances, we waive the request."

"I should think so," the judge said. He looked at Robert. "Now, as to the charge of murder in the first degree against Robert Price, how does the defendant plead?"

But before Eli could respond, Robert jumped up from his seat at the defendant's table.

"I did it, Judge! Leave Mumsy out of this! I killed that girl, and I'll kill again!" he yelled, the duck's ass bobbing up and down. "Give me the gas, the gas, the *gaaaaaassss!*"

CRACK, CRACK, CRACK, CRACK. "Counsel, do you specialize in mentally unstable clients? Bailiffs, *remove the defendant!*"

The bailiffs, having just returned, dragged Robert out of the room.

"Sorry, Your Honor. The plea is not guilty," Eli said, putting some papers into his briefcase and snapping it shut. Smiling like Bre'r Rabbit in the briar patch.

"This court is in recess!"

I waited for Eli in the lobby. He exited the courtroom surrounded by reporters peppering him with questions. I ducked behind a column, hiding in the shadows and watching the show.

He addressed them for a few minutes, making the usual declarations of his clients' innocence, along with his heartfelt belief that they would be acquitted, yadda yadda yadda. I couldn't believe anybody listened to the statements made by defense lawyers on the courthouse steps, let alone reported them. After all, what was he supposed to say—*My clients are scumbags! They should be hung up by the thumbs!?*

Eventually, the reporters got their fill of canned lawyer responses and Eli broke away, angling for the front door. "Psssst," I said, waving him over to my corner.

"Hey," he said, grinning at me. "You made it!"

"Wish I hadn't."

"Yeah, well—I told you how it would go down."

"Funny, I don't remember any mention of a Monty Python sketch. Do you have time for a bite? I want to talk to you about something."

"Sure. Let's go to the cafeteria. They got great tiramisu."

Tiramisu in a courthouse cafeteria? Only in Malibu, I thought.

We went through the line and Eli helped himself to a serving of fancy Italian cake and a coffee. I bought a tuna salad sandwich and iced tea. When we sat down at a table, Eli sliced a fork down the middle of the cake, scooped up one of the halves, and cantilevered it into his open mouth.

"So you happy with that outcome?" I asked him.

He grinned, the espresso-soaked lady fingers turning his lower teeth brown. "It was perfect."

"I guess I have to trust you on this strategy," I said dubiously.

"Damn straight. So, what's shakin'?" he said, forking in the other half of the tiramisu. He picked up his paper napkin and dabbed his lips daintily as he swallowed.

"Have you ever heard of Frank Steinmetz?" I asked.

"Yeah," he said. "Big-time producer."

"Is he mob-connected, as far as you know?"

He nodded. "Pretty sure, yeah. Why?"

"Oh, just want to know how terrified I should be."

"How come?"

"He hired me and Terry on a very hush-hush matter."

"Hush-hush, my mustache. What's up?"

"Really, I can't say, except to tell you that we may have a line on the killer through him."

His eyebrows went up. "For real?"

"Yeah, I think so."

"Great. Meanwhile, I've got Greg working on a motion for suppression of the confessions." Greg Adams was Eli's brilliant law clerk and investigator.

"And what about the mental-incompetence motion?"

"He's working on that one, too. Calls it 'Habeas Bats in the Belfry.' It should tie up the proceedings for a while. I did it once for a mob guy I represented."

"Oh really? How'd that turn out?"

"He didn't go to prison."

I found myself cheered by this. "Excellent."

"He died of a stroke before the trial."

"Oh."

"But I got a shrink on the line that will swear up and down that they're suffering from a dual psychosis, a thing that sometimes happens in families—shared delusions brought on by congenital mental conditions."

I had to laugh. "I *guess* that's good news."

"It's perfect," he said, downing his coffee in one big slurp. He patted his lips again with the napkin. "Look, I gotta take off. You keep me up-to-date as much as you can."

"Okay."

He stood up from the table. "By the way, did you see the *Times* yesterday?"

I gave him an innocent look. "No . . . why?"

"Apparently, there are some redheaded twins going around town on a pink Harley, beating up bikers. Hell of a coincidence, huh?"

"Yep."

Eli gave me a knowing wink, then waddled on out of the cafeteria.

I knew I should be staking out Heather's house, but I couldn't stop thinking about Terry at the rehab clinic and what she might encounter there. I decided I needed more background information on the Children of the Cosmos, so I went back to Reba's to do a little online research with Robert's computer.

After reading for an hour, I was surprised I'd never heard of the group before. Their leader, Abaddon, was a former advertising executive named Morton Fayson, a man with enormous expertise at stoking the publicity machine. His right-hand woman had been a professor of genetics at Brown University, a specialist in DNA, who was in charge of their own private Genome Project. They were seeking to isolate alien chromosomes from the human ones, revealing our true identities at last.

As Shannon had said, they had several big names associated with them, people whose show business careers had taken a turn south but who still had lots of money as a result of their former fame. They lived in Bel Air and Beverly Hills and Brentwood, and had entrée to others in their financial stratum. I couldn't find a definite address for the cult's headquarters, but mention was made of a mansion in Pacific Palisades.

Strangely, considering all the publicity he generated, Abaddon seemed to be very shy about personal appearances. Try as I might, I could find no record of his showing up in public.

He'll come to you, Heather had said.

I was sure she'd tell him we were looking for him, but would he materialize as promised? I shuddered at the idea of looking into the hypnotic eyes of some crazed Rasputin of the Third Kind.

I didn't know exactly where I stood on the subject of aliens. Mine was the usual complaint—although there were lots of eyewitness sightings, there was never any hard evidence left behind.

Just as with the "higher power" issue.

Oh sure, there was the occasional burning bush, but usually only one person standing by to witness it, right? And there were tablets etched with the Ten Commandments—but the actual stonework was done offstage, and again, only one person to testify as to its origin.

But what about Grizzie? She wasn't exactly Moses the Lawgiver, but you could look high and low for a more truthful soul and you'd never find one. And there she was, telling us with a straight face that she'd been beamed up.

Maybe Abaddon was just who he said he was, an emissary from an advanced civilization somewhere out there in the universe. But if they were the Masters of the Earth, what did that make us?

Their slaves?

With Terry gone, the dead air was deafening. I had no ideas coming at me, no one to bounce my ideas off of. I was starting to realize just how much I depended on her rock-hard skull to hone my thoughts on. I knew we were missing something, but *what*? We couldn't move forward until we could name it. What was the thing that tied all of this together—Heather, the Cosmeteers, Frank, Candy . . . ?

I needed to talk it through with someone. Someone I could trust, who could help me put it all together.

Boatwright.

Sure, he was hot, but he also had the cop's mind, the street smarts, the bloodhound's nose for a criminal scent. I told myself I was motivated solely by a desire to solve the case, but somehow I think my libido might have had something to do with it, too. With each thought of him, I experienced a phantom whiff of his aftershave. And this time, Terry was in no position to interfere.

He answered after one ring of his cell phone.

"I've been waiting for your call."

"How'd you know it was me?"

"Cop intuition. And caller ID."

"So where are you?"

"I'm in Beverly Hills."

"Could we meet for coffee? I want to bring you up-to-date on our end of the investigation."

A beat. "How did I know you'd be conducting your own investigation?"

"You don't really think my aunt and cousin murdered that girl, do you?"

"The DA does."

"I know, but—"

"And they have some pretty compelling evidence."

"Sure, planted."

"Well, if you can tell them who it was planted by, then you might have a chance."

"Well, that's what we're trying to find out. But I need some help. I'm kind of out of my depth here. Have you heard anything?"

There was a pause. "Not on the phone."

"Where do you want to meet? How about Hamburger Hamlet?"

Hamburger Hamlet was a famous, midpriced Los Angeles restaurant that was a hangout for minor movie stars, producers, and other entertainment-industry types. You could almost always count on a celebrity sighting of the has-been kind. Just the place if you were looking to spot someone whose career peaked in the eighties or earlier.

"I'll be there in an hour, depending on traffic."

"Oh, come on," I teased. "Use your cherry."

He laughed. "See you there."

I took Reba's Mercedes for comfort and arrived at the restaurant on Sunset Boulevard before Boatwright did. I had just ordered coffee when he walked into the room, sporting wraparound black sunglasses and a three-o'clock shadow, running a hand through his dark windblown hair.

Be still my hormones.

Unfortunately, this time he was also the enemy. The Law. The System. Part of the fraternity that had locked up my aunt and my cousin. He spotted me and smiled—and for a moment I seriously considered defecting to the enemy side.

"Sorry I'm late," he said, slipping into the U-shaped booth.

"I know, I know. You had a triple homicide."

"No, I had a squad meeting that ran over." He pushed the sunglasses up on top of his head, drawing me into his deep-blue eyes. "It's really good to see you." My skin went tingly. "You gonna eat?" he asked.

I shook my head. "Just coffee."

"That's okay, I'm not hungry," he said, adding with a wink, "for food, anyway."

That was laying it on a bit thick, I thought.

Just then, the waitress came up beside the booth and asked if he wanted coffee. "Yes, please," he said, flashing her the killer smile. She stumbled back like she'd run smack into an invisible sex field, then remembered to make a note on her pad before scurrying away.

"You have a way with waitresses," I observed.

"Women always want me," he said, grinning, "until they get to know me."

"Cheers to that." I smiled and lifted my cup.

"Hey, you don't know me well enough to dislike me. It usually takes people weeks to peel away enough of my facade to realize it."

"I'm a quick study."

He smiled again, laugh lines creasing his cheeks. "No, see, I got you pegged. You're a contrarian."

"I am not. I'm a Pisces."

"You know what I mean. Whatever you think you should do, you do the opposite."

"You're talking about my sister. I always do what I think I should do."

"In your bass-ackwards way. I know how it goes—you're attracted to me, so you think you shouldn't be attracted to me."

"Oh, is that a fact?"

"But eventually, you'll have to succumb."

I was thinking of succumbing right there on the floor of the restaurant—the back seat of his unmarked car, at the very least—but I wasn't going to give him the satisfaction of saying so. "Why *have* to?" I asked him.

He gave me a look that a lion might give to a gazelle trapped under its paw. "Because it was meant to be."

I clenched my teeth to keep my jaw from dropping.

Meant to be?

While I was wondering how the hell to respond to that little bombshell, the waitress arrived with his cup. She fumbled it and the coffee sloshed over onto the saucer.

"Oh, I'm so sorry! I'll get you another one—"

He put a hand on her arm, and she instantly turned to goo. Was that for my benefit? I wondered. A demonstration of his magnetic charm?

"It's fine, don't worry." He tipped the coffee from the saucer into the cup and took a sip. "Hon, that's a great cup of coffee," he said to her, as she tittered giddily and skipped away.

"If you're done slaying the waitress, can we talk about my little problem?" I said.

He gave me an impish grin. "Sure."

"I need your take on our case."

"In what way?"

"Something's not right. They jumped right into an indictment, and the arraignment was this morning. I don't want to say 'rush to judgment,' but—"

He flinched. LA cops *hate* that expression. "Then do me a favor—don't say it."

"Okay, but doesn't it seem that they were a little quick on the draw?"

"Not really, if they think they have a case."

"But the lead detective doesn't even buy Reba and Robert as suspects. He told us so himself."

Boatwright shrugged. "Not his call. It's the DA's."

"Yeah, but he implied he could even get in trouble by continuing to look into it. Isn't that strange? I mean, wouldn't you want to be sure you had the right people before bringing charges? Wouldn't you give the lead detective credit if he thought something was amiss? Let him continue investigating?"

He stirred his coffee. "Look, your cousin walked in the door carrying the girl's head. Your aunt had her body wrapped in a Turkish rug. It's not often you get evidence like that handed to you. I'm not surprised they're moving quickly. It's a big crime for Malibu. High profile. They want to sew it up."

"But obviously they were framed. Where's the motive?"

He shook his head. "Not that it matters—they don't need motive—but your aunt is covering up for your cousin, who's a head case, no pun intended. He went out with some young girl and had his way with her, then chopped her up. The DA probably figures your aunt knows all about it, which makes her an accessory after the fact. He thinks he can make her crack by bringing charges against her, too. When she decides to talk, he'll give her a deal."

I thought about what he'd said. "Wait, did you hear about somebody 'having his way with her'? They didn't charge him with rape. What are you talking about?"

He leaned in and whispered. "This is confidential."

"Cross my heart." I did it with my finger.

"She'd had intercourse."

"So there's DNA evidence that could exonerate Robert!"

"I heard your lawyer friend was going for not guilty by reason of insanity. He's not even gonna argue the evidence. Besides, she could have had sex with anybody."

"Including a serial killer."

"Is that your theory of the crime—serial killer?"

"No. We've been working on a dumped-wife-who-belongs-to-a-wacky-cult-and-who-tried-to-blackmail-her-husband-with-the-body theory of the crime. But we've been wrong before."

He laughed. "And you wonder why the DA is going with what he's got?"

"Listen, I want to tell you the rest of it, but you have to swear on your badge that you won't tell anyone, for any reason."

He put a hand to his breast. "Swear."

"Okay, here's the thing. There's a big producer by the name of Frank Steinmetz who lives next door to Reba and Robert. Someone sent him a tape of him with the victim, a working girl named Candy, then hit him up for two hundred fifty thousand to buy it back."

"After she was killed?"

"No, that's the interesting thing. This was while she was still alive. The tape's real kink-o-vision, if you know what I mean—very embarrassing. They threatened Frank with exposure, but he wouldn't pay. Then Candy ended up dead."

"In your aunt's house."

"Yes, but think about that. If you wanted to scare someone into paying, what better way than stuffing the body right next door? Demonstrating how close you can get, without directly jeopardizing your mark, the money person . . . ?"

He pondered that for a second. "But why cut her head off?"

"I'm kind of stuck there," I admitted. "Maybe they were holding it in reserve, like—'the body's next door, and if you don't pay up, we'll put the head somewhere that will incriminate you.'"

"But they didn't do that."

"I know—that's why I'm stumped. Now I'm thinking maybe they chucked it in the canyon so no one *would* find it. Only problem being that someone did—Cousin Robert."

"I have to admit, you've just moved up on the plausibility scale."

"From what to what?"

"Zero to three and a half."

"Thanks a lot," I said, heavy on the sarcasm. "The other problem is that the blackmailers haven't hit Frank up for more money, so I can't figure out what they're up to."

He looked off in the distance. "Okay, let's think this through. What does the head represent?"

"Well, it represents her identity," I said. "Her face."

"Right. So why would they toss it away?"

"I thought at first that they didn't want her identified. But that's out, because Frank's only on the line for blackmail if the body's identified as the girl in the tape."

"But the girl *was* identifiable even without her head," he said, eyes coming back to my face. "By her sister. She recognized the tattoo, various birthmarks, et cetera."

"So maybe they hadn't counted on the sister. Didn't know about her existence, perhaps."

I thought about her now . . . *Twink*. Was it coincidence that she was working for our prime suspect? Or did she suspect that Heather may have had a hand in the murder and start investigating on her own?

Boatwright interrupted my thoughts. "Maybe when they saw that somebody else was going up for the murder, they thought they had nothing left to threaten Frank with, so they gave up on the blackmail and got rid of the head. I mean, they couldn't have foreseen that the people they planted the body on would jump up and confess."

"But Reba and Robert only became suspects *after* the head was found. So it was dumped prior to that for some reason."

He took a deep breath and leaned back. "Okay, so they wanted to threaten Frank with the head, but they didn't have the nerve to hang on to it. It's a pretty incriminating little item to be caught with."

"Yeah, that makes sense, I guess."

"Any leads on the blackmailer?"

"Like I said, we're thinking Heather Granger, Frank's soon-to-be ex. Very ugly divorce in progress. She's doing some underhanded things, like selling his horses without his knowledge. She may have murdered the girl to up the ante."

He made a face like he wasn't buying.

"What?" I said.

"Cutting off heads . . . that doesn't strike me as a female crime. Too brutal. Too straightforward. Women tend to be more passive-aggressive. They like poison, stuff like that."

"Oh, passive-aggressive like the chick in Texas who ran over her husband six times?"

"She used a car, not a hacksaw."

"True," I said, sighing. "So you don't think it's a female?"

"All I can say is it doesn't feel like one."

"And now there *is* this business of the DNA, which might indicate a male doer—"

"That means nothing, now that you tell me the girl was a pro."

"Not that kind of pro. She plays dress-up with her customers, metes out punishment as a dominatrix."

"Doesn't mean she can't mix it up a little. Some guys actually *enjoy* normal sex," he said with a meaningful grin.

I had to smile back. It's always heartening in LA to hear that someone you're interested in is not a sexual deviant—normal guys being in alarmingly short supply.

"But if Eli knew there was DNA, he might rethink his mentally incompetent strategy," I said. "It'd be something to work with, at least. Isn't the prosecutor supposed to give him that information as part of discovery?"

"Yeah, theoretically. But if it doesn't support their case, they might lose it or forget they ever saw it."

I sat back in the booth, shaking my head. "This isn't the way the justice system is supposed to work. They're supposed to go after the bad guys, not the nearest luckless bystander without an alibi. And they're supposed to present *all* of the evidence."

"Not if it doesn't serve their purpose." He sipped his coffee. "Speaking of abnormal sex, where's your sister?"

I gave him a look. "I'm gonna pretend you didn't say that."

"I didn't think you two went anywhere without each other."

"Terry's doing some undercover work right now."

"Where?"

"At the rehab place where Robert was before all of this came down, New Horizons. They've been infiltrated by these cult members, the Children of the Cosmos, and the directors want us to find out how they're getting in."

He shook his head in amazement. "Can't you two work one case at a time?"

"Funny part is, it may all be tied in. Heather Granger is a member of this cult. She's been funneling Frank's money to them for years, and after the divorce, she's not gonna have Frank's money anymore. At least not as much of it—which makes her a prime suspect for the blackmail." I stopped, frustrated. "But she's a female, which rules her out, according to you."

He laughed. "What a crazy, cocked-up scenario."

"I know, huh? Why can't life be like an Agatha Christie novel, where everybody in the village has a motive for the murder, and they all oblige you by hanging around looking suspicious and making self-incriminating remarks, then you figure out who the bad guy is because he uses the wrong pronoun or something—*Aha! You said 'I.' Not 'he.' Therefore, you, Mr. Vicar, are the murderer!* And then everybody sits around having a sherry while they wait for the constable to come and collect him."

He burst out laughing. "I think you'd better lay off the mystery novels. Too much of that stuff will rot your brain."

"Yeah," I said, rolling my eyes, "like real life *won't*."

He stood to go and dropped a ten on the table. "I gotta get back," he said, then leaned over and kissed me on the top of my head.

What the hell?

He caught the look on my face. "What?"

"A kiss on the scalp. How very stimulating. I think my hair follicles just had an orgasm."

"Knucklehead." He laughed and ruffled my hair.

"Whoa! Multiple hair-follicle orgasms!"

"You want a real kiss?" he said, eyes going all dark and smoldery.

Now I wasn't so sure.

"Maybe . . ."

"How do I know you're not Terry, trying to trap me?"

I gave him a wicked smile. "The only way to tell us apart is a birthmark."

"Oh yeah? Where?"

"Wouldn't you like to know. . . . *Buh-bye!*"

"Smart-ass," he grumbled.

"Good guess!"

He threw back his head. "It's on your . . . ? Ha! That's great."

Then, before I even knew what was happening, he leaned

in suddenly and gave me a long kiss, ending with a delicate bite on my lower lip.

He pulled back and I slumped down in my seat, electrified and limp at the same time.

He grinned at the kiss's effect. "By the way, anytime you want to tell me about your secret life as the Pink Menace, I'd love to hear about it."

With that, he turned and left, waving good-bye to the waitress as he went. Her expression melted as he passed, and she followed him all of the way out of the restaurant with her eyes, much to the annoyance of a couple who were trying to order their lunch.

I slapped my forehead.

The Pink Menace. Holy cannoli.

sixteen

S till thrilling to Boatwright's kiss, I headed back to Reba's to dress for the afternoon's activity: staking out Heather Granger's house. We had found out whatever we could about her through other means, and now it was time to do the old-fashioned gumshoe thing. I was also hoping I could get close enough for a word with Candy's sister, although that was obviously a situation that had to be handled very delicately.

I didn't want to plunge right in and ask her direct questions; on the other hand, I didn't want to waste an opportunity, should one arise. Nor did I want her to take me into her confidence only to discover that I had an ulterior motive. No, I definitely wanted to keep her on my side.

Trying to look the part, I pinned my hair to my head and made a do-rag out of one of Reba's Versace scarves. Then I borrowed some oversized black Valentino sunglasses, threw on some hip-hugging white shorts and my Pucci-print bikini top, with a jean jacket for a cover-up, slapped some zinc oxide on my nose, and looked at myself in the mirror.

My own mother wouldn't know me. Or own up to knowing me.

I stuffed Frank's phone under a beach towel in a straw carryall, placing the pups on top on the towel. The dogs made for excellent cover. With them and the getup, I looked like a slightly deranged Malibu native out to enjoy the afternoon.

"We're going to the beach, babies," I said, and they almost wagged the tails off their behinds in excitement.

I loaded everybody into Reba's Mercedes and headed out to Zuma, the sunroof open all the way. Paquito was in the front seat with his paws up on the armrest, nose straining toward the fresh ocean air that was streaming in the window. Muffy was performing the same time-honored canine ritual in the back.

"What are you picking up on the radar, kids? Mackerel? Shark? Jellyfish?"

It was pretty festive. And a gorgeous day. I could almost forget I was on my way to spy on a potential murderer.

When I got to Zuma, I took one pass by Heather's house to get the lay of the land. There was a small orange Toyota in the drive next to an elephantine green Esplanade. I pegged the SUV as Heather's, and I knew the smaller car belonged to Twink.

Good. She was still working here.

There were other cars parked the length of the block, most of them luxury cars like BMWs or Mercedes, alternating with high-end SUVs—Lexus, Infiniti, and the like. Looked like some kind of tony gathering was going on. I saw a large white commercial van parked directly next to Heather's driveway. As I passed, I glanced at the side panel of the truck.

Hungry Boys Catering.

It was the same one we'd seen heading to EquiSpa the other day, with the cartoon man shoveling a forkload of food into his mouth. This time the picture reminded me of Eli eating tiramisu, and it made me giggle. I gathered they were the ones to call, hereabouts, if you were serving finger sandwiches. Maybe Heather was hosting one of her alien to-do's.

"Call Hungry Boys," I sang, making up a commercial to entertain the dogs. "For all your finger-food needs . . . call Hungry Boys. . . . These boys are eager to please . . ."

The dogs didn't seem all that entertained, but they weren't the least bit bothered by my singing, either. I could pretty much do no wrong in their eyes, and I had to admit, that was one reason I loved the little boogers so fiercely. I got a half-mile down the street and made a U-turn, then took another slow run by the house. As I did, I saw Twink heading up the drive to her orange Toyota.

"What a stroke of luck, pups."

They agreed, wagging their tails.

I stopped at the corner and waited for Twink to pull up behind me. After a few moments she did, then sat patiently waiting for me to turn. Instead, I waved her forward.

She hesitated, then pulled around the Mercedes to make her turn in front of me. When she got even with my window, I waved at her.

"Excuse me?" I said like a lost wayfarer.

She leaned over and cranked down the window on her passenger side. "Need directions?"

"No, actually, I was hoping to talk to you."

Her smile was instantly replaced with a look of confusion. I raised my sunglasses so that she could see my eyes. She made the same gesture, but there was no recognition on her face.

"I saw you the other day, when you went to work for Ms. Granger?"

She arched her eyebrows and nodded. "Oh, you're one of those twins on the front porch?"

"Yeah. I wonder if I could talk to you for a few minutes."

Her eyes darted sideways. "What about?" she said, frowning now.

"I'm sorry to say it this way"—meaning I didn't like to be shouting this through a car window—"but I need to talk to you about Candy."

The sunglasses went down on her nose. Her head snapped around to face the road. She jammed her car into gear and wheeled around the Mercedes, speeding down the road perpendicular to Heather's, churning up dust.

"Well," I said to the doggies. "That could have gone better."

Their tails drooped in sympathy.

I watched Twink disappear down the hill toward PCH. Then she screeched to a stop at the next intersection. I waited for her to peel out again, but the car sat there idling for a long minute . . .

Then it started backing up.

I didn't need any more encouragement. I wheeled around the corner and caught up with her halfway down the road. I pulled the Mercedes up on her left and looked through her window. Tears were running down her cheeks behind the sunglasses. She didn't say anything, just pointed down the street ahead of her.

I understood I was to follow her. I nodded, and she took off.

We went left on PCH and pulled into a Malibu strip mall facing the ocean. There was a Sunglass Hut/Bikini Boutique, a New Age bookstore, a few high-priced gift shops with handmade ceramics and little crystally things hanging in the windows. Across the road was a Pet and Equestrian Supply store, fronted by a huge statue of a horse.

I pulled in next to her and walked up to her car. "I'm sorry," I said through the open window. "I didn't mean to upset you."

She laughed bitterly. "You didn't think I'd be upset by a total stranger coming up and asking about my dead sister? What the fuck business is it of yours? Are you a reporter or something?"

Had to tread lightly here—the girl was obviously hurting. "No. I'm an investigator."

She studied me from behind her sunglasses. "You're a cop?"

"Private investigator. My aunt and my cousin have been indicted for Candy's murder. I know they didn't do it, but I need proof of that or they're going to be locked away for a crime they didn't commit. Which means the person who *did* commit the crime will get away with it."

She thought it over, drumming her fingers on the wheel. "I can't be gone long. I'm supposed to be getting supplies. . . ."

"This won't take long. Can I buy you a coffee?"

Twink shrugged and got out, rolling up the window before locking her car. Then she noticed the anxious little mugs pressed against the window of Reba's car, begging to be included in the coffee klatch.

"Oh, how cute," she said, her face softening. "Can they come with us?"

"Sure." I grabbed the Pomeranian out of the car. "This is Paquito," I said, handing him to her. Next I grabbed the pug. "And this is Miss Muffy." I closed the door but didn't bother to lock it. We'd be sitting at an outdoor café not a hundred feet away.

"They're adorable," she said as Paquito licked the salty trail of a tear on her cheek. "Dogs are the best, aren't they?"

"They beat the pants off of people."

"I heard *that*."

"She hadn't been doing this stuff long," Twink said, stirring the whipped cream, chocolate sprinkles, and cinnamon she had polluted her coffee with. "She was actually a pretty good actress. But 'pretty good' and no contacts gets you bupkiss."

I nodded in sympathy. "I've met so many disillusioned actors and actresses in this town. I don't know why so many people get sucked in—it's a dog's life anyway." I glanced over at Muffy and Paquito. "No offense," I added for their benefit.

"She was auditioning for commercials, exercise videos, stuff like that. She'd get work occasionally, but she was having trouble paying the bills. I think her first 'job' in this other area was some online thing—just video, no real contact with the . . . What do you call them, *johns*?"

"We call them losers."

This got me a short laugh. "Yeah, well . . . I guess she got correspondence from some of these guys, offering her lots of money to do it in person, so she went for it." She rubbed at her eyes behind the shades. "She was a cheerleader, for chrissakes!"

I didn't volunteer that I considered it a short drop from cheerleader to Kitten with a Whip. Instead, I nodded.

"Did you know any of her customers?" I asked gently.

She shook her head. "She knew I didn't approve. I even said once—and I kick myself every time I think of it—I said, 'Don't tell me anything about it. I don't want to know.' Now I think if she *had* told me something, if I had known who she was involved with . . . I mean, one of the sick sons-a-bitches killed her!" She pounded the table with her fist, startling the dogs. Muffy let out a perturbed "Woof."

Why hadn't it occurred to me that there might be another john out there that Candy had punished too lustily, or maybe someone else she had tried to blackmail? Someone who had dealt with her very harshly as a result. We had been fixated on Heather, and Frank's animosity toward his ex-wife had seemed to confirm our suspicions.

"Don't beat yourself up," I said when I realized no one had spoken for minute. "I think anyone would have the same reaction to a sister going into that line of work. It was only a rejection of her choices, not of her as a person."

She grabbed a bunch of paper napkins from the dispenser and blew her nose. "But I did reject her. I was so harsh. I called her a prostitute. Next time I saw her, she was . . . she was . . ."

Headless.

Both of us thought it. Neither of us said it.

Twink threw the used napkins into the trash bin. "Your aunt and cousin"—she scratched Paquito behind the ear—"they aren't into . . . ?"

"The kinky stuff? God, no. Reba's idea of sadomasochism is getting her legs waxed and her eyebrows tweezed in the same appointment, and Robert's just a big teddy bear of a lush. To quote their maid, he's completely sexless."

"Then I wonder why . . . ?"

"The DA is bringing a case against them?"

She nodded.

"I wonder the same thing."

"I mean, couldn't somebody have . . . put Candy's body there to frame them?"

I was starting to like this girl. "Yeah, we think that's what happened."

"But why?"

"That *is* the question. Listen, I assume that when the police interviewed you, you told them about Candy's profession."

I got a blank look in response.

"You . . . didn't tell them about it?" I tried to keep the shock out of my voice, but there it was anyway.

"I . . . I didn't see the point," she said, sniffling. "They had arrested somebody already. Why tell them about the other stuff? They'd just make it sound like she brought it on herself, like she deserved to be murdered because of what she was into."

"True, they do tend to blame the victim in cases like this. But at the same time, it can be a source of leads for the police."

"But they were already sure they had the murderers."

I leaned into the table. "I don't know how I can convince you of this, but I swear on the lives of these dogs that my family members had nothing to do with your sister's death."

She looked down at the dogs with the smile of an animal lover. "You just convinced me."

I exhaled in relief. "And I know it sounds like a cliché, but if the real murderer isn't caught, somebody else's sister could be next."

She sat with this for a moment, then straightened up in her chair. "Okay, what can I do to help?"

Music to my ears, an ally in Heather's employ. But I didn't want to play the Heather card right away. Might seem like too much of a stretch for her to be behind the murder. Anyway, I was beginning to have my own doubts about the actress's involvement.

"If you can think of *anyone* Candy may have mentioned to you, someone she was doing business with that she didn't trust, or—"

Twink shook her head. "I told you. We didn't talk about it."

"Do you know the Web site where she did her thing, or do you have access to her computer or her e-mail account?"

"I could get her computer. I don't know her passwords, but we could probably figure them out." She was perking up for the first time since we'd met. "It'd be fairly easy to get onto her hard drive and retrieve that stuff, wouldn't it? I mean, I don't know how to do it, but there are people who do. . . ."

I was nodding like a maniac. This might be the biggest break in the case so far. "Yes. When do you think you could get it?"

"I don't know . . . tomorrow? Would that be okay?"

I would be at New Horizons the next day. "I'll be tied up. Could I have my sister contact you?"

"Sure. What's her name?" Then she laughed, embarrassed. "What's *your* name?"

"I'm Kerry McAfee. She's Terry."

"Same last name, I guess."

"Yeah, same last name. Same freckle constellations. Same shoe size—"

"You guys must have a good relationship," Twink said, then the thought backfired on her, the sadness dropping down like a curtain over her big brown eyes. "Candy and I had a good relationship . . . I mean, when we were kids."

"Where are you guys from, originally?" I asked, trying to lighten things up.

"Riverside." She gave a derisive laugh. "Pickup country. Trucks, that is."

"We're from Burbank. But I've been *through* Riverside."

"Everyone's been through it. No one goes *to* it. They just breeze through on their way to Palm Springs."

"Busted."

Twink glanced at her watch, then took a pen out of her purse and wrote on a napkin. "Here's my cell phone number," she said. "Have your sister call me on this. I have to get back or Heather will have a cow."

I made it sound like casual interest. "How did you come to work for her?"

"She hired me from a place called EquiSpa. Her husband Frank had his horses in the clinic there. She's trying to sell them, so she wants them in tip-top shape. I'm keeping them exercised and groomed, showing them to potential buyers."

"Did Candy meet Heather or Frank at EquiSpa?"

Twink shrugged. "She might have, at an open house or something. When I was trying to keep our sisterly relationship intact, Candy would sometimes meet me at the stables. Why?"

"No reason." No point in complicating the issue right now, I figured. But if Candy *had* met Frank at EquiSpa, she might have met other rich pervs there as well, all of whom could be considered suspects. I couldn't wait to get my hands on that client list. This thing could blow Miss Heidi Fleiss's skinny butt right out of the water.

"Listen, Heather doesn't know about Candy being my sister," Twink said, interrupting my thoughts. "And I don't want her to know. I don't want . . . the looks . . . you get from people, know what I mean?"

"Oh, sure. I understand. She's kind of an odd duck, isn't she? I mean, all that alien stuff?"

"Tell me about it. She's having one of her meetings with them right now. She invited me to come in and listen, but no way I'm getting involved with people like that."

"She has them over to her house?"

"Yeah, has the whole thing catered and everything. And they have a satellite hookup to watch some quote-unquote *transmission* from the big leader."

"From where, the Mother Ship?"

She chuckled. "I don't know, and I don't want to know. This is my last job here, then I'm moving back to Riverside. Life's a little too strange for me in Malibu."

"Yeah, I hear ya."

We got up from the table and walked back toward our cars. She hesitated, giving Paquito a kiss on the top of his head. "Sure you don't want to leave him with me?"

"The Pomeranian stays," I said like Tony Soprano.

I opened the door to the Mercedes, placing Muffy in the back seat, taking Paquito from her to put him in front.

"Can't blame me for trying," she said, waving to him.

"Nope."

We stood there awkwardly for a moment.

"I'm very sorry about Candy," I said.

Twink looked down at the pavement. "Thank you," she said in a barely audible voice. Then she got in her car with a strangled little sob and drove across PCH to the feed store.

I zoomed back to Reba's as fast as the Mercedes would take me, which was pretty damn fast. Fortunately, I didn't attract the attention of any Malibu black and whites in my haste. I rushed to get the pups some food and water, then called Eli's office.

Priss told me he was out but promised he'd call me back on his cell phone. "Have him call right away, okay?" I said to her. "It's really, really important."

"Sure thing," she said before hanging up.

I paced around for ten minutes, trying to get everything straight in my head so I could present it to Eli in a coherent fashion.

Finally, the phone rang.

"Yo, Ker. What's up?"

"Eli, you gotta put the brakes on this mental-competency thing. All kinds of things are popping up. Big things. I'm getting the dead girl's computer tomorrow, and I need an expert to dig some things off the hard drive—and I figure you have access to someone for that—and it turns out the victim was a dominatrix with lots of clients who could also be potential suspects . . . and to top everything off, the District Attorney has DNA evidence that he's not even sharing with you—" I stopped and took a breath. "Eli? You there?"

"What DNA evidence?"

"I have it on good authority that they found semen on the victim."

A beat. "Where'd you hear that?"

"Can't say, but it's a reliable source. The prosecution's supposed to let you know if there's exculpatory evidence, aren't they?"

"Yeah, it's mandated by the Brady doctrine, but they don't actually have to come forward with it until the pretrial conferences. I don't know if you've considered this, but it could also be *incriminating* evidence."

"It's not Robert's," I said firmly.

"Let's hope not. You sure they got it?"

"Like I said, reliable inside source."

"They've probably got it out for analysis. But this is good to know. If we don't see it, we'll know they have something up their sleeve."

"Can you get me a computer expert for the hard drive?"

"I'll get Greg on it right away. You think she's got a kinky client list on the computer?"

"It's worth looking into, isn't it?"

"Definitely."

I heard the call-waiting click. "Gotta go—another call."

"Okay," he said. "Good work."

"Thanks." I clicked over and heard Terry's voice:

"Hey."

"Hey, sis, how's it going in there?"

"Academy Award–winning performance, if I do say so myself. Golden Globes, at the very least. I give good junkie. I said my parents were threatening to cut off my trust fund if I didn't get help for my drug dependence. Young, vulnerable, loaded—yours truly."

"Notice anyone interesting yet?"

"Yeah, there's a woman named Dawn who's glommed on to me. Our age, weighs about eighty pounds. Skinny enough to be a junkie, but doesn't have the haunted look. I think she's a garden-variety bulimic."

"What did she say she was into?"

"Meth. But she's not twitchy. I smell a rat. Anyway, we made a date for herbal tea later. I'll let you know if she says anything suspicious."

"Good. Listen, I met with Twink today. Candy's sister, remember?"

"Do I *remember*?"

"Down, girl. Anyway, I want you to contact her tomorrow. I've got her cell phone number. She believed me when I told her that Robert and Reba aren't guilty, and she's going to bring us Candy's computer so we can get stuff off the hard drive, like her client list and e-mails."

"Great! Leave all the information at the house."

"And there's more good news."

"What?"

"A little birdie told me that the prosecutor has DNA evidence from the victim—semen."

"Was this a *studly* little birdie by the name of Boatwright?"

I laughed. "Yeah."

"So you're back on with him?"

"No! I just . . . went to him for some advice."

"*Mmm-hmmm.*"

"Terry, don't you see what this means? There's direct evidence of the killer, and it will have to come out sooner or later."

"Let's just hope it's not Robert's."

"It's *not Robert's!* God, I'm surrounded by cynics!"

"Yeah, and I'm surrounded by lunatic drug addicts, so we're even." When she heard me sigh, she added, "I'm sure it's Jack the Ripper's jizz, okay?"

"Yeah, yeah."

"So see you tomorrow morning? Shannon says come in through the kitchen and meet us in her office for the debriefing, nine o'clock."

"Okay. Have a nice evening."

"And *you* have a nice evening there at Murder Central. Be sure to lock the windows, leave broken glass in front of the doors, and change all the speed-dial buttons to 911."

"I'm not scared."

"My *ass.*"

"Bite me," I said, and she hung up laughing.

$\mathcal{I}$ *spent the* night with Reba's cell phone on my pillow, the lights burning, CNN blaring on the TV, the pups in the bed with me, and two—count 'em, two—butcher knives on the nightstand.

I probably slept for only three hours total, but fortunately, Mr. Stephen King made no more appearances. And neither did the Mangler of Malibu Canyon.

seventeen

t nine A.M., I was back in Shannon's office at New Horizons. She and Terry were talking when I got in, and I sensed an easy rapport between them. Shannon motioned me to a chair across from Terry's.

"Something to drink?" she said, her assistant, Tad, hovering nearby.

"Vodka, please. Straight up."

Tad's eyes bugged, but Shannon laughed. "I'm afraid our stock of hooch is a little low here at the rehab facility." Tad finally got the joke, giggling behind his hand.

"Water would be fine," I said. Tad scurried off to get some.

"Terry was just filling me in on group therapy," Shannon said to me.

"I've got a couple of candidates," Terry said. "The girl Dawn that I mentioned to you, Ker, and a woman in her fifties by the name of Belinda, with red hair in ringlets, who dresses in muumuus. A real nutcase. She followed me back to my room, and when I remarked that we were housed on the same floor, she got all flustered and said, 'Oh, am I on the second floor? My room's on the first,' then she ran away. So keep an eye on her."

"How was your tea with Dawn?" I asked.

"I was just telling Shannon about that. She asked a ton of questions. Where did I go to high school? How much money did my parents have? How much money did I have? Wouldn't I like to find the solution to all my problems in one place, the ultimate answer to all of life's questions?"

"Sure sounds like she's setting you up for a cult."

"Either that, or she's selling Amway. I'll be looking into her background and Belinda's while you're in here."

"So how did you present yourself?"

"I stuck pretty close to the truth. Said I grew up in Burbank, but embellished when it came to the family finances. Said my father was a movie producer and made a ton of money, so we moved to Beverly Glen when I was in my teens."

I nodded. Sounded simple enough.

"And oh," she added, jerking her cheek muscle. "You've got a twitch. You know, just to look like you're the real thing."

I tried to do a twitch, and Shannon and Terry burst out laughing.

"You're supposed to be nervous," Terry said, "not a total spaz."

"Okay, the twitch comes and goes, if anybody asks," Shannon said. "You ready?" I nodded again. "Group therapy starts at ten. Lunch at twelve. Free time or games in the common room from one to two o'clock. Your choice of t'ai chi or yoga meditation from two-thirty to four. Free time or Ping-Pong from four to five forty-five. Dinner at six. Group therapy again at seven. Free time from nine o'clock to lights-out at nine-thirty. Okay?"

"Gee," I said. "Just like Girl Scout camp."

"More like girls' lockup," Terry said.

"So where can we talk?" I said after we'd left Shannon's office.

Terry pointed to the kitchen. "In there."

"Is the music piped in there, too?"

She laughed. "It's *everywhere*. It's about to drive me back to drugs."

We snuck into the kitchen and huddled next to the huge industrial refrigerator, speaking in whispers.

"Here's Frank's cell phone," I said, handing it to her. "Let's hope he doesn't call while I'm in here. And you can keep our cell phone, because I have Reba's. You have her number, right?"

She nodded.

"So," I said, "you think these two women have something to do with the cult?"

"*Something* has messed with their brains. Might be the cult. But they're not the only ones who are whacked."

"Gee, I'm really looking forward to the next twenty-four hours."

"It's not all bad. In fact, I think I might have got something out of the group therapy, as far as managing my anger."

I looked at her in shock. "Really? It helped you?"

"I think so. All that talk about unflinching honesty, it kind of got to me. Maybe I should go in for more therapy—you know, when we're done with this case."

Well, blow me down.

"Hey. I'm really proud of you, sis. That would be . . . that would be a big step."

She shrugged. "Yeah, I'll think about it."

Fantastic, I thought. Maybe we'd get Robert off booze, and Terry off rage, and everybody off murder charges, and we'd be a normal family when this was all over!

Nah.

"I think *you'll* enjoy group therapy, too," Terry said with a smile. "It's really interesting."

"I'm sure I will."

She moved toward the back door, pink helmet in hand. "You keep your eyes open."

"I will," I said, waving good-bye. "Don't get into any fights."

She pushed through the door. "Who, me?"

Ten o'clock, and time for group. A bunch of us sat on big comfy couches and pillows on the floor. A thin guy in his twenties chewed his cuticles, large blue eyes darting around the room as he gnawed away on himself. A skinny, mousy blonde who was missing some patches of hair had smiled at me when I entered the room. *Dawn.* I nodded to the blowsy woman with her hair in copper ringlets, wearing a baggy dress. *Belinda.*

Terry had been right on with her descriptions of them.

A man who looked seventy but who was probably only forty-five sat cross-legged on the floor, leaning against a wall. A goateed rock 'n' roll heroin junkie whose name was James. The woman in the armchair with cat's-eye glasses and black hair in a bun was Dr. Gustafson.

"Hello, everybody," Dr. Gustafson said, consulting her notes. "Shall we pick up where we left off?"

We all nodded.

"Fine. Now, Faith"—Dr. Gustafson looked straight at me—"you were telling us about your first crush on a girl."

All eyes turned in my direction.

I am going to kill Terry with my bare hands.

"Right," I said, searching my brain for some memory of Terry's painful history as a baby lesbian. Was this some sort of punishment? Was she setting me up for being less than a perfect sister? For not paying attention to her stories of early yearning? Then, as the panic was rising, a name came to me out of the mist. . . .

"Barbara . . . *Deedler!*" I said too loud.

A couple of people leaned back into the sofa cushions.

Dr. Gustafson cleared her throat. "Yes, you were telling us about your and Barbara's first kiss."

I am going to flay Terry's flesh and feed it to the dogs.

"Oh, yes. Our first kiss . . ." I tried desperately to remember my first kiss from a boy, thinking I'd substitute my story for Terry's. Problem was, I had remained unkissed until my sixteenth birthday, and I was sure Terry was stealing same-sex kisses as early as kindergarten.

Oh, just go with it, I told myself. *You're a junkie. You can't be expected to remember what happened to you before you cooked your brain.*

"Yes, Barbara Deedler," I improvised. "It was in the second grade—"

"Third," Belinda said.

"Huh?"

"You said yesterday it was in the third grade."

"Oh, yeah. That's what I meant," I said, twirling my forefinger next to my temple. "*Hoo-hoo.* Fried synapses." I cleared my throat. "Anyway, I'll never forget Barbara. She had the cutest pigtails . . ."

Several of the patients frowned.

"I thought she was bald on account of the chemo," Dawn said.

"*Yes*. The chemo, right! *After* she had the chemo, the pigtails were history, of course. But when first I fell in love with her—oh, it must have been somewhere around the first grade—she had two little pigtails . . . right here on her head."

I stuck my fists up to the sides of my head to demonstrate.

The goateed guy with the craggy flesh looked up at me from the floor, one eye narrowed.

"So anyway," I reminisced, "there I was with my very bald, very brave little girlfriend—a cancer survivor in the third grade, can you imagine?—and we were holding hands under the bleachers—"

"You were in the back of her mother's van," Cuticle-chewer said.

"*Right . . . you . . . are*. Now I remember. We were on our way to the video arcade—"

"You were on your way to see *The Lion King*. You said you'd never forget it!" Belinda was becoming indignant at my cavalier attitude toward first love.

I looked around the room and exploded: "Look, if you're all experts on my life, why do I even have to tell the story?"

Dr. Gustafson blinked in my direction. "Well, I think we were all kind of wondering how it went at the orthodontist."

"The orthodontist?"

"To get your braces unlocked."

And after I feed her to the dogs, I am going to burn all of her photographs.

"Yes, well, it took two hours, but ultimately they were able to separate us with wire cutters. And that's the end of the story."

"Gee," Cuticle-chewer said, "that's kind of anticlimactic."

I shrugged. "Story of my life."

"Very well, then," Dr. Gustafson said. "Now, who else wants to share a story of first love?"

Dawn waved her hand in the air. "I do! I do! I do!"

Cuticle-chewer rolled his eyes. "Dawn's gonna try to dominate the group again."

"Am not!" Dawn said.

"Are too," said Belinda.

"People, people," Dr. Gustafson said. "We're all here for each other. Dawn, you may begin today."

And thus began Dawn's rambling tale of supernatural love.

"*Could you believe* that story?" Belinda slammed her tray on the table next to me, plopping down noisily into her seat. She unfurled her napkin with a *thwap* and shoved it into her lap.

Lunch was chicken in creamy basil sauce with pasta on the side. Not bad for institutional food, I'd been thinking. Glad to see you get something for your ten thousand smackers.

"Story?" I said to Belinda. "You mean the one about Dawn and the visitors?"

She made a big show of rolling her eyes. "I mean, please. The girl's in the wrong place. She needs a rubber room, not a rehab facility."

"Strange things have been known to happen," I said, forking in a mouthful of pasta.

"Right. The aliens abduct her to do experiments on her, and one of them is so smitten that he begs the others to keep her on board and make her his mate. And when they refuse, he jumps ship and she hides him in her bedroom closet until they come and force him back to the ship. Sound like any movies you've seen in the last century?"

"Well, it's no more far-fetched than, say, the Barney and Betty Hill story, and people believe *that*."

She dropped her fork, looking at me like I'd just set fire to the Bible. "Excuse me?" she said. "You don't believe Barney and Betty?"

I'd read about them in my online research. Barney and Betty Hill were a mixed-race couple who told one of the first and most harrowing stories of alien abduction in the sixties. The couple's story came out under hypnosis: Their car froze somewhere out in the country, then they were beamed up to a spaceship where the aliens performed probes of a very unpleasant nature on them. Barney and Betty's experience was kind of a watershed for most alien enthusiasts, or believers, or whatever you wanted to call them. The first nationally publicized incident.

And though it had happened when Martian movies were the rage, the beings the Hills described weren't big papier-mâché rock-monsters or tinfoil-covered Frankensteins or big green blobs. They more closely resembled "Grays." The ones with the big heads and luminous black eyes and small bodies. The ones Grizzie had described as her abductors.

The Hills didn't get *that* from a movie. Subsequent Hollywood depictions of aliens resembling Grays came directly from reports like the Hills'. And Belinda's reaction to my offhanded remark told me she was a true believer.

"I'm not sure I'd believe anything said by a couple named after the Rubbles," I said, deliberately provoking her. "You think there's a little *Bam Bam* Hill out there somewhere?"

Belinda set her jaw. "Betty and Barney's abduction came *before* the Flintstones."

"Okay, okay. But it always comes down to the same thing. Where's the proof?"

She stared at me, as if debating whether to divulge some top-secret info. Finally, she whispered, "The proof . . . is all over the place."

I chewed some chicken. "Yeah, sure. Eyewitness accounts. But where are the nuts, the bolts? Where's any evidence that these advanced civilizations have actually been here in their spaceships?"

She shook her ringlets in disgust. "What makes you think advanced civilizations use nuts and bolts? Look, if we went back in time and visited the cavemen, and one of them tried to tell one of his skeptical buddies about it, don't you think the skeptic would say, 'Oh yeah? Where're their buffalo hides and spears? Where's one of their supposedly smooth skulls? Upright beings without brow ridges—*ha!*'"

I laughed. "Uh, yeah. But Belinda—the fact is, we haven't gone back in time. So that's kind of a dumb analogy."

She stared at me as bright red splotches flamed on her cheeks. Her eyes bugged and her lip quivered and her head began shaking like a paint can mixer. "DON'T CALL ME DUMB!" she screamed.

Everyone turned to look at us. Open mouths full of food.

Belinda shook uncontrollably. She slammed her palms down on the table, then turned her head toward me with jerky little motions, ratcheting it one inch at a time, like some sort of twitchy robot. I instinctively covered my knife with my hand.

"All right?" she said in a tight little voice, squeezing off a demented smile.

I gulped. "All right. Sorry."

She grabbed up her tray and stalked off. I leaned back in my chair and put a hand to my palpitating heart.

Sheesh. What a scary witch!

I took a few minutes to pull myself together before bussing my own tray. Then I stuck my head out of the double doors, looking for her. She was nowhere to be seen, so I headed back up to the common room on the second floor, where I planned to get some soothing chamomile tea.

The only person there was James the junkie. He sat on the couch staring at the TV, a rerun of *Law & Order*.

I poured myself some tea and sat on the opposite end of the couch, setting the cup on the coffee table to cool. After listening to Dawn's bizarre *ET*-esque fantasy and witnessing Belinda's complete personality disintegration, it felt strangely calming to be sitting there next to an avowed heroin addict. He hadn't said much during group—how could he, with Belinda blabbing about her abusive childhood and Dawn going on and on about her alien Romeo? So I hadn't heard his story.

I looked over at him. He didn't look back.

Fine with me. I'd had enough talking for a while, and there was more to come tonight. I started getting into the story on TV, where an Aryan Nation type was yelling about his constitutional right to live surrounded by white people. *The guy should move to Malibu,* I thought. *Nobody here but us honkies.*

"You're lucky," James said quietly.

"Huh?" He'd spoken so softly I wasn't sure I'd heard him correctly. "Lucky?" I said.

"No tracks. You didn't mess up your hands." He looked down at the knobs of scar tissue between his fingers. "How are your arms?"

I pulled on the cuff of my sleeve self-consciously. "Oh. Pretty messed up."

Without warning, he sprang like a cat across the couch, grabbing me at the elbow. He shoved up my sleeve and exposed the skin, which bore no evidence of drug abuse.

Oops.

I thought quickly. "I shot up between my toes."

He bored into my eyes with his own, releasing my arm. "That's what I thought. You're no junkie." He collapsed back on the arm of the couch and stared at the TV.

I was getting hot under the collar, though I knew I shouldn't let myself. This could be it—a cover-blowing moment that could jeopardize the whole operation. Thing was, I'd noticed that a lot of the people here had anger-management problems—Terry and Belinda being prime examples—so I could blow my top and stay right in character.

"What?" I yelled at him.

He kept his eyes on the screen. "You're a liar."

It was true, but it still felt like a personal insult. I wasn't a liar in real life! But wait—my sister was, and that's who I was supposed to be at the moment.

"Dickhead," I said, because that's what Terry would have said.

He turned hate-filled eyes to me. "Lying bitch. What are you doing here?"

"I don't have to explain myself to you," I said, jumping up from the couch.

He grabbed my shirt and pulled me to him. "Yes, you do. 'Cause we're all supposed to be open and honest here as part of our recovery, and we're supposed to feel okay about that 'cause this is a 'safe place' where everyone is telling the truth, and yet there's one of us in here that's lying about who she is and what she's doing here—"

I wrenched my shirt out of his hand, getting down in his face.

"Touch me again and I'll rip your fucking nose off," my sister said with my mouth.

Then I marched out of the room, his eyes burning holes in my back.

I decided to get away from the madding crowd. Hanging out with addicts was proving to be more than a little nerve-racking. I'd noticed that no one spent much time in the lobby. I thought maybe I could hang out there for a while and read a magazine in peace.

But there was no peace from the grating music.

If I had to listen to this mind-bending garbage much longer, it was going make me lose my last remaining marbles. Nineteen hours and counting. I might make it if I could find a way to turn down the volume.

I crept down the hallway on the opposite side of the lobby from the executive offices. Sure enough, there were rooms along the corridor dedicated to building maintenance. An office that said *Engineer*, a closet that said *Supplies*, and the one I was hoping for . . .

Sound System.

The door was unlocked. I pushed it open, prepared to break into a "Is this the ladies' room?" routine if anyone was inside.

The small room was empty. Of humans, anyway.

One entire wall was dedicated to an array of electronics that could stock a whole department at Circuit City. There were dozens of tape decks with toggle switches and knobs, hundreds of lights and buttons, even a microphone for making building-wide announcements.

I ran my finger over the labels underneath the switches. *Intercom, Music,* and, hello—what was this?

Reinforcement.

I thought of the stereo system at EquiSpa and wondered if they did some sort of subliminal reinforcement here under the music. That would certainly explain why you couldn't get away from it. If they could follow you everywhere, constantly impressing your subconscious mind with the idea that you wanted to be clean, it might help to reprogram you into an addiction-free unit. I reached for the volume knob.

The door to the room swung open.

In walked a janitor. He wore a green maintenance man's jumpsuit, and had leaky blue eyes in a sallow, chinless face. A few tufts of hair stuck up from his scalp in greasy shafts. He smelled like he'd just wandered in from a chicken coop, and he looked like the type to have deep, meaningful relationships with the chickens.

"You're not *thupposed* to be in here," he lisped.

"I'm sorry. The music was driving me crazy. I just wanted to turn it down."

He grabbed my wrist and ripped it away from the switches. But he didn't release it. He pulled me to him, our faces close. Then he blasted me with enough halitosis to singe my eyelashes.

"Nobuddy touches the thwitches, exthept for Mr. Peavey," he said in a trailer-park twang. "Go talk to him, you got a problem, hunney."

I broke his hold on my wrist and tried to move past him. But he wouldn't give me room. For an agonizing few seconds we stood there, chin to chin. Was he going to turn me in? Cop a feel?

"Would you move?" I said angrily.

"Sthurely." He gave me a gap-toothed leer, then he moved back to give me just enough space to get to the door. And as I squeezed past him, I would have sworn he thrust his pelvis forward to ensure my hip making contact with his . . .

Ewwww. I ran from the closet and tore across the lobby floor, brushing frantically at the chicken-lover cooties on my hip. Thank God for the annoying music. I couldn't hear myself think about the number of hideous ways that little encounter could have turned out differently.

I needed to talk to Terry right away. It was a scary state of affairs when I felt the only way to restore my sanity was by talking to my psychotic sister. I hurried upstairs to my room to call her.

eighteen

"*W*hat did you do to these people, anyway? They all hate me!"

A moment's silence, then Terry said, "Um, are you being me, Ker? I mean, are you trying to act the way you think I would?"

"Well, yeah. Makes sense, doesn't it?"

"Yes, except that I played it the way I thought *you* would. You know, wimpy and stuff."

"WIMPY?"

"Yeah, like I'm someone going through withdrawal and having a hard time of it."

I gave an exasperated sigh. "You could have *told* me! I've been acting all hard-shelled and bitter and sarcastic."

"Thanks a lot."

"And you could have told me about getting your braces stuck with Barbara Deedler in the third grade! I thought you were so moved by the unflinching honesty! We never had braces!"

Terry laughed. "Hey, I have to have *some* fun, don't I?"

"You said she had cancer! That was for fun?"

"God, don't you know anything about storytelling? You gotta really grab people."

"Never mind. We've got bigger problems."

"What?"

"That guy James confronted me and accused me of not being a junkie."

"What guy James?"

"The Keith Richards look-alike."

"He wasn't there yesterday."

"Are you sure?"

"Sure, I'm sure."

"Well, he got onto me pretty quick. He pulled up my sleeve to look for tracks and accused me of lying. He asked me what I was doing here."

"Shit. Maybe you'd better tell Shannon."

"Not yet. Let me see what happens in group therapy tonight."

"Okay, but be careful around him."

"I will. By the way, those two women you mentioned? They're total alien freaks. No, alien *superfreaks*."

"Dawn and Belinda?"

"Yeah. You think they're the recruiters?"

"Look, if they were recruiting for Abaddon, they'd be more subtle, don't you think? Otherwise, Shannon would have been on to them a long time ago. I don't think they're who we're looking for. This James guy sounds interesting, though."

"He doesn't exactly fit the profile. He's got scars all over his hands, and I don't think he's rich."

"Then how's he paying for it?"

"Hmm. Good question. I'll see what he does tonight."

"And remember . . . *wimpy*."

"Right."

There was a knock at the door. I almost dropped the phone.

"Someone's here!" I whispered to Terry, then disconnected. I shoved the phone under a pillow.

"Yes?" I said through the door.

A young male voice: "It's me, Kent."

Kent? I opened the door to Cuticle-chewer. I hadn't even registered his name in the group therapy session.

He gave me a shy smile. "Hi."

"Hi."

"Are you busy?"

I let my eyes go sideways. "Uh, not really." He struck me as very familiar in his tone and body language. *Now* what had Terry neglected to tell me—that Kent was her new best friend?

"I thought we could have another discussion about"—he drew a breath and lowered his chin, eyes locked onto mine— "*roses*."

Well, at least he didn't want to talk about aliens. I supposed I could talk a little horticulture for a while. Terry said she'd played vulnerable, so maybe she had a long conversation with this poetic-looking guy about American Beauties or something.

"Sure," I said, opening the door. "Come on in."

I sized him up as he entered. Five feet seven, a hundred and thirty pounds at the most. I could take him if I had to. I noticed that he was carrying a scented candle on a saucer. He pulled the curtains closed, darkening the room. Then he sat and lit the candle, placing it in front of him on the cot. He gave a theatrical wave of his arm, indicating that I should sit across from him.

Okay, I thought. *We're having a séance.*

"Sit, and we'll talk about *roses*." He pronounced the word slowly, like it was some sort of code I was supposed to pick up on. I sat on the cot and saw the candle flame reflected in his dark blue eyes. The shadows gave him a gaunt, dangerous look.

"Roses are . . . pretty," I said as an opening salvo.

The room was getting darker around the flickering candle-light.

"We're surrounded by rose petals," he said in a low, heavy voice. "Can you smell them? Can you smell their heady per-fume?" I had no idea what to say, so I nodded. "Let me know when the scent fills up the whole room."

I closed my eyes and took a deep breath, and . . . damned if I didn't smell roses!

Oh, it's the candle, you moron. After a few seconds, I opened my eyes. "I smell them," I announced.

I finally realized what was going on. He was trying to hyp-notize me. No, he was trying to rehypnotize me. This was our second session—maybe even our third—which meant that he had been through this before with Terry. The word "roses" was no doubt a verbal cue planted in Terry's mind during a previ-ous session. A hook designed to make her more susceptible and obedient.

"Just close your eyes and drift," he said softly.

I really wanted to do just that. His voice was lulling me, forcing my body to go limp.

"Let your whole body relax. . . ."

I felt my shoulders loosen. The breath went out of me.

"That's it. Forget all of your problems and let the tension go. . . ."

My head wobbled forward, then bounced back up. I was going under.

Damn, he's good.

I had to resist, to think nonrelaxing thoughts. I had to keep my mind on edge, while making like a rag doll on the outside.

In my imagination, I stepped on a rusty nail. I got an overdraft notice from the bank. I pictured my hands closing around Terry's throat, her eyes bugging. "You think it's funny now, huh, huh?" I yelled at her.

Kent went on for some minutes, walking me down a staircase in my mind into a dark basement, counting backward as I went. With each step, he was directing me farther into the black cavern of the subconscious. I found I was less and less capable of resisting his tempting suggestions to *drift.* . . .

After an indeterminate period, he asked in a whispery voice, "Are you there? Are you in your special place?"

Where was I? It was dark in here. The sound of his voice echoed as if in a water-filled grotto, bouncing off the rock walls. Had I gone under in spite of myself? I'd lost time somewhere.

"Are you there?" he asked again.

I wasn't sure where I was, but I nodded in response to his question.

"Good. Are you ready to accept what I'm going to tell you?"

"Yes."

"Remember what I told you yesterday?" he said in a high sweet voice, as if to a small child. "Are you ready to hear more?"

"Ready," I said in a thick, sleepy voice.

"Abaddon is the one true prophet. Abaddon is bringing the truth of our genesis to the masses. . . ."

"Yes . . . Abaddon brings the truth."

"His work is the only thing of importance in the world today. . . ."

"Yes . . . important work."

"And he has chosen you as his bride."

"Me?" I asked through a sodden haze.

What the hell kind of pickup line was this?

"He prizes your beauty. And above all, your intelligence and sensitivity. He wants to lift you up above the earth monkeys. He wants you to join him as he carries out his millennial mission . . . to share in the secrets of the universe. Will you do that? Will you join him in the work of a lifetime? Will you dedicate yourself, body and soul?"

Now I was sure I was fully conscious, because I wanted to slap him. What a shameless manipulator! Putting women in an altered state and asking them to be some sort of bogus bride—which probably meant bride-for-a-night. But I had to go along, to see what he was up to.

"I will," I said like someone who'd been hit with a tranquilizer dart. I lifted up my cement arms, reaching for him.

He gently pushed my arms back down. "No, you don't give yourself to me, you give of yourself to the mission . . . but thanks for the offer. You will soon be able to throw off the yoke of your earthly life . . . ridding yourself of all those burdensome physical possessions and all that filthy lucre—"

"Yes, I want to unburden myself and be free."

"Good, good . . . so you shall be . . . you will divest yourself of these obstacles to enlightenment. . . . You won't need them where you're going. . . . Now do you remember what you are to do in order to remove the obstacles?"

I was stuck. What could I say?

I nodded.

"Good," he said. "You will liquidate your holdings, then you will be given instructions on where to wire the money."

"Yes, I will divest . . . I will wire the money."

"Excellent. Now remember, if anyone asks you about any of this, you say nothing."

"I say nothing."

"You have never heard of Abaddon or the Children of the

Cosmos. You will have no memory of our conversations until you hear the music signal."

"I will have no memory of our conversations."

He sounded satisfied. "Abaddon will be so happy that you have decided to join him. I will be your contact. When you pick up the phone, you will hear this. . . ." He began to hum a tune: *"Hm hmmm hm hm hm hm hmmmm hmm hmmmm . . ."*

I couldn't quite place it. An old Rat Pack song, maybe?

"Hm hm hm hmm hm hm hmm hm hmmmm . . ."

I got it! "That Old Black Magic."

What kind of guru was this, recruiting millennial foot soldiers with Sammy Davis, Jr.'s greatest hits? I hummed along with him, mostly to avoid giggling, as I remembered the lyrics:

> *In a spin,*
> *Lovin' the spin I'm in,*
> *Spinnin' that old black magic called . . .*
> *LOVE!*

And Kent signaled the end of the session by blowing out the candle.

"In five minutes, you will awake refreshed, with no memory of our conversation." He opened the door, looking both ways down the hallway. "See ya in group, Faith," he said, as he disappeared through the door.

As soon as he was gone, I fell off the cot laughing. I rolled around, one hand clutching my abdomen, the other pressed against my mouth. I rocked back and forth until I finally had control of the giggles.

"See ya in group, Sammy, Jr.!"

I got up and looked at myself in the mirror. My mascara had smudged itself into raccoon eyes. How long had our little session lasted? I noticed for the first time that there were no clocks in the room.

Then I remembered that the cell phone had a clock. I reached under the pillow and pulled it out. The LCD screen was illuminated. Had I left it on? I put it to my ear and heard an open line.

"Terry?" I said into the phone. "Terry? Are you still there? Can you hear me?"

"I will have no memory . . ." she intoned like an automaton.

"I know, wasn't that great? This guy's a hoot! Why didn't you tell me about becoming the Bride of Abaddonstein?"

"I have never heard of Abaddon or the Children of the Cosmos," she said in a thick, sleepy voice.

Oh shit. She wasn't kidding. Terry had listened into the whole session and had been rehypnotized. I had to snap her out of it!

"Terry! Wake up!"

"I have no knowledge . . ."

I did my best impersonation of our dear departed mom: "Theresa Elaine McAfee! You stop that nonsense this instant, young lady!"

There was a pause, then she whined, "I didn't do it, Ma! It was Kerry!"

"Terry, it's me. Listen, you've been hypnotized, do you understand?"

"You like her better than me!"

"It's your sister, *Kerry!* Listen to me very carefully. . . . You've been hypnotized and I need you to snap out of it . . . *right this minute!*"

There was another momentary silence while her brain switched gears, then: "Huh? Oh . . . hi. How's it going?" she asked in a normal voice.

I released my breath. Thank God—she was back with us. "Ter, something funky's been happening to you. Here's what I need you to do—stay exactly where you are. Don't move a muscle until I get there. And whatever you do, do *not* answer the phone. I won't call you again, I'll just show up."

"But you can't leave now. We're not done there yet."

"Oh yes, we are. I found out what's been going on. I'll tell Shannon and I'll be back home in an hour, okay? Sit with the dogs and don't speak to anyone else. Promise me!"

"Okay, but chill out, all right?"

"Wait for me," I said, and disconnected carefully.

I gathered my things in the knapsack, as I reflected on how the Cosmos Kids were operating. Kent was probably one of several agents who wormed their way into the rooms of the patients and hypnotized them. Then when they left the place, their victims were clean and sober, and to all outward appearances, ready to become responsible members of society again.

Only now they'd have a secret mission. They'd clean out their bank accounts and wire all their money to offshore accounts that belonged to the Children of the Cosmos.

Insidiously brilliant, and possibly the key to Robert's missing days. He might have been hypnotized and sent on some mission that was beyond his conscious ability to recall—set up to take the fall for Candy's murder.

Flush with my success, I closed up the knapsack, threw the lock on the door, rushed out into the hallway, and—

A hand grabbed my arm. Another hand pressed a cloth against my nose and mouth, with an oddly pleasant smell.

Chloroform.

Oh shiiiiiiiiiiiiiiiiiiitttttttt . . .

nineteen

$\mathcal{I}$ woke up in the darkness of a shroud, hands and feet bound, mouth gagged. I was curled up in the fetal position on the floor of a moving vehicle. A van of some sort, I thought. How long had I been unconscious?

Were we going north or south? I thought I felt a rise in elevation, so that must mean north. What's north, Santa Barbara? But there were a lot of twists and turns. We could be in the Sierra Nevadas by now.

I had to concentrate on getting out of these bindings.

What my kidnapper didn't know was that I had a secret weapon: double-jointed fingers and thumbs. As a kid, I'd been able to hold my fingers rigid and bend only the first joint, giving the other kids hours of squealing pleasure.

Freak-o fingers! Deform-o hands! they'd shouted in grossed-out glee.

And I could pull my bottom thumb joint in, so that the thumb appeared to be sprouting from the inside of my palm. . . . I got even bigger shrieks of delighted horror from that.

Until now, this had always seemed like more of a curse than a blessing. Now I was giving thanks to whatever higher wisdom had bestowed these weird digits on me, and made a solemn vow never to complain about my freckles or my bra size again.

I pulled my left thumb joint in and began to work the heel of that hand through the rope. If I could just get it all the way through before he came back, I'd have a chance to . . .

What? Brain him with a tire iron?

The van came to a stop. *Damn.* He got out and slammed his door. I heard him walk around the back of the van, then he slid open the side door and jerked me by the arm, dragging me across the floor. He grabbed me up in his arms, carrying me up some steps, then opened a door and went into a building.

I thought I detected the scent of creosote. We might be in the middle of the desert. The middle of nowhere.

Great.

The door sounded like wood on wood, but that didn't tell me anything, except that it was probably not a commercial building.

He shoved me down on the floor against a wall. I heard him toss something down next to me—my knapsack. Then he whipped the canvas bag off of my head.

I swear to God, if I live through this, no bag is ever coming within ten feet of my head again!

"Ugh!" I said through the drool-soaked gag.

My vision cleared and I beheld my kidnapper.

James! The burnt-out rock 'n' roll junkie. Boy, if kidnapping, gagging, and bagging women was his idea of "unflinching honesty" . . .

"I'll be right with you, babe. Hold your horses," he said, then exploded with laughter. "Ha! I'm fucking funny. I should say, hold your *horse*."

We were in a cabin. But it was a finished cabin. Nice wood paneling, good rustic furniture. I leaned against the wall, hands behind my back.

And I almost had the binding loose.

He squatted down in front of me, snapping on some latex gloves. "Okay, doll face. Now we're going to get you those tracks on your arms. . . ."

"Ugh! Ugh!" I said through the gag.

"You want to know why I'm doing this?"

I nodded.

"Well, you don't really need to know, do you? Now, I'm just gonna roll up your sleeve. This won't hurt a bit."

I looked down in horror. He was holding a hypodermic needle. Dammit, this was twice in one year somebody had pulled this shit on me, and it was making me *very* angry!

"You've never done intravenous drugs in your life, have you? You little liar."

"Ugh hunh!" I grunted indignantly. Seemed like some creep was *always* shooting me up with something or other.

But why this time? Last time, I thought it was in order to frame me for a murder. But it turned out the maniac had actually intended to kill me. . . .

Oh dear.

"That's right," he said, reading the fear in my eyes. "I'm gonna kill you. But it's gonna look like you got high and shot yourself." He looked up at a walnut-handled Beretta and a hunting rifle that hung over the fireplace.

"First things first," he said, rising to grab the Beretta. He wrenched my right arm toward him. Fortunately, my shoulder wouldn't give too much, so my left hand was still concealed behind my back and was almost, by this time, free. . . .

He pressed my right palm around the butt of the gun, then grabbed my forefinger and mashed it against the trigger.

"There. That should do it. A nice big print from your sweaty little finger."

He laid the pistol down and began readying the hypodermic. "You're gonna go out on a cloud of bliss," he said, looking at the needle fondly. "Ahh . . . maybe when I'm done with you, I'll have a little taste, just for old times' sake." He wrapped a rubber strip around my left biceps, pulling it tight, then slapped the inside of my arm to raise a vein.

I was furiously working my left hand. He took it for a struggle to avoid the needle. "I said it wouldn't hurt," he warned, "but it will if you keep moving."

A vein presented itself, plump and blue.

He jabbed in the needle. I screamed through the gag. He pushed the plunger home just as I got my left hand out of the rope. . . .

I slammed a left hook into the side of the head. He went over, sprawling on the floor, taking the needle with him.

I whipped up my bound feet and brought them down hard on the side of his skull. He hollered in pain.

I pulled my feet back again, legs to my chest, then slammed the soles of my boots straight into his face. His head snapped back and hit the hearth of the stone fireplace.

His eyes stared, open but unseeing. Blood gushed from his nose and onto the floor. I didn't know if I'd killed him or just knocked him out.

Then I got the rush. *Ahh, morphine for the soul.*

I felt myself take flight—all was bliss. I marveled at the sudden beauty that flooded my senses and thought about lying down on the perfect, perfect floor. . . .

No, Kerry. Untie yourself! Get up! You've been drugged!

I tried, but my fingers were rubbery. Almost useless. Through a gigantic force of will, I got them working and untied the knot around my ankles. But I felt myself getting heavier, sleepier . . .

Get up! Get up and run! He could wake up any minute!

I saw my knapsack on the floor. I hooked my elbow through its strap, lurched to the door, and slammed my wrist into the knob. Then I remembered: *Fingers. Use your fingers.*

Somehow I threw the bolt and got the door open, stumbling out into the clear twilight air. I'd been gone for hours. Surely, they'd be looking for me by now.

I started down the road, dragging my uncooperative feet.

A pickup truck whizzed by. I waved my arms and said, "Ugh!"

I still had the gag in my mouth.

Either the driver hadn't seen me or he'd decided to pass me by.

I started working on the tight little knot at the back of my head. I couldn't begin to untie the gag—not enough manual dexterity. But my saliva had caused the fabric to stretch, so I was able to yank it down over my chin.

I tried to work some of the stiffness out of my jaw. I wiggled it around, stretching my bottom lip up toward my nose. I probably looked like Billy Bob Thornton in *Slingblade*. I'd probably sound like him, too, if I said anything.

I gave it a try:

"Can ouuu heppp meee, missther?" (Drool.) "I bin ki-napppp . . ."

Never mind. I'll use sign language.

I glimpsed headlamps through the trees below. Cars. Civilization. But they were far away, at the bottom of the mountain. I thought I could make it.

I stumbled down the rocky road toward the lights. And got as far as a house around the next bend. . . .

The front door was open. Someone inside would help me!

I got myself up the stairs and staggered inside to see a welcoming blaze in the fireplace. I shuffled toward it, then saw a door to my left. Maybe the homeowner was in there. . . .

I pushed open the door and saw a large bed covered in a soft downy comforter.

Mmmm . . . bed, I remember thinking.

It was my last conscious thought until I woke up in the slammer.

twenty

"*Y*our lawyer's here," said a gruff woman's voice.

I sat up painfully. "Huh? Where am I?"

"You're in Disneyland, Snow White. And I'm your old pal Grumpy. Now, come on, move it."

I looked at my watch. Two A.M. I rubbed at scratchy eyes that felt like somebody'd let the air out of them.

The guard grabbed me by the arm and dragged me through the door of my cell. "Have a nice nappy-poo?"

"Can you tell me what happened? I don't remember anything after—"

"After what, you killed your party buddy?" This caused her to hawk up a laugh. "No, don't tell me. Your lawyer'll just make a big stink about it."

She opened a windowed door into a small interrogation room. "All yours," she said, tossing me inside.

I stumbled over the threshold and saw Eli at the table, battered briefcase open in front of him. "Eli! I killed him?"

He grimaced and drew his fingers across his lips.

"I didn't hear that," the guard said, as she withdrew, slamming the door behind her.

Eli got up from the table and took me in his arms.

"It was self-defense, I swear!"

"Shhh, sweetheart," he said, patting my back. "I know that. But you'd better have a seat, and I'll tell you how it looks."

I fell into a chair across from him, arms on the table. My head was wobbly on my neck, and I felt like a jackhammer was going to town on my brain. "How does *what* look?"

"Well, whoever you were partying with—"

"Partying with! I was kidnapped!"

"I'm telling you what it *looks* like, please. We'll get to your story in a second."

"Sorry," I said, pinching the shrieking muscles at the base of my skull.

"Okay, you were partying with some guy in a cabin in Malibu Canyon . . ."

So we'd never even left Malibu.

". . . there was some kinky sex play . . ."

What? I swallowed a scream.

". . . you had this knotted kerchief around your neck and rope burns on your wrists. You were high as a kite. Things got a little rough. You took the pistol down from the fireplace and you either bashed him on the head with the butt of the gun or you shot him—"

"Somebody *shot* him?"

"They don't know. There's no body."

"Then how—?"

"The gun had been fired."

"I didn't do it!"

He waved a hand impatiently. "Then you ran, panicked, but the drugs got to you and you broke into somebody's house and crashed. They found you curled up with your thumb in your mouth like Goldilocks, sleeping in their bed. They were able to trace you back to the original cabin and found your prints all over the pistol on the floor."

"Duh! 'Cause he put them there!"

"I *said* you'd get a chance to tell your side of the story." He sat back in his chair and folded his hands over his stomach. "G'head."

"They think I killed him?" I asked shakily.

"Like I said, they haven't found a body or a bullet. But there's blood on the fireplace stones and lots of it on the floor."

"Did they give me a gunshot-residue test?"

"No, they were waiting for you to wake up. Now, go. This oughta be good."

"First tell me—is Terry okay?"

"Sure she's okay. After they booked you, they called her and she called me. They noticed you were missing at New Horizons when you didn't go to group therapy at seven o'clock. They were looking for you frantically when Terry got the call."

"And Terry . . . was she acting strange at all?"

He shrugged. "No stranger than normal."

"Who called her?"

"Your pal Detective Thomas."

I cringed to think that Thomas had seen me dragged into the station, drooling and out of my mind. But I had absolutely no memory of it.

"Why didn't they question me? I haven't spoken to anyone that I can remember."

"They can't interrogate you when you're obviously high—

your statement wouldn't be worth anything to them. They had a doctor check you out, and he told them to let you sleep it off. They'll want to talk to you now, but I'm not letting 'em near you."

"Thomas will believe me! He knows I'm investigating the murder."

"Even if he does, what's he supposed to do? You were caught with your pants down, so to speak."

"Eli, you gotta believe me. I kicked him in the face, but I swear I didn't shoot him. I was just trying to get away!"

"Look, it makes no difference to me. Frankly, I think it's refreshing that someone from your family is willing to claim innocence."

I slumped back in my seat. "*Claim* innocence? It makes no difference to you if I'm a murderer or not?"

He gave me a stone-blank stare. "So your story is that you kicked him in the face. That works for me."

"My story *works* for you? Well, that's great, 'cause it's the truth!"

"Whatever."

God, he was exasperating!

"Eli, he's no buddy of mine. His name is James. He was in my therapy group in the morning. He accused me of not being a real junkie, then he came to my room, chloroformed me, and dragged me to the cabin and shot me up with heroin."

"People are always doing that to you."

"I know. Pisses me off."

"Okay. So then what happened?"

"He told me he was going to make it look like a suicide. He pressed my fingers against the trigger, but I managed to get my hands free because I'm double-jointed in my hands, and I kicked him in the face. He hit his head on the fireplace, then

I hauled myself down the mountain and I guess I—I ended up in somebody's bed."

"Okay, I believe you!" he said with a broad smile of appeasement. "But the police won't. Now, here's what I'm going to do. If they bring murder charges against you—"

"Murder charges? You said there's no body!"

"That doesn't mean they can't bring charges. Especially if they can identify the guy and he's gone missing. I hate to say it, but they're looking at you with a very jaundiced eye after what happened with Reba and Robert."

I sank forward, arms on the table, utterly depressed.

"Hey, it's not all bad news. I can plead insanity for you, too. And baby makes three, see? It plays right into my family-psychosis defense."

"No!"

"Whaddaya mean, no?"

"I mean I'm not going to plead not guilty by reason of my gene pool!"

"Look, there are no murder charges yet. I'm just trying to give you a worst-case scenario."

"Thanks a lot. What do they have on me now?"

"Under the influence, two counts of attempted burglary. Strictly chump charges. I'll have you out later this morning on bond."

"Burglary? How does that figure? You said I was asleep."

He shrugged. "Theft of clean sheets? I don't know. You're accused of entering someone's dwelling with the intent to commit larceny. It's just your bad luck that you fell asleep before you could rob them."

I sighed. "Terry's got money for the bond."

"Don't worry, you're covered."

"I'm good for it, I promise. I'll pay you back every penny."

"Oh no, not me. Your friend at the rehab place is picking up the tab."

"What friend?"

"Your employer, Shannon Voss. I spoke to her before I came over here. She said to tell you how sorry she was, and she promises that she'll get to the bottom of it."

"She can identify James! She can tell the police I'm not lying!"

"See? Nothing to worry about."

"For now, I need you to get me out of here. You sure you can do it?"

He frowned, stung to the core. "Hey. They don't call me the Great Bondini for nothing. I got a strategy that can't lose."

I squinted at him. "Not the 'apple doesn't fall far from the tree' thing."

"No, something else. But listen, I want you to take it easy for a while after you get out, okay? You've made a big, hairy mess of things, babe."

I gave him a sardonic smile. "Yeah, well, sharpen your razor. 'Cause things are gonna get a *lot* hairier."

"Good morning, Counsel." We were back in court, only this time I was seated at the defendant's table.

Eli and Harlon Pinchbeck stood to acknowledge Judge Ratliff's greeting.

"Morning, Judge," they said.

They asked me to confirm my name and address. I did so as well as I could, considering that spelunking gnomes were chipping away at the inside of my skull with vicious little chisels. They read the charges against me: violation of California Penal

Code, Section 459, attempted burglary in the first degree . . . entry of an inhabited dwelling with the intent to commit larceny . . . under the influence of a controlled substance . . .

Finally: "How does the defendant plead?"

I stood. "Not guilty, period."

"Period?" the judge said.

I swallowed. "I mean not guilty, but not for some . . . reason like . . . family insanity."

Shut up, Kerry.

Eli stood to help me out. "My client pleads not guilty, Your Honor."

"There. That was easy, wasn't it?" Judge Ratliff said to me, smiling.

"We'd like to request bail, Your Honor," Eli said.

"We'll hear from the people."

Harlon Pinchbeck stood up and looked down at the toe of his leather wingtip as if to gather his thoughts, then cleared his throat and looked up again with fire in his eyes.

"If it please the court, I would like to point out that this"— a bony finger flew in my direction—"is the third member of the same family to be arrested on felony charges this week. Your Honor, the Price-Slathertons and Ms. McAfee here are all fruit of the same rotten tree."

Arrrgh. I *knew* that tree business was going to get in here somehow.

The judge looked at Eli, his eyebrows peaked. "She's one of *that* family?"

Eli nodded. "Ms. Price-Slatherton is Ms. McAfee's greataunt."

"Your Honor," Pinchbeck said, "I submit that this entire family represents a danger to decent, law-abiding society—"

The judge lifted a silencing hand. "The matter before us is *State v. McAfee.*"

Pinchbeck's body twisted back and forth, like he was trying to screw himself into the floor, his voice rising to a fever pitch. "The defendant was found *drugged out of her mind*, having broken into an inhabited dwelling with intent to commit robbery and who knows what other forms of mayhem. Her prints were found on a gun at another house up the road, and blood was found in large quantities on the floor!"

The judge frowned at me, then looked down at the complaint. "There's no mention here of an assault."

"We haven't established the identity of the victim in that incident, Your Honor. But as I indicated, we have the defendant's fingerprints on a handgun at the location. We need to keep her in custody until the full nature of this incident can be ascertained."

"I see," said the judge.

"Presumably, the defendant has access to her aunt's offshore bank accounts and real estate. She's an extreme flight risk and a danger to the community." Pinchbeck glared at me, hatred rising off him like steam off a dog turd on a cold morning. "I implore Your Honor, for the safety of this city, for the welfare of our women and children . . . this family of cold-blooded killers must not be allowed to freely roam the earth!"

Jesus, he made us sound like a family of tyrannosaurs.

Pinchbeck sat down quickly, then his whole body shivered, as if he'd just looked evil in the face.

Eli turned to me, giving me an avuncular smile, and patted my shoulder. "Please the court," he said, standing, "the defendant is indigent. She's too proud to take a penny from her rich relations."

I wanted to roll my eyes, but I was afraid it might be interpreted as contempt of court.

"I'm acting as counsel at the behest of her current employer, and as her previous employer myself, I can attest to her high moral fiber, her absolute trustworthiness, and her deep and abiding ties to the community. She has no prior convictions, Judge." He paused, gripping his hands together at his chest. "Plus, she's a national hero. One of the Smith twins . . . you know, the ones who creamed the hijackers on that Hawaii flight!"

Groan.

"She is?" the judge said. "Good work, young lady. Wish we had more like you. Very well, I will grant bail at ten thousand dollars."

"Thank you, Your Honor," Eli said.

He grabbed up his briefcase and hustled out of the courtroom to post bond. The prosecutor flung eye daggers at me as the bailiff ushered me out the side door and back to the holding cell to await my release.

Within an hour, I was back on the street in front of the jail. I heard the thrumming of a motorcycle engine and saw my twin waving to me from the pink Harley. Awash in relief, I grabbed Eli around the middle and hugged him.

"Thanks, Eli. I can't believe you turned the judge around like that. Even I thought I was Jeffrey Dahmer after the prosecutor's statement."

"Nothin' to it."

"I didn't want to exploit the hijacking thing, but if it's my get-out-of-jail-free card, I guess I shouldn't complain."

"Right. You gotta use whatever you can. Now, remember what I said? Don't do nothin' stupid."

"Have a little faith, Eli."

I ran to the motorcycle and grabbed a helmet from Terry.

"Coffee!" I yelled over the roar of the engine.

She nodded. I hopped on the back of the bike, and we were off for some post-incarceration java and jawing.

twenty-
one

$\mathcal{W}$e sipped cappuccinos at the same coffee shop in Malibu where Twink and I had met previously. I gave Terry the short version of what I'd been through, and she whistled in awe.

"Wow, Ker. You were honest-to-God kidnapped! That is some scary shit!"

"I know."

"Are you okay?"

"Sure."

"How did you get out of the bindings?"

"I used the old 'deformo-thumb' trick," I said, demonstrating. She gave me a double-jointed high five. "Brilliant, baby!"

"Elementary, my dear Twatson."

"So . . . we think it was the Children of the Corn that had you kidnapped?"

"Children of the *Cosmos*," I corrected her.

"Whatever. We think it was them?"

"No. Here's why: One of their guys came in and tried to hypnotize me into being a follower of Abaddon just before I was kidnapped. Now, why would they bother converting me if immediately afterwards they were going to kill me?"

"Then who is this James person? Who's he working for?"

"Don't know. But the fact that I was kidnapped means that someone besides the Cosmos Kids is up to something at New Horizons. And somebody on the inside has to know about it."

"But who? Peavey?"

I shrugged. "We need to get over there right away and talk to Shannon."

"Right, so . . . hypnosis? That's how they get people?"

"Yeah," I said, studying her face. I wanted to know if Terry had any lingering posthypnotic suggestibility, but I didn't know how to test her for it. I couldn't just come out and ask her; she'd only deny it.

"Yoo-hoo!" She waggled her fingers. "You're staring at me. It's kind of creeping me *out*."

I began to hum "That Ol' Black Magic":

"Mmm hm hm hm hm hm mm hmm hm hm . . ."

She frowned. "Are you having a stroke?"

I put more feeling into it. *"Mmm hm hm hm hmm, hmm hm hm mm mm . . ."*

"Can you talk? Nod if I should call 911."

I shook my head impatiently. "Wouldn't you like to talk about *roses*?" I intoned like Boris Karloff.

She lowered her chin and answered slowly. "All right. Let's talk about . . . *roses*."

I stared straight into her pupils, bending her to my will. "The roses . . . do you smell them?"

She breathed in. "Yes, I smell the roses . . ."

"And will you now do my bidding?"

"Yes, I will do your bidding . . . right after I smack the shit out of you!" She bonked me on the head. "What are you *doing*?"

I laughed. "It's okay, take it easy. You're all right."

She gave me a puzzled look. "What do you mean?"

"Listen, the guy who tried to hypnotize me had already hypnotized you, as far as he was concerned. I was checking for posthypnotic suggestion."

"What guy?"

"Kent. The guy with the bloody cuticles. It was obvious he had been to your room and had a session with you."

"No way."

"Yes way."

She shook her head, arms crossed. "Ker, I can't be hypnotized. I'm too stubborn."

"He told both of us that we'd have no memory of the sessions."

"Then how come you remember this alleged session?"

"Because I figured out what was happening and I didn't let myself go under."

She gave me a snide look. "Oh, yeah. You're so brave and strong and true, nobody could hypnotize *you*."

"Terry, this isn't a competition. I suspected something was up from his strange use of the word 'roses,' like it was a psychological hook or something. It put me on guard. And yeah, I think if you weren't tipped off, somebody could easily trick you into it. So just imagine, if they go into someone's room every day and do this number on them, reinforcing the idea day in and day out that they want to hand over all their money to Abaddon, then when they get to the end of the rehabilitation period—"

I stopped as a terrible thought occurred to me.

"What?" Terry said, seeing the look on my face.

"Um, I was just wondering. Where's our money—the money Frank gave us?"

She shrugged. "It's . . . it's—"

"Where is it? You had it."

She blinked rapidly. "I . . . I can't remember, right offhand."

"Oh shit! What have you been doing while I was away? Did you get the computer from Twink?"

Her mouth hung open. "No, she blew me off. Said the police had already confiscated the computer."

"So what else? What did you do the whole time I was in jail?"

"This and that . . . stuff, you know."

I jumped up and grabbed her by the collar. "What stuff?"

"I don't remember!" she wailed in agony.

I released her shirt. "Terry, is it possible you went to the bank and deposited Frank's money?"

"No!" she yelled, then looked at me desperately. "Could I have?"

I began rummaging through her pockets, yanking out a couple of bank receipts. Sure enough, there was a deposit slip for twenty thousand dollars.

"You put the money in the bank, enough to tip off the government, and you think it was *your* idea?"

She grabbed the receipt from me and stared at it, stunned beyond speech. I looked at the other receipt and my worst fears were confirmed.

"It's been wired to another bank. Probably in the Caymans or somewhere."

"The Caymans? We don't have a—"

"The Cosmeteers probably do. And, oh no . . . Reba does,

too! Oh boy, I hope the prosecutor doesn't get wind of this. Eli said I was indigent."

"The prosecutor? What about the IRS? We're gonna report cash we got paid by a mobster, and pay taxes on it besides? With what? That's the only money we had!" She threw herself down on the tabletop. "Oh my God, I was hoodwinked!"

"Now you know how it feels. Look, we have to go to someone and get you deprogrammed."

"Why? What's the point? They can send me to the bank all they want—we don't have a dime!"

"Maybe they can get you to sell the motorcycle or sign over the deed to the house. . . . Anyway, you can't have our cell phone anymore. That's how they do it. They call you and send you a signal over the phone."

She reached into her jacket and handed the phone to me, shame-faced. I slipped it into my knapsack. "I'll take Frank's phone, too." She gave it to me and it went into my jacket pocket.

"What are we gonna do? Go to the cops?" Terry said, on the brink of tears.

I shook my head. I didn't think we'd get a sympathetic ear from the police, not with our record lately.

And then it came to me, in a flash of inspiration that pierced the clouds of my mind like a crack of lightning. And a voice spoke to me from above, telling me precisely what to do.

I found Dwight Franzen's business card and slapped it on the table in front of Terry. "No, not the cops, Clarice. We're going all the way to the *F* . . . *B* . . . *I!*"

"Yeah!" she said, sitting up like a little dog.

"But first, we're going back to New Horizons to talk to Shannon Voss."

$\mathcal{T}he\ guard\ leaned$ out of his shack with the phone still at his ear. "Ms. Voss can't see you," he said, a superior smile on his fat face.

Terry grabbed the phone from his hand. "This is bullshit!" she yelled into the receiver. Then she dropped the phone, angled the bike, and gassed it, popping up onto the curb on the right side of the barrier. She ran over the grass, bumping down off the curb on the other side. I looked back at the guard and saw him staring at us openmouthed.

He charged out of the shack, wrestling his gun from the holster. Terry screeched up to the front door and killed the engine. We calmly got off the bike and rang the bell. The guard reached us just as Amanda Exeter opened the door.

"Freeze!" he yelled, pointing his gun at our backs.

Amanda threw her hands in the air. "It's okay!" she said to him. "They can come in!"

He reluctantly lowered his gun. "You sure?"

She nodded. "Go back to your post."

"I can call the cops," the rent-a-cop said breathlessly, drooling at the prospect of being embroiled in a real-life police matter.

Amanda glared at him. "Nobody's calling the cops, okay? Now get your lard ass back in that shack this second!"

Whoa. Ms. Goody Two-shoes had an edge.

The guard shuffled back to his shack, holstering his gun as he went. "Let me know if you want me to call the cops or anything," he muttered over his shoulder.

"I'm so sorry about that," Amanda said to us, instantly morphing back into Miss Professional. "I know Ms. Voss is most anxious to see you, but she isn't here just now. Can we make an appointment for you at a later time?" She consulted the ever-present notebook. "How's tomorrow at three o'clock? I'll have to confirm with her assistant, of course."

Terry gave her The Look. "Oh, see, Amanda. That's not gonna work for us, because my sister got kidnapped from this place, and I think maybe somebody needs to talk to us about it sooner than that, like *right now*."

Looking into Terry's eyes, Amanda evidently decided to can the über-assistant act. "I'm sorry, she's not here. Honest, I"—a little fear crept into her voice—"I really don't know where she is. She isn't answering her cell phone, her home phone, or her pager."

Terry looked at me. "Have you called the police?"

Amanda shook her head. "No, I mean . . . if it turned out she was shopping or something . . . She can be pretty tough when you get her mad. Her assistant was afraid to call them, actually."

"Why don't you have Peavey call?"

She laughed nervously. "He's afraid of her, too."

"Then how about we have a meeting with Mr. Peavey," Terry said. "Somebody around here needs to talk to us." She shoved her way past Amanda and into the lobby, and I followed, Amanda trotting along beside us.

"Okay, but I want you to know, he's pretty shaken up, what with all that's happened," she said with a guilty look.

"Not half as shaken up as I am," I assured her.

Amanda ran ahead of us and knocked on Peavey's door, pushing it open simultaneously. "Mr. Peavey?"

"No calls!" came the shout from inside.

"The McAfees are here—"

"I'm in conference!"

Terry rolled her eyes, then thrust open the door, striding into the office. "Sorry, Wendell. But you're here. And you need to do some talking."

He sprang up behind the desk, his mouth hanging open, then looked at Amanda accusingly. "Oh, the *McAfees*. You really must learn to enunciate, my dear. I thought you said 'a pack of thieves.' Ha. Thought you were joshing me."

She gave him an *Eat dirt, boss* look, then ducked out of the room.

"Please, sit down," Peavey said, plopping his butt down in his executive chair. "I'm sorry, Ms. Voss isn't here to talk with you."

"Where is she?" Terry said, not one to let a squirming body off the hook so easily.

"I expect her shortly. She had personal business to attend to this morning."

"Uh-huh," I said. "I assume she kept you informed of our activities here with regards to the investigation."

"Well, I had a vague idea, but you know, I've been very busy. . . . There's so much paperwork in this job, you can't imagine. The state wants everything in duplicate and triplicate and—"

"Let us fill you in," Terry said, cutting him off. "This is what we're going to be telling the FBI as soon as we leave you. You had an alleged patient here by the name of Kent. I don't know what his cover story is, but the real story is that he's a recruiter for Abaddon, the intergalactic prophet of doom. These Children of the Cosmos come in here and hypnotize your patients right under your nose, and you supposedly know nothing about it. They brainwash them into giving Abaddon the money to fund his arsenal or build his bunker or buy him a Ferrari to take him back to his home planet—"

"The FBI?" Peavey said, stuck on what she'd said at the start of her harangue. "Well, surely there's no reason to get them involved. I'm certain we can settle this thing without all that folderol."

"Settle this thing?" Terry said, aghast.

"Yes, I understand that you underwent a certain amount of pain and suffering during your ordeal." He gave her a look of deep sympathy, but she pointed at me. "Sorry, *your* ordeal," he said, turning the sorrowful pig eyes in my direction.

"It would have been more of an ordeal if she'd been killed," Terry said.

"Yes, thank goodness for that. Now, I'm sure we can arrange to compensate you for all the bother. . . ."

I couldn't believe it. Wendell Peavey wanted to buy us off and sweep the whole thing under the rug?

"If I'd had any inkling that this little . . . investigation would be physically dangerous for anyone," he rambled on, "I'd have put a stop to it before it began. I'm frankly surprised that our own head of legal affairs has put us in such a precarious position in terms of liability."

Again with the liability. This guy had a one-track mind.

"You are really missing the point, Mr. Peavey," I said firmly. "You have a criminal enterprise operating at your facility. And on top of that, one of your alleged patients kidnapped me and tried to kill me. Now, it's imperative that you bring in the law-enforcement authorities to deal with the situation. Are you getting this?"

"And the first thing you need to do is turn over your patient records so we can find out who 'Kent' and 'James' are," Terry told him.

Peavey blanched, slumping back in his chair. "But those records are strictly confidential. Why, if we started giving people access to patient records, we could be sued."

Terry gave me an *I am not believing this* look.

"Wendell," she said. "They weren't real patients—they have no right to confidentiality."

He looked down at his wedding ring and gave it a little twist. "I have only *your* word for that."

Terry gave a grunt of incredulity. "Yes, but you people hired us specifically to get that information! You said it yourself—they were infiltrating the place!"

Peavey looked back up at us, and I saw that his face was different; he no longer wore the look of distracted befuddlement. "Yes, yes, yes. And you allege that one of our patients kidnapped you, but we've no proof of that either, have we?"

My jaw dropped, and I looked over at Terry. Her head was shaking in disgust over what she was hearing.

"And I'd like to point out that *I* didn't hire you. Shannon Voss did," he said, venom icing the mention of the woman's name. "I would *never* hire a pair of drug addicts to do a sensitive investigation. I wouldn't hire a drug addict to mow my lawn. I know too much about them."

I couldn't believe we were hearing this from the head of an organization supposedly dedicated to rehabilitating those addicts.

Peavey stood and hitched up his trousers as he walked over to the window. He looked out on the rolling green lawn, his bulbous posterior facing us.

"I know you must be shocked, hearing this from me. But my philosophy is—once an addict, always an addict. It's not a question of *if*, it's only a question of *when*. They all relapse eventually—frankly, that's why this is such a good business."

I found myself breaking out into a sweat. Where was the bumbling, harmless factotum we all knew and loved? The sudden bitterness bubbling up in the man was making me extremely uncomfortable. Not to mention that he was more or less openly accusing us—especially Terry—of being untrustworthy.

He turned and showed us his little gray teeth, sneering. "Isn't that right, Terry? Don't you feel the pull of it all the time, calling to you . . . *Take me*, it says . . . *get wasted . . . forget all that crap about recovery . . . you know you want me . . .*"

Terry jumped out of her chair, arm poised to strike. I leaped up and caught her hand as it was headed for Wendell's shiny red cheek. She let me stop her, but her arm muscles were trembling, her breathing hard.

"I went cold turkey, Wendell. In prison. And there wasn't any pretty little recovery program there to help me. So you can just cram it up your big fat fanny!"

Peavey laughed. "Yes, yes, very good. You trot along to the FBI. Trot, trot, trot. But there is no record of a 'Kent' or 'James' enrolled here, so I'm afraid what you're going to look like is a couple of hysterical little drug users. And, of course, I can corroborate that assessment when asked. A couple of scammers who tried to con the management of this facility into hiring you under false pretenses."

I got a sudden cold rush—the cold prickles of a premonition on the back of my neck. "Where is Shannon Voss?" I said. "The truth this time, Wendell."

He shrugged, inspecting his fingernails. "I'm afraid we had to let her out of her contract. She was a very competent attorney, but far too inclined to waste the institution's money on her fanciful investigations."

Terry gave me a devastated look.

"I want her address," I said.

He shook his jowls, the liver lips set in defiance.

"Come on, Kerry. Let's go," Terry said, her voice thick with emotion as she stalked out the door.

"I'm not leaving without Shannon's address." I sat back down, glaring at Peavey.

He watched Terry leave. "Best of luck with the FBI," he called after her, chuckling, then he came around to my chair, grabbed my elbow, and yanked me up, hustling me out through the open door. Amanda was at her desk in the outer office, her eyes going wide when she saw him manhandling me.

She spiked up from her chair. "Shall I call security?"

"Yes," he said, shoving me past the desk. "I want them to be certain that the Misses McAfee leave the grounds." He sneered at me, then turned and rumbled back into his office like a triumphant killer elephant.

I shot Amanda a hateful look as I turned to go, but was surprised to see that she had her finger over her lips, shushing me. She leaned over her desk and stuffed a small piece of paper into the palm of my hand as she picked up the phone.

"Hello, Security?" she said, giving me a jerk of the head to send me on my way. "Mr. Peavey would like you to escort two young ladies off the grounds."

I gripped the scrap of paper and hurried out into the corridor, where Terry was waiting with tears in her eyes.

"Let's get the hell out of here," she said.

From the other side of the lobby, two security guards sprinted our way, heads down. We swung open the doors and ran toward the bike in the front drive. I glanced down at the paper in my hand, then looked back over my shoulder. The security guards were on the porch, hands on their hip holsters, glaring at us like we were a couple of fleeing bank robbers. One of them spoke into his radio, probably to the guard in the shack.

"I've got Shannon's address," I whispered to Terry when we got on the bike. She gave me a quick thumbs-up.

The guard jumped out of his shack and crouched in a firing position, his firearm aimed at us, as we roared past the upraised barrier. Terry rode out of the driveway with no hands on the handlebars, her arms thrust in the air, third fingers extended in a good-bye salute to New Horizons and Wendell Peavey.

twenty-two

One PCH Plaza was a complex on the east side of the Pacific Coast Highway, built directly into the cliff above the road. It was a round building that gave all of the condominiums a view of the coastline. The reflector windows were full of golden afternoon light. I wondered if it was sweltering inside those million-dollar apartments, or if millions of watts of air-conditioning managed to deflect the heat.

We couldn't make out where the entrance was, so Terry took a left onto the shoulder of the road next to the ocean, parking between two cars. We'd have to run across the highway, taking our lives in our hands to get to the other side. We saw a break in the traffic and went for it.

There was a subterranean garage that had an entrance at street level, with an automatic iron gate. A staircase led up to a double door at the base of the building. The door was embedded in the rock. We buzzed the intercom and a male voice asked us our business.

"We're here to see Shannon Voss," I said.

"Is she expecting you?"

"No. Can you please call her and tell her the McAfees are here to see her?"

We waited a moment, then the voice came back on. "There's no answer at her apartment."

Terry stepped up to the intercom. "Actually, that's why we're here. We're private investigators in Ms. Voss's employ. Can you let us in?"

"Can I see some ID?"

Terry looked at me, then turned back to the intercom. "Uh, you want to tell us how?"

"Camera, up to your left."

Sure enough, there was a tiny lens angled at us to the left of the door. I took out my wallet and opened it to my license, holding it up to the lens. We heard the buzzer and the double doors slid open. We entered and were surprised to find ourselves in a shiny metal compartment—an elevator.

"It's a first for me," Terry said, pushing the button marked *Lobby*. "The only way into the building is through the elevator?"

"Guess so."

"What happens when it breaks?"

I shrugged. "There must be a back door, too."

The elevator doors opened onto a lobby done lavishly in marble, with potted palms in brass planters lining the walls. A guard on the street side of the room stood sentinel behind a large concierge desk. He was short and scrawny with a vicious case of acne, his uniform so large on him that he looked like a Cub wearing an Eagle Scout's uniform. His gun resembled a Super Soaker next to his little hip.

"Hi, I'm Terry McAfee," Terry said. "This is my sister, Kerry."

"Can I see a badge or an ID from Ms. Voss's workplace?"

My, we are big on IDs.

"It's classified work, under the radar," Terry said confidentially, leaning on the desk. "We're paid in cash, know what I mean? That's not unusual in the PI business."

He fluffed the feathers on his pigeon breast, the tin badge rising as it expanded. Probably fantasizing about a career that involved flashing a license to snoop. Might be more rewarding than standing at attention, buzzing people into an elevator all day.

"Well, like I said, she's not answering."

"A colleague of hers was concerned," Terry said. "She gave us the address so we could come here and check on her. Do you have the ability to open her apartment?"

He debated whether to exaggerate his importance in the scheme of things or to downplay it. Not sure which would get him into more trouble. When in doubt, he chose the middle ground. "I have the ability, but not the authority. Unless it's an extreme circumstance, a matter of life or death."

"Look," I said. "She's not answering her pager, her cell phone, or her home phone. She's a professional woman, a lawyer. She doesn't normally play hooky from work, and especially not in the middle of a"—I tried to think of something that would resonate with him—"situational investigation. So unless you'd rather we called the police and had them come here to bash down the door, I really think you ought to give it a go."

He gave us a helpless look. "There's no one else to buzz people in. Bob doesn't get here until eight. I'm alone 'til then."

"It'll just take a minute," Terry said. "You'll be up and down within seconds."

"I can't open her door and leave you there! You could rip her off!"

I sighed and read the name tag on his uniform. "Andy, just open the door so we can determine that Ms. Voss isn't inside bleeding to death from some household accident or something, and then you can lock the place up, and we'll come right back down with you, okay?"

The bleeding-to-death proposition did it. He grabbed the master key ring from a hook and scrambled out from behind the desk. "Okay . . . if it's potentially a matter of life or death."

We took the elevator up to the seventh floor, where Andy bounded out the door into the hallway, circling to the right. We followed him to apartment 705. He rang the bell. No answer. He knocked tentatively several times, calling out, "Ms. Voss?"

"Life or death," I said to give him nerve.

He brought up the keys with trembling hands and unlocked the deadbolt, then the knob. The door opened but stuck on a chain. Andy glanced over at us. "L-locked from inside. Someone's in there."

"Shannon!" Terry yelled through the open door.

There was no sound. The only thing we could see was a section of the floor that was illuminated with a rainbow pattern of color from a piece of stained glass in the front window.

"Should I go call the police?" Andy said, now openly looking for guidance from us.

"Yeah," Terry said. "Do that."

She waited until Andy had rounded the corner, then she backed up a few paces and hurled herself against the door. The chain lock snapped and Terry tumbled forward onto the floor of the living room into the circle of blue and red and yellow lights, looking like a freckled Madonna in a church window. She quickly rolled back up onto her feet.

Andy heard the noise and came running. "You shouldn't have done that!"

Terry looked off in the distance. "Yes, Andy, I should have," she said quietly.

I walked into the apartment, and she pointed me to the kitchen. There was a marble-topped counter with a built-in stove. On top of the stove, a large aluminum pasta pot. And out of the pot, long ash-blond hair streamed down to the stovetop.

"Oh man," I said. "Not again."

Andy stared, uncomprehending, his head shaking as from palsy. His lips moved, but the only sound he made was "*Uh? Uh?*"

"I think the rest of her is in there," Terry said, pointing into the bedroom. I looked inside and saw a naked foot with bright pink toenails at the end of the bed.

Andy crept up to the stove and peered inside the pot. Then his eyes rolled up in his head and he keeled over backward, hitting the tile floor with a noisy thudding of his skull and sloshing of his brains.

Terry rushed over to check on Andy. "Ker, you want to call the police?" she said, grabbing his wrist to feel his pulse.

"Where are we, Malibu?"

"Santa Monica, I think. Or Pacific Palisades."

"Thank God for small favors," I said, heading for the phone.

We took some ice cubes from Shannon's freezer and wrapped them in a dish towel for Andy's head—the only things we disturbed in the apartment—then sent him back down to the service desk.

The uniforms got there first. Two cops rushed into the apartment with guns drawn.

"Police!"

Terry and I instinctively put our hands in the air. "We're private investigators," I said quickly, waving the license at them. I'd already removed it from my wallet in order to have it free for the first officers on the scene. I was glad I had. I didn't expect them to be so jumpy.

A short, solid African-American cop whose name tag said *Murray* took the license from my hand. He looked it over and handed it to the tall, fair-haired officer, Ventura. Murray gave me a quick pat-down while Ventura held his gun on us, then did the same with Terry.

"We found the body, Officers. We didn't kill her," I said. "Check with the security guard downstairs."

Ventura looked at me over the top of his gun. "He told us you were behaving suspiciously. Said you knew there was a body in here."

Terry rolled her eyes. "The chain lock was on. I busted through it. We had information from the woman's workplace that she wasn't answering her phones."

Ventura kept his gun trained on us, moving over to inspect the busted chain lock. The wood was splintered, the lock plate hanging from the chain with one screw still clinging to it. The other screw lay on the floor.

"Check the stove, Officer," I said.

Ventura walked over to the stove while Murray kept us covered. He took one look, then spun around, eyes lit up like a pinball machine. "Steven. Check it out."

Officer Murray hurried over and looked, whistling softly. Then both of them turned to us. "Is there another body in here?" Ventura said.

"Not that we've seen," I said.

"Then who . . . how . . . ?" Murray sputtered.

"Who cut off her head and locked the door from inside?" I asked.

They nodded.

"I think the man you're looking for is named Harry Houdini."

"Or Harry the Stick Insect Murderer," Terry said.

We waited downstairs in the lobby while the detectives, crime-scene techs, and coroner's people did their thing—processing the crime scene, interviewing the neighbors, removing the body to the morgue.

Andy was quivering with excitement, breathlessly informing returning residents that there'd been a grisly murder—not on his watch, mind you, on Bob's watch—and warning them away from the seventh floor. He kept volunteering to escort residents to their apartments for safety, but every single time he got a queasy "No, thanks, Andy" and the resident hurried off on his or her own.

The buzzer rang. Boatwright announced himself as a police detective over the intercom. I'd called him right after notifying the local cops, but it had taken him a couple of hours to get there.

"Sir, hold up your ID to the camera, please," Andy said.

"Oh, for God's sakes, Andy," I said, reaching around him to push the button release on the door.

Andy gave me an indignant grunt. "I'm in charge of the security for the residents of One PCH Plaza! You just let a potential murderer in the building!"

"He's Beverly Hills PD. Get over yourself."

The elevator doors opened. "Well, hello there," Boatwright said, breaking into a grin when he saw me. "Here we are again, in deep doo-doo."

"Your ID, sir," Andy persisted.

Boatwright tossed it to him, but Andy fumbled it and it dropped, skittering across the polished marble floor. He dived for it, losing his balance and landing sprawled on the floor with his face on top of the ID. He lay there for a few seconds, nose pressed against the badge, then looked back up at Boatwright. "Everything seems to be in order here, sir."

"Thank you." Boatwright picked up his ID and extended a hand to Andy, pulling him to his feet. "Way to keep the world safe from cop impersonators." He turned to Terry and me. "You all done here?"

I shrugged. "We gave a statement."

"I'm gonna have a word with the local dicks, then I want to talk to you two. Give me ten minutes."

"Okay."

He went up in the elevator and Andy resumed his post, trying to salvage some dignity by readjusting his belt, badge, and gun.

"Can't believe they let that guy carry a gun," Terry whispered to me.

"It's America," I said. "Any loser can carry a gun."

We waited on the couch, leafing through magazines. Boatwright came back into the lobby ten minutes later, as promised.

"Okay, you're clear," he said. "Let's go."

"We could sure use some coffee," I said.

He pushed me toward the elevator. "What you could use is a spanking."

We got a table outside at Gladstone's, a half-mile down the road. It was too late in the day for coffee, so we ordered beers. The sun was a golden goose's egg in the process of sinking into the ocean, the sky above it a deep indigo.

I grabbed several handfuls of circus peanuts from a large oak barrel and tossed them on the concrete tabletop. Gulls circled menacingly overhead but were prevented from actually dive-bombing our peanuts by the wires stretched over the tables. They were decorated with bright-colored little flags, fluttering noisily in the gale-force winds that had suddenly whipped up. Glass windbreaks around the outdoor patio kept the wind from blowing our heads off, and the sound of the waves crashing against the shore was doing a lot to calm my nerves, as was the beer.

"Okay, spill it," Boatwright said. "How'd you get on to yet another murder?"

"First," Terry said, "doesn't it look good for Robert and Reba that there was a similar murder in the neighborhood while they were incarcerated? Another blond woman decapitated?"

He took a swig of beer. "It could be a copycat. Same MO, different creep."

"Yeah, but at least it provides an alternative theory of the original crime," I said. "And it puts some pressure on the locals. They don't want to look like they let a serial killer slip through their fingers."

"Right, in theory. Now, last time I heard"—Boatwright pointed at Terry—"*you* were going undercover at some rehab place."

"Yeah, New Horizons," she said. "I was there for one day, then Kerry took over. What we discovered is that there's a guy named Kent pretending to be a patient, who finds rich, vulnerable addicts, hypnotizes them, then recruits them for this cult called Children of the Cosmos."

"And what did you do with this information?"

"Nothing, yet," Terry said.

"We didn't get a chance," I interjected. "I was on my way

out to share the information with Terry when I was chloro-formed and kidnapped. A scary-looking junkie named James who I'd met at New Horizons took me to a cabin somewhere in Malibu Canyon and shot me up full of heroin. I managed to escape and ended up in someone's bed, where I was arrested and charged with burglary and being under the influence of a controlled substance."

Boatwright looked up at the sky. "Unbe-*liev*-able!"

"Yeah, and that's not all. When we confronted the director of New Horizons with this, he tried to buy us off. When that didn't work, he had us thrown out."

"That's when we found Shannon," Terry said. "She was the one who originally hired us, and when Peavey blew us off, we came here to talk to her and found her . . . like *that*."

"Oh, well, that explains it." Boatwright cracked open a peanut and popped it in his mouth. "I thought people in your family just had some kind of homing instinct for dead bodies."

Terry and I shrugged at each other.

"By the way, how did they get out and lock the chain behind them?" I asked him. "Any ideas?"

He shook his head. "I guess that's one for *Unsolved Mysteries*. There was no other way out of the apartment. Windows don't open. And the only exits are the front elevators that go down into the garage, and a fire door in the back with an alarm."

Terry let out a frustrated little sigh.

"So," Boatwright said, "that director threw you off the grounds, huh?" He thought about it for a second. "Well, he can't throw *me* off the grounds."

Terry and I smiled at each other. "You're going to help us with this?" she asked.

"I'll see if I can sneak in a few hours. Might be tricky, though. Number one, it's against departmental policy. Number two, the Captain has me working on a high-profile vehicular murder."

"Vehicular murder?"

"Yeah, a jilted girlfriend who ran over her plastic surgeon boyfriend with a Jaguar *he* gave her. That's gratitude, huh?"

"Now, there's a total copycat crime!" I laughed. "Was she trying to outdo that woman in Texas? I'll show you how to do it with class, my dear—we in Beverly Hills kill our men with *Jag-u-ahs*."

"Yeah, amazing how these things go in waves," Boatwright said. "Somebody figures out a new way to do somebody in, and every homicidal maniac in the country goes, 'Oh, *good one.*'"

"And it makes no difference to them that the original criminal didn't get away with it?" Terry said.

He shrugged. "They're not thinking. They're going on pure adrenaline, or 'passion,' as it's sometimes known. I'm telling you, there's nothing more dangerous than a woman who's been dumped. They make the gangbangers look like amateurs."

"We thought Heather Granger was one of those dangerous dumped women," I said, "until now."

Boatwright looked at me curiously. "Why until now?"

"Well, we had a motive for her with the first girl, the dominatrix—jealousy or blackmail or both. But what did poor Shannon do to deserve her fate?"

"Not so fast," Terry said. "Shannon was investigating the Children of the Cosmos, Heather's group. And we were about to expose their techniques . . . so there's a connection right there."

"True," I said.

"On the other hand," she went on, "Peavey himself turns out to have quite a dark side. He said he fired Shannon. Maybe he didn't want to give her 'severance' pay."

Boatwright groaned.

"Shit!" I said. A seagull squawked in response, taking flight. "It's all too complicated!"

"Always is with you two," Boatwright said, then glanced at his watch. "Look, I gotta go. I want you girls to lay low until I can talk to this director at New Horizons—what was his name?"

"Wendell Peavey," I said.

He noted it down. "I'm sure the local cops will be talking to him since the dead woman worked for him. I'll tell them what I know and see if I can tag along. In the meantime, keep your noses clean." He threw down a twenty and gave me a quick kiss on the cheek.

Terry stuck out her cheek as well.

"Last time I kissed you, I got in big trouble," Boatwright said.

"It's okay," I told him. "Just keep your tongue in your mouth."

He smiled and gave Terry a peck. "Remember, no more snooping until I can get a line on Peavey."

I gave him a little wave, then we watched him jog across the parking lot to his car, carrying his sport coat draped over one arm. Long stride, shoulders back, nice rounded buns moving under the khaki pants.

"I could go for that," Terry said.

"Keep your hands off him!"

She grinned mischievously. "I meant as a brother-in-law."

"Oh," I said, flushing slightly. "I knew that."

"Nuh-uh! You thought I was hot for your cop!"

I rolled my eyes. "Did not."

"Did so!"

"Anyway, you're getting way ahead of yourself," I told her breezily. "I'm not sure I even like the guy."

"Oh, *you* like him."

"Oh, shut up and drive."

We walked over gravel to the Harley, which stood alone on the shoulder of the road, gleaming under the streetlamps.

Terry jerked a thumb in the direction of the parking lot. "You didn't tell Boatwright about the wire transfer, I noticed."

"Well, I mean—I present him with an alien cult and a kidnapping and two decapitation murders *and* a hypnotized sister? How much strain can a new relationship be expected to endure?"

She laughed and smacked me on the side of the head.

"Ow! What was that for?"

She shrugged. "'Cause I'm glad you're back."

"Oh," I said, rubbing my ear. "Thanks, I guess."

She threw her leg over the bike. "Hey Ter," I said in my most diplomatic voice. "You know your idea about going into therapy?" She looked at me and nodded. "I think that might be a good thing."

"Why do you say that?"

"Well, because I've noticed you express anger and affection in the same way—by smacking people."

She gave the idea some consideration. "Kerry, when I said that about going into therapy . . . ?"

"Uh-huh?"

"I was just fuckin' with ya." She broke into a wicked grin.

"Oh."

Then she laughed and smacked me again to drive the point home.

twenty-
three

*W*e were headed back to Reba's when Terry stuck out her arm suddenly and made a hard right onto a side street. She pulled onto the rocky shoulder of the road and killed the engine.

I took off my helmet and scooted around for a handlebar conference. "What are we doing here?"

"I've got it, baby!"

"What?"

"The lock—I know how they did it."

"*How?*"

"Look, if they know that someone's going to suspect foul play and bust in, they figure the someone who's busting in is going to do what I did, which is back up and make a run for the door, right?"

"Right." I had actually thought it was kind of a macho TV police maneuver but hadn't said anything at the time.

"So the lock doesn't even need to be screwed all the way in, you know? If you're going to throw your whole body against the door, you wouldn't even notice if the chain was already loose, you'd just assume you had broken it with your momentum."

"Oh *yeah* . . ."

"So what they did, they pried the lock plate out of the door, and then when they left, they hooked the chain back *in* the plate and stuck it on the door with some kind of adhesive or something. There was plenty of room for a hand to go in there and do the job."

"Right, right! And then, once you were inside, you looked over and all you saw was screws that had been ripped out of the door and the lock plate hanging down. That's what you expected to see, so you wouldn't be looking for adhesive!"

"Good, huh?" she said, grinning.

"Masterful." I gave her a high five. "But why bother? Were they being cute? Or did they want to hang the cops up on that little mystery to buy some time?"

"Yeah, they'd be racking their brains on how the murderer got out, since the windows don't open."

"Or maybe . . ."

"Maybe?"

"Maybe it was to deflect attention from the way they *actually* got out."

"Which is how?"

I grinned, shaking my head at the simple brilliance of the scheme. "They went down in the elevator, just like everyone else. There's no other way out!"

"Whoa!" she said, her eyes going wide. "Are we good, or what? Let's go back and check out our theory." She reached for the ignition.

"Sis," I said solemnly, putting a restraining hand on her arm.

"Yeah?"

"That was a total *Columbo* moment. Savor it."

"I'm savoring, I'm savoring," she said, then opened up the throttle for a victory roar.

We zoomed back to One PCH Plaza and rang the buzzer.

"Can I help you?" a man's voice, but not Andy's voice, said.

"We're investigating the murder of Ms. Voss," I said into the speaker. "Are you Bob?"

There was a moment's silence. "I've already talked to the police. Who are you?"

Story of our lives. Stonewalled by rent-a-cops.

"We're private investigators," I said, holding my ID up to the camera. "We worked for Shannon."

The elevator doors opened without more ado.

"He's more cooperative than Andy," I whispered, as we were conveyed to the lobby.

"Yes, he is." Terry waved at the camera in the upper right-hand corner of the elevator.

The lobby was empty except for a good-looking, dark-haired guy behind the concierge desk. He filled out his uniform nicely, I noticed. A strapping young buck with a wide smile and broad masculine features.

He slipped a girlie magazine under the desk.

"Evening," he said. "I'm Bob. How can I help you?"

We shook his hand and introduced ourselves.

"We were wondering," Terry said. "Can we have another look at Shannon Voss's apartment? There's something we'd like to confirm."

"What?" he wanted to know.

"Something to do with the chain lock," I said. "If you'll let us up there, we'll show you."

He shook his head. "Sorry. Crime-scene tape's up. And the cops told me not to let anyone near it."

"Are they still here?"

"They just left. I told them everything I knew, which was nothing."

Terry took on an intimate tone. "Tell you what, Bob. You look like an easygoing person, unlike your colleague Andy—"

He gave an involuntary snort of laughter. "What about it?"

"Well, Andy didn't want to let us up there, either. And there was Shannon, dead inside the apartment, while Andy was pulling his 'I don't have the authority' thing. The woman's rotting away, and the killer's out there kicking up his heels because Andy's afraid to let anyone in. See what I mean?"

His thick eyebrows came together in a frown. Where was this leading?

"But that's just the way ol' Andy is," Terry said with a *tsk*. "He's so obsessed with the rules, I have a feeling nobody could get past *him*—he almost didn't let the police in here. Know what I'm saying, Bob?"

"Nooo," he said slowly, crossing his arms over his chest.

"Well, here's what I think." She tapped the desk. "I think somebody walked right past this desk, took the elevator upstairs, killed Ms. Voss and rigged the lock on the door, then walked right past this desk again and went out the front door . . ." She paused for effect. "But I don't think they walked past Andy."

His eyes were beginning to light up with panic, but his voice remained steady. "I told the police. Nobody except the residents and their guests are allowed in here, and all guests have to sign the register." He backed up against his padded stool, leaning one hand on the seat in a vain attempt to look casual. Terry reached out and grabbed his magazine from the back of the desk.

Playboy.

"Good articles in here," she said, flipping through the pages. "I guess that's what you read it for, the articles?"

He grabbed it back from her and chucked it into a trash can. "It gets a little boring sitting here all night. Excuse me for wanting a little entertainment."

I was wondering if I should jump into the fray, but Terry seemed very much in command, so I let her continue on her own.

"Ever leave your post when you're bored?" she said. "Did you leave your post last night? For a little, I don't know, *entertainment* of some kind?"

"I think you better leave," Bob said, hand twitching toward his hip holster.

"No," Terry said.

"Now."

"Uh-uh, Bob."

The two of them stared each other down.

When Bob couldn't stand it anymore, he yelled, "What do you want from me?"

"It was a woman, wasn't it?" Terry said quietly. "The one who paid you to look the other way?"

He glanced over at me, eyes begging for mercy. I gave him no comfort.

Terry leaned on the desk, her face flush with excitement. Her quarry was now within striking distance.

"Bob," she said, "we're going to the police with this. If you tell us now, it'll go better for you, I swear. Time is of the essence. The murderer is still out there, and if you don't come clean, someone else may die . . . tonight."

He rubbed his eyes, face cracking underneath. "I knew I shouldn't do it. I am so *hosed*."

"Tell us," I said sympathetically. "Terry's right. It will be better for you if you do."

He sank back on his stool and sighed. "She approached me outside on my way to work. She was wearing a coat, which was kind of weird—I mean, a long fur coat in May . . ."

I looked at Terry excitedly. "And what was she wearing underneath?"

He made a face of pure anguish. I was actually beginning to feel sorry for the guy. "I don't know. Some Victoria's Secret outfit in leather."

I felt my breath coming quicker. "And what did she look like? Was she pretty?"

He laughed sardonically. "I wasn't exactly focused on her face. Blond hair, average height, bitchin' bod."

"She came up in the elevator? Would there be video of her?"

He shook his head. "I turned off the fire alarm, let her in the back door."

"What time?" Terry said.

"Around two in the morning."

"Okay, but what did she look like?" I asked him. "Can't you remember anything about her facial features?"

It took him a second to respond. "She wore a mask," he said finally.

"A mask?" Terry and I said together.

He flinched with embarrassment. "Yeah, you know, like Zorro. Said she was a present, a 'Hookergram' or some shit. She was going to Mr. Keith's apartment, number 715. Some of his office buddies had set it up."

"So you just let her in," I said, shaking my head.

"Yeah. I mean, if somebody set up a surprise for me like that, I wouldn't want some pissant security guard messing it up."

"Very considerate of you," Terry said. "You didn't tell the cops about this, did you?"

He cast his gaze to the floor. "Mr. Keith is entitled to his privacy."

"And you're entitled to yours, aren't you, Bob?"

He looked up at her from beneath long dark lashes. I was feeling sorrier and sorrier for poor Bob. "Wh-what do you mean?"

"She took care of you, didn't she? Blow job . . . ?" His eyes went sideways and he bit his lower lip. "Was it before or after?"

His head drooped like a wounded dog's.

"Bob, I don't know what this is going to do to your fantasy life going forward," Terry said, "but you got your knob polished by a decapitation murderess."

He slumped forward on the desk, put his head on his arms, and began to weep right onto the sleeves of his uniform.

"I don't think we need to see that lock, do you?" I said to Terry.

She shook her head. "Listen, Bob. We know a great criminal lawyer, name of Eli Weintraub. We'll have him call you, okay?"

But he didn't answer. We left him there, crying his heart out, and walked to the elevator without looking back. Terry punched the call button.

"Jesus, that was rough," I said to her, as the elevator doors closed.

"Yeah, but now we know—our killer is a woman."

"No, we don't know that. Someone else could have come in

the back door while Bob was being serviced. What I want to know—was this woman connected to the babe who went to see Frank the other night? The one in the fur coat?"

"What are you saying? You think Frank had something to do with Shannon's murder?"

I blew out a sigh. "No. Why would he?"

"Maybe Shannon was the one who was blackmailing him?"

I punched the wall of the elevator with my fist. "God, we need a Ouija board to figure this out!"

"Hey, sis," she said, as the doors opened, "they can run, but they can't hide from the dreaded Smith twins."

And with that we took our overheated little selves out into the fresh ocean air.

twenty-four

$\mathcal{W}$e were on our way back to Reba's to call Boatwright about Bob's mystery date, when Frank's phone rang in my jacket pocket. I felt it vibrating, and my heart went cold in my chest. I tapped Terry on the shoulder and she pulled off the road.

I had the helmet off and the phone open in a flash. "Frank!" I said perkily. "How are you?"

"How *am I?*" I cringed all the way down to my toes—it *was* kind of a dumb opening. "What are you bimbos doing for your money?"

I tried to sound upbeat and confident. "Well, actually, we've been doing quite a lot—"

He cut me off. "I got hit up again . . . this time for a million."

I mouthed *a million dollars* to Terry. Her eyes bugged.

"Get over here. I need you to make the drop."

Yikes.

"We'll be there," I said. He hung up without another word, and I snapped the phone shut. "They demanded a million this time," I told Terry. "Frank wants us to make the drop. He asked what we've been doing for our money."

"Shit. We don't even have his money anymore."

"Like that's our biggest problem right now."

"Did he say where they want it dropped?"

I shook my head.

"Okay," she said. "It's go time."

We rang Frank's front doorbell. There was no answer. The house was dark.

"He's not here?" I said, my heart full of hope.

Terry scoffed at me. "He's here, don't worry."

She led the way around the side of the house, down the stairs to the sand, and across the terrace. We entered the house through the open back door.

Frank sat on the couch, looking irritated. "You ring the door-bell? What are you, the Avon Investigators?"

"Sorry," I said.

He was dressed in a black track suit and athletic shoes, one leg slung over his knee. The house was silent and empty. One crookneck lamp burned behind the couch, framing Frank in a triangle of light. A brown leather suitcase sat next to him on the couch.

"Is that it?" I said, pointing to the suitcase.

He nodded—*Duh, stupid.*

"Where'd you get so much cash?" Terry asked.

"My associates prefer to deal in cash whenever possible. I got it from them."

"You told them about the blackmail?" I said.

"No. I told them I needed it to pay off an actress who was sexually assaulted by one of our stars on a movie set. It's a true story, except for the money part."

I looked at him curiously. "What's true? She was raped?"

He leered at me for an uncomfortable few seconds. "Yeah, according to her, but I didn't offer her money to shut her up."

"What'd you do?"

He flashed a Cheshire-cat grin. "I promised to make her a star."

Terry and I groaned simultaneously.

"We gonna sit here chitchatting all night? Or are you gonna get moving?" Frank said, slapping the suitcase.

"Where do they want the drop?" Terry asked.

"You're gonna love this—at a rehab facility."

"New Horizons?" Terry and I said at once.

"Who are you now, Frick and Frack?" Then his face turned suspicious. "How'd you know that?"

I gave a shrug that I hoped looked innocent. "It's the only one nearby."

"Who called you?" Terry said. "I mean, man or woman?"

"Woman."

"Old or young?"

"Young. What the hell difference does it make?"

I tried not to look confused. "Well, where? Where should we drop it?"

"The front door? I don't know! I'm paying *you* to figure it out!"

"I've got to talk to Kerry about this, Frank." Terry jerked her head to the side of the room. I followed her into a dark corner, out of Frank's earshot.

"What does this mean? Is Peavey behind everything?" I said, trying without success to cast him as the archvillain in my mind.

She bit her bottom lip. "Has to be, right? He was probably a customer of Candy's. I can see him getting into that masochistic stuff." I felt a stab of envy for the person who got paid to whip Peavey's butt. "He knew about Frank . . . maybe got hold of the tape during one of their sessions, killed Candy, and went for the blackmail. He's got one of the other kinky girls working with him, the one who got past Bob to kill Shannon. . . ."

"Yeah, it's possible. He also tried to kill *me*."

We stood there for a second, pondering that one.

"Listen, it makes sense now," she said. "He knew about Reba's house because Robert was in the program. He was probably putting those Cosmeteers on the patient rolls, too—getting a payoff for letting them in. That's why he wouldn't let us see the records. But now things are getting too complicated. He had to kill Shannon because she was onto him. Now he wants to take the money and run." She stopped, out of breath and out of rationalizations.

"But Peavey, a criminal mastermind? His fingers in all these pies? He doesn't seem smart enough."

"Maybe he's just been playing dumb."

"Hey, are you done over there?" Frank said. "I ain't got all night."

"One minute, Frank," Terry said. "We're coming up with a plan."

"Look," I whispered to her, "if we know it's him, then we should tell Frank and go to the police. If Peavey's arrested for the murders, then the blackmail is off, right? Frank has nothing to worry about, and neither do Reba and Robert."

"Oh, I hadn't thought of that."

"Come on, let's tell him."

We walked back over to the couch.

"So what's your *plan*?" Frank said sarcastically.

I sat down a few feet away from him. "Frank, it may not be necessary to pay them off. The tape may not have the same value anymore."

"Oh yeah? Why not?"

"There's been another murder. One just like Candy's. And strangely enough, the victim worked at New Horizons. Her name was Shannon Voss. We think your blackmailer just might be a serial murderer by the name of Wendell Peavey, director of the facility."

"And if they determine that the same killer did both women," Terry continued, "and if you can provide an alibi for last night—the night of Shannon's murder—then they can't nail you for Candy's death, tape or no tape."

He shook his head disgustedly. "I already knew about the Voss murder."

My, but bad news travels fast in Malibu.

"How did you know?" Terry said, frowning. "How?"

"They told me about it when they called and asked for the million. Why do you think I'm willing to pony up?"

"Well, there's nothing connecting you to that one—" I started to say, then stopped myself. *"Is there?"*

He nodded slowly, his eyes on mine. Cold, staring eyes that sucked up all the light.

"What do they have on you?" Terry said, squinting at him. "Another tape?"

"For fuck's sake, I had to hire Charlie's Angels. Look, just go give them their money and get the tape and don't worry about the rest of it."

There was definitely something fishy going on here.

"Tell us what the connection is, Frank," Terry said, crossing her arms, "or there's no drop."

He stared at her for a few seconds, then finally looked away.

"They say they planted some DNA evidence on the Voss woman . . . some of *my* DNA."

"What kind of DNA?" Terry demanded.

He sneered at her. "Do I have to spell it out for you, sweetheart?"

"Semen?" I said.

He narrowed those dark eyes at me, giving me a brusque nod.

Suddenly, I had an attack of amnesia. I forgot who I was and who I was talking to. I jumped up, yelling, "You son of a bitch!" Frank's eyebrows fused together and his hands went to his face protectively. "You did kill them!" I shouted.

"N-no, no," he stammered, scared shitless. Scared of *me*. I hate to admit it, but it was a heady feeling making him cringe in fear. "I swear I didn't!"

"Then how did they get your . . . stuff?" I demanded.

"I don't know," he muttered through clenched teeth.

Terry's head began bobbing up and down as understanding dawned. "It wasn't one of your stars who raped that actress, was it, Frank?" she said slowly. "It's a true story except for the paying-off part . . . and the *who did it* part."

He looked out the door, head cocked as if tuned to the pounding surf. "Where are you getting this?" His tone implied that we were stupid little girls, but the conviction had gone out of his voice.

"Is that it?" I said. "They got the DNA from your victim? Or is it 'victims'?"

"Okay, I get a little carried away sometimes, but I didn't even *know* that chippie at New Horizons—"

"How many?" Terry said, her eyes burning. "How many have you had your way with, promising to make them stars?"

He bared his teeth in a sneer. "Do you know who I am?"

"HOW MANY?" Terry screamed at him.

"A dozen, maybe." He rotated his eyes to the ceiling. "But I swear on my dear mother's grave, I had nothing to do with killing those two women. Sheez, I'm no *murderer*."

Terry and I stood there paralyzed with revulsion. Up to our ankles in scum.

"Where's her grave?" I asked him.

"Huh?"

"Your mother's."

"Yonkers," he said in a barely audible voice.

"Good," I said, "then you can't hear her rolling over in it."

I grabbed the handle of the suitcase. Frank's face lit up like that of a mischievous kid who had successfully dodged his due punishment. "You gonna do it anyway?"

"Yeah," I said, "but something tells me this isn't the end of your problems, Frank. Your associates, the money people—you said they're Italian, right?"

He didn't answer, just stared at my mouth like he dreaded what might come next. He'd clearly thought of this himself.

"They don't think much of rapists, do they?"

His eyes flashed in desperation. "Don't tell anyone, please. Keep your mouth shut. Don't say nothing, and I swear . . . I swear, I'll make you a—"

"Save it," Terry said.

We turned and walked out the terrace door, hauling the conscience of Frank Steinmetz in a million-dollar valise.

*T*he suitcase was so heavy on my lap I was afraid my femurs
would snap. Terry pulled into an unlighted side street and
parked in the dark.

"Okay, we came off real tough back there," she said. "But
what do we do now?"

I had been thinking the same thing. Peavey was turning out
to be a serious killer—would he stop at snuffing the go-
between, especially when he saw that it was us? "It's a public
place, practically," I said. "What's he gonna do, kill us with all
those people there?"

"He could ambush us in the parking lot and stuff us into the
trunk of a car. Maybe with a little help from your friend
James."

"I don't know. That wouldn't make much sense. He's been
pretty clever so far, setting up other people for his crimes. He'd

be taking a big risk, killing and disposing of two more people. He probably wants to get away clean. Got a private jet set up to take him somewhere or something. . . ."

She heaved a sigh. "Wish we had a gun."

"Or a bodyguard."

We looked at each other, and our eyes widened.

"Lance!" we both said at once.

Terry immediately thought better of it. "No, that's no good. He's a total wimp."

"Yeah, but he's huge. It'd be like having a walking, talking scarecrow. They won't know he's harmless."

She considered it a moment. "Yeah, okay, go ahead," she said. "See if you can reach him."

I punched in Lance's number. He answered on the first ring.

"Lance Manley here." He was all business. I could hear the clanking of forks on plates and the tinkling of wineglasses in the background.

"Lance, it's Kerry. I'm sorry to interrupt your dinner—"

"Hey, Herman Munster!" someone yelled in the background. "Your order's up!"

Then I heard Lance's voice, muffled through a hand over the microphone. "Hey, man! Give me a break. It's a call about an audition!"

"Audition, my ass!"

Lance came back on the line. "Oh, hi, Kerry," he said casually. "I'm out to dinner with my agent. What's up?"

"Shake a leg, Munster! It's gettin' cold!"

I winced. It was painfully obvious what was going on. "I'm sorry, Lance. I needed a favor, but if you're tied up with your agent—"

"Agent, schmagent. . . . It's only show business. You need me, I'm there."

A dish crashed in the background.

"So," I said, "where are you having dinner?"

"At i Cugini on Ocean Boulevard."

Good. He was only fifteen minutes away. I told him to meet us at the Pier View Café. It was half a mile down from New Horizons and the closest landmark I could think of. I said we'd wait for him in the parking lot.

"Be there in fifteen," Lance said.

"Pick up this order or your ass is fired!"

"Well, if you're sure—" I said.

"My agent works for *me*, right? *Ciao*."

Then I heard Lance yell, "Hey, Guido! Take this job and shove it!" followed by a dial tone.

We waited in a dark corner of the parking lot at the Pier View, away from the highway.

"I don't know if it was such a good idea to meet here," I said, flashing back to the over-the-railing incident with the biker.

"We're in the dark," Terry said quietly. "No one can even see us. Besides, that guy would never show his face here again—he'd be too humiliated."

I looked at my watch. "I thought Lance would be here by now."

She sighed and shook her head. "We really shouldn't be doing this."

"That's what I was *saying*."

"No, I meant we shouldn't be making Frank's payoff. Covering up for his abuse of women."

I'd had the same thought. "I know."

"If we went to police with this money and told them what was going on, maybe *he'd* go up for the murders."

"But he didn't do them. We can't send him up for crimes he didn't commit just because he's a scuzzball."

"Boy, you have some strange code of ethics, you know that? You can't do a bad thing to a guy who should be locked up for two hundred years on rape charges?"

"I mean two wrongs don't make a right. And it's not like I invented that concept."

"Yeah, but he needs to be off the streets, and it's never gonna happen, 'cause he's a big producer and he's got mob money to throw around. He'll do it again, you know."

"Hey, if our karma can catch up with us, surely his can catch up with him."

And no sooner were the words out of my mouth . . .

A tricked-out hog rumbled into the parking lot, moving down to the end of the row. It turned left, its headlamp raking across our bike. The driver slowed, angling back toward us.

"Oh shit," I said.

He pulled up in front of us, idling. He wore a black helmet, black leather pants, and black hobnail boots for stompin' ass. Even in the darkness, I could see a smile breaking on his face, just below the Hitler mustache and above the thin strip of beard.

He turned off his engine and the rumbling ceased. "Well, hello again, ladies. Care for a little rematch?"

He swung a muscular leg off the bike and started toward us.

"Run for it!" I yelled to Terry.

She didn't move.

"Go!" I reached through her arm and tried to turn the key.

She grabbed my wrist with one hand and pointed to the parking lot entrance with the other. A tiny Hyundai was pulling into the lot. And inside the tin can of a car was a huge body with a jarhead in a brush cut.

Lance.

The biker turned to see what we were looking at, just as the headlamps on Lance's car swung into our line of vision. The three of us—Terry, the biker, and I—were momentarily blinded by the lights.

The Hyundai stopped. The driver's-side door opened. A hulking figure got out, moving to the front of the car. With the light radiating out from his gargantuan silhouette, he looked like the robot descending the spaceship ramp in *The Day the Earth Stood Still.*

The biker took a step back. His eyes jerked back and forth between Lance and us. The sight of this huge guy dressed nattily in a waiter's tux seemed to have completely fried his circuits. What sort of animal was this?

"Hi, girls. Hello, sir—how can I help you?" Lance said, smiling. Then he casually cracked his knuckles.

That did it. The biker jumped on his bike, kicked off the stand, and burned rubber out of the parking lot without looking back, disappearing in a plume of exhaust.

"Where's your friend going?" Lance asked, watching him leave.

"To get his leather pants dry-cleaned," Terry said, laughing. We reached out to hug our savior.

"Did I do something good?" Lance said with a goofy grin as he gave us a squeeze.

"Yeah, dude," I said, "you did something *very* good."

"So what's up?" Lance said. "Was that it?"

I pointed to the suitcase. "No. We have to make a delivery up the road."

"Cool," he said. "Want me to carry it?"

"No," Terry said, "here's what we'd like you to do. We want you to come in with us and look tough. That's all you have to do. You know, like your movie role where you played the

Secret Service agent. Square jaw, teeth clenched, hand in your pocket like you've got a gun . . ."

Lance's eyes lit up. An acting job, after all.

"Like this?" He went into steely-eyed mode, jaw muscles flexed, hand concealed inside the tux jacket.

"Perfect," I said. "And they're supposed to give us a tape. A small digital tape. If they don't, we're not giving them the money."

"A digital tape for a suitcase full of money? Sounds like spy stuff. Are you guys working for Her Majesty's Secret Service now?"

We laughed, but he continued to stare at us curiously, waiting for an answer.

"Lance, Her Majesty's Secret Service is in England," I said, getting a blank look in return.

I tried again. "Where the Queen is . . . ?"

Mt. Rushmore.

"Her *Majesty*, the *Queen of England* . . . ?"

"Oh," he said finally, nodding. "Gotcha."

Terry slumped over the handlebars, shaking her head. I gave Lance directions to New Horizons in case we lost him in the half-mile from here to there.

"We'll wait for you out front," I said.

"Okay, see ya there," Lance said, hunkering down and cramming himself into the Hyundai like a giant clown getting into a circus car.

"How does he drive that thing?" Terry wondered.

"He probably took out the back seat."

"Right," she said, reaching for the key. "Okay, here goes nothing."

●　　●　　●

There was no guard on duty when we pulled up to the gate. The barrier was up, the windows dark. The place looked deserted. Terry pulled around to the front door and parked.

I got off the bike. "Where is everybody? It's only eleven."

"Lights out at nine-thirty."

"Oh yeah. I guess I had my lights knocked out before the official lights out."

We waited a minute or two, then Lance pulled in. He parked behind us, turned off his engine, and opened the door, squeezing himself out of the car like tuxedoed toothpaste. He straightened his coat, ran a hand through his hair, and stuck the other hand inside his jacket.

"Let's rumble," he said, nodding toward the front door.

"Lance," I whispered. "We don't expect anything to go wrong. But if it does, just take care of yourself, okay?"

He frowned. "What do you mean?"

"Well, I mean, if there's any . . . gunplay . . . or anything like that."

I saw him gulp, but he steeled himself with Method acting techniques. "Don't worry," he rasped like Eastwood. "Lance has your back."

The three of us crossed the front porch. The door swung open before I could ring. It was opened by Amanda Exeter. But something was very different.

She had bleached her hair blond and she'd lost the glasses. Wearing jeans and a midriff tee, not her usual dress-for-success camouflage. I couldn't help looking her over. Who knew she was hiding such a hot body under the suits?

"Mr. Peavey is waiting for you," she said, officious as ever in spite of the new look. "In his office."

We nodded and followed her down the hallway, Amanda looking over her shoulder at Lance. "Who's the lug?"

"Our bodyguard, Lance," I said. "He's armed."

She shrugged. "No problem. This will be a businesslike exchange. No need for firearms."

"Sure," Terry said. "But it never hurts to be covered."

"Are you in on this, too?" I said to Amanda.

"In on what?" she singsonged.

"Don't play innocent. How much is Peavey giving you? Ten percent? Fifteen?"

She pushed open the door to Peavey's office and gestured for us to go inside. We stopped cold when we saw blood on the wall. At the base of the bloody wall were two tasseled loafers sticking out from behind the desk, toes up.

"No," Amanda said, breaking into a smile. "He's giving us *all* of it."

Twink stepped out from behind the door, pointing a semiautomatic at us, a silencer attached to the barrel. She was gripping it with latex-gloved hands.

"Hi again," she said, smiling.

"Keep the big guy covered," Amanda said. "He's got a gun."

Lance raised both hands in the air. Amanda slammed the door behind us, patting Lance down quickly. "He's got no gun!" she scowled.

"Nobody *told* me to bring a gun," Lance whined.

Amanda laughed. "Wow, you girls came here unarmed? You are so unbelievably stupid. Your whole damn family is so stupid it makes me want to vomit!"

Twink shook her head. "So stupid, and yet so capable of messing everything up for us."

"Not anymore," Amanda said, and the two of them exchanged satisfied smirks.

"Is that Peavey behind the desk?" I asked in a weak voice.

"What's left of him," Amanda said, giving a sort of sexualized shudder. "*God*, that felt good!"

"What are you, lesbian lovers?" Terry asked, trying to put it together in her mind.

The two women howled with laughter. "No, we're sisters," Twink said. "Just like you, only much, much smarter."

Terry and I gaped at each other.

"You have a *third* sister?" I said to Twink.

"No, just the two of us," she said with a curtsy. "Twinkle and Candy Starr."

What did this mean? Amanda Exeter was *Candy* the dead dominatrix . . . ? I tried to force my brain to process this information, but it was too shocked to comply.

"But then, who . . . whose body . . . ?" I stammered.

Amanda rolled her eyes. "I guess this is where we lay out our master plan, giving you time to think of an escape while we display our diabolical brilliance for you to admire in your final moments on earth—"

"Forget it," Twink said. "Not gonna happen." She looked around the room like an interior designer sizing up a living room. "Now I need *you*"—she pointed to me—"right over here."

I didn't move. She waved the gun at me. "Come on, come on!"

"I could scream," I said.

"And I could shoot you before it got out of your mouth. Anyway, the place is virtually soundproof. Nobody heard Wendell yelling his stupid head off."

I moved over slowly, my eyes never leaving Terry's. When I got even with Peavey's body, I forced myself to look down. It was a horrible sight. Half of his head had been blown away. My stomach flipped over and the blood drained from my face.

Twink moved me by the shoulders, a fraction of an inch. "Right there, please."

Amanda grabbed her own gun from the desk, also fitted with a silencer. I'd been so stunned by her appearance I hadn't even noticed she was wearing latex gloves as well.

"I like your new look, Amanda," I said.

"Glad you approve," she said sarcastically.

"I'll bet you're a knockout in fur."

She narrowed her eyes at me. "What's that supposed to mean?"

"Your little costume, the one you wore for killing Shannon," Terry said. "Only, fur's not very PC these days, is it?"

"I wouldn't worry about it. It's fake."

It wasn't an outright confession to murder, but it was close. Not that it made much difference at this point.

"Where is everybody?" I said in order to keep her talking.

Amanda pointed the gun at Terry, making a mental calculation of the bullet's future trajectory. I realized they were busily manufacturing a false crime scene—Peavey and the rest of us dying in some wild shoot-out.

"The patients have all gone beddy-bye, and the night staff is tied up in the refrigerator," she told me. "You should know—you put them there."

Twink chuckled and bent down to pick up some bags at her feet. She held them up for us to see—*WH Smith*.

"Cripes," I said.

"Told you we were smart," Amanda jeered. Then she pointed Terry to the side of the door. "Stand over there. Next to the door, please. Thank you."

Terry stood just inside the door as instructed.

"Now, we thought someone might come with you, but not this *big* a someone," Twink said, thinking it over. "I guess he could be next to that plant over there, huh?" she asked Amanda.

"That'll work," said Amanda.

Lance shuffled obediently to a potted palm a few feet down the wall from Terry.

"Hey, Amanda," Terry said softly, looking directly into her eyes. "I know why you're doing this. I know Frank Steinmetz raped you."

Amanda's head made an involuntary little hitching movement. "What are you talking about?"

"I know he assaulted you. But did you have to go this far to get revenge? All of these people . . . dead?"

Lance began to whimper. *"I don't want to die—"*

"Shut up!" Amanda yelled at him, then whipped around to Terry. "It's none of your fucking business! And my name's *Candy.*"

"Candy," Terry said, nodding sympathetically. "I think a jury would be inclined to give you a break if they knew the whole story."

"Oh, let me see . . ." Candy said, putting the gun barrel to her chin. "Do I walk away with a million dollars, or do I go tell my sad story to a jury? Grow up, Kerry!"

"Terry."

"Whatever! We wouldn't have had to kill everyone if it wasn't for your stupid aunt and cousin. Where did they get off, confessing to a murder they didn't commit?"

Terry looked at me for the answer. I shrugged and offered the only explanation I had. "They did it out of love."

"Oh *puhleeeze,*" Twink groaned.

"Okay, that's enough of that," Candy said. "Everybody ready? Why don't you tell each other how much you love each other before I blow you away?" she added with a snicker.

"I love you girls," Lance said, sniffling. "It's an honor to sacrifice myself for you."

"I love you, too," I said to Lance. "And I'm so sorry we got you into this." Then I turned to Terry. "And I love you most of all, Ter."

Terry nodded and gave me a sad little smile. But she said nothing in reply.

Candy waited, looking at her. "Well?" she said impatiently.

"Well what?" Terry said. "Go ahead, shoot."

"Aren't you going to tell her you *wuv* her?" Candy mocked, but Terry only offered her a blank face in return.

"She can't express herself verbally," I said. "She needs therapy before she can do that."

Candy hooted with laughter while Twink raised the gun. "Okay, here comes the *doctor*. . . ." She pointed the muzzle right at Terry's heart, squeezing the trigger.

BAM!

The door to the office flew open, slamming into Twink's arm as the gun fired. My head spun in the direction of the shot. I saw Candy falling against the wall, framed by blood spatter, her eyes wide in shock, her mouth working soundlessly. She looked down at the red stain spreading on her chest, then back up at Twink.

"Sis . . . ?" Candy wheezed.

Then her legs gave way and she crumpled to the floor.

"Shit!" Twink screamed.

Terry dived for the gun in Candy's limp hand. In a split second she had whirled around with it in her own hand and had it aimed at Twink.

A standoff.

Only then did I look to see who'd come in.

Dawn and Belinda, in their nightgowns.

They stood in the doorway taking in the scene, their eyes bugging out to the stems.

"What are you doing here?" Twink shrieked at them.

Belinda pointed to Terry and me. "W-we came here to confront them. We saw them come in the front door."

"Yeah," Dawn said indignantly. "You're not one person. You're two people. Your names probably aren't even Faith."

"And I'll bet you never got your braces locked with that little chemo girl, either," Belinda said, jutting out her lower lip.

Twink's face was contorted in confusion. "What the *hell* does that mean?"

Dawn got a wounded look. "They weren't unflinchingly honest with us!"

It started like a choking sound. Or severe hiccups. Twink began to convulse, her whole body spasming. Finally, out of her mouth came a long, horrible scream, like the shrill plaint of the peacock.

"Are you telling me . . . that my sister is *dead* . . . because of these two . . . complete . . . motherfucking . . . IDIOTS?" she wailed.

Belinda's eyes got wide. Her lip quivered. Her head began to shake.

"DON'T CALL ME AN IDIOT!" she screeched, launching herself at Twink.

Twink was too hysterical and too surprised to react. And Belinda outweighed her by sixty pounds. The large redhead landed on the frail blonde and the two of them crashed into Peavey's desk, tumbling to the floor. They rolled around in a tangle of thrashing limbs, first one on top, then the other.

"I'm NOT an idiot!"

"Get off, you cow!"

"TAKE IT BACK!"

"Idiot!"

"*AM NOT!*"

"Stupid bitch!"

Twink's gun was twisting around in her hand, pointing first this way, then that. The rest of us made like boxers, ducking and weaving as the barrel flashed perilously in all directions.

Then, without warning, Lance sprang into the air like Greg Louganis. He sailed across the room in a swan dive, arms out, then tucked and plummeted, landing on top of the two women with the sound of a grand piano dropping on two air mattresses.

WhussssgggggHHH!

The thrashing ceased.

I thought I'd heard the sound of a few ribs snapping, as well.

Twink's fingers went limp, her hand releasing its grip on the gun.

I rushed over to snatch it up, aiming the silencer directly at her pretty little nose. "Well, Lance," I said, shaking my head in amazement. "You did it again."

Lance looked up from the body pile. "I did good?"

"Yeah, boy," Terry said, picking up the phone to call the cops.

twenty-
six

Candy had been taken away in an ambulance, alive but just barely. I hoped she'd make it so she could stand trial for her heinous crimes. And I hoped she'd end up being prosecuted by Harlon Pinchbeck, with the Honorable Jay Ratliff presiding. Twink was in police custody at this very moment, on her way to the Malibu jail.

She gave up the digital tape without a struggle when she realized there was no way out. She was actually more concerned with the welfare of her sister at that point, as unbelievable as that may seem. At the end of the day, a few human genes go into the makeup of every monster.

Peavey's body had been removed to the morgue, and the staff had been released from the refrigerator—chilled, shaken, a little stir-crazy, but basically intact. Dr. Gustafson was among them, having been on night duty, so she was able to quell any incipient outbreaks of hysteria in the patient population.

Belinda had her rib cage wrapped but declined painkillers on the grounds that it was a slippery slope back to dependency. She would tough it out, she said, while Dawn patted her sympathetically on the back, assuring her she could make it.

When the patients were finally shooed off to bed, I filled Dr. Gustafson in on everything that had happened. When I asked her about the "reinforcement" channel of the stereo system, she claimed to have no idea what I was talking about.

She located the keys to the sound system closet, and after fiddling with the knobs, we were able to turn down the music and hear the channel underneath. As I'd come to suspect, subliminal messages were being piped into every room of the institution at every moment of the day—but they weren't therapeutic in nature:

"Abaddon is the one true prophet . . . Abaddon holds the key to the universe . . . Abaddon's work is of paramount importance . . . Join Abaddon's millennial mission . . ."

Gustafson was shocked, convincingly so. I believed she had no involvement with Peavey's devious plot to control the minds of his patients, turning them into unthinking cash machines for the Children of the Cosmos, and by extension, for himself.

Two hours later, Terry, Lance, Detective Thomas, and I sat in the conversation pit in the lobby, tying up loose ends. Thomas made no pretense of being the big-guy-in-charge. He just sat there asking us questions and taking notes.

"So who do you think the dead girl was? The one they passed off as Candy?"

I'd been thinking about that ever since it was revealed that Amanda actually *was* Candy, disguised as Executive Assistant of the Year. "I think you'd better look into the fate of a girl named Becky Madrigal."

He wrote the name down. "Who is she?"

"She worked with Twink at EquiSpa. Supposedly, she took off to pursue a musical career, but my guess is she's singing in the heavenly choir right now. Probably had no family to speak of, nobody to report her missing. They dyed her hair blond so she could pass as Candy, or maybe she did it herself to fit in better at the beach."

That was what my nightmare had been trying to tell me. The girl with dark roots and no singing ability was the one who had been killed, whereas Candy was still alive. That would teach me to pay attention to my dreams.

"And that reminds me of something that went right over my head," I said. "Twink told you they were transplants from the east, but she slipped up and told me they were from Riverside. I never even noticed the discrepancy in her story. Becky's probably the one who's from out of town, the one with no fingerprints on file because she didn't have a California driver's license."

Thomas shook his head with grudging admiration for the sister fiends. "Pretty clever. They must have known it would take a couple of weeks to get fingerprints from the national database."

"And by that time they planned to be on the road," I said. *With a million dollars.*

"So they kill Becky, then Twink files a false missing-person report on her sister," Terry continued. "All Twink has to do is go to the morgue in tears, saying she recognizes the dragon as her sister's tattoo."

"We'll check with all the tattoo parlors. See if we can con-firm this Madrigal woman's identity," Thomas said. "Twink was pretty good at those tears, I have to say. It was a real piti-ful scene when she ID'd her 'sister.'"

"Yeah," I said. "They're a couple of fine little actresses."

"But then, what about the head?" Thomas wanted to know. "Why did it show up with your cousin?"

I shrugged. "Maybe they took Becky out in the canyon, the one closest to the rehab facility here, and killed her there. Then they chopped off the head to hide her identity. Buried it, only to have it dug up again by wild animals. Our cousin was in the habit of sneaking out to the canyon to watch for . . . *um* . . . to look at the stars at night. He fell asleep, or went into some kind of fugue state, and when he came out of it, there was the head."

"Then it was Candy who dressed up as a 'Hookergram,' got past the night watchman at One PCH Plaza, and killed Shan-non Voss," Terry said.

"Why couldn't that have been the other sister, Twink?"

"The guard's description," I told him. "He said she was 'aver-age height,' with a great body. Twink's at least six feet tall and model-thin, not *Playboy* material like Candy."

"All right," he said. "So now we're only missing one piece of the puzzle. One damn big piece—*why'd they do it?*"

Okay, this question required a little finesse. If we told him about the blackmail, the money would be confiscated, Frank would be interrogated, and all roads would lead back to the mob.

I was well aware that lying to a police officer in the course of an investigation was a punishable offense, but I was also sure that Frank's buddies had ways of punishing people that might be even less pleasant than anything the law could threaten us with. Cement shoes vs. time in a cement block.

"Well, the sisters killed Shannon Voss to implicate Peavey," I said slowly, as if I was just figuring it out, which I was. "It would look like he murdered her to keep her from spilling the beans on the Children of the Cosmos. Then they killed Peavey to implicate us, setting it up to look like we were honing in on his action . . . all of us dying in a blaze of gunfire."

"Okay, but why kill Becky, if that's who she was, in the first place?"

I looked at Terry. *Take it, sis.*

"We're not sure," Terry said.

The biggest, fattest liar in the free world, and that's the best she can come up with?

Thomas's mouth formed a skeptical line. "How did they get you here tonight? On what pretext?" he said, looking directly at me. Damn it, everyone was looking directly at me. Even Lance had an expectant look on his big face.

I sat there for a moment, my butt balanced precariously on the horns of a dilemma. Perjure myself? Obstruct an investigation and live to see another day?

Or tell the truth about Frank.

"We have a client," I said finally. "We can't disclose his name. They were blackmailing him. We came here to negotiate on his behalf. He was their main target—everyone else just got in the way, including us."

Thomas gave me a stony look. "I need his name."

"Why? You don't need motive," Terry said. "You've got an airtight case without it."

He shook his head. "This is a murder investigation. I'm gonna need his name."

"It'll probably come out anyway, once you start working on the girls," I pleaded with him. "Give us a few hours, at least."

A few hours to give Frank his money and wash our hands

of him for good. Then the chips could fall wherever they wanted to.

Thomas sat there for a second, thinking it over. His eyes traveled down to the suitcase at my feet. "Okay, I'll give you twenty-four hours. If we're not solid by then, I'm coming back to you."

Terry and I sighed in relief.

He closed his book. "I want to say—you did some real good work here, ladies. Really good work."

A little whimper escaped Lance's throat.

"And you, too," Thomas said, giving Lance an appraising look. "Say, you got a job, son?"

Lance pointed to his chest. "Me?" There were no other men around.

Thomas nodded.

"I . . . I just quit a job tonight," Lance said.

"Well, we could use a man of your stature and courage on the force, if you'd be interested."

"Would I!" Lance squealed in excitement. "Would I!"

"Um, do you have to take . . . an intelligence test, or anything like that?" Terry inquired casually.

Thomas shrugged. "It's real basic. Come by my office tomorrow and we'll talk," he said to Lance, who was rocking back and forth on the couch, hands between his knees.

"A cop, oh man . . . a cop . . . I get to wear a cowboy hat—"

"Oh, Detective Thomas?" I said. "One question."

"Shoot." He made a face. "Sorry, what?"

"The girls planted DNA evidence—semen—on their victims as a backup strategy. Did you ever do any analysis of it?"

"We discounted that right away. Looks like they took a sample from somebody and froze it to keep it from degrading. The cells had all burst in the process. According to the lab, if you don't do it just right, the ice crystals melt and the cell explodes. We knew it was planted evidence from the get-go."

Terry looked at me, shaking her head.

"Funny," Thomas said, "everything else they did was so dang clever. But I guess they didn't do their homework on that one. It was kind of a dumb move."

"Well, they *are* blond," Terry said.

Thomas laughed and started to walk away. "Anyone need a ride?"

"No, thanks." I waved him off. "We're set."

"You guys gonna take it easy for this rest of this evening?"

"Sure," Terry said. "After we run a little errand."

He glanced at the suitcase again but let the question go unasked. He smiled, tipped his sheriff's hat, and headed west.

Out the front door.

We said good-bye to Lance on the front porch. He could barely stand still, so anxious was he to get home and bone up on his reading, writing, and math skills for the officer qualifying exam.

"Thanks again, Lance," Terry said, grabbing his hand in a shake.

"Don't mention it," he said, pumping her hand up and down.

I pulled his head down for a kiss on the cheek. "You're the best, Lance."

"Cut it out," he said, blushing, then he bounded down off the porch and jammed himself into the Hyundai. "Wish me luck!" he yelled through his open window before firing up the clown car and pulling out of the lot.

"Knock 'em dead!" I called, waving to his taillights.

When he was gone, I looked at Terry hopefully. "You probably don't have to know where the Queen of England resides to be a Malibu cop."

"Or even President of the United States," she said, and grinned.

We headed back to Frank's, the suitcase weighing heavily on my lap and heavier on my conscience.

Frank was getting his money back.

And his victims? Would they ever be compensated for their pain and suffering?

I told myself we couldn't solve all the world's problems, not in one night anyway. At least we'd found our murderers.

As before, the back door was open for us.

We walked in, calling, "Frank?"

No answer.

"I'm not in the mood for this," Terry grumbled. "Frank!"

Again, no answer.

I dropped the suitcase on the floor. Terry went to the study and looked inside. "He's not here," she said.

"What do we do? We can't just leave the money in the living room with the house unlocked."

"Well, I'm not waiting for him to get back. We'll take it over to Reba's and hold it for him there."

I shook my head. "I want to be done with this. I want this money out of our hands."

"Okay, I'll take a look upstairs. Maybe he's asleep."

I got a queasy feeling as soon as she cleared the top landing, and started up the stairs after her. "Terry, no! Wait! Let's call the police!"

But she ignored me, going into the master bedroom. I stood

in the middle of the staircase and watched the lights come on inside the room. Then I heard the scream I'd been waiting for.

"Oh my God!"

I bounded up the remaining stairs two at a time, my heart about to explode. Terry stood outside the open bathroom door with a sickened look on her face.

The bathroom tile was covered in red liquid.

"Jesus, Ker," she said, backing up, clutching her stomach.

I forced myself to look inside. Frank was nude in the bathtub, arms floating in the red water. They had been opened from the wrist to the elbow. The dark edges of the wounds gaped like the holes in Robert's canvases, tendons glowing white inside. A safety razor lay on the tile next to the bathtub.

I turned away, horrified and strangely saddened.

I wished I hadn't looked. I wished I wasn't going to have that image burned in my brain, along with Peavey's mangled head and Shannon's decapitated one.

We walked slowly back down the stairs.

"Think it was his money pals?" Terry said softly. "Or did he do it to himself out of guilt?"

"It doesn't really matter," I said. "The operative word here is *guilt*. Everything comes back to you, sooner or later."

The call to the cops would have to wait. We couldn't leave a million dollars of mob money in the house for the sheriff's deputies to find. It might make Frank's financiers cranky. We took the suitcase back to Reba's.

We conjectured that Frank's "associates" had gotten wind of what he really wanted the money for, and had visions of lawsuits coming down the pike from injured actresses. Or maybe they're just not the sort of people who enjoy being lied to. So we took the bold and possibly suicidal step of leaving a note on Frank's coffee table:

To retrieve your investment, please see us next door. We're on the deck. (And kindly dispose of this note carefully.)

We had no idea if it would reach the right people. We planned to stay out on the deck for at least an hour. If the money people hadn't shown up by then, we'd go back and dispose of the note ourselves, calling the sheriff from Frank's house. We hadn't quite worked out what we were going to say about what had brought us there, but we had given ourselves an hour or so to come up with something.

We sat in the dark for no more than twenty minutes, when a gruff voice drifted up to us from below the deck, making us jump. We'd never even seen him coming.

"You got the money?" the voice said.

"Yes," I said, standing to look over the rail.

"Sit down!"

I complied at once.

"Kick the bag over the edge."

Terry and I braced ourselves on the deck chairs, then each of us put a foot to the suitcase and pushed. The bag cleared the edge and fell to the sand with a loud *whump*.

"It's all there?"

"Yes sir," I said. "We didn't even open the suitcase."

God, I hoped it was all there.

We heard the suitcase fasteners snap, then waited a few agonizing minutes while the money was counted. I tried to regulate my breath, forcing myself to inhale and exhale in time to the waves pounding in the distance.

Something flew up on the balcony. Terry ducked, and I jumped out of my chair, hitting the deck. Expecting what—a hand grenade?

It was a thick stack of bills, held together with a rubber band.

"The boss says good work with the terrorists, girls."

Then nothing. Not another sound.

He'd disappeared into the night.

I got to my feet, my whole body shaking. After a moment, I felt the nausea slowly subside.

"Terry?"

She was already counting the money. "Yeah?"

"Can we—"

"You don't even have to say it. We'll get a safety-deposit box."

I closed my eyes and fell back into the deck chair.

"Good," I said.

twenty-
seven

$\mathcal{D}$etective Thomas didn't seem thrilled to hear from us again so soon. He was still at the station, busy with the paperwork on the bloodbath at New Horizons. Terry called him while I listened in on the extension.

"Is this night ever gonna end?" he said with a heavy sigh. "What were you doing at his house?"

"We saw the back door standing open. It was late and there was no movement in the house. So we did the neighborly thing and went in to check on him."

There was a moment's silence, as Thomas weighed her credibility. "You sticking to that story?"

"Yuh-huh," we both said at once.

"Where were you going tonight when you said you had an errand to run?" he asked suspiciously.

"Needed to pick up some tampons," Terry said, "that's all."

"And you needed a large brown suitcase to carry them in?"

"We like to shop in bulk."

"Sheesh, you girls are something else. Where you go, trouble follows. Okay, I'll send out some deputies. They'll be there in ten minutes." And then he hung up.

Maybe we *were* a magnet for trouble. It sure seemed that way lately. Or maybe we had a homing instinct for dead bodies, as Boatwright had said—drawn to them like those proverbial moths to the flame.

The deputies arrived, joking that Malibu had a much higher mortality rate since we had come to town. I let Terry do most of the talking, since she had a demonstrated knack for making perjurious statements convincingly.

Several hours later, with the dogs nestled around us, we finally got to bed.

Having lived through the longest week of our lives.

twenty-eight

 e were watching the local news coverage of the incident at New Horizons the next morning when the phone rang. It was Eli, jubilant through the crackling of interference. I made out the words ". . . released this morning!"

"What? You're breaking up!"

He passed back into range of the communications satellite. "Reba and Robert are out. The prosecutor dropped the charges!"

I sank to my knees, on the verge of laughing hysterically or crying hysterically, I didn't know which. "They're free? Where are you?"

"Downtown LA. They're being processed at the Inmate Reception Center. They'll be released to me and I'll bring them home. Be there as soon as I can."

I disconnected and yelled at Terry, "Reba and Robert are out. The charges have been dropped!"

"Yay!"

We did a little dance in the middle of the floor, the dogs yapping and spinning around with us. Today, doggies, there would be treats all around.

Forty-five minutes later, the waiting was making me nuts, so I decided to burn off some excited energy. I let the pups out and we took a run down the beach (in the opposite direction of Frank's house). When their little legs got tired, I picked them up, one in each arm, and continued running.

After pounding the sand for another ten minutes, I was completely exhausted. I put the dogs down in the surf and they frolicked in the waves, yapping and nipping at my feet as we made our way back to Reba's.

Terry was on the deck drinking coffee. The pups ran up the stairs to greet her, then began to shake the water off their fur (I think Muffy honestly believed she *had* fur, instead of a doggie buzz cut). They shook and shook and shook and shook, then the sliding door opened and Reba dashed out.

"Darlings!" she sang, running into my arms.

"Reba, I'm so happy you're home!" I squeezed her, but not so tight as to snap the fragile bones.

Next she ran to hug Terry. "You're my heroines!"

"All in a day's work," Terry said, blushing a little.

Eli stepped out into the sunlight wearing reflector shades. Reba threw him an adoring look. "And my hero . . . !" She leaped into his arms, laughing gaily and kicking her feet, sending her Ferragamos flying. Terry and I ducked the airborne leather slip-ons.

"The sand," Reba said. "I must feel the sand between my toes! The wind in my hair! The salt on my lips . . . I'm FREE!"

Eli lumbered down the steps with her and out toward the water's edge. He lowered her to the sand and she took off, skipping through the surf in her colorful caftan with her arms waving, Eli chasing after her like Big Bird in pursuit of a flighty little Mrs. Bird.

Here we go again, I thought. *Mating season for seniors.*

Reba stopped and Eli went crashing into her. The two of them landed in the surf, splashing and rolling around in each other's arms like Deborah Kerr and Burt Lancaster in *From Here to Eternity.*

Then I suddenly remembered. "Hey, where's Robert?"

Terry and I ran inside and found him standing at the picture window.

We threw ourselves into his arms for a bear hug. "Welcome home!" we cried.

"Thank you, sweets. So good to be home!" He pointed to Eli and Reba thrashing around in the waves. "You don't suppose they're going to disrobe and begin coupling in the surf?" he asked with a nauseous look on his face.

"Let's lower the blinds, just in case," I suggested.

"Excellent thinking," Terry said.

I started to pull the blinds just as Grizzie stomped into the kitchen with a broom. Grizzie was back, too! She peered out the picture window over my shoulder and caught sight of her mistress lying on the sand, making out with Eli.

"Holy mo'er o' God, have ye no SHAME?" Grizzie yelled, then tramped back out of the room muttering imprecations à la Popeye.

"Welcome home, Griz!" Terry said.

"Huh!" she grunted from the other room.

Robert laughed, his big shoulders shaking. "Such warmth and humanity in the woman. Say, is there any fresh coffee?"

"Of course," I said. "Would you like some?"

"Love some! And I've got just the thing for dunking," he said, dashing off to raid his bedroom closet.

Between the three of us, we polished off a pot of coffee and six packages of Ding Dongs. While we dunked, we quizzed Robert about the day he disappeared, but he maintained that he still had no memory of it. He acknowledged that he'd spent time in the canyon with Bunga but denied taking any drugs.

"And did you see anything . . . *interesting* . . . in the skies?" I said.

He winked at me.

"Well?" Terry pressed him.

"I saw some interesting phenomena."

"What?" I said. "What did you see?"

"Tell you what. I'll take you out there one day soon so you can see for yourselves."

"Thank you very much," I said, shaking my head, "but I've been there, and I'm not going back. Especially not at night."

"Then I guess you'll remain a nonbeliever," he said, yawning.

"I guess I will."

"Earth monkey."

"What?"

"Heretic."

"Heretic?" Terry said, frowning at him. "This is a religion for you now?"

Robert blinked a few times. "I'm sorry—what were we saying?"

"You were calling me names," I said.

"Nonsense. I have but one name for you two, and it's my

darling Nancys Drew. Now, old Cousin Robert is bushed. I'm dying to sleep in my own bed."

And with that he trundled off to his studio for a nap.

I shot Terry a look. "We really have to get you guys to a specialist. You're still under the influence."

She shrugged. "Something tells me the Cosmos Kids aren't going to be a problem much longer."

Reba and Eli came running back up the stairs, wet clothes askew, staggering like a couple of drunks. Due to her recent tattooing, Reba's makeup was perfect even after a roll in the sand and sea. She whipped back her wet hair like she was auditioning for a shampoo commercial.

"Nothing like the salt air to get a man's blood pumping, girls!" she panted. "Make a note of it!"

Eli popped her on the behind with his leather belt, and she erupted into giggles, then took off running. He chased her through the living room and down the hallway, then the bedroom door slammed behind them—

BAM.

After a few seconds, Grizzie called out from the dining room. "Is it safe?"

"It's safe," I said.

She came stomping back in, muttering what sounded like "Shame, shame," and began to sweep up the sand that Reba and Eli had tracked so thoughtlessly into the house.

And thus was a nice, relaxing morning spent at home with our lawyer, our dogs, and the folks sprung from jail.

twenty-
nine

$\mathcal{T}$ wo weeks later . . .

"My, my. You clean up nice," I said to Terry. "When was the last time you wore a dress?"

"Barbara Deedler's bat mitzvah," she said, tugging on the sides of the green silk Nicole Miller sheath. She pinched the fabric of the dress and pulled it out, looking down the front. "It's uncomfortable," she said, wiggling around. "Scratchy."

"It's only for a couple of hours."

What was the occasion for the momentous donning of a dress? you ask.

Reba's engagement-cum-release-from-murder-charges party.

I had used our earnings from Frank's associates to purchase a fabulous pink number from BCBG. It was sleeveless with a delicate floral pattern and a shimmery organza wrap that you could either wear around your shoulders or as a scarf.

"Come on," I said, approaching Terry with a mascara wand. "Just a touch."

She backed off like I was coming at her with a machete. "No!"

"It'll make your eyes stand out—"

"All right, if you *must*." She closed her eyes and stuck out her face.

"Moron, your eyes have to be open."

"Oh." She squinted as the wand came toward her. "I hate shit coming at my eyes."

"Trust me, okay?"

I managed to dab a little black on the blond ends of her lashes. Then, before she could protest, I grabbed a lipstick and smoothed some shiny pink on her lips. I spun her around, and the two of us looked at ourselves in the mirror. I had my red curls piled on top of my head, Reba's diamond studs in my ears. Terry had insisted on wearing her hair down, but the makeup was a definite improvement.

"Now you look like a proper lipstick lesbian," I said.

"And you look like Cinda-fuckin-rella."

I laughed. "Maybe I'll find my Prince Charming at the party."

"Yeah, you never know what interesting men might show up," she said, smirking.

"You never know," I agreed.

We $went$ $outside$ to join the festivities. Beautifully dressed people milled around under a large canvas tent a hundred feet from the water. The tent was garlanded with hanging wisteria, like bunches of perfumed grapes. A dozen small tables with white folding chairs sat at discreet intervals inside the tent, and each table boasted a centerpiece of edible flowers, a stuffed robin redbreast on a twig, and an ice sculpture of a honeybee.

"Springtime for lovers," Reba had said, announcing her theme. "There'll be flowers . . . there'll be birds . . . there'll be *bees!*"

She was scurrying around attending to last-minute details, greeting the guests, and barking instructions to the cute, clean-cut guys in waiters' uniforms, who were dancing as fast as they could with their silver trays held aloft.

Grizzie had the afternoon off because the event was being catered. She was in her apartment with her feet up, watching *Wall Street Week*. Cousin Robert was in his studio, painting. He was still committed to sobriety, he said, and didn't want to be tempted.

On the buffet table was a fount of temptation—a terraced silver urn bubbling with champagne, run on a battery pack hidden by a spray of chrysanthemums. Eli stood next to the table, stuffing shrimp into his mouth directly from the serving platter.

Reba scooted up to him carrying an appetizer plate garnished with a yellow flower.

"Oh dearest," she sang, holding out the plate. "Wouldn't you rather fill up a nice little dish of your very own?"

Eli gave her a look laced with cyanide.

I ran over to referee the situation, laying a hand on each of their shoulders. "Now, didn't we agree that nobody's going to try to change anybody in this relationship? Didn't we say that it's the best way to get along with somebody we're going to be married to? Complete acceptance of the other person just as he or she is?"

Eli nodded, cheeks bulging with shellfish. "Sh'right. Th'what we said, dearesʼht."

"Agreed," said Reba, taking a long, cleansing breath. "Here, dear, try an edible flower." She held up the golden blossom for Eli to sample.

He swallowed two cheekloads of shrimp, frowning. "You want me to eat a flower? What do I look like, Daisy the Cow?"

She waved it in front of his nose. "You'll love it. It has the most delicate flavor. It's called a *cal-en-du-la*," she said, exaggerating the syllables.

"And I sure ain't eatin' a flower named *Count Dra-cu-la*."

I gave him a stern look. "Now, Eli. What did we say about trying new things? Being open to things our mate is interested in?"

"I didn't know that included eating the centerpiece," he protested.

"Well, that's the whole point. It's something new . . . something you haven't done before, and something you just might like if you gave it a try."

He grabbed a gladiolus stem from the arrangement on the table and turned it sideways like a leg of mutton, ripping off the petals with his teeth and chewing noisily. "Mmmmm. That's great. Got any barbecue sauce?"

Reba slapped his arm playfully. "Oh, *you*."

He crammed the flower back in the vase and picked up a shucked oyster. "Tell you what, I'll eat about twenty of these, then we'll see what happens, eh? See if we come up with anything *new*?" he said, his eyebrows waggling lecherously.

Reba put a hand to her mouth and giggled, bony shoulders shaking in glee. "Be-*have*," she said, blushing an attractive pink. She took me by the arm and dragged me away, leaving Eli to pour bivalves down his throat.

"Now, dear," she said to me, "I want to discuss your fee."

I shook my head adamantly. "Uh-uh. No payment."

"Don't be silly! We're free because of you. We owe you our very lives!"

Oh no, not another eternally grateful person, I thought, looking over at Lance, who was doing duty behind the bar. He was wearing his tux, shaking a martini pitcher while he studied an open workbook on the bar. *Fun with Dick and Jane?*

"I won't hear of it, Reba. Case closed."

Terry wandered up to join us. Reba took one look and gasped in awe. "My dear, you look absolutely fabulous!"

"Thanks." Terry tugged at her dress self-consciously.

"Terry dear, I want you to talk your silly sister into taking payment for all that you've done."

I was ready to jump down Terry's throat, sure that she would take Reba for all she could, but she shocked the hell out of me. "Reba, no. We can't do that. You're family."

"Nevertheless," Reba insisted.

"Uh-uh," Terry said. "That would be very bad juju, taking money to help a family member."

"Oh, very well. Perhaps you'll accept a little present, then."

"Maybe," I said. "Depends on how little."

"Well, I was thinking you might like a nice Turkish rug for your living room floor—"

"NO WAY!" we yelled, and a dozen heads spun around to look in our direction.

Reba's eyes popped out to the whites. "For Heaven's sake, I was *kidding.* Is everyone around here allowed to have a sense of humor but me?"

Our jaws dropped in tandem. Reba was developing a sense of humor?

Terry began to sing à la David Byrne: "This is not my beautiful aunt . . ."

"Look who's here," Reba said excitedly, pointing to the door. "It's Heather Granger. I wasn't sure she would show."

I smiled at Terry. "Oh, I thought she might."

Terry winked at me and nodded.

"Excuse me, dears," Reba said, fluttering away. "I must go say hello."

We watched as Reba approached Heather, who was the picture of serene beauty in her gauzy black widow's dress. They chatted for a minute, then Reba dragged Heather over to the bar to get a drink.

"Thank you *so* much for the recommendation," we heard Reba say. "The caterers are sublime."

"I'm so glad you like them," Heather replied.

Terry leaned into me and whispered, "By the way, we got a call from the mayor's office."

My mouth flew open. "The mayor of Los Angeles?"

"No, the mayor of Munchkin Land." She rolled her eyes. "Yes, the mayor of Los Angeles."

"Well . . . why are they calling us?"

"They want to give us a citizenship medal. Two medals, actually. For the hijacking thing."

"Oh no."

"Oh yes."

"Well, I guess we can get Lance to pick them up for us or something." I pointed behind Terry, who turned to look. "Hello, Heather!"

She breezed over to us, highball in hand. A young waiter passed her with a serving tray and she stopped to take a canapé, giving him a nod and a smile.

"Hello, girls," Heather said in her most melodious voice.

"Nice to see you." I lowered my own voice to the sympathy register. "How are you holding up?"

"Oh, fairly well, considering." She cast her lovely eyes downward.

"We're so sorry about your husband," Terry said.

"Thank you. It was . . . such a shock," Heather said, then brightened again instantly. "But here we are, the sun is shining, and life begins anew." She looked around the tent, daintily polishing off her canapé. "Which is so beautifully expressed in the theme of the party."

"Yes, springtime for lovers," Terry said. "Reba's idea. You got your birds, you got your bees—"

"And your dolphins!" Heather sang. "Look out there!" She pointed to a family of dolphins in the bay. "Now, there's a good omen! Let's have a look, shall we?"

She kicked off her shoes and skipped out from underneath the tent onto the sand, heading for the water's edge.

We followed her out and watched the dolphins gamboling playfully in the waves. It *was* a good omen, I decided, a sign that things were on the mend. Heather looked back over her shoulder to gauge the location of the nearest guest.

When she determined that no one was within earshot, she turned to us, eyes sharp as broken glass. "Okay, you little bitches. Where is it?"

Terry and I blinked. "Where is what?" Terry said.

"Oh, don't give me your little Pollyanna act," Heather snapped. "Where's the money?"

"What money?" I said.

"The million you got from Frank!"

Terry and I stood dumbstruck for a few seconds.

"W-we don't have it," I stuttered.

"Bullshit! You think you can get away with keeping it, you little birdbrain? You didn't think I'd come for it? After all I went through, you thought I'd let you *keep* it?"

"All *you* went through?" Terry said, frowning at me in confusion.

Heather scowled, her skin stretching like Saran Wrap over

the prominent cheekbones. "You saw what I did to Frank. Just imagine what I'll do to you. . . . Before I chop off your heads, I'll personally scrape every last freckle off your smug little faces!"

"*You* chopped their heads off?" Terry said. "I . . . I thought that was Twink and Candy!"

Heather gave her a smirk. "And who do you think gave them *their* orders?"

"You'll never get away with it, Heather," I said, then grimaced. *That was a little hackneyed*, I thought.

She shook her auburn mane. "Don't be a dope. There's absolutely no evidence tying me to those murders. And the police are convinced that Frank was done in by his mob buddies. They were kind enough to share their suspicions with me, and of course I wasn't the least surprised. 'Lie down with dogs,' I said, 'and you're sure to get—'"

"You lay down with him long enough," Terry said. "And then you killed him for a lousy million."

"It wasn't for the money, you twit. That was supposed to go to the girls. It was all their idea, anyway. They came to me and told me about Frank's string of victims. But the asshole wouldn't pay up, so I expanded on their idea. Showed them how they could kill that girl and *really* make him pay. Make no mistake, Frank got what he deserved."

"And the victim, Becky?" I said. "She deserved it because . . . ?"

Heather breathed a sigh. "She was a nobody going nowhere. . . . Sometimes it's kinder to put people down, like a horse with a broken leg."

"They try to save horses with broken legs these days," Terry said. "It's more humane. But I guess you wouldn't know a lot about being humane, would you, Heather?"

Heather glared at Terry, her eyes narrowed. But she offered nothing in her own defense.

"I guess they put Wendell down for you too, huh?" I said. "Your patsy Mr. Peavey? He was getting scared, wasn't he? Afraid your little cult scam was going to come to light?"

"Yeah, well, it was a great business until you stuck your noses in, blowing the whole operation. In another year, I'd have had enough to buy a castle in the Loire Valley."

"France?" Terry said. "Why France?"

"Because they appreciate mature beauty in France!" Heather said, baring her porcelain teeth. "Now I need that money!"

"Why?" Terry said. "I don't get it—what about all the money you and Abaddon soaked people for?"

"They froze our accounts, also thanks to your meddling."

"Really sorry to hear that, Heather," I said, trying to sound calmer than I felt. "Listen, if we had the money, we'd give it to you. We returned it to Frank's financiers."

"What? I'm not buying that!"

"Well, you'd better," Terry said. "'Cause that's what happened."

Heather stepped in closer and lowered her head. "Nice try. I'm not leaving here without it. Or you're a couple of dead redheads."

"You're threatening us with all these people around?" I said.

"They'll be leaving when the party's over," Heather said with an evil little chuckle, "but the caterers won't." She gave us a smile that was pure gloat. "They're *mine*. And each one of them has a gun in his cummerbund."

"And a gun at his back," Terry said, her face breaking into a grin.

"Wh-what?" Heather said, blanching.

"Check it out," I said, pointing inside the tent.

The party *was* over.

Every cute little guy in a waiter's outfit was matched by a sheriff's deputy or an FBI agent brandishing a gun. The male and female guests, all of them undercover cops dressed beautifully in party clothes, holding out their badges and their weapons and looking very mean. And my three crushes—Boatwright, Franzen, and Thomas—on the outskirts of the crowd, radios in hand, jointly supervising the whole operation.

Lance, temporarily deputized that very morning, pointed the barrel of a Smith & Wesson .38 at the nose of a waiter whose finger sandwiches were tumbling off his tray.

"Do I get to say it?" Lance called out to Detective Thomas.

"Go!" Thomas called back.

Lance whipped out a cowboy hat from behind his back and plunked it on top of his head, bellowing, "YOU'RE UNDER ARREST, SUCKERS!"

Whereupon Ms. Heather Granger, pioneering woman doctor, former socialite, bogus cult member, and cold-blooded murderess, dropped into a very fashionable heap on the warm Malibu sand.

Terry reached down the front of her green dress and yanked the hidden microphone off her chest.

"That's better," she said. "That wire was bugging the hell out of me."

thirty

"I've always wanted to do this." I poured water over one of the ice sculptures to watch it melt. Streams ran down what was left of its face like little honeybee tears of anguish.

"That was a cute idea of Reba's," Terry said. "Bumblebees for *The Sting*."

"She *is* developing a sense of humor. Who'd have thought?"

We were alone in the tent, candlelight flickering in the chill night air. The officers and agents were long gone, and Reba and Eli had been inside for hours performing God only knows what acts of oyster-inspired perversion.

The party and mass arrest had been a rousing success.

I put my feet up on one of the folding tables. Terry refilled her glass from the bubbling champagne fountain. She took a sip, scratched the delicate itch at the tip of her nose, and began to sing:

"*Ti*-ny bubbles . . ."

I chimed in with the chorus:

"Bubbedy bubbedy bubbles . . ."

"*In* the wine . . ."

"*In* the wine . . ."

"Make me happy . . ."

"Make me happy . . ."

"Make me feel fine."

"I don't real-ly feel fine . . ." I sang, taking up the lead.

"Bubbedy bubbedy bubbles . . ." she chorused. "Why-*y-y* not . . . ?"

"'Cause we don't know . . ."

"'Cause we don't know . . . ?"

"Where Abaddon is." I looked over at her. "Can we stop now?"

She shrugged. "Yeah."

"It's hard to discuss everything in Tiny Bubbles-ese."

"Takes practice," she said, then took another drink. "Don't worry about Abaddon, they'll nail his ass."

"I hope so, the bastard—taking advantage of all those people, of their need to believe in something."

Terry spun the champagne glass by the stem. "You know what I don't get?" she said.

"What?"

"Why were you kidnapped by James, if Heather was in charge of the whole operation? I mean, while they were attempting to kill you, they were hitting me up for money. So they had to know we weren't the same person."

"Maybe the girls had me kidnapped on their own. And the regular Cosmos Kids weren't in on that angle. They just did what they always do, hypnotizing and brainwashing and cashing in, like the well-oiled machine that they were."

"So the left hand didn't know what the right hand was doing?"

"That'd be my guess," I said. "But we'll probably never know, exactly. Nor will we ever find out what happened to James."

"And I guess when they set up the second phase of the blackmail, Candy had to disappear, so Heather changed her into Amanda and leaned on Peavey to hire her, knowing that she'd eventually use Amanda to wipe him out."

"Brilliant deduction, Sherlilocks."

We sat in silence, gazing out at the ocean through the open side of the tent. A school of phosphorescent organisms glowed green in the waves, as from a spotlight on the ocean floor. And farther out, millions of other creatures lurked in its depths, gobbling up their fellow travelers, biting them in half, swallowing them whole, trapping and ambushing and chasing them to the death.

But not for money's sake. Not out of jealousy, or for a thrill. And certainly not over religion.

No, we humans had a lock on killing for the wrong reasons. They did it for survival. Part of the real "Plan."

"I don't know if I could live at the beach," Terry said finally.

"Well, I'm pretty sure you'll never be able to afford it." Then I realized what this meant. "Hey, what about Lailannii? What about sunsets under the coconut trees and walks by the water?"

She shrugged. "She threw me over for a fire-eater. I got a postcard yesterday."

"Oh, sorry."

"No biggie. It was only a fling. Speaking of which—you and Detective Good Buns . . . ?"

"Boatwright? I don't know." I frowned as I thought about it. "Franzen was pretty cute at those FBI briefings, wasn't he?

So forceful, up there with his little pointer and his overhead transparencies . . ."

She shook her head. "Not my type. Too wholesome."

"Yeah. I think he's probably Mormon."

She sat up, interested. "Hey, I never thought of that. If he's Mormon, we could *both* marry him. We could be *sister wives*."

"Gag me!"

She threw a chrysanthemum at my head, laughing. "They don't really do that—not the normal ones, anyway. Just a few wackos out in the Utah bush."

"I knew that."

"So what *about* Boatwright?"

"I don't know. He's got an edge. He scares me a little."

"Even better! I like a little danger, a little excitement."

"I know *you* do. . . . Anyway, I don't think he's interested."

"Why on earth do you say that? He's obviously interested."

"Well, he didn't say much to me when he left today."

"He had fifteen people under arrest!"

"Well, if that's more *important* than saying good-bye . . ."

She rolled her eyes. "You need to get over yourself."

"Well, you need to get into therapy."

"Well, you need a fat lip!"

"Well, who's gonna give it to me?"

"I AM!"

"You and what army?"

"Me and Dick Armey!"

"Well, me and Jerry Falwell can kick your and Dick's ass!"

"Well, you and Jerry Falwell can suck my and Dick's—"

"HEY!" a man's voice came from the side of the tent. Boatwright pushed back the canvas flap and walked in, smiling adorably.

"Am I gonna have to separate you two?" he said.

Good ol' Jen. She developed a sudden migraine and took herself right off to bed, leaving Boatwright and me alone together in the tent.

What, you want details?

Well, okay, voyeur. But I'm not going to get all graphic. I'm not some kind of slut.

Much.

Boatwright wriggled out of his jacket. I think he knew the effect his shoulder holster had on me. Really, I had been prepared to hold out on him, making him wait for an expensive night of dinner and theater. But he cheated, unleashing the big gun, so to speak.

I felt a rush of warmth when I saw the leather straps digging into his chest, the lethal power nestled next to his pectoral muscle.

Mamma fucking mia.

Humphrey Bogart cool and Colin Farrell cute. A deadly combination of seductiveness and the color of authority. What red-blooded, law-abiding woman could resist?

"I've always wanted to do it in a tent," he said, grinning.

"I've always wanted to do it with someone who said 'do it.' It's so . . . animal."

He laughed. "I heard you're getting a medal from the mayor."

"Looks that way."

"I've always wanted to do it with a medal winner. Of course, I always figured it would be an Olympic skater in a tight sequined outfit."

"Sorry to disappoint you," I said. "I'm only a national hero."

He ran a finger down the front of my dress. "Wanna show me how you took down those terrorists?"

"Think you're up to it?" I knocked his hand away to mask my quivering reaction to his touch.

"Sure. C'mere, show me."

He came at me in a wrestler's crouch. I went around behind him and put my arms around his neck. "I grabbed him like this—"

Before I knew what was happening, I was flipped over his head onto my back, landing with an ungainly thud on the sandy canvas.

"Ugh!"

Boatwright quickly knelt at my side. "Wow, I'm so sorry! I didn't mean to throw you that hard. You're lighter than I thought." *Oh sure, flatter me to make up for slamming me to the mat.* "You know, you really should put on a few pounds."

So much for flattery. "Fine. Go get me a bucket of chicken wings. Forget all this romance stuff."

I started to sit up but groaned and fell back down, clutching my side.

"Are you hurt?" There was real concern in his voice.

I was fine, but I figured on milking the situation. "Yes," I whimpered. "It hurts."

"Where?"

"All over."

He leaned over me. "Want me to kiss it and make it better?"

"Mmm-hmm."

"Does it hurt here?" He touched the side of my neck.

"Yes," I said. "Pretty sure it's whiplash."

He gave me a series of little kisses up and down my neck, turning my stomach muscles into mush.

"Here," I breathed, pointing to my breastbone.

I felt a feathery brush of his lips over my heart. Then he dragged them across my chest, dotting my breasts with little kisses through the fabric.

"Does it hurt down here?" He took the sides of my dress and started to pull it up over my hips—

"Here." I grabbed his ears like jug handles and pulled his face up to mine. Lips to lips. Teeth to teeth. God help me, tongue to tongue.

And then it was a free-for-all.

Hands clawed at clothing, ripping it off like radioactive material. The pink dress was whipped over my head. Buttons flew from his shirt. Zippers went south. When he was down to his underwear, I grabbed his hand and returned his jujitsu move, flipping him over onto his back.

"That was too easy," I said him. "You know, you really ought to work out more."

"Oh, I'm not hard body enough for you?"

I jumped on top of him in my bra and panties, my hands cupping pecs that felt like hockey pucks. "Pretty flabby, Boatwright."

He laughed, then slid his fingers under the straps of my bra, working them off the shoulders and down the sides of my arms. A lazy index finger made its way softly to the edge of my bra cup. Then it slipped inside and made contact with my nipple. Nerves ran with the baton, handing it off to each bundle down the length of my body, yelling in their tiny nerve voices: "Get ready! Here he comes!"

I was ready in microseconds. I was about to drown in readiness.

My groin ached from wanting him, and there was a maddening ringing in my ears.

Wait. That was a phone.

Boatwright's hand stopped halfway on its journey down my stomach. "Sorry," he said.

I rolled off of him, tears of frustration springing into my eyes. Not the first time this had happened, folks. He jumped up and grabbed the phone out of his jacket pocket. I almost sobbed at the sight of him in his briefs, a sight I knew would be all *too* brief.

"Yeah," Boatwright said into the phone. "Where? Okay, be there in twenty." He snapped the phone closed and gave me an apologetic look.

"Sorry, occupational hazard," he said sheepishly. "Crime never rests."

"Tell me about it," I said, rolling over on my side. "I'm thinking of dating a banker. They clock out at three. Better yet, a kindergarten teacher. They're off after the twelve-o'clock nap."

He laughed. "Sounds sexy." He pulled on his khakis and reached for his shirt. I grabbed the shirttail and held on to it, refusing to let go.

He pulled on the shirt hand over hand until I was lifted to my feet, then he took me in his arms and kissed me gently, while his hands brushed sand from my backside. His palms were surprisingly soft.

"I could probably spare ten minutes, but I don't suppose that's the way you want our first time to be."

"Bingo."

"I'm really sorry."

I sighed. "I understand, darling."

I understand, darling? Was I auditioning for Mrs. Homicide Dick?

He shook the sand out of his shirt and put it on, then strapped his piece back to his chest. I stood there watching him, feeling like prime, grade-A idiot meat. Stranded in my underwear with my thwarted passion.

Was this what I wanted from life?

He leaned in for a short kiss, pulling my bra straps back up to my shoulders.

"I'll call you," he said.

"Uh-huh," I replied.

He threw on his jacket, shoes, and socks, blew me another kiss, then let himself out of the tent like a desert warrior going out to subdue the Infidel.

Fine. Leave the little missus here with the goats while you make the world safe for true believers.

I looked around the tent, shaking my head. Now what?

Go wild, a voice said in my head. *Run down into the surf in your underwear like the feisty heroine from some romance novel. Let your inner goddess be ruled by the moon.*

Sure, I said to the voice. *But first, Champagne.*

I picked up a clean glass from a server's tray and held it under the bubbling fountain.

This is kind of adventurous, I thought, warming up to the situation. *Who would ever suspect me of drinking champagne in a tent in my skivvies, having almost done the deed with a homicide detective?*

The thought caused me to laugh out loud. Before I knew it, I was laughing so hard I blew champagne out my nose, which sent me over the edge into hysterics.

"What's so funny?" a man's voice said outside the closed flap.

He's back!

Of course he couldn't stay away—even his sworn duty couldn't keep him from me! I'm more of a femme fatale than I knew. One taste of me and duty be damned!

I ran to the side of the tent and threw open the flap, coming face-to-face with Special Agent Franzen of the FBI.

"Catch you at a bad time?" he said, looking me up and down.

epilogue

*I*n the days that followed, after we cleared away the empty champagne bottles and I finished shaking the sand out of my pink dress, the other pieces of the case fell into place one by one.

Kent and the rest of the Hungry Boys were booked as accessories to murder. They were Heather's little foot soldiers, gaining entrance to the houses of the rich and famous with the catering company, and checking into rehab clinics to prime people for fleecing by the Children of the Cosmos. At my suggestion, the cops tested their truck for forensic evidence, and sure enough, they found it—Becky Madrigal's hair and traces of her blood. The Boys had transported her body at Heather's behest and stashed it in Reba's house.

Meanwhile, the FBI made a high-profile arrest of Abaddon on the tarmac at Santa Monica airport. He had been waiting for

Heather and her million dollars in a private jet, with a flight plan for the Bahamas, but she cut a little deal for herself by ratting him out. Abaddon is facing RICO charges, and Heather is facing reduced charges of racketeering and second-degree murder. Even with the breaks, she'll be behind bars 'til the cows came home to her birthing clinic on the open plains.

The prosecutor dropped my charges when he heard that the mayor of LA was honoring us with citizenship medals. Plus, they found James's body a few days later in a stall at EquiSpa, where he'd worked shoveling manure. The official story was that he'd been trampled by a horse with impulse-control issues, but Terry and I both suspected that Twink and Candy somehow had a hand in it. As for our other friends from New Horizons, Dawn and Belinda, the arrest of Abaddon led to their fifteen minutes of fame. They were all over the media with their story—*Oprah, The Today Show, Catherine Crier*—talking about their experience as survivors of a brainwashing cult. They intend to launch a whole new recovery circuit, offering therapy and rehabilitation for victims of similar experiences.

Lance began working in a civilian capacity at the LA County sheriff's office in Malibu, pending his successful completion of the officer qualifying exam. They're cutting him a little slack by letting him retake it. Fingers crossed that the eighth time's a charm.

As for Eli and Reba, they postponed their wedding, deciding to try couples therapy to work out a few kinks in their relationship. So far they've had six scheduled appointments, of which Eli has missed the last five. (I think Reba's got a crush on the therapist, but it's probably just transference.)

As for me, I made sure that Terry and Robert went to a specialist in hypnosis deprogramming, so they wouldn't run out and wire money into offshore accounts every time there was a rerun of a Rat Pack movie on TV. Happily, this had a surprising outcome: Robert was finally able to account for his two missing days. He claimed that while lying in the canyon coming down off a sugar high, he'd seen a blinding light in the sky and was beamed up onto a spaceship peopled by little gray men who had performed . . . well, it's not really polite conversation. I will only say that Robert claimed not to be traumatized in the least. He said he actually enjoyed the experience (especially the probes).

I ran to Grizzie with the news, thinking she'd be overjoyed at having her story validated. But she burst into laughter. "Blarney, blarney," she said over and over again.

"What do you mean, *blarney*?" I said.

"It's what Irish bulls do in the meadow," Terry informed me.

"I know *that*. You lied to us?" I cried indignantly, but Grizzie only laughed all the harder. "We really thought you were abducted!"

"Don't ya know about us Irish?" she said. "We're storytellers for centuries back."

I pouted. "We thought you were telling the truth."

"Well, me darlin' lasses, there's an old sayin' where I come from," she said, wiping away tears of mirth. "It's true, even if it didn't happen."

~~THE END~~

Don't believe anything Kerry says about me in here. It's all bull blarney.

THE END

Read on for a sneak peek at
The Vampire of Venice Beach,
the next installment in the series featuring
the McAfee twins, by Jennifer Colt, available from
Broadway Books in January 2007.

"Is this payback?" I said as I jogged alongside a powder blue hearse in a zippered black jumpsuit and Reeboks, panting in the eighty-degree heat. "This is payback, right?"

Terry tossed me a pitying look. "Save your breath," she said. "We'll talk about it after we pick up our check."

She was jogging on the passenger side of the hearse and seemed to be having an easier time of it—cool and comfortable and quite the bad-ass in her wraparound, black Christian Dior sunglasses.

"Is it because I forced you to wear mascara and laughed at you in a dress?" I said, wiping at the sweaty white makeup on my forehead. "That's it, isn't it?"

She pulled down her glasses so I could see her eyes rolling. "Zip it, okay? We'll talk about it *later.*"

The two of us were doing our impression of secret service agents guarding the presidential limousine. We were supposed to be crowd control, but I suspected we were more like window dressing for the motorcade making its way down Main Street in Venice, California. We aren't trained fighters, we don't carry weapons, and we aren't all that imposing physically. An unruly mob could flatten us like bunnies under a bulldozer. But we'd earned an inflated reputation for toughness after thwarting a hijacking a while back (long story), and Terry was all for exploiting it.

The occasion was the *Coming Out of the Coffin* parade, a celebration of the vampire in contemporary society. But it was also a publicity stunt for the new Dark Arts Gallery, a collection of businesses that would sell clothing, artwork, and furniture to the Gothic demographic. Venice has long been a quirky beachside city that is home to artists, body builders, chainsaw jugglers, tarot card readers, gangbangers, street basketballers, punks, hippies, scads of homeless persons, and a few yuppies. Now with the influx of Anne Rice devotees, you could officially add vampires to the list of subcultures thriving here.

"Coming out of the coffin?" I'd said when Terry first told me about the job. "Are these gay vampires?"

She gave me a look. "Why am I the world's expert on gay people?"

I just stared at her.

"Okay, then as the world's expert on straights—why do you guys always insist on knowing if someone's gay?"

"Well, the name kind of implies—"

"It's none of your business what they do in the privacy of their own coffins!"

"Okay . . . you're right," I agreed, with mock seriousness. "I don't care if they perform same-sex sucks. It's really unimportant in the scheme of things."

She gave me a *You're so unenlightened* look. "They're just regular people with a little different fashion sense and different preferences in recreational activities."

"Recreational activities? Oh, of course," I said, putting a finger to my cheek. "Let's see, shall we go boating on Lake Arrowhead today or go chomp on someone's jugular? It's so lovely out, let's go jugular-chomping!"

Terry explained to me in a tone usually reserved for very small retarded children that the occasion was for throwing off the yoke of oppression, an opportunity for vampires to come out into the light and assert themselves as an unappreciated and misunderstood minority.

"And what *about* the light?" I asked. "Don't they disintegrate if they go out in the sun?"

"They're not real vampires, moron. They're *social* vampires."

"Oh. So what you're telling me is that vampirism is a 'lifestyle choice' now."

"Right."

"And we need to be more tolerant of people who make this lifestyle choice."

"Right."

"Just like gay people."

An exasperated sigh. "This is exactly why I took the job," she said. "You're so judgmental. You need to broaden your horizons a little."

And there you had it. The reason we were working for vampires was that I needed horizon-broadening. I'd let her bully me into it rather than appear prejudiced against an oppressed minority. Now as I slogged forward in a black microfiber outfit that stuck to me like tar on asphalt, my lips and nails painted in matching obsidian, carrying a silver-tipped walking stick to ward off dogs and vampire hunters, I was feeling the tiniest bit silly for getting sucked in (sorry).

The sidewalks were full of summer crowds milling in front of vintage clothing stores, massage parlors, cafés, and neighborhood bars. People dressed for the season, I noted with envy. Sandals and shorts and tank tops, arms and legs free to breathe.

They turned to watch us pass. Even in jaded, seen-it-all Venice this merited a glance: a motorcade of multicolored hearses trailing black and red bunting with two redheaded twins dressed like refugees from *The Matrix* jogging next to the lead car. Three giant bodybuilders, also clad in black, ran alongside the hearses behind.

"Anyhow, I couldn't turn down an old friend," Terry said over the hood of the hearse.

An old friend?

I was still reeling from the news that we'd been hired for this gig by Darby Applewhite, the onetime homecoming queen of Burbank High, now reigning as Ephemera, Queen of the Undead. Our former schoolmate was a real fixture on the Goth scene, according to Terry—lead singer in a band called *Flatlining Femmes*. For some reason, Terry had kept this little tidbit from me until this morning when we went to Darby's house to pick her up in her coffin. I could only guess why.

Did my sister have a secret life? Maybe when I'd been out on dates she'd been transforming herself into Batgirl and flying off in pursuit of forbidden thrills. No one who knew her would put it past her.

"I'm not buying the *old times' sake* BS," I said to her. "Since when do you care about Darby Applewhite? You hated her in school."

"Shhh! She'll hear you."

"Oh, she's gonna hear me through the walls of a hearse and a mahogany coffin? Does she have supersonic vampire ears? She didn't in high school. How do you go from being the Princess of Perkiness to the Queen of Darkness, anyway?"

Terry shook her head. "People change, you know. It's not like we're poured into some mold at birth that defines us our entire lives."

There was no talking to her when she was in righteous mode. And I had to concentrate on oxygenating myself before

I collapsed and was carted away by one of the hearses on parade. I glanced in the window of the blue hearse and got a thumbs-up from the driver.

He was one of Darby's two male roommates, a wraithlike blonde, five feet five, with heavily lined blue eyes, who went by the name of Lucian. Her other roommate, Morgoth, was driving the tiger-striped hearse. He was a chubby little thing with thick black hair in a widow's peak that he enhanced with shoe polish so it reached halfway down to his eyes. With Darby they formed the odd trio, sharing a dilapidated house festooned with human skulls, iron torture implements, and body parts floating in formaldehyde. The place had made my blood curdle even in the bright light of a July morning.

The motorcade slowed to round the corner at Main and Rose. Only three blocks to go.

We traveled past rundown Craftsman houses, weed-clogged yards, low-cost housing, and the occasional luxury condo looking like it had gotten lost on its way to Santa Monica. Then our destination came into view, a warehouse looming over the mixed neighborhood like a blue airplane hangar. There was a gaggle of local news types on the curb eager to get a sound bite (sorry) for the nightly broadcast.

I could hear it now. "Would you buy a used hearse from these people? Venice vampires open the Dark Arts Gallery on Jim Morrison's old stomping grounds."

The procession came to a stop by the curb. A black satin bow was stretched across the front door of the warehouse for the ribbon-cutting ceremony. Goth groupies started pressing toward the motorcade. Time for crowd control.

"Move back, everybody! Stay clear of the hearse, thank you!" I pointed at a man in a black satin cape who was trying to peer inside the car. "You sir, could you move away from the hearse, please?"

I checked in with the crew. "This is Red One to Bruce One," I said into my walkie-talkie. "Do you copy, Bruce One?"

The black box crackled. "Copy."

"We're about to unload the first hearse. Keep the crowd back from the vehicles and don't let them block the cameras. Publicity is the whole point, here. Bruce Two, you in place?"

"Roger that."

"Bruce Three?"

"These people have fangs!" said a panicked falsetto.

I rolled my eyes. "Easy, Bruce," I said in a calming tone. "They're here to shop, not to feed."

We had commandeered a group of actors to help out for the day—cohorts of our friend Lance Manley, who was now a rookie in the Malibu sheriff's department. These guys weren't the brightest bulbs in the bug zapper, I'd discovered, and though they were billed as martial arts experts, they were clueless about bodyguarding. Terry had suggested they imitate an action hero as a Method acting technique, and it turned out they all wanted to be Bruce Willis. Not an Arnold Schwarzenegger or Jackie Chan or Vin Diesel in the bunch. When fists were about to fly over the issue, Terry settled the matter by making them all Bruce-for-a-day.

"Bruce Three, was that a copy?" I asked.

Crackle. "Back! Back, bloodsuckers!" I heard Bruce Three shouting.

I signaled to Terry that I'd be back and jogged down the line of hearses past the mob that was cheering and howling, demanding an appearance by the vampire queen. Bruce Three was stationed next to a royal purple hearse with a matching coffin inside. My first thought on seeing it was that Elizabeth

Taylor had given up the ghost, but I was told that the hearse belonged to a famous artist named Viscera Vicious, who was also partial to purple.

On the curb, black-clad arms were flying. A vamp with a bicycle chain looped through one side of his nose, shoulder-length maroon hair, and Freddy Krueger torso rippers attached to his fingers was slashing at Bruce Three. Bruce dodged the spikes, brandishing a large wooden crucifix.

"Back! Back, thou fiend of the dark!" Bruce yelled at the vampire.

I guess Bruce had had some classical theater training.

"Hey!" I ran up to the brawlers and jammed my walking stick between them. Steel spikes clanged on the stick and the crucifix slammed into the shaft hard enough to crack wood.

"Way to go, Bruce," I said. "Crack the crucifix."

"He was trying to bite me!" Bruce Three was six feet four inches of bulging muscle, blond hair, and tanning-parlor skin. You wouldn't think he'd be threatened by the anemic-looking Goth who barely came up to his shoulder, but I guess you could say the same thing about me and spiders.

"Both of you, chill . . . !" I said, turning to the vampire. "Sir, did you attempt to bite my bodyguard?"

"Shyah. Like I want a mouthful of steroids," the vamp grumbled, then added, "He was waving a cross at us!"

"Bruce, what are you doing with a crucifix?" I scolded him. "That's so politically incorrect. You provoked them!"

Bruce Three looked down at his shoes. "I brought it just in case," he said petulantly. "You never know with vampires. They can transfix you with their eyes and turn you into their sex slave."

The vampires protested, screeching and brandishing their long nails. With visions of a riot breaking out, I decided I had to act quickly. I clicked on my walkie-talkie. "Bruce Two, do you copy?"

"Copy."

"Come replace Bruce Three at the purple hearse."

"Rrrrroger."

I grabbed Bruce Three by the arm and dragged him away. His muscled black replacement, Bruce Two, jogged by with a snappy little salute. I didn't think the vamps would give *him* any trouble. He looked like George Foreman when he was still throwing punches, before he started pitching barbecues.

"These people give me the creeps," Bruce Three said with a shudder.

"They're not real vampires," I said. "You don't fight them off with crucifixes. That's a Hollywood myth."

"What do you fight them with?"

"Nothing!" I said, spouting the party line. "They're harmless slackers dressed up like Dracula. They're no different from you or me."

He gave me a skeptical frown.

"Okay they're different," I conceded. "But they're not necessarily monsters."

We arrived at the first hearse just as Lucian and Morgoth were unloading Ephemera's coffin. Next they'd move to the tiger-striped hearse and unload Vlad the Retailer, whose name was a pun on Vlad the Impaler, the real-life inspiration for the fictional Count Dracula. Vlad had been a fifteenth-century Romanian prince who enjoyed skewering Ottoman invaders like cocktail shrimps and staking their squirming bodies across the countryside before consuming their flesh and blood.

Hence Dracula's bad rap.

I hadn't actually met Vlad or Viscera, nor had I seen the so-called Ephemera when we'd picked up her coffin this morning. They'd be revealed to me in all their glory at the same time as the audience. After a few words for the camera, Ephemera would move to the front of the gallery and cut the black ribbon, after which the whole crowd would move inside to drink bloodred cocktails, which I hoped were grenadine, and to consume finger food, which I hoped was not actual digits.

The drivers stood Ephemera's casket on end and began to unlatch it.

A cutie-pie reporter chirped into a video camera. "We're here at the culmination of the *Coming Out of the Coffin* parade in Venice, where well-known vampire personality Ephemera will be emerging from her coffin for the grand opening of the new Dark Arts Gallery, catering to those whose tastes run to the macabre . . ."

The coffin lid swung open on a nightmare vision of Snow White in a poison apple coma. The big blond hair I remembered from high school was now raven black and hung in raggy shanks down the front of her crimson gown. Her lips were purple, her sun-starved skin like boiled potato. She had a black widow spider tattoo high on her right cheek, eyebrows that were inverted black V's, and fang caps on her canines that dug into her bottom lip.

It looked like she'd had a makeover in Hell.

One of her acolytes blared on a bullhorn, "Ephemera, Queen of the Undead! Awaken to the world of the living! Grace us with your unearthly presence!"

The crowd went insane.

I guessed Darby hadn't caused this much of a sensation since the regional playoffs, when instead of the regulation underpants she'd worn a red thong under her cheerleading outfit. Although she claimed it was an honest wardrobe malfunction, it got her butt kicked right off the squad. But nothing could keep the Applewhite juggernaut from the homecoming court. Darby was too popular, too pretty, and too obliging to the football team to be deprived of the honor, and her coronation took place the very same week of her thong disgrace.

Now she had reinvented herself as a vampire goddess. I looked at her reclining in the coffin surrounded by white satin, hands clutching a gleaming set of shears, and thought about how strange life could be. As the noise from the crowd reached a deafening roar she slowly began to lift her arms, head nodding as if she were awakening from a deep, blood-drugged sleep.

Then her whole body pitched forward and she hit the asphalt face-first, the shears skittering away on the street.

Someone screamed. A girl in a ripped-up wedding gown fell over in a faint. I charged through the crowd, shoving my way through the vampires to get to Ephemera, who was sprawled flat on her face, arms akimbo. Her red velvet skirt was hiked up over her black fishnet stockings.

"Call 911!" I yelled, kneeling at her side.

Terry whipped out her cell phone and punched in the number. "We need an ambulance! The corner of Rose and Fourth!" she shouted at the dispatcher. "Vampire down! I repeat: vampire down!"

The Bruces tried to contain the crowd, pushing the noisy peasant throng back from its fallen queen. I ignored the mayhem breaking out around me and turned Ephemera over onto her back, feeling for a pulse.

Her arm was cold as lunch meat.

I brushed the hair away from her face and winced when I saw that her nose had been smashed on the street. Her makeup lay like a layer of sex wax on her bloodless face. I lifted her wrist and the delicate hand flopped like a bag of bird bones.

"What happened?" Terry crouched next to me. "Did she suffocate?"

"I don't think so. Look at this."

I pointed to two gaping puncture wounds on her neck. They were several millimeters in diameter with black edges, surrounded by a painful-looking purple hickey.

Terry drew a sharp breath. "Omigod. She was bitten?"

"She was more than bitten," I said. "She was sucked dry."

This queen wasn't undead.

She was dead dead.

About the Author

Jennifer Colt is a screenwriter in Santa Monica, California. She has written for Dimension Films and Playboy Enterprises and has worked in the nontheatrical division of MGM/United Artists in LA.